Praise for Dianne

"Book after book, Duvall brings her readers romance, danger and loyalty."

"Duvall's storytelling is simply spellbinding." —Tome Tender

"Dianne Duvall does an amazing job of blending paranormal with humor, romance, action, and violence to give you a story you won't want to put down." —The SubClub Books

Praise for Dianne's Immortal Guardians Books

"These dark, kick-ass guardians can protect me any day!" —Alexandra Ivy, *New York Times* Bestselling Author

"Fans of terrific paranormal romance have hit the jackpot with Duvall and her electrifying series." —RT Book Reviews

"Crackles with energy, originality, and a memorable take-no-prisoners heroine." —Publishers Weekly

"Full of fascinating characters, a unique and wonderfully imaginative premise, and scorching hot relationships." —The Romance Reviews

"Fans of paranormal romance who haven't discovered this series yet are really missing out on something extraordinary." —Long and Short Reviews

"This series boasts numerous characters, a deep back story, and extensive worldbuilding… [Ethan boasts the glowing charms of Twilight's Edward Cullen and the vicious durability of the X-Men's Wolverine." —Kirkus Reviews

"Paranormal romance fans who enjoy series like J.R. Ward's Black Dagger Brotherhood will definitely want to invest time in the Immortal Guardians series." —All Things Urban Fantasy

"Ms. Duvall brings together a rich world and a wonderful group of characters… This is a great series." —Night Owl Reviews

"It was non-stop get-up-and-go from the very first page, and instantly you just adore these characters... This was paranormal at its finest."

—Book Reader Chronicles

"Full of awesome characters, snappy dialogue, exciting action, steamy sex, sneaky shudder-worthy villains and delightful humor."

—I'm a Voracious Reader

Praise for Dianne's
The Gifted Ones Books

"The Gifted Ones series is nothing short of perfection itself. I can't wait to see where she takes us next!" —Scandalicious Book Reviews

"I enjoyed this world and can't wait to see more crossover as the series continues... You will smile, swoon and have a lot of fun with this."

—Books and Things

"Full of danger, intrigue and passion. Dianne Duvall brought the characters to life and delivered an addicting and exciting new series. I'm hooked!" —Reading in Pajamas

"The Gifted Ones by Dianne Duvall combine paranormal romance with historical medieval keeps, magic, and time travel. Addictive, funny and wrapped in swoons, you won't be able to set these audios down."

—Caffeinated Book Reviewer

"Ms. Duvall excels in creating a community feel to her stories and this is no different... A Sorceress of His Own has a wonderful dynamic, an amazing promise of future adventures and a well-told romance that is sure to please." —Long and Short Reviews

"I loved this book! It had pretty much all of my favorite things — medieval times, a kick-ass heroine, a protective hero, magic, and a dash of mayhem."

—The Romance Reviews

"A great beginning to a new and different series." —eBookObsessed

"A must read!" —Reading Between the Wines Book Club

BLADE OF DARKNESS

NEW YORK TIMES BESTSELLING AUTHOR

DIANNE DUVALL

*Immortal
Guardians*

For my family

Acknowledgements

I'd like to thank the many readers who have requested Aidan's book. I've wanted him to find a HEA ever since I wrote the "lotto" scene in *Night Unbound* and was thrilled when I found the perfect woman for him. More thanks go to Crystal and my fabulous street team, as well as the bloggers, reviewers, and wonderful readers who have picked up copies of my books and helped spread the word about them.

I would also like to thank Syneca for translating my imaginings into such a beautiful cover. I'd also like to thank my editor, proofreader, formatter, and the other behind-the-scenes individuals who helped me bring you *Blade of Darkness*.

And, of course, I'd like to thank my Facebook friends who share in my excitement with every release and make me laugh and smile even when I'm stressing over deadlines. You're the best!

Chapter One

THE THUMP OF AIDAN'S HEAVY boots echoed off the walls as he followed Chris Reordon down the long white corridor on Sublevel 5. Chris presided over the East Coast division of the network, which encompassed thousands of human employees who helped Immortal Guardians protect humans from psychotic vampires.

What looked like a large-screen television took up almost the entire wall at the end of the otherwise barren hallway. If Aidan wasn't mistaken, it displayed a live video feed of the sunny meadow beyond the network's parking lot, like an oversized window.

"That's new," he commented.

Chris nodded without looking up. "Melanie hoped it would make living five stories belowground a little more palatable for the vampires housed here. If they like it, we'll add similar faux windows to their apartments."

The doorways to Aidan's right opened into Dr. Melanie Lipton's office, a lab, an infirmary, a break room for employees, and Dr. Linda Machen's office. The doors on the left marked a half dozen or so vampire apartments.

"Tell me again," Chris grumbled, "why I should give you an apartment here when my team put so much time and effort into providing you with a nice, comfortable house in the country."

Aidan shrugged. "Melanie and the other doctors were tired of me bunking in the infirmary."

"Why the hell don't you bunk at your house?"

Aidan stared at the back of Reordon's head. Chris pretty much loathed him. "Because I like it better here, where I can hang out with the vampires."

He had never done that before—befriended vampires. Those he encountered on his nightly hunts were always either raving lunatics or halfway down the road to insanity with no interest in avoiding the destination.

But the vampires here were still lucid. And getting to know them was a new venture.

When one did the same old same old every night for nearly three thousand years, *new* was good.

No. He'd borrow a word from Cliff. New was *awesome*.

Chris stopped before a heavy titanium door that had an electronic pad beside it. "This is your key card." He held up a card. "You'll need it and the code I wrote on the back to get inside." His cell phone chirped. "Hang on." Tugging it from his back pocket, he answered with his usual brusque, "Reordon."

"Mr. Reordon!" a woman nearly shouted from the phone. "It's Veronica Becker. I work in— " Snarls erupted on the other end. She shrieked a curse. "I work in IT at the network!"

Chris frowned. "I know. What's—?"

"I got a flat tire," she interrupted breathlessly, "and two vampires— Shit!"

"Where are you?" Chris demanded.

"Sax-Beth Church Road just off Highway 54."

Chris looked at Aidan.

"I know where that is." Aidan pictured the location in his mind. The hallway around him darkened as a feeling of weightlessness engulfed him. Fresh air ruffled his hair as he found himself standing at the intersection of Saxapahaw-Bethlehem Church Road and Highway 54.

A full moon dominated a cloudless sky. The croak of frogs, hum of insects, and rustling of other nocturnal creatures filled the night. As did raucous laughter.

He looked to the west.

Vampires. Taunting their intended victim until howls of pain split the night.

Aidan's nose twitched at the sharp scent of pepper. Running up the winding, two-lane country road, he traveled at speeds most drivers would deem unsafe. Two headlights appeared in the distance. Stationary. Flickering as bodies moved back and forth in front of them.

"Please hurry," he heard Veronica cry. "I can't hold them off much longer. And I think one just— " She swore again.

There. A woman. Small. Perhaps five feet two inches tall. Armed with a tire iron and the biggest can of pepper spray Aidan had ever seen.

He grinned. Smart woman.

Her cell phone lay on the hood of the car behind her. Chris's voice swam out of it, expressing concern without tipping off the vamps that an Immortal Guardian now hunted them.

Two vampires danced around her, flashing fangs, their eyes glowing bright blue. When one blurred and sped toward her, she doused him with pepper spray. To a vampire with extremely heightened senses, it would feel like flames searing his eyes, nose, and lungs.

The vamp bent forward with a yelp and scrubbed at his eyes.

Veronica bashed him on the head with the tire iron, then pepper sprayed and whacked his friend. But the vampires recovered quickly and weren't as stupid as they looked.

Even as Aidan raced toward them, one of the vampires tossed the woman a sneer and backed away to the other side of the car.

Michael!

Aidan heard her panicked thought and noticed for the first time a toddler slumbering in a car seat inside.

Fury rose. If the madness that afflicted vampires hadn't fully taken hold, the vamp would use the child to torture the mother. And if the madness *had* fully taken hold…

Aidan stopped running long enough to focus his energy and send a sharp telekinetic push.

Both vampires flew backward, away from the car and Veronica.

Drawing his short swords, Aidan swept forward.

Scrambling off the ground, the vampires drew long bowie knives and lunged at him.

Neither scored a hit as Aidan tore into them, his blades opening major arteries.

Unlike immortals, vampires tended to bleed out very quickly when they suffered such wounds. Much like these, who sank to the ground and—seconds later—gasped their last breaths.

The odd symbiotic virus that infected them began to devour them from the inside out in a last, desperate bid to live despite the cessation of blood flow. By the time it finished, nothing would remain of the two but their clothing, watches, and dental fillings.

Silence fell in the wake of the brief battle. Even the insects made no sound, as though they were stunned by the violence they had just witnessed.

Aidan turned to face the woman. "Veronica?"

She gave him a shaky nod. "Yes."

"I'm Aidan. Are you okay?"

"Yes. But I think the tall one might have called…" She trailed off as Aidan raised a hand.

Tilting his head, he listened carefully.

A few insects nearby tentatively made their presence known.

In the distance, several figures raced toward them at preternatural speeds.

Aidan swore. "Get in the car."

The woman lunged for the driver's door and yanked it open. "Are more coming?"

"Yes."

She scrambled into the car and slammed the door shut.

Door locks *snicked* even as she swung around to check on the boy in the back seat.

The toddler's face scrunched up in a frown as he slumped deeper into his car seat and continued to sleep.

"Sit tight," Aidan said, loud enough for both Veronica and Chris to hear. "I've got this." Leaping over the car, he plunged into the forest and barreled toward the vampires. This would go better if he stopped the vampires before they caught sight of the car and its occupants.

Tall trees thickened and blocked the moon's illumination as he continued forward, leaving him in darkness his preternaturally sharp eyes had no difficulty penetrating.

Tiny lights flickered in the distance. Blue. Green. Silver. Always in pairs.

The faces that housed those glowing eyes swam into focus seconds before the vampires struck.

His own eyes glowing amber, Aidan swirled and struck and fended off blows. Though they outnumbered him six to one, he actually had the advantage. Aidan had been born in a time when *all* wars were fought with blades. He had begun training with master swordsmen as soon as his noble Celtic father had deemed him old enough to hold a wooden sword.

And he had been born with advanced DNA that bestowed upon him special gifts. Teleportation. Telekinesis, which aided him in deflecting blows whenever he had a second to focus his energy. Telepathy, which warned him of the vampires' next moves. And the ability to heal with his hands.

That advanced DNA also shielded him from the more corrosive aspects of the vampiric virus that infected him. Humans were not so lucky. Humans infected with the virus turned vampire and suffered progressive brain damage. So even the kindest amongst them swiftly turned into psychopathic killers.

Like these. They knew a woman and child waited somewhere behind Aidan. The vamp who had called them had told them as much. And their plans for the duo sickened him.

Blood sprayed when Aidan sliced two of the vampires' carotid arteries. As they stumbled backward, their hands going to their throats, Aidan severed another vamp's arm and opened the femoral artery of another.

Four down. Two to go.

The fifth went down easy. The sixth took off running.

Cursing, Aidan raced after him. No way would he leave that monster alive to prey on other innocents.

Dashing through the forest at preternatural speeds could be dangerous, particularly if one became distracted.

Reaching into his coat, Aidan drew a dagger and let it fly.

The vampire grunted as the dagger buried itself in his back. Glancing over his shoulder without slowing, he ran headlong into a tree.

Aidan winced at the sound of bones snapping and puncturing organs. Skidding to a halt, he watched as the vamp sank to the ground.

The heart inside that battered body still beat.

Aidan crossed to him, then lopped off the vampire's head to spare him a slow, torturous death. Poor bastard. He might have been a good man before the virus had taken its toll.

Once he'd wiped the blood from his blades, Aidan sheathed them and teleported back to the car.

Veronica shrieked when he abruptly appeared beside the driver's door. Wilting with relief, she thrust open the door and stepped out into the night. "Are you all right?"

"I'm fine. And you?"

"I'm okay."

"Were you bitten?"

"No."

"Good."

"Aidan?" he heard Chris Reordon call.

His eyes went to the cell phone on the hood of the car. Picking it up, he held it to his ear. "Yeah?"

"Did you kill the vamps?"

"Aye. Two of them on the road and six more in the forest to the west."

"Does Ms. Becker require medical assistance?"

Aidan examined her again. "Do you require medical assistance?"

Eyes wide, she shook her head. "No. I'm okay."

"She's fine," Aidan told Chris. "Just a little shaken up. I'll see that she gets home safely."

"Thank you. I'll send one of my guys to collect the vampires' weapons."

"You have the location?"

"Yeah. We LoJack all employee cars. I know where she is and can have a guy there in five minutes."

"Do you want me to stay until he arrives?"

"No. That won't be necessary. Thanks again for helping Ms. Becker."

"Happy to do it." Aidan ended the call and handed Veronica her phone.

Her fingers trembled as they closed around it. "I left it on the car." It took her a couple of tries to get the phone in her pocket.

"When you told me to get in the car, I forgot to grab the phone first."

"Don't worry about it. I know movies like to pretend otherwise, but people rarely think clearly in an emergency. Although I have to say, the pepper spray was a brilliant move."

"Thank you. I hoped it would hurt more with their heightened senses."

He smiled. "I'm sure they found it quite painful." His own eyes burned a bit just from being near it.

"I can't seem to stop shaking," she said with a hint of embarrassment.

"That's normal. Try taking deep breaths." He drew in a long deep breath, held it, then released it to demonstrate.

She followed his example.

If he weren't splattered with blood, he would've offered her a hug to help calm her. "May I ask you a question?" he asked instead, hoping a distraction would help.

She nodded.

"What does LoJack mean?"

She smiled. "Did Mr. Reordon say he'd LoJacked my car?"

"Yes."

"It means he can track the location of the vehicle at all times and get the GPS coordinates."

"Ah." Aidan and his fellow immortals spent their nights hunting psychotic vampires, so they had little time left over to learn all the fascinating things the latest technology could do. "Well, he's sending someone to clean up our mess here and said we've no need to wait for him." He motioned to the car. "If you don't mind my dirtying up your front seat a bit, I'd be happy to escort you home."

Her pretty features smoothed out with relief. "Thank you. I'd appreciate that."

"Would you like me to drive?" he offered.

She shook her head. "I'm okay. I'm not shaking so badly now."

"Then give me a minute to change your tire and we can be on our way."

Reaching into the car, she popped open the trunk.

Aidan changed the flat in less than a minute, then tucked the old tire and tools in the trunk and closed it.

As Veronica got back in the car and closed the door, he glanced at the first two vampires he had slain.

All that remained were their clothes and weapons.

Aidan kicked the lot of it off the road, then circled to the passenger side and settled himself in the car.

"So," Veronica said as she started the engine and drove forward. "Why were you late?"

He raised his eyebrows. "Late?"

She nodded. "When I realized I had a flat tire, I expected you to be right along to change it for me."

He stared at her.

"After several minutes passed, I figured you must have gotten held up and started changing it myself. Then the vampires showed up."

"You thought I'd appear and change the tire for you?" he asked.

"Yes. That's what you did for Kimberly and Dawn."

His stomach sank. "You, uh… you know about that?"

"Yes. I have to admit I was surprised to discover I'm on your list." Glancing over at him, she grinned. "You look dumbfounded."

"I suppose I am. You know about the list?"

"Of female *gifted ones*? Yes, I know about it."

Hell. "*How* do you know about it?" he asked. Only a handful of immortals knew Aidan had inspired Chris's wrath and come damned close to being executed by Seth, the Immortal Guardians' leader, for breaking into network headquarters and stealing a list of female *gifted ones* in the area.

Gifted ones were men and women like himself who had been born with advanced DNA, the source of which they still didn't know. Only *gifted ones* could be transformed by the virus without descending into insanity. And, after nearly three thousand years of loneliness, Aidan had defied Seth and acquired the list so he could arrange chance meetings with the women in hopes of hitting it off with one and—at long last—finding someone who would love him enough to transform and spend the rest of eternity with him.

Again she smiled. "Dawn gushed over you for days after she got a flat tire on the way home from work and you miraculously showed up to change it for her. Then Kimberly got a flat tire and"—

she grinned—"a certain Celtic immortal appeared like a knight in shining armor and took care of it."

He grimaced. Perhaps flattening the women's tires, then gallantly showing up to aid them hadn't been the wisest way to arrange a chance encounter. But the odd hours he kept made it hard for him to bump into them at the grocery store. "You're saying I need a new MO."

She laughed. "Yes, you do. But don't worry. I think I'm the only one who has put two and two together. And I only guessed it because I happen to know that they're both *gifted ones*."

"Oh." He didn't really know what else to say.

"So, why were you late?" she asked again.

"Actually, I didn't flatten your tire tonight," he admitted, fearing it might offend her. "You aren't on my list."

"Oh. Well, that's a relief." She frowned, then laughed. "And yet I feel oddly insulted, which makes no sense whatsoever."

He smiled. "It isn't because I don't think you're worthy," he assured her. "I love strong women. And you showed great courage tonight, standing against those two vampires. I admire intelligence as well, and Cliff says you're brilliant."

She blushed. "The vampire Cliff?"

"Yes." Cliff had been amongst the first vampires to surrender to the Immortal Guardians and seek their help, hoping the scientists at the network would be able to stave off the madness that would soon claim them. "Since he lives at network headquarters and has heightened hearing, he pretty much knows everyone's business."

She shook her head. "Poor guy, listening to everybody's drama all day."

Aidan shrugged. The vamps all viewed it as an ongoing soap opera or reality show and found some entertainment in it. "Cliff told me you lost your husband last year," he said, broaching the subject gently.

Grief darkened her features.

"He also told me you loved your husband a great deal, so I assumed your heart still belonged to him."

Her throat moved in a swallow. "It does." She blinked quickly several times as moisture welled in her eyes. "I'm sorry. I still can't talk about it without crying."

"No need to apologize."

Silence fell as she navigated the dark country road.

"Does it bother you?" he asked curiously. "The list?"

"No." She cast him a curious glance. "Is it true you're almost three thousand years old?"

He released an exaggerated sigh. "Yes, it is."

She laughed. "I heard one of the other immortals at the network say that immortal/human love affairs always end badly."

"They do. The human ages while the immortal remains young. Even if bitterness over that fact doesn't worm its way into the relationship, the mortal dies and leaves the immortal alone to grieve for centuries."

She shook her head. "So you've been by yourself all this time?"

He shrugged. "I've had the friendship of Seconds." Mortal men assigned to guard him during the day, provide companionship, and offer a semblance of normalcy to neighbors and anyone else who might be paying attention.

"But no wife?" she prompted softly. "No lovers?"

"No wife. And it's difficult to take a lover for more than the briefest amount of time when I must hide my abilities and so much of my life from her."

She slowed the car to a stop at a red light. The low rumble of the car's engine filled a comfortable silence until she spoke. "You know, Tom and I only had nine years together. He worked at the network, too. And when we ran into each other the first time… something just clicked. It was like we became instant best friends. We wanted to spend all our time together from then on and would spend hours laughing and talking in the cafeteria after our shifts ended. Then we started going out to dinner and…" She shook her head. "He was *it* for me. He was the one." When she gave him a sad smile, tears glistened in her eyes. "People keep telling me that I'm young. That I'll move on and find love again. I smile and nod. But I know in my heart that I won't. I'll never find someone I can have that deep a connection with again. And the knowledge that I'm going to spend the rest of my life without that—without Tom, without love—is unbearable sometimes."

Aidan read her thoughts and knew her sorrow to be true.

He also heard the words she didn't speak aloud: *How have you lived for three thousand years with that sorrow and that loneliness when I can hardly bear the notion of living another forty or fifty years with it?*

She cleared her throat. "So I get it. I get the list."

Nodding, he murmured, "I see that you do."

The signal light turned green.

Driving forward once more, she forced a bright smile. "Any luck so far?"

"Nope." He returned her smile. "But as it happens, I have an appointment in" — he consulted his watch — "thirty-five minutes with a lovely psychic in Carrboro."

"Ooh, a psychic," she repeated, her voice full of intrigue. "Maybe she's seen you coming."

"If she had," he countered with a wink and a grin, "she would've canceled the appointment."

Veronica laughed.

⌖

Thirty-five minutes later, Aidan stepped out of his Tesla Model S and studied the small shop in front of him. It was half of what appeared to be a duplex that had been converted into two businesses with homes above them.

Closing the driver's door, he pocketed the keys.

A tingle of excitement fluttered in his chest. Anticipation rose. As did hope.

It made him feel young again and brightened spirits that had been dark for too many years to count.

He knew this was a long shot but savored the moment nonetheless.

Gifted ones born in previous centuries had always refused to be transformed. Even those who had fallen in love with immortals had steadfastly remained mortal, fearing what transforming would mean for their soul. The church had long deemed vampires minions of Satan. And until modern medicine had enabled immortals to better understand why they were the way they were, immortals had assumed the same rules applied to *them*. So they had never pushed the women they loved to transform for them because they didn't want to be responsible for damning them.

But in the past century or so, their mortal doctor and scientist friends had identified the virus that infected both immortals and vampires as well as the advanced DNA that made *gifted ones* and immortals different, easing their fears.

Then Sarah Bingham had shocked the immortal world by doing what Aidan and the others had believed no mortal ever would. She had asked to be transformed so she could spend the rest of eternity with Roland Warbrook.

And hope had surfaced.

All Aidan had to do was find the right *gifted one* — a woman he could love, who could love him in return and who would be willing to transform for him — and he could view the future as more than just an endless stretch of days in which he slew vampires every night, then went to bed alone.

Strolling forward, he pushed open the door. A bell dinged as he ducked and stepped inside.

~⊗⊗⊗~

At the sound of the bell, Dana Pembroke turned around and felt her jaw drop.

Holy crap.

The man who stood just inside the door had to be three or four inches above six feet. His thick black hair was short and so wavy it almost curled. But it by no means lent him a feminine air. His strong jaw bore just a hint of a five-o'clock shadow. Deep brown eyes captured hers and sparkled with amusement beneath dark brows.

Because she was drooling over him?

She let her gaze dip lower.

What woman *wouldn't* drool over him? He was freaking hot.

A black T-shirt stretched taut over broad shoulders, revealing a very muscled chest and thick biceps. Casual black slacks hugged slim hips, what she guessed would be a really nice ass if he turned around, and muscular thighs.

His lips stretched in a friendly smile. "Good evening."

His lovely bass voice flowed through her like hot chocolate on a cold winter's night.

Straightening, she struck a dramatic pose and touched her fingertips to one temple in much the same way Shawn Spencer did in the television series *Psych*. "Aidan O'Byrne?" she intoned.

His smile broadened, revealing straight white teeth. "Aye. Let me guess. You saw me coming."

Grinning, she abandoned her pose and shrugged. "Kind of hard not to when you make an appointment."

He laughed. "Would you be the charming lass I spoke with over the phone then?"

Damned if she didn't feel a little blush of pleasure heat her cheeks as she strode forward and offered her hand. "That would be me." And his accent was even sexier in person. "Dana Pembroke."

He took her hand in his much larger one and brought it to his lips for a kiss. "It's a pleasure to meet you."

She didn't think a man had ever kissed her hand before. Why did that make her insides go all gooey?

Staring up at him, she offered no protest when he didn't immediately release her hand.

Damn, he was handsome. And he had one of those smiles that made it impossible to resist smiling back.

Until blood abruptly splattered across his face and neck.

She gasped.

A deep slash opened on his chest. Another opened on his left arm, then his right. The hand holding hers grew slick with warm, wet blood.

Fear streaking through her, Dana yanked her hand out of his grasp. She looked down at her trembling fingers.

No blood stained them, but she could still feel the warm wetness of it.

When she looked up, Aidan was as he had been before she had touched him, his handsome face clean, his clothing flawless, his flesh unmarred. No blood. No cuts.

Her heart slammed against her ribs.

His smile faltered. "Dana?"

Had she just seen the future? *His* future?

"Are you okay?" he asked, concern darkening his pretty brown eyes.

The future had never come to her so quickly or clearly before.

She forced a smile. "I'm fine. I'm sorry."

He tilted his head to one side, his gaze turning watchful. "You saw something."

For once she found herself at a loss for words. Normally she would have denied it, unwilling to inform a client she had just met that she'd foreseen his death. But something told her this man would recognize the lie. "Yes."

"It disturbed you."

"Yes."

"Past or future?"

She considered it a moment. "I'm pretty sure it was the future."

"But you do sometimes see the past?"

"Yes."

"Did you see me wounded?"

"Yes."

"Badly?"

Her eyes clung to his. "Yes."

He nodded, strangely unconcerned. "I'm guessing you saw a slash across my chest. About here." He drew a line across his chest. "A couple more on my arms." He traced two paths on his arms exactly where she had seen the cuts in the remarkably clear vision.

Relief suffused her, relaxing the muscles she hadn't even realized had bunched up in her shoulders. "Yes." She smiled. "So it was the past. Good."

He smiled.

Realizing what she'd just said, she hastened to clarify, "I mean, not good that you were wounded. I just…"

"Thought you were about to lose a client?" he suggested with a wink.

She laughed. "Well, I didn't think you'd want to come back if the first thing I told you was that you're going to be seriously, perhaps fatally, wounded."

He grinned. "I was in the army in my youth. And since then I've been working in the private security business. Both have proven to be dangerous on occasion, so I've had my fair share of nicks and bruises over the years."

That had been one hell of a nick. "Private security?" She motioned for him to accompany her and began strolling toward the back of her small shop.

He shrugged. "There always seems to be someone out there who wants to kill or kidnap someone else. I, and my brothers, offer protection to those who need it."

"Your brothers? Do you have a big family then?"

"They're brothers in spirit, not by blood. Most of us don't have families of our own, so we consider each other family."

Dana had no family of her own either, so she could appreciate that. An only child, she had lost all her grandparents before she turned seven. Then, after reaching adulthood, she lost both parents in a car accident. "Is this the first time you've consulted a psychic?"

"I admit," he said with another smile, "this is the first time I've ever made an appointment with one."

She had thought so. "Well, usually clients seek me out because they have concerns or questions they would like answered. They're often stressed and worried, not to mention nervous about seeing a psychic for the first time. So I do things a little differently than other psychics." She opened a door and stepped into what used to be a sizable dining room before the duplex apartment had been converted.

Since purchasing her half, she had painted the walls in soothing earth tones. Large plants flourished in every corner. In front of the central window, she had created a garden with sand and stones, a variety of plants, and a rock waterfall. At one end of the long room, she had placed a small round table with two comfy chairs in what would make a great reading nook. Two more chairs were parked on the opposite wall beside a bookshelf that held books, puzzles, paper, crayons, and markers for clients who brought children with them.

And at the other end of the room, she had installed a comfortable massage chair.

She motioned to that now. "I usually start things off with a massage to relieve some of the tension and ease nerves."

He arched a brow. "And because touch strengthens your gift?"

She regarded him with surprise. He was the first one to guess that. "Yes."

He eyed the contraption warily. "I'm supposed to sit on that?"

"Yes."

"I hate to tell you this, but I don't think I'll fit."

She laughed. "You *are* taller than most of my clients"—and heavier with muscle—"but I can adjust it to accommodate you."

He continued to look doubtful. "I don't think that's such a good idea."

"It's actually very comfortable," she coaxed.

"I still don't think it's a good idea."

"Why?" Did he really think it wouldn't support his weight? She might not have any clients who were as muscular as he was, but she had had clients who weighed more than she guessed he did and hadn't had any problems thus far.

"Should I be blunt," he asked, "or would you prefer I sugarcoat it?"

"Blunt," she responded without hesitation.

"As you will." He drew in a deep breath. "I don't think it would be wise because I'm attracted to you."

Surprise and pleasure warmed her.

"And if I park my caboose in that chair—"

She laughed. "Caboose?"

He grinned. "My friend has a two-year-old daughter who only seems to repeat the naughty words she hears, so I've had to clean up my language a bit."

Too cute. "I'm sorry I interrupted. Go on."

He dipped his head in a slight bow. "As I was saying, I'm attracted to you. And if I park my caboose in that peculiar chair and let you put your hands on me, I fear my body may react in ways that will embarrass you."

Was that another blush heating her cheeks? "Oh."

He winced. "I should have sugarcoated it, shouldn't I?"

"No. No, it's fine," she said. "I just…" A brief self-deprecating laugh escaped her. "I just have no idea how to respond to that. Almost all my clients are women. And now I'm blushing like a teenager, aren't I?"

He grinned. "Yes. I find it quite fetching."

Something about this man just made her feel lighthearted. Comfortable. Almost as if they were good friends who simply hadn't seen each other for a long time.

Perhaps it was his old-world mannerisms. Kissing her hand. Using words like *fetching*.

But she couldn't seem to stop smiling. "You know what? It's fine. Don't worry about it." Brushing her hands together, she motioned to the chair. "Go ahead and park your caboose in the chair. I'll adjust it until you're comfortable. And if your body responds to my touch, I'll just pretend not to notice." Yeah, right. Because she had been *so* successful with not blushing when he had broached the subject. "I really do need to touch you though in order to give you the most accurate reading."

"As you will," he said again.

Chapter Two

DANA MADE THE NECESSARY ADJUSTMENTS to the chair, then showed Aidan how to sit and where to place his face and arms.

"This is supposed to be relaxing?" he queried, doubt in his deep, warm voice.

Grinning, she moved to stand behind him. "You'll see. Before I begin, are there any medical conditions or injuries I should know about?"

"No."

"Just making sure." She rested her hands on his shoulders.

Aidan chuckled.

"What?" she asked as she began to stroke his back.

"It's my warped sense of humor. I was tempted to let out a long, loud moan as soon as you touched me just to see how you'd react."

Dana laughed. She really liked this guy.

Beginning with some open-palm compressions, she worked her way down either side of his spine, then switched to loose-fist compressions.

Usually the muscles in the client's back and shoulders were tight with stress. But Aidan's muscles were surprisingly loose and relaxed.

Kneading her way up to his shoulders, she began to work contralaterally, holding his shoulder with one hand while she applied pressure to his scapula with the heel of the other.

Minutes passed. And with each she relaxed a little bit more herself.

No more flashes of Aidan covered in blood struck her.

That had been unnerving. And she had feared, more than a little bit, that the same would happen as soon as she touched him again.

"Let me know if I use too much pressure," she said as she began forearm compressions. "Or not enough."

He grunted. "Feels wonderful. I think your other customers have been lying to you."

"About what?"

"I think they come here for the massage and the psychic reading is just icing on the cake."

She chuckled.

His back was so broad. Had she ever touched a man who was so ripped with muscle before?

None of her other clients could compare. And she sure as hell had never dated any man who was so physically fit.

Thin? Sure. Strong enough to hoist her over his head with one arm? Definitely not.

Feeling all of that lovely muscle under her hands affected her in very unprofessional ways. She moved to his side, lifted one of his arms and draped it in the crook of her own, then began manipulating his shoulder.

Her heart began to pound. *Get a grip, Dana*, she scolded herself as she stroked and kneaded his big biceps with both hands, working her way slowly down his arm to his hand. His large, smooth, tanned hand that could easily encompass both of hers.

How did he work out without getting calluses?

She kneaded his hand, stroked his fingers. And suddenly saw those fingers cup her bare shoulder and slide down to clasp her breast.

Her breath caught at the vision. It was so clear! She could see and feel everything as if it were real.

Aidan knelt before her on a huge bed. Both of them were naked.

His big hand squeezed her breast. His fingers and thumb teased her nipple, sending fire dancing through her. Dark head dipping, he lowered his lips to her other breast and took the tight peak between warm, soft lips.

Aidan jerked his hand from her grasp.

The vision vanished.

Kneeling beside him, Dana fought to keep her breath regular. Her heart thudded in her chest. Her pulse raced as arousal slithered through her body.

Still in the massage chair, Aidan reached up with the hand he had removed from her grasp and rubbed the back of his neck.

Dana stared at him, glad the face cushion blocked his view of her. She hadn't moaned or gasped or anything like that, had she? What the hell had that *been*?

It certainly hadn't been a vision of the past. So… what? Her gift was telling her that she and Aidan were going to be lovers?

Aidan lowered his arm to the armrest.

But Dana didn't move.

What was happening here? Visions never came to her this clearly. And it had happened twice now with Aidan.

"Everything okay?" he asked, no doubt wondering why she had ceased the massage.

Was his voice a little deeper than it had been before?

"Yes," she said, but sounded shaken even to herself. "Everything's fine."

"Should I not have moved?" he asked. "I didn't mean to break the flow of things."

Hell, if he hadn't broken the flow of things, the vision would've likely continued and let her see and feel them making love until she orgasmed. It had felt *that* real.

"No. It's fine." Except she was afraid to touch him again. Even though she *really* wanted to touch him again. Holy crap, his hand and lips had felt good on her. She hadn't been with a man in a long time. And Aidan's touch had electrified her.

"Did you see something again?" he asked when she didn't resume the massage.

"No," she lied. What was she supposed to say? *Actually, yes. I saw the two of us naked on a bed about to have what looked and felt like it would be hot, sweaty, never-want-it-to-end, never-felt-this-way-in-my-life sex.*

Yeah, right. And have him think her a total perv who only used the massage thing as an excuse to fondle her clients while she fantasized about having sex with them? *I don't think so.*

"I was just going to move to the other side," she said, forcing a light, friendly tone. Rising, she moved to his other side and stared down at his strong shoulder.

"You're worried I'm going to break your chair, aren't you?" he asked. "Is it creaking beneath my weight?"

She smiled, relaxing a bit. "No." Taking a deep breath, she lifted his arm and rested it in the crook of her own.

No naked flashes. No visions of his mouth on her breast.

Dana began to manipulate his shoulder, breathing a little easier every second she didn't have another vision. *Get it together*, she counseled herself again and rushed through the rest of the massage. "All done," she pronounced.

Aidan sat up, rolling his broad shoulders. "Can't remember the last time anything felt so good."

"That's what I like to hear." She motioned to the comfy chairs in the corner. "Would you please have a seat over there?"

"As you will."

When he rose, towering over her, she studiously kept her gaze from dropping below his waist. She wasn't sure how she would react if the massage had aroused him as much as that vision had aroused her, so she thought it better to leave that a mystery.

As he seated himself in one of the chairs, she reached up and retrieved a box from the top shelf of the bookcase. Carrying it with her, Dana sat in the chair opposite him and placed the box on the table between them.

She felt his gaze like a touch as she opened the box and withdrew her tarot cards. Placing the box aside, she glanced up. "Would you shuffle the cards, please?"

Nodding, he complied. "Since your gift stems from touch, do these really help you? Or do you use them because your clients expect it?"

The words carried no sarcasm, only curiosity.

"A little of both. If I tell them what I see when I touch them, they have only my words. If I tell them what I see in the cards, they have a visual confirmation of sorts."

"Seeing is believing," he murmured.

"For many, yes."

Aidan watched Dana lay the cards on the table one by one. He nodded and feigned interest as she explained what each card meant but in truth had difficulty concentrating.

His heart still hammered against his ribs. His pulse raced. His body burned.

If seeing was believing, then he might have at last found the woman for whom he had been searching. Because Dana had *seen* the two of them engaging in love play.

Aidan's telepathy enabled him to read her thoughts. So he had seen it as vividly as she had. Had felt it, too, and been so swept away that he had had to break contact with her to bring the vision to an end while he fought the desire to dive off her odd chair and reenact the scene with her.

"Do your visions always come true?" he asked, interrupting her explanation of the chariot card. "The ones of the future?"

She hesitated. "More often than not I don't so much *see* things as *know* them. My client will ask me a question and— "

"But when you do see them? When you do have visions? Do those visions always come true?"

Color invaded her cheeks as she ducked her chin and dealt another card. "Yes. They always have in the past."

Elation filled him. Not just because she had answered him truthfully even though the question clearly flustered her. But because they would be lovers.

Lovers and something more?

It took every ounce of concentration to keep his eyes from glowing. Younger immortals couldn't prevent the involuntary response. Any deep emotion, good or bad, tended to make their eyes glow vibrant amber, something that immediately tipped off mortals that they weren't human. But Aidan was quite old and had more control over the response.

She frowned, her blush fading. "It looks like you have a very formidable enemy in your future, Aidan."

He grunted. "In my business, I tend to attract them like flies."

Dana shook her head. "This one is different."

She must mean Gershom. That powerful bastard was determined to kick-start Armageddon. And the Immortal Guardians were having a hell of a time bringing his arse down.

She set the cards aside and reached across the table. "Let me see your hand."

Eager to touch her again, he extended it toward her.

Taking it in her own, she turned it palm up. "You have a very long lifeline."

His should be the longest lifeline she had ever seen.

Her brown eyes flickered up to meet his. "You've lived much of your life alone."

He shrugged. "I've had friends. Men I consider brothers."

"But no wife?"

"I haven't been so fortunate, no."

And she could feel the loneliness that plagued him. He saw it in her thoughts and felt a little lighter when she wondered how the hell that could be possible, having experienced a tiny hint of the passion he could bring a woman in her vision.

Resting her palm on his, she returned her attention to the cards. "I'm seeing deception. A *lot* of it." She shook her head. "Divided loyalties. Betrayal. Something's coming, Aidan. And when whatever happens goes down, you aren't going to know who to trust."

He frowned. She made it sound as if he would face whatever turbulence came alone. What of his immortal brethren? Why would they not be by his side?

The only time he had ever lost faith in any of them or eroded theirs in him was when he had broken into network headquarters and stolen the list of *gifted ones*. Seth had mistakenly believed Aidan had sided with the enemy responsible for Lisette's near death. The powerful immortal leader and longtime friend had actually wanted Aidan dead until Aidan had clarified things.

But they were good now. Had been for a while.

Sure Chris Reordon still bore a grudge against him, but even *he* trusted Aidan to take care of business when someone needed help. So why did Dana believe Aidan would face whatever fight lay ahead without them?

He curled his fingers around hers, holding her hand as she frowned down at the cards.

Her skin was so soft. Her fingers so small.

Those fingers abruptly tightened on his, clamping down in an almost painful grip.

Reading her thoughts, Aidan saw the cards and table disappear, replaced by light.

Two men swam out of the brightness, engaged in fierce battle. Aidan didn't notice where — if they were inside, outside, in the city or in the country — because he was too shocked by the combatants themselves.

He and Seth fought each other with a ferocity that filled his blood with ice. Their eyes glowed — his amber, Seth's gold. Each clutched swords in both hands and swung them mercilessly, remaining in constant motion, their faces twisted with fury and determination as they did their damnedest to slay each other.

Dana yanked her hand from his grasp and leapt to her feet. Stumbling backward, away from the table, she tripped over one of the legs and nearly fell but regained her balance quickly enough to remain upright.

Stunned, Aidan slowly rose. And damned if his hands didn't begin to shake as violently as hers did.

What the hell?

Dana said nothing, just regarded him with wide eyes, her lips parted in shock.

"Dana?" he forced himself to say in the most even tone he could muster.

She didn't know he had just seen everything *she* had. She didn't know he could read her thoughts, which now scrambled for purchase as they chased themselves around and around in her head.

"Did you see something?" he asked her.

She nodded. "You and another man trying to kill each other with swords."

He swallowed. *Think quickly. Think quickly. What would the younger immortals say?* "I..." He feigned a chagrined smile. "I hate to mention this, because I don't want you to think I'm a" — what was the word Cliff would use? — "a geek. But I'm a member of a reenactment group."

He supposed it wasn't technically a lie. He did spar regularly with immortal warriors who fought with blades the way battles had been fought centuries ago. Wouldn't some consider that reenacting?

Her mouth closed. Her eyes lost some of the deer-in-the-headlights look. "Like a… like a medieval reenactment group? With swords and that kind of thing?"

Roland and Marcus were from the Middle Ages. He sparred with them. "Yes."

She drew in a deep breath. "Okay." She nodded, trying to rationalize it, make it work. "Okay. So you do the sword-fighting thing on a regular basis?"

"Yes." That was certainly no lie. He fought vampires every night. But it didn't explain the glow she had seen in his and Seth's eyes.

Mankind's inability to believe in magic or the fantastical came to his aid there. Even as he sought some way to explain it, she began to question whether or not she had actually seen it. *Had* his eyes and those of his opponent glowed? Or had it merely been a trick of the light?

Fortunately for him, neither he nor Seth had flashed fangs in the vision.

"Okay," she repeated, her heartbeat slowing. "I gather you take that pretty seriously? I mean, you guys really looked like you were trying to kill each other."

Yes, they had. And Aidan's stomach clenched at the knowledge. "You think I'm a geek now, don't you?" he jested.

She relaxed a little more. "No."

"First I say *caboose*. Now this."

She smiled. "Actually, I thought your caboose was cute." Her eyes widened. "*The* caboose," she corrected hastily. "I thought *the* caboose was cute. Your *saying* it, I mean."

He winked. "I prefer the first one."

She laughed. "I bet you do." She motioned to the table. "Do you want to continue the reading?"

He shook his head. "I think I'd better take my leave before I say or reveal anything else embarrassing."

She nodded at the cards. "I'm sorry I couldn't tell you exactly what's coming, just that it's not good."

He and Seth engaged in what appeared to be a battle to the death was a wee bit worse than *not good*. "I appreciate the heads-up."

Aidan followed her out of the room and to the front of the store where he retrieved his wallet from his back pocket and handed her his credit card. "Would you be averse to my making another appointment?"

She smiled up at him. "Not at all."

"Excellent."

"Any particular time of day?"

Just tell her anytime is good. Don't rush things. "I know you now see me as a geek with a dangerous job, G-rated language, and a penchant for swords," he began, cursing his own eagerness, "but is there any chance I could take your latest appointment and coax you into joining me for dinner afterward?"

She stared up at him.

"Or coffee?" he suggested. "Maybe some pie or ice cream?" He frowned. "What is it that women like to do when they're testing the waters and deciding whether or not they want a man to court them?" No, that wasn't right. "Or want to date him," he corrected. "I meant date him."

She grinned. *He is just too freaking cute.*

He relaxed when that thought came through, loud and clear. Cute was good, wasn't it?

"How about Wednesday night, seven o'clock?" she suggested.

He grinned back. "Wednesday night it is." Offering her a quick good-night, he left her shop feeling more lighthearted than he had in centuries.

Until he thought of her last vision.

What the hell was he going to do that would make Seth want to kill him?

Again?

⸻◈◈◈⸻

Aidan jerked awake.

Though the room around him was dark, he had no difficulty seeing. His preternaturally sharp vision allowed him to make out objects in the lowest light conditions, though color could be difficult to discern.

Glancing around, he found nothing out of place. No one had invaded his new apartment. No doorbell chimed.

So what had woken him?

Voices filled his head. Louder than the voices of the employees who worked the day shift at network headquarters. Uglier voices. Craving violence. Urging the recipient of their cries to commit it.

Cliff.

Rising, Aidan drew on pants, a shirt, socks, and boots.

Cliff had once been a follower of the British immortal Sebastien Newcombe. Bastien had thought himself a vampire for two hundred years and had gathered together an army of vampires he had pitted against the Immortal Guardians in an attempt to destroy them all.

Cliff had been a member of that army, as had two other vampires, Vincent and Joe. All three had wisely chosen to surrender in the final battle Bastien had waged. And while Seth had forced Bastien to join the Immortal Guardians' ranks, Cliff, Vincent, and Joe had come to live at the network, hoping the doctors and scientists here would be able to prevent them from descending into madness, or at least slow the decline. None had wanted to become like those who had turned them, torturing and killing innocent victims with glee.

But Dr. Melanie Lipton and her colleagues had not yet found a way to slow the progressive brain damage the virus wrought in humans or to prevent the madness.

Vincent and Joe had long since lost their battle with insanity and forfeited their lives.

Other vampires had sought the network's help since then. But only Cliff remained of the initial three.

Aidan took a moment to brush his teeth, then wet his hands and finger-combed his tousled hair, trying to smooth the damned waves and curls.

Cliff had been transformed by a vampire against his will when he was in college. If one discounted the world-weariness that darkened the young man's eyes, Aidan thought he looked to be about twenty-five years old. Most vampires only retained their humanity for a couple of years. If they were particularly strong, fought hard, and weren't subjected to poor living conditions or torture that could exacerbate things, they might last four years before the madness turned them into monsters.

Cliff's bright, healthy mind had waged its battle for six years now, valiantly fighting the effects as the virus chiseled and carved away at it. He had astounded all who knew him by remaining honorable all this time, fighting alongside the Immortal Guardians and helping them conquer their enemies. None had dared hope he would last this long.

But he was beginning to lose the battle.

Seth knew it because he could read Cliff's thoughts and saw the mayhem in them. Aidan knew it for the same reason. He suspected Bastien knew it. Cliff was like a brother to him. And Bastien took Cliff vampire hunting with him each night, hoping to give Cliff an outlet for the increasingly strong, violent impulses that struck him.

Aidan suspected Melanie knew it as well. She toiled for longer and longer hours in the lab, desperately seeking answers and a way to prevent the inevitable.

She would blame herself when they lost him.

If they lost him, he mentally corrected, reluctant to give up hope.

Even if she could cure the virus with some new medication that would kill it, they would still lose Cliff. The first thing the virus did when one transformed was conquer and replace the body's immune system. So if Melanie found a way to destroy the virus, Cliff and anyone else treated with the cure would be left with no viable immune system and would die.

And if—by some miracle—Melanie found a way around *that*, she still had no way of reversing the brain damage, no way to repair the tissue the virus corrupted. Even powerful healers like himself and Seth could not heal some forms of brain damage. The brain was just too complex.

Leaning out of the bathroom, Aidan snagged his cell phone, then ducked back inside and closed the door.

Shortly after Cliff, Vincent, and Joe had come to live at the network, Chris Reordon had brought in a construction crew and had every bathroom in the building soundproofed so the vampires would stop complaining about having to listen to employees *pee, fart, and shit* all day.

Aidan dialed Chris's number.

"Reordon," Chris answered.

"It's Aidan. Can you get to a quiet room?"

"Just a minute."

Aidan waited while Chris ducked into his office bathroom and closed the door so the vampires and immortals in the building wouldn't hear their conversation.

Aidan could have saved Chris the trouble by simply speaking to him telepathically, but Chris had reacted so badly to Aidan's tampering with some of the network guards' minds a couple of years ago that he thought it best to leave the mortal's mind alone.

"Okay. What's up?" Chris asked.

"Cliff is struggling."

He swore. "How bad is it?"

"Bad. I'm going to teleport him out and take him hunting to help him work off some of the aggression that's building."

"Is Bastien going with you?"

"No. I don't want to trouble him."

Chris made a sound of understanding. "When will you be leaving?"

"In the next five minutes or so."

"Okay. I'll turn the alarm off for ten minutes. Call and give me a heads-up when you're ready to return and I'll turn it off again." Chris's techno-wizards had installed an alarm that blared anytime someone teleported in or out of a room at network headquarters. Aidan didn't know how it worked, but it had alerted them the moment Gershom had made an unexpected appearance at the network last year.

"Will do." Pocketing his phone, Aidan left the bathroom, then his apartment, and strode down the hallway to Cliff's door.

A dozen guards, all armed with automatic weapons and tranquilizer guns bearing the only sedative known to affect vampires and immortals, manned the end of the hallway, blocking the sole elevator and stairwell. Only employees with the highest security clearance could enter this floor, the farthest underground. And no vampires could leave without either an immortal escort or an armed escort to ensure they didn't harm any of the network employees or — should they suffer a psychotic break — escape.

Aidan nodded to the guards. "Gentlemen."

They nodded back. Unlike their boss, all were friendly toward Aidan, but there remained a subtle distance inspired by their awe over his age and power.

Aidan knocked on Cliff's door.

Cliff didn't answer.

"It's Aidan. I'm coming in," he announced without raising his voice.

Vampires' hearing was nearly as acute as that of immortals, so Cliff would hear him even if he whispered.

Cliff still didn't answer, but Aidan heard a welcome amidst the vampire's turbulent thoughts.

Drawing a keycard out of his pocket, he swiped it, then punched in a security code. Reordon had refused to give him such until Bastien and Melanie had asked him to.

A metallic clank sounded.

Aidan pushed the door—as thick and heavy as that of a bank vault—open and stepped inside, closing it behind him.

Every vampire who had sought the Immortal Guardians' aid had been given a luxury apartment and pretty much anything he wanted to make it feel like home… except for sharp implements. (The utensils in their kitchens were limited.) The nicely painted walls, however, were reinforced with titanium and several feet of concrete that would keep the vamps from tunneling out and escaping during psychotic breaks.

Aidan glanced around.

One might expect a man battling insanity to have a cluttered, chaotic home. But Aidan thought Cliff's apartment was tidy enough to please even the obsessive-compulsive television detective Adrian Monk.

Cliff rarely slept more than a couple of hours at a time now and constantly sought activities to keep both his mind and hands busy.

Maintaining an immaculate living space appeared to be one such activity.

Today Cliff sat on a cushy sofa, elbows on his knees, head in his hands, his fingers curling into fists and clutching his shoulder-length dreadlocks so tightly that Aidan worried he might pull his hair out.

Cliff didn't look up as Aidan approached.

Aidan sat down beside him.

The voices were louder this morning, the internal battle the young vampire waged fiercer than ever.

Aidan listened to those voices and felt his heart sink.

Though Cliff hated to admit defeat, he was considering asking Bastien to end it for him. To kill him now before he lost the last of his lucidity and became the equivalent of a rabid dog.

Cliff would end it himself but didn't want Melanie to find him… or whatever would be left after the virus devoured him from the inside out.

Aidan rested a hand on Cliff's shoulder. "Do you trust me?" he asked softly.

"Yes," Cliff whispered in a pained voice one might expect to hear emerge from the lips of someone with a pounding migraine.

"Stand up."

Lowering his clenched fists, Cliff did so and raised glowing amber eyes full of anguish.

"Don't be afraid," Aidan murmured, then teleported them to a beautiful vale in Scotland.

Cliff cried out as bright afternoon sunlight bathed them.

Aidan tightened his hold on the vampire's shoulder to keep him from bolting for the trees. "Don't."

Cliff threw up his hands to shield his face. The violent voices in his head shrieked and wailed, then went silent in the face of the fear that struck him.

A moment passed.

Aidan's hand heated where he touched Cliff as his healing gift went to work.

When the vampire's flesh didn't begin to blister from exposure, Cliff slowly lowered his hands. Squinting against the brightness, he stared down at his exposed arms.

His smooth brown skin remained healthy. No blisters formed. No pain struck.

Cliff looked up with wide eyes, his heart beginning to pound. "How is this possible? Am I hallucinating? Is this…? Am I having another psychotic break?"

"No." Aidan smiled. "I can heal with my hands and am using my gift to heal the damage the sun is doing in real time."

"You can do that?" Cliff asked with astonishment.

Aidan nodded. "I wasn't sure I could until I tried it with Ethan.

I can't say he was very pleased about being my guinea pig, but he owed me."

A little huff of laughter escaped Cliff. "Well, you *did* transform his wife for him so she'd be superstrong."

The Immortal Guardians had come to understand in recent years that, unlike those transformed by vampires, *gifted ones* who were transformed by immortals tended to become as strong and durable as those who transformed them. So Ethan's wife Heather was now as fast and strong as Aidan and even had his greater tolerance for daylight, something Ethan couldn't have given her had he transformed her himself because he had only been immortal for a century or so.

Cliff closed his eyes and tilted his face up to the sky. "It's warm," he murmured. "I'd forgotten how warm sunlight is. And that you can feel it on your skin."

"With your heightened senses, you feel it a little more now."

Cliff shook his head. When he opened his eyes, tears glistened in them. "I never thought I would feel it again. Not unless…"

Not unless he decided to end it that way, by walking into the daylight and letting the sun sear the madness — and his life — away.

Aidan squeezed his shoulder. "Every day you hold out, Cliff, every day you keep fighting, I'll give you this. I'll give you the sun."

Cliff's Adam's apple bobbed up and down. "Doesn't it hurt you?"

Aidan shrugged. His skin prickled unpleasantly as he took the damage the sun did to Cliff and absorbed it into his own body, keeping Cliff healthy. The longer they remained, the more it would hurt. "It's a mild discomfort at most," he lied.

But Cliff was a smart man. He knew better. "Why would you do this for me?"

"Because you're my friend. My brother. And this is what brothers do for each other." Aidan knew Cliff would've done the same for him. The two had become good friends since Aidan had transferred to North Carolina.

Cliff nodded. "I *would* do it for you."

Aidan didn't doubt it. Cliff was an extraordinary man. "You hear that?"

Cliff cocked his head to one side, listening. "What?"

Aidan grinned. "I think we shocked the voices into silence." No cries for violence filled the young vampire's mind.

Cliff laughed, his shoulders loosening with relief. "I think you're right. My mind hasn't been this quiet in a long time." He took in the beautiful scenery. "Where are we?"

"My home in Scotland."

"All this land is yours?"

"Yes."

"Wow. You're a lucky man." He sent Aidan a sly glance, appearing more at ease than Aidan had seen him in months. "Are you sure you aren't just trying to keep me alive longer so I can help you find a wife?"

Aidan laughed. "You've caught me. That's exactly why."

Since Cliff had heightened hearing and spent most of his time at the network, he knew a lot about the *gifted ones* who worked there and had been sharing that information with Aidan in hopes of aiding him in his quest to find love.

"Any luck yet?" Cliff asked, watching a hawk float above them on the breeze.

Aidan shrugged. "I met Veronica Becker."

"You did? I thought you had crossed her off the list because she's still mourning her husband."

"I did. But she got a flat tire."

Cliff gave him a pointed stare.

"It wasn't me," Aidan protested.

"Sure it wasn't."

Aidan laughed. "It truly wasn't, but she thought it was."

Cliff grinned. "Figured it out, did she?"

"Yes, and kindly suggested I find another MO."

The vampire laughed. "I told you so. North Carolina is like a small town. Word gets around."

"Well, when I didn't show up to change her flat tire, she got out to do it herself and was attacked by vampires."

Cliff's smile vanished. "Is she okay?"

Aidan nodded, trying to ignore the stinging pain that intensified in his skin. "She's fine. I escorted her and her son home, then went to see Dana Pembroke."

"The psychic?"

"Yes."

"How'd that go?"

"She had a vision of the two of us making love."

Cliff's eyebrows flew up as his face brightened with a smile. "That's awesome!"

"Aye. And she agreed to go out to dinner with me tonight."

"Do you think she's the one?"

Aidan shrugged. "I don't know. But I like her."

"And she's psychic and saw you two naked together. Holy hell, that's a good sign."

Aidan grinned. "I hope so."

The hawk's shadow swept across them as it took off after whatever prey had caught its attention.

Cliff surveyed the countryside around them. "It's weird. The things you take for granted. The things you wouldn't expect to miss much if they were taken away."

Most Immortal Guardians could tolerate at least a few minutes of direct sunlight and several more of indirect sunlight. The older the immortal, the more powerful they were and the more sun exposure they could tolerate.

Aidan was quite old.

But vampires began to blister as soon as the sun's rays touched their skin. They couldn't tolerate any exposure at all.

"I've always been a night owl," Cliff mused. "So when I realized I couldn't go out in daylight anymore, I didn't think I'd miss it." He continued to drink in the bright light. "But I do. I really do."

"Not anymore," Aidan vowed.

Minutes passed.

"Listen," Cliff began, "there's something I need you to do."

"Name it."

"I wouldn't ask," he added, his reluctance evident. "I had hoped I wouldn't have to." His face turned pensive. "But Bastien can't teleport and — "

"What would you have me do?" Aidan interrupted.

Cliff drew a folded piece of paper from his jeans pocket and held it out. "I need you to go to this address."

Aidan took the paper with his free hand. Flipping it open, he read the address.

Understanding dawned.

He nodded. "Consider it done."

"You know what I'm asking?" Cliff pressed.

"Yes."

"I'd ask Richart, but I don't really know him well. And Seth…"

"You'd rather Seth not know, if he doesn't already."

"Yes."

"I understand." Aidan tucked the paper into his back pocket. "Shall I go tonight?"

"No. It doesn't have to be tonight. I don't want you to cut your date short. Just… soon."

Aidan smiled but knew it didn't reach his eyes. "I'll take care of it."

"You don't have to bring me out in the sun again."

"I didn't *have* to bring you out into the sun today. I did it because I wanted to," Aidan told him. "And I'll do it again tomorrow for the same reason. And every day after that as long as you continue to fight."

"You're a good man, Aidan."

"So are you, Cliff. Nothing that happens in the future will ever negate that."

"You don't know how much I want that to be true," Cliff said, his face somber.

Chapter Three

DANA GAVE THE MIRROR ONE last glance. "You look nervous," she told herself.

She felt it, too. When was the last time she had gone on a date?

A moment's thought made her grimace. Graham Walsh. Four months ago.

Ugh. What a jerk. All hands. No brain. Smarmy little bastard.

Why couldn't her gift tell her ahead of time which men would suck as companions and which ones wouldn't?

She paused. Well, it *had*, sort of, this time. Hadn't it?

Heat coursed through her as she recalled the vision of Aidan touching her bare body.

Was she crazy to let that vision guide her instead of the other two, which had been so frightening? The man had a violent past.

What soldier hasn't? her inner voice countered. *Especially if they did tours in the Middle East?*

True. But Aidan had freely admitted that he had a violent present as well.

Not really, the voice denied. *He said he has a dangerous job. Dangerous, not violent.*

She bit her lip. He liked to hack at other men with swords in his free time. That was violent, wasn't it?

Isn't that better than parking his ass on the couch and playing video games all day or drinking with his buddies all night?

She supposed so. It certainly kept Aidan fit. All those lovely muscles…

But what about the tarot cards? They had confirmed that

something bad was on Aidan's horizon. Did she really want to start something with him when she knew something awful was coming?

When is something bad not *on the horizon? That's life.*

Also true. How many times had bad things happened in *her* life?

Too many to count. And her damned gift hadn't prevented any of it.

Her damned gift that hadn't bothered Aidan in the least. Usually when she told guys she was psychic, they assumed she was a flake, or mentally off, or—in a few cases—thought her a tool they could use to win the lotto. And they tended to really hate that she saw things about them that they preferred to keep hidden.

Aidan, on the other hand, had been refreshingly unfazed by it all.

And he had made her laugh. She loved that about him. He had a very appealing sense of humor.

"You still look nervous," she told her reflection.

She supposed that was better than looking desperate.

Aidan hadn't mentioned where they would be dining, so she had had worn her trusty black dress that could pass for either casual or dressy, depending on the shoes and accents she wore with it.

She'd add those after she saw what he was wearing.

A bell dinged downstairs.

Her heart leapt.

Switching off the light, she left her bedroom, hurried down the hallway, and skipped down the stairs that led to the shop.

When she spotted Aidan, she damn near tripped over her own feet.

He stood just inside the door, his hands in the pockets of his slacks as he calmly waited for her to appear.

She even liked that about him. People seemed to have less and less patience every day, wanting to have whatever they wanted the minute they wanted it and getting pissed at even a minute's delay.

Aidan seemed perfectly content to wait, as though he had all the time in the world.

A faint smile tilted his lips as he studied the comfortable waiting area in front of the bay window.

Tonight he wore a dress shirt, tie, and jacket—all black—and looked even more handsome than he had last week. No five-o'clock shadow darkened his strong jaw. His wavy hair had been carefully tamed. Mostly.

She grinned when she saw a few curls already starting to rebel.

When he glanced over at her, his smile widened. "There you are."

"Hi."

His gaze went to her own carefully tamed brown locks and swept a slow path to her toes. His eyes twinkled when he saw her shoes: black Converse Chuck Taylor high-top sneakers.

"Don't worry," she said as she approached him. "I'll change them before we leave. These are just more comfortable for work."

When she stopped in front of him, he took her hand in his and raised it to his lips. "You look lovely." He kissed her hand again. "And I've seen the shoes women torture themselves with today. I'd rather you be comfortable. The Chucks are fine."

She stared up at him, her heart trip-hammering in her breast. "Seriously?"

"Of course."

That was a first.

The image of a pretty, petite redhead flashed through her mind.

Fighting a frown, Dana withdrew her hand. "You don't, by any chance, have a redheaded girlfriend who wears Chucks, do you?"

His eyebrows flew up. "You saw her when we touched?"

She nodded, disappointment striking.

"Do you remember the toddler I told you about?" he asked.

"The one who inspired you to say *caboose*?"

He grinned. "That's the one. Her mother and father are friends of mine. And her mother does indeed have bright red hair and wear shoes identical to yours."

"Oh." She relaxed. "Good."

He winked. "Thought I was a geek *and* a womanizer, did you?"

She laughed. "I don't think anyone would mistake you for a geek, Aidan."

"A womanizer either if they knew my past," he said with a wry smile. "Your gift is far stronger than I thought it would be when I made my first appointment."

She shifted, wishing she had pockets of her own. The formfitting black dress left her with no place to tuck her hands when she felt awkward. Like now. "Honestly, visions this strong are pretty rare for me. I don't know why, but I seem to see things more clearly with you. It's unusually"—what was the word she wanted?—"effortless."

He tilted his head to one side. "That's a good thing, isn't it?"

Smiling, she shook her head. "I don't know yet."

"Well, let's hope it is. And I appreciate your candor."

She shrugged. "Since I'll likely see more about you than you want me to, I figured honesty was only fair." She motioned to the open doorway behind her. "Shall we begin your reading?"

"As you will."

She reached past him and turned the lock on the front door, then led him to the earth-toned room.

"Should I remove my jacket and tie?" he asked.

"Yes, please."

Why did it feel so intimate, watching him doff them?

Taking the clothes, she hung them on coat hooks tucked behind the door. When she turned around, she found him unbuttoning and removing his dress shirt.

She stared. "I don't think I've ever seen a man wear a black T-shirt under a dress shirt before." Usually they either wore a white T-shirt or nothing at all.

He offered her a sheepish smile. "I can never seem to keep my white shirts white."

She grinned. "You and me both." Taking the shirt, she hung it beside his jacket and tried to ignore the appealing scent it bore.

Aidan folded his large body onto her massage chair with a grimace. "I definitely heard it creak this time. If I keep coming here, I'm going to have to lose a few pounds."

"Don't you dare," she admonished, then bit her lip.

He arched a brow, lips twitching.

A blush heated her cheeks as she laughed. "You have an uncanny way of making me say things I should only think."

"I beg to differ," he said with another wink. "They'd be far less entertaining if you didn't speak them."

Dana moved to stand behind him. "Any new injuries or health

conditions I should know about?"

"Not a one."

"Good."

She began to stroke his broad, muscular back. Her pulse picked up, pleasure winding its way through her in a way it never did with her other clients. "No long, loud moan?" she teased.

He chuckled. "I thought I should contain myself."

Dana smiled as she worked her way down either side of his spine, then up again. She had wondered if she would again have visions of the two of them in bed. But as the minutes passed, lust didn't fill her. Concern did. "Something's happened since I last saw you," she murmured. "Something that's troubling you deeply."

He said nothing.

"You're worried about losing someone."

He swore faintly. "Your gift *is* strong. Did you *see* that or sense it?"

"Sensed it."

He shook his head. "A friend of mine is ill. He's struggling."

"I'm sorry to hear that," she said softly. "It's something brain related?" Her gift told her as much.

"Yes. We're hoping the doctors will be able to save him, but time is growing short. And he's losing hope."

"But you're helping him," she murmured. "I don't know how, but whatever you're doing is helping him." She frowned. "*Will* help him. It's something you just started doing recently?"

Straightening, he looked over his shoulder at her. "You saw that?"

She shrugged. "More like felt it."

He stared for a long moment, unspeaking. And she got the impression he wanted to ask her a question but feared the answer she might give. "Will it be enough?" he asked finally. "Will it keep him going until the doctors can find a way to heal him?"

Moving closer, Dana cupped Aidan's face in both hands. His jaw was as smooth as it looked. His skin warm. His eyes tormented. Her pulse picked up at the contact, but she ignored it and focused her gift, searching for the answer he wanted.

A minute passed.

She sighed. "I don't know. I'm sorry. It's just not coming to me."

He covered one of her hands with his and held it to his cheek. "Thank you for trying."

The room around them fell away into darkness. Now Aidan stood before her, looking down at her while she cupped his face in her small hands.

His head dipped. His lips met hers, *claimed* hers in a kiss that stole her breath and sparked heat. He wrapped one arm around her waist and drew her up against his hard form, then slid his hand down her back and over her ass to press her hips into his and let her feel his arousal.

Gasping, Dana dropped her hands and broke contact.

The earth-toned walls of the room resurfaced. Aidan still sat on the massage chair.

While she gaped at him, her heart pounding, body tingling from the vision that had come upon her so unexpectedly, he reached up and rubbed closed eyes with the hand that had held hers, almost as though he had a headache.

"Everything okay?" he murmured, probably wondering why she had jerked her hands back.

She nodded, then realized he couldn't see it with his eyes closed. "Yes." Forcing a smile, she poured every ounce of *normal* into her voice that she could muster. "Is your head hurting?"

"No. My eyes were just…" He shook his head and smiled as he lowered his hand and met her gaze. "They're fine now."

"Okay. Would you like to skip ahead to the reading?"

He smiled. "Is your gift already warmed up then?"

Among other things. "Yes."

He stood. "As you will."

⤙◈◈◈⤚

Body burning, Aidan watched Dana cross to the bookshelf and reach up to grab her tarot cards. He could not stop his gaze from following a path down her back to her narrow waist, full hips, and the bottom he had clutched in her vision.

Once more he felt the heat of her body as he had pressed her against him and ground his hips into hers. Damn, it had felt good. And it had felt so real that he had actually been surprised to find himself still sitting in her massage chair when she broke contact.

If you don't stop thinking about it, your eyes will begin to glow again, he counseled himself as he reached over to the coat hooks and grabbed his dress shirt. Drawing it on, he fastened the buttons down the front and left the tail untucked to hide the arousal Dana wouldn't miss if she glanced at his slacks.

"Are there any other questions you'd like me to try to answer tonight?" she asked as she claimed one of the chairs and motioned for him to take the other.

Sitting across from her, Aidan took the deck she offered, cut it, and shuffled it several times. "Not really. Just curious about my future, I guess."

The vision had shaken her. But she did a fair job of hiding it as she began to lay out the cards. Her brow furrowed. "Something bad is definitely coming, Aidan. Has anything happened that could give you a clue as to what it might be? The more I know, the more I may be able to *see*."

He shook his head. "No." He had even spent a couple of days at David's place, which had become the hub of the Immortal Guardians' world here on the East Coast, to see if he'd catch any *weird vibes* as Cliff would say. But Aidan had felt nothing off when he encountered Seth this past week. He had found no clues at all that might help him guess why Seth would apparently soon want to kill him. "Not so much as a hint," he murmured.

Frowning down at the cards, she slid her hand across the table.

Aidan clasped it in his, eager to touch her again.

How long had it been since he had held a woman's hand?

A moment's thought couldn't uncover the answer.

He had taken a lover here in the United States in the 60s. A lot of immortals had. The era of free love and the prodigious use of hallucinogens had, for once, made it easy for them. No need to worry about their lovers freaking out over glowing eyes and fangs when such could be blamed on the drugs.

But it had been a casual affair. All about sex. No emotional connection. No hand-holding or snuggling. No real spark, not like the one Aidan felt each time he saw or touched Dana.

"I still can't see what it is," she said, raising frustrated eyes to his. "Just that it's going to be bad."

"I've seen bad before and lived to tell the tale."

Her gaze dropped to his chest. "I guess you have. But you had men at your back you could trust then, didn't you?"

He slid his thumb across her hand, loving her soft skin. "You still believe I'll face whatever is coming alone? That my brothers won't be by my side?"

She glanced down at the cards. "I don't know if you'll be alone. But I keep feeling like you won't know who to trust. Or that someone you *do* trust may turn against you..." Her fingers tightened around his.

Aidan delved into her thoughts as another vision gripped her.

Two men, indistinct at first, hacked at each other with swords.

Him and Seth again?

No. As the figures swam into focus, Aidan had to clamp his lips together to prevent an expletive from bursting forth.

Roland Warbrook swung his swords with furious precision. Nearly a millennium old, he was a formidable opponent, matching Aidan in skill. And Roland appeared to be as determined to kill Aidan as Seth had been in Dana's previous vision.

What the hell?

Roland's mouth moved in a shout that went unheard in the silent vision. But Aidan had little difficulty reading the British immortal's lips.

You killed her, you bloody bastard! You killed *her!*

Dana yanked her hand back, leapt to her feet, and again stumbled away from the table, nearly knocking over her chair.

Aidan's heart pounded in his ears.

Killed whom? Killed Sarah—Roland's wife?

His blood went cold. Who else but Roland's wife could Aidan kill that would drive the reclusive, antisocial immortal to seek Aidan's death?

He swallowed hard.

Aidan would never harm Sarah, let alone kill her. She was the one who had given him hope again. She was the reason he believed he might actually one day find a woman who would love him and transform for him. *Nothing* could make Aidan slay Sarah. It just didn't make sense.

"Okay," Dana blurted, eyes wide as she pointed a trembling finger at him, "you have *got* to stop sword fighting in your spare time. Because that crap is going to get you killed!"

If Seth and Roland both wanted Aidan dead, there was a damned good chance it *would* get him killed.

She drew in several slow, deep breaths to calm herself, then retook her seat. "Aidan?"

Try though he might, he couldn't find a lighthearted response.

Her brow furrowed. "I'm sorry Aidan. I didn't mean to shout. And I shouldn't have said that. I don't really think your reenactment thing is crap. I just — "

"Had another vision that startled you," he interrupted, unoffended.

"Yes, but I didn't actually see you get killed, if that's why you look so worried. It was just another vision of you and one of your reenactment friends going at each other with swords. But it was so vivid that it caught me off guard and scared me." She smiled wryly. "Again."

He nodded.

"I'm sorry. I overreacted. I didn't see you die. I really didn't. So please, stop looking like I just told you the exact date and time of your death."

He wished she *could* tell him the exact date and time he would die. Then he would know how long he had to head off whatever the hell was going to make Seth and Roland want to kill him.

He smiled and forced his shoulders to relax. "No worries."

Her lips tilted up in a smile as a twinkle entered her eyes. "I don't know why so many people think men who do the whole reenactment thing are nerds. What I just saw was like something you'd see in the League of Assassins or something. Very impressive."

He winked. "Does that mean you'll still go to dinner with me?"

"Absolutely."

"Good." He stood.

Her eyebrows rose. "You mean now? Don't you want me to finish the reading?"

He shook his head. "Another time perhaps." If she saw much more in her visions, she'd know they had nothing to do with a reenactment group. He would like to get to know her better — and for her to get to know *him* better — before he risked all and tried to explain the whole *I'm-immortal-and-kill-vampires-for-a-living* thing.

Rising, Aidan crossed to the coat hooks and retrieved his tie.

"I'll go change my shoes," Dana said as she headed for the doorway.

"You're welcome to wear those," Aidan reminded her, glancing at her Chucks.

She laughed. "Maybe on our *next* date." Her eyes widened. "I mean, if there *is* one."

Aidan winked when color flooded her face. "Too late. You've already promised me a second date. I'm going to hold you to it."

Laughing again, she ducked out of the room.

<hr/>

The restaurant Aidan had chosen was owned and operated by the network.

Chris Reordon apparently was the human equivalent of Seth. The man could do *anything* and had a finger in *everything*.

Aidan had learned in the two years since he'd transferred to North Carolina that Chris was one of those stellar individuals who went above and beyond the call of duty. The network head's job was to ensure that the existence of immortals, vampires, and *gifted ones* remained a secret by cleaning up the messes immortals and vampires made, keeping Immortal Guardians supplied with bagged blood (donated by network employees), providing them with new identities each time they outlived their current one, forging whatever other documentation they needed to move from country to country, giving them new homes, safe houses for emergencies, an impressive income, and the like.

The network head also had to oversee the thousands of mortal employees who aided the Immortal Guardians by studying the virus that infected them, monitoring the internet for any videos or mentions that might out the immortals, posing as emergency-response crews when things got messier than usual, managing the Immortal Guardians' money, infiltrating certain agencies that were swathed in secrecy so they could gain more intel and provide Immortal Guardians with real-time satellite-surveillance images when the immortals launched the kind of large-scale battles they had in recent years, serving as Seconds (or mortal guards who each served a particular immortal, handled business for them during daylight hours, backed them up in battle, and kept them from living too solitary an existence), and more.

But Chris considered all that par for the course and went even further.

Chris didn't just want the immortals to maintain anonymity and be comfortable. He wanted them to be happy and have as close to a normal life as possible, even though they spent their nights in the very abnormal pursuit of hunting vampires.

So Reordon built restaurants like this one that served humans in the main dining area and immortals and their Seconds in a smaller room boasting a VIP label that led humans to assume the men and women guided back there were simply wealthy individuals who wanted special treatment. That way Seconds could enjoy a meal they didn't have to cook themselves and talk about the job without worrying about being overheard. And immortals could use their gifts without ending up in videos posted online.

Aidan had, of course, called ahead to let Sergio — the manager — know that he would be dining with a human woman, so Sergio wouldn't slip and mention Aidan's occupation.

Pocketing his keys, Aidan strode around the back of the car.

Dana stepped out before he could reach her.

"Aren't men supposed to open car doors for women?" he asked.

She wrinkled her nose. "I don't know. It always felt weird to me to sit there and expect someone else to do something I was perfectly capable of doing myself. So I never waited to see if the man would do it."

He closed the door for her. "When I look at it from that perspective, I suppose I would feel the same way." Placing a hand on the small of her back, Aidan tried to keep his eyes from fastening on the lovely hint of cleavage the neckline of her dress exposed as he escorted her to the door. "I trust you'll let me open *this* door for you?" he teased, reaching for the handle.

She laughed. "Yes, thank you."

The interior of the restaurant was nice. White tablecloths. Candles and warm lighting. A plethora of plants that added color and provided privacy for couples who wanted such.

A man in a suit as expensive and finely tailored as Aidan's

greeted them with a smile. "Good evening. Aidan O'Byrne?" he asked, tilting his head back to look up at Aidan.

"Yes."

"Excellent. I'm Sergio, the manager of this establishment. Would you and your guest please follow me? I've had a table prepared for you in our VIP section." Sergio turned and started toward a door on the far side of the restaurant.

As Aidan and Dana followed, she leaned in close and whispered, "VIP section. Ooh la la."

Aidan laughed.

The restaurant seemed to do a bustling business. The tables they passed were full of human couples and families.

Sergio opened the door to the VIP area and stood back to let them enter. Closing the door behind them, he guided them down a short hallway that opened into a smaller dining room.

For some reason, Aidan had expected the dining room to be empty. But it wasn't. Three Immortal Guardians—Étienne, his wife Krysta, and her brother Sean—dined with an older couple Aidan had come to know as Krysta's mortal parents. Both parents were *gifted ones*, but Aidan couldn't remember the nature of their gifts.

All turned at Aidan and Dana's entrance and smiled, issuing a chorus of greetings.

Aidan paused by their table.

"Who's this?" Krysta's mother, Evie, asked cheerfully.

The Immortal Guardians in the area all adored Evie because she fussed over them and treated them all like sons and daughters, something most hadn't experienced in hundreds—if not thousands—of years.

"This is Dana Pembroke," he said. "Dana, this is Étienne, his wife Krysta, her brother Sean, and their parents Evelyn and Martin."

Dana smiled and nodded. "Nice to meet you all."

Each offered a "Nice to meet you, too."

"Call me Evie," Krysta's mother said, then smiled up at Aidan with twinkling eyes. "I'd ask you if you'd like to join us, but I can tell you'd rather have Dana all to yourself."

Krysta groaned. "Mom, don't embarrass him."

Dana laughed and sent Aidan a flirtatious glance that made his heart do a funny little leap in his chest. "You want me all to yourself, do you?"

He grinned. "Absolutely."

Murmuring goodbyes, they left the group and followed Sergio to the other side of the room.

Two Seconds monopolized another table, laptops open amidst platters of more food than Aidan thought two humans should be able to consume. Sheldon served as the French immortal Richart's Second or human guard. Tracy served as Richart's sister Lisette's Second.

Aidan nodded to them. "Sheldon. Tracy."

Sheldon nodded. "Hey, man." His eyes shifted to Dana and widened. "Dude, are you on a date?"

He didn't have to look so damned surprised. "Yes. And I'm trying to impress her, so don't be"—he waved a hand in a circle in front of Sheldon—"you."

Tracy laughed. "Don't worry. I'll keep him in check."

Sheldon gave Dana a friendly smile and held out his hand. "Hi. I'm Sheldon."

Dana returned his smile and shook his hand. "Nice to meet you. I'm Dana."

"Nice to meet you, Dana. This is Tracy."

Dana shook Tracy's hand. "Nice to meet you, Tracy."

"Nice to meet you, too."

Dana looked up at Aidan. "Is Sheldon one of your adopted brothers?"

Aidan chuckled. "No. Sheldon is more of a… weird cousin to us all."

Sheldon grinned. "Proud *of* it!" Then he frowned. "Hey. Wait a minute."

Everyone laughed.

As Aidan and Dana moved away, Sergio waved them over to a table in the corner with romantic lighting and plants that partially hid them from the others' view.

Aidan held Dana's chair for her, then seated himself across from her.

Sergio handed them each a menu and vowed to return in a moment.

Dana's eyes twinkled with amusement as she opened her menu and studied him above it.

Aidan offered her a sheepish smile. "Apparently surrogate family members can embarrass one as much as blood relatives can."

Étienne, Krysta, and Sean laughed, their preternatural hearing allowing them to catch the comment.

Dana smiled. "I take it some of the others were the brothers you mentioned you work with?"

He nodded. "Étienne, Krysta, and her brother Sean are part of the private security group I work with. Out of the lot of us, I think Krysta and Sean are the only ones amongst us with family still living. So Evie and Martin have sort of adopted the rest of us. They treat us all like kin, mothering and fathering us every chance they can get."

Dana smiled. "And you all love it."

"We eat it up like candy," Aidan admitted with a grin.

"I envy you that. I lost my parents in a car accident several years ago and really miss all the worrying and butting in — the telling me not to waste my time with this guy or that one — that drove me crazy when I was in high school and college." Her eyes darkened with sadness, then lit up again. "Ooh. I bet my mom would've been able to answer all your questions. Her psychic gift was much stronger than mine."

"Your mother was psychic, too?" Aidan asked with interest. One of the oddities he'd come to understand about *gifted ones* was that they didn't always share the same gift their mother or father possessed.

Dana nodded. "So was my dad, if you can believe it. They used to joke that they never bothered to date anyone else because they knew years before they met that they would end up together."

Both parents had been psychic *gifted ones*? No wonder her gift was stronger than he had expected. Many *gifted ones* born in recent decades possessed gifts that were so muted by thousands of years of *gifted ones* DNA being diluted with ordinary human DNA that they didn't even realize they were different.

Aidan opened his menu and perused the offerings. "Anything look good to you?"

Dana eyed the menu. "Are you kidding? Everything looks good to me."

He set his menu aside. "In the movies, the man sometimes orders for the woman, but I'd much rather you choose what you want yourself. If that's everything"—he smiled—"then I'll have Sergio bring us a little bit of everything."

She stared at him a moment, then lowered her menu. "May I ask you something personal?"

"Of course."

"How long has it been since your last date?"

He laughed. "Longer than I care to admit. It shows, does it?"

Her slender shoulders lifted in a slight shrug. "Maybe a little."

"And here I was hoping to make a good impression."

"You are. A *very* good impression. But more than once you've referenced what you thought men were supposed to do on a date instead of just sort of going with what you've always done, so I thought maybe it had been a while."

Far longer than a while.

"Which I find very hard to believe," she continued, "because— with your good looks and charm—I would think women would fall all over themselves to get your attention."

In the rare instances he followed vampires into bars or clubs, women could be quite bold in their pursuit of him. But Aidan wasn't looking for an easy lay. He'd had his fill of women who could make him hard but otherwise bored the pants off him. He wanted someone who could hold his attention when they *weren't* in bed. Someone with whom he enjoyed talking. Someone who made him laugh. Someone who challenged him intellectually. Someone who made him feel young again.

Sergio returned with a waiter who placed two glasses of water and a basket full of bread on the table. The waiter took their order, then left.

Sergio migrated over to Étienne's table, asking if everything had met their expectations as the group prepared to leave.

Aidan and Dana waved as the group exited.

"I hope I didn't make you feel self-conscious or anything," Dana said, a question in her pretty hazel eyes. "I haven't dated in a while either."

"Because of your gift?" he guessed.

She nodded and toyed with the basket. "When guys find out what I do for a living, they tend to assume I'm nuts. The few who *don't* usually consider me a tool they can use to win the lotto or get rich playing the stock market."

"Imbeciles, the lot of them," Aidan declared.

She smiled. "Thank you. But even those who accept it, or at least appear to..." She shrugged. "I don't know. It's hard for them, I guess, my knowing things about them that they would rather keep hidden. It makes them uneasy. Sometimes it makes them angry."

"Or afraid?"

"That, too, though they would never admit it."

"And I'm guessing your gift often lets you see things you really wish you hadn't." He sure as hell saw a lot in people's *thoughts* that he would rather not. But when he was tired he sometimes couldn't block them.

She grimaced. "That, too. Being psychic makes dating pretty hard."

"I understand."

She cast him an uncertain look. "It really doesn't freak you out, even a little bit, knowing I can see things from your past, present, and future? Knowing that the more time we spend together, the more I'll see and the more I'll know about you that you may not *want* me to know? Because I *will* see stuff you don't want me to, Aidan. I always do. And it *always* ruins things."

Leaning forward, Aidan crossed his arms and braced them on the table. What he contemplated was no doubt very unwise, but he couldn't seem to stop himself from saying, "It doesn't freak me out at all, Dana, because I'm in the same boat."

Chapter Four

DANA FROWNED. "WHAT?"

Aidan took one of those pauses that made her think he questioned the wisdom of speaking. "I'm in the same boat," he repeated. "I haven't dated in a long time because I was born with gifts similar to yours that tend to make others uncomfortable."

Disappointment filled her. Seriously? He was *mocking* her?

"You look a bit like you want to hit me over the head with the breadbasket," he stated, brow creasing, "so — to keep you from thinking whatever it is that's making your eyes flash with fury — I'll tell you that I'm telepathic and can prove it if you'll give me permission to read your thoughts."

Hell yes, she was furious. This was Jason all over again. That asshole had pretended he had psychic abilities like hers in a lame attempt to get into her pants. He hadn't realized she actually *was* psychic and would see through his bullshit.

Dana leaned back in her chair and crossed her arms. "You're telepathic?"

"Yes."

"Prove it."

"I can read your thoughts?"

"You tell me," she countered, a blatant dare. *Read my thoughts, my ass*, she mentally grumbled. She had thought Aidan was different, but to mock her like this by pretending he had a special gift, too? What a disappointment.

"I *am* different," he insisted. "And I'm not pretending. I do have a special gift. More than one, if you're to know the truth of it."

She frowned. Had he just read her thoughts?

"Yes," he said.

She narrowed her eyes. Yes, what? Yes, he had read her thoughts? Or was he just guessing the path they would naturally take?

"Yes, I read your thoughts," he said. "And yes, I could've guessed the path they would take, but I didn't."

She stilled. Okay. That was a little spot-on.

"And to prove it," he continued, "I'll tell you that, although I have not been listening to your thoughts on our date, I *did* give them a listen both times you gave me a reading and know that you've had two visions about me that you failed to mention."

Her heart began to pound. How did he know that?

"In the first one," he said, lowering his voice, "we were naked in bed and I was touching your — "

"Holy crap," she whispered, dropping her arms and gaping at him.

His lips twitched. "I was going to say breast, but— "

"How do you know about that?" she blurted.

"The same way I know that in the second vision, you were cupping my face in your hands — as you did earlier — and I kissed you and pulled you up against me, sliding my hand down over your lovely bottom. I read your thoughts and saw it as clearly as you did."

Speech eluding her, Dana stared at him so long that her eyes began to burn.

"Blink," he instructed.

She did.

"I know it's a bit of a shock," he murmured, eyeing her with some concern.

"A bit of a shock," she parroted numbly.

"I know it feels… intrusive. But I didn't read your thoughts the whole time. Most of the time I can control what I hear and don't hear and can block others' thoughts fairly easily." Younger telepathic immortals weren't so lucky. "But when the visions struck you, I saw them as clearly as *you* did without even trying. I think because we're both gifted."

She hadn't told anyone about those visions. There was no way he could've known about them without reading her mind. "Holy. Crap."

His eyebrows rose.

"Are you reading my thoughts right now?" she asked.

"Yes. They're a little chaotic. I'm sorry I've shaken you up so much. I just wanted you understand why I haven't dated in so long and hoped you'd appreciate my honesty."

Honesty! He had read her thoughts! He had apparently been reading them all this time, saying exactly what he knew she wanted him to say and—

His brows drew together. "Now wait a minute. That's not true. I would never use what I saw in your thoughts to manipulate you. If that had been my intent, I never would've told you I'm telepathic."

"Dude," a voice interrupted, "you told her you're telepathic?"

Aidan swung around and shot a glare at Sheldon.

Dana guessed Sheldon was in his early twenties. Tracy looked to be thirty or thereabouts. Both eyed her and Aidan with great interest as they gathered their laptops and gear and stopped by Dana and Aidan's table on their way to the door.

"Sheldon," Aidan growled, definitely a warning.

"You know he's telepathic?" Dana asked his friend.

"Yeah," Sheldon responded simply. The woman at his side nodded. Neither seemed to view it as anything extraordinary, as if she had just asked them if they knew Aidan could play the piano.

"It doesn't bother you?" Dana pressed.

Sheldon gave a dismissive shrug. "Nah. Aidan's a good guy. He almost never reads my mind."

Aidan grimaced. "Because there's too much porn and weird shite up there."

Tracy laughed and gave Sheldon's shoulder a shove. "Freak."

Sheldon grinned. "You know it." Then he caught Dana's eye. "I'm surprised he told you. People don't usually react well when they find out he's different. I'd think you'd understand that since you're different, too."

He knew she was a psychic? "How did you—?"

"I heard a rumor that Aidan was smitten with a psychic." He shrugged. "When I saw you two together, I assumed you were her."

Aidan frowned. "Where'd you hear that?"

Sheldon hesitated. "Cliff let it slip while we were playing video games. You won't hold it against him, will you? He didn't mean to. He was just… more distracted than usual. And Tracy is the only person I've told."

Aidan shook his head. "It's fine."

Tracy smiled. "We'd better go before Sheldon says anything else that will embarrass you." Taking Sheldon's arm, she urged him toward the door. "You two have a nice evening."

"What'd I say that embarrassed him?" Sheldon asked, puzzled.

She whispered something to him.

Sheldon snorted. "Yeah, right. Like she didn't already know he's smitten. It's so obvious."

Tracy pushed him into the hallway and closed the door after them.

In the wake of their departure, Aidan swung back around and met Dana's gaze with obvious reluctance. "Apparently there's something else I failed to tell you that you should probably know."

Seriously? Something *else*? "What's that?" she asked, unsure she wanted to hear it.

He sighed. "I *suck* at dating."

Dana laughed. She couldn't help it.

Sergio and the waiter returned with platters of food that smelled so delicious Dana's stomach growled.

"Thank you," she murmured as the two smiling men backed away, then exited.

A heavy silence fell.

Dana picked up her fork and speared some salad. "So." Tucking the crunchy veggies in her mouth, she chewed and swallowed. "You're smitten with a psychic, are you?"

Relief smoothed the lines in Aidan's brow. His lips tilted up. "Very much so."

"Because of the visions?" she asked, trying not to blush.

His smile grew as he picked up his own fork. "I was smitten before the visions. The visions just gave me hope that you might one day be smitten, too."

And damned if her heart didn't give a little jump in her chest.

"Don't read my thoughts!"

He chuckled. "I won't. I'm afraid if I do, I'll find you trying to think of a diplomatic way to end our date early."

Better that than him finding her mentally reviewing the visions of them making love.

"You're blushing," he said with a wince. "Did I guess right? Are you wanting to end our date?"

"No. I was just…" She shook her head with a smile. "Having those visions about you was already weird. Your *knowing* about them just makes it…"

"Even weirder?" he suggested.

"Yes."

"You've never had erotic visions before?"

"No. Not even about the men I slept with."

He winked. "Perhaps they simply weren't very talented in bed."

Laughing, she lowered her eyes to her plate and nudged the food around with her fork. "I don't know." How to explain it without scaring him off? "It almost feels like…"

"Your gift is telling you we're meant to be together?"

"Yes," she answered finally. And she didn't know how to feel about that.

Risking a glance up at him, she found him regarding her with understanding. A far cry from the *Holy-crap-she's-talking-about-marriage-on-our-first-date* look or the *Hot-damn-I'm-gonna-get-laid* look she had expected to find.

"I can see how you might find that a bit unsettling," he told her, unperturbed.

A bit unsettling was an understatement. "What did *you* think when you saw the visions?" she asked, curious.

His eyes twinkled with mischief. "You mean besides wanting desperately to see those visions play out?"

She grinned. "Yes, aside from that."

He seemed to think about it for a moment. "I was surprised the visions were so clear."

"They usually aren't."

"And when you told me your visions always come true, I wondered the same thing you did—if your gift was telling you we're destined to be together."

She carried another forkful to her lips, chewed, swallowed. "It isn't just the nature of the visions. It's that this has never happened before. Usually I get feelings or impressions or cloudier visions of *other* people's futures. But I've *never* been given such vivid glimpses of my own. I just don't know how I feel about it."

A twinkle of mischief entered his deep brown eyes. "You've seen your own future and can't decide whether or not you're happy with the choices you're going to make?"

She smiled, feeling another rush of amusement. "No. It isn't that. It isn't *you*. I don't know how to explain it."

"I think I know what you mean." He paused to consume a bit of mouthwatering chicken, then sighed. "I've been alone for a long time, Dana. But the fact that I haven't been dating doesn't mean that I've not been searching for someone I could love. Someone whose company I can enjoy so much that I never want to be without it. Someone I could easily imagine spending the rest of my life with." He set his fork down. "And now that your visions are telling me I may have found her. Found *you*. That *you're* the someone I've been searching for…" He gave her a wry smile. "I find I'm a bit torn."

That shouldn't hurt, should it? Because it did. Enough to surprise her.

Leaning forward, he braced his forearms on the table. "Part of me is overjoyed. Part of me is thrilled that I may have finally found someone who makes me laugh and feel happy in a way I haven't in a very long time. Someone I can look forward to spending all my days and nights with."

Her treacherous heart began to pound again.

Lowering his eyes, he touched a finger to the breadbasket. "But there's another part of me that I have to admit, much to my surprise, wants to dig in his heels. Because somehow acknowledging the visions and going along with them feels like I'll be forfeiting free will."

"Yes!" Relieved that he really did seem to understand, she set her fork down and leaned closer. "That's it exactly. You've described it perfectly. I like you, Aidan. And I like the idea that we may find something meaningful together if we keep seeing each other. But the idea that I may not have any choice in the matter just doesn't sit well with me."

Smiling, he rested a hand on the table, palm up in invitation.

Dana placed her hand in his and felt that tingle of excitement she always did when she touched him.

He curled his fingers around hers. "You have choice."

Her heart leapt when he slid his thumb across the back of her hand in a soft caress.

"You just have to decide which part of you is speaking the loudest."

The one that wanted to see him again. "Which part of *you* is speaking the loudest?"

He smiled. "The part that wants to see you again. The part that enjoys your company."

Happiness and relief filled her, until she realized he had just echoed her thoughts. "Wait. Are you reading my thoughts again?"

His eyebrows flew up. "No. I said I wouldn't. Why?"

She sent him a wry smile. "Because you just echoed them perfectly."

A boyish grin lit his face. "So you're saying I *don't* suck at dating?"

She laughed. "No, you don't."

He winked. "Then let's abandon all thought of fate and just enjoy each other's company, shall we?"

She nodded.

Giving her hand a squeeze, he released it and tucked into his meal once more.

Dana did the same. And as the night progressed, she tried to remember if she had ever had a first date—or *any* date for that matter—in which her companion had enchanted her more.

Aidan was charming and funny and so damned handsome. He was smart, too, which she found as great a lure as his physical appearance. Ignorance had always been a deal-breaker for her. If she had to pick one or the other, she would always choose brains over brawn. But with Aidan, she didn't have to.

Once he finished his dinner, he reached across the table once more and clasped her hand in his. Such a simple touch. His thumb caressing the back of her hand as he laughed over a story she shared about the time in high school she had had a vision of a male acquaintance getting pantsed by his so-called friends. She had tried to warn him, only to find herself accused of being the mastermind behind it when the vision came true.

And she, in turn, laughed when he admitted that whenever his brothers didn't want Aidan to read their minds, they pictured themselves naked to dissuade him.

Dana didn't realize how much time they had spent talking and laughing together until Sergio returned to ask them if they'd like to order another dessert.

They had already devoured two, something she would likely regret when she got on the scale in the morning. But she had been having a wonderful time and hadn't wanted it to end.

"What do you think?" Aidan asked. "Would you like to try something else?"

She glanced at her watch. Her eyes widened. "We've been here five hours?"

Aidan grinned. "Time flies when you're having fun, doesn't it?"

Yes, it did. And they had been having a lot of fun. But it was probably time for the restaurant to close.

She looked at Sergio. "No, thank you. I'm good."

Aidan rose and held out a hand. "Shall we go then?"

Nodding, she rose, looped her purse strap over her shoulder, and placed her hand in his.

His was so much bigger than hers that the whole of her hand could fit in his palm. But it felt absurdly wonderful when he twined his fingers through hers and escorted her after Sergio.

The large front room was deserted as they passed through it.

Once ensconced in Aidan's car, Dana began to feel both nervous and excited.

Since he had seen the vision of the two of them naked in bed, would he expect her to make love with him tonight?

Quite a few of Dana's friends and acquaintances wouldn't have hesitated. But she had never ended a first date with sex before.

Granted, she'd never gotten to know a man so well on a first date. Another novelty about Aidan was that he had not looked at his cell phone once during the five hours they had talked and dined. He hadn't taken any calls. He hadn't texted. He hadn't scanned his social media feeds or anything else of that nature. He had instead given her his full, undivided attention.

You could learn a lot about a person over the course of five hours of conversation.

Aidan parked in front of her shop. "I believe dinner and a movie is a standard first date. I'd say I'm sorry we didn't get to see a movie" — theaters closed fairly early in North Carolina — "but I enjoyed your company too much to complain."

She smiled. "I enjoyed yours, too."

Opening his door, he stepped out into the night.

Dana opened her own and got out as he strolled around the back of the car. Closing the door, she unzipped her purse and withdrew her keys.

Aidan placed a hand on her lower back as they walked toward her front door. "So. What's the proper way to end our first date?"

"I'm not having sex with you," she blurted, then bit her lip.

His eyebrows flew up. "Ever? Or tonight?"

"Tonight." She gave him a self-deprecating smile. "I'm sorry. It's just, I know you saw the vision of the two of us in bed and was afraid you might…"

"Expect you to invite me in so we could reenact it?" he finished for her.

"Yes."

He frowned. "Is *that* how couples end first dates now? I was just hoping you wouldn't think me too forward if I asked you for a kiss."

Amusement sifted through her, soothing her nerves. She had discovered tonight that his speech and attitudes were a very entertaining combination of modern and old-fashioned. "A kiss sounds good."

He smiled. "You don't know how happy that makes me." Sliding one arm around her, Aidan drew her close.

Her pulse increased with anticipation as she looked up at him.

Dipping his head, he touched his lips to hers.

Her breath caught. Her heart stopped, then began to pound in her chest so loudly she wondered if he could hear it.

He tilted his head, increased the pressure. And that first tentative caress soon became a fiery exploration that made her whole body burn.

Dropping her purse and keys, Dana slid her arms around him and flattened her hands on the muscles of his broad back. A deep rumble of approval emanated from him as she leaned into his hard form, pressing her breasts to his chest and washboard abs.

Never had she been so turned on by a kiss.

Wrapping his other arm around her, he tightened his hold, pressed her closer, let her feel his growing erection.

She parted her lips.

He slipped his tongue inside to stroke and tease her own.

Dana moaned. He tasted so good. Felt so good. She didn't want it to end. Wanted to jump up and wrap her legs around his waist.

Aidan ended the kiss. Eyes closed, he pressed his forehead to hers. Both fought for breath, their chests rising and falling quickly. Bodies still pressed together.

Then he released her and took a deliberate step back. Sliding his hands into his pockets, he drew in a deep breath, held it, then let it out slowly.

Dana stared up at him, trying to calm her racing pulse, stunned by the intensity of the desire she felt for him. One kiss and she was ready to say, *You know what? Forget what I said a minute ago. Let's get naked.*

And he appeared to have been just as affected as she.

He opened his eyes. Such a deep, dark brown. "Well." His lips turned up in that winsome smile she found so irresistible. "I don't know about you, but the part of me that was digging in his heels earlier is now telling me he's all in."

She laughed. "Mine is, too."

Bending down, he picked up her purse and keys for her.

"Thank you."

Drawing his own keys out of his pocket, he touched her arm with his free hand and gave it an affectionate squeeze. "I'd better leave before I go back on my word and ask for more than a kiss."

She nodded.

Dipping his head once more, he pressed his lips to hers in a light caress. "Good night, Dana."

"Good night."

Withdrawing his touch, he walked backward toward the driver's side of the car, as if he was loath to let her out of his sight.

"Would you by any chance be amenable to my seeing you again tomorrow night? Or would that be too soon?"

She smiled. "Tomorrow night sounds good. Seven o'clock?"

Grinning, he offered her a gallant bow. "Seven o'clock it is." He opened the car door. "I'll wait to leave until after you're inside with the door locked."

And she'd thought he couldn't appeal to her more. "Thank you." Unlocking the door to her shop, she stepped inside. "Good night, Aidan."

"Good night."

Closing the door, she locked it and watched through the window as he ducked into his car and started the engine.

Tossing her a jaunty wave, he backed out of the parking space and drove away.

Dana couldn't wait to see him again.

———◦◦◦———

Aidan stared at the quaint home before him. Off the beaten path, it was small and painted a pale, cheery yellow with white trim. In front of it, a picture-perfect lawn bore edges as straight as a blade. A row of dark shrubs butted up against the house on either side of the stone sidewalk. Flowers in every color of the rainbow proliferated in front of them and poured over the sides of hanging baskets on the front porch. Bright white window boxes offered even more colorful plants, proclaiming the homeowner's green thumb.

A heart beat, slowly and steadily, inside the house.

"Stop procrastinating," he grumbled to himself and strode up the walk, the setting sun at his back.

His boots produced thumps as loud as a bass drumbeat in the night's quiet as he scaled the wooden steps and ducked under the porch's roof. Raising a fist, he knocked on the front door.

Nearly silent footsteps carried to his ears as the individual inside crept over to the front door. Aidan bent his knees a bit so she could see him through the peephole.

He knew the moment she did. Her heart began to slam against her ribs.

A full minute passed.

He sighed. "I can hear your heartbeat through the door, so pretending you aren't home isn't going to work, Emma."

A whispered curse. "What do you want?"

"I need to speak with you. Open the door, please." When she made no move to do so, he sighed again. "You know who and what I am, so you know no locks can keep me out. I'm asking you as a courtesy."

Another quiet moment passed, then the *click* of locks being unlatched intruded upon the night.

The door swung open.

Aidan stared down at the woman illuminated by the porch's light.

She opened the door only the width of her body and held it there, indicating she had no intention of inviting him inside.

He fought a smile.

She was lovely, with smooth, flawless skin the color of Melanie's favorite chocolate bars. Eyes as dark a brown as his own filled with anxiety as they rose to meet his.

He guessed her height to be in the neighborhood of five feet five inches. Her thick black hair was drawn back from her face in intricate braids he had heard Cliff call cornrows, until about the place where some women and girls wore headbands. Then it sprang free in an Afro that looked as soft and fluffy as cotton candy.

Narrow shoulders bared by a tank top stiffened as she braced herself and clenched her jaw, gearing up for a fight. Her slender arms ended in hands that gripped the door and doorframe so tightly he could see the tendons in her knuckles. Small breasts. A barely there waist. And full hips clad in yoga pants that clung to shapely legs.

"You know who I am," Aidan stated again.

She gave him an abrupt nod. "You're Aidan. I've seen you around at the network."

"And Cliff has mentioned me."

She seemed to debate the wisdom of answering that one. "Yes," she responded, voice neutral.

"As I said, we need to talk."

After hesitating another moment, she stepped back and opened the door wide enough for him to enter.

Aidan stepped inside and glanced around while she closed the door behind him, leaving it unlocked. They stood in her living room. Small, but tastefully decorated. Beyond it lay a modern kitchen and a breakfast nook that housed a treadmill instead of a table and chairs.

"So?" she prompted, folding her arms just under her breasts.

"So," he parroted and wondered how to begin. "You've been seeing Cliff."

Something flickered in her eyes, and he could almost hear the debate waging inside her. Should she deny it? Feign ignorance? Brazen it out?

"How did you know?" she asked finally.

"Cliff is my friend," he told her. "I sleep at the network during the day and have spent a lot of time with him since transferring to North Carolina." How could he put this delicately? "You know that immortals and vampires have heightened senses."

She nodded.

"Well, I couldn't help but notice that, on the nights Bastien takes Cliff hunting with him and lets him roam alone for a few hours, Cliff always returns carrying a woman's scent."

Her lashes lowered as she looked down at her small bare feet.

"I catch the same scent each time I pass your office at the network. And even if I didn't, I'm telepathic and see you in his thoughts."

A muscle twitched in her jaw. "If you're here to tell me not to see him anymore, you can— "

"That's not why I'm here," he interrupted, cutting her off before she could tell him to go fuck himself. Cliff had chosen well. This woman would fight long and hard to remain by his side. "Because I'm telepathic, I also know that Cliff is always in better shape mentally after spending time with you. He's calmer. More at peace." Aidan shrugged. "I'm his friend. I wouldn't take that away from him."

She lowered her arms, all defensiveness fleeing. "He says I quiet the voices."

"You do." Damn, he hated to be the bearer of bad news. "But Cliff is struggling, Emma."

Her throat worked in a swallow. "He's been struggling for a

long time now."

Aidan shook his head. "Yesterday was different."

Fear and dread returned to her brown eyes. "What happened? He didn't come by last night. Did he have another break?"

"No," Aidan told her. "But the voices clamoring in his head were so loud that they woke me from a sound sleep. And when I went to him…" He really hated to tell her this. "He was contemplating ending it."

All strength seemed to leave her legs.

Aidan hastily grasped her upper arms to keep her from sinking to the floor.

Emma gripped his forearms with desperate hands, fingers twisting the material of his sleeves. Moisture welled in her eyes. "Is he…? Did he ask Bastien to…?"

"No," Aidan hastened to assure her. Cliff must have told her about Vincent.

When Vince's madness had progressed enough that he had flown into a rage and hurt several network employees, he had asked Bastien to end it before he lost himself altogether and hurt anyone else.

Though it had torn him up inside, Bastien had broken into network headquarters, fought his way to Vince's side, and decapitated his friend.

Bastien still relived that horrid moment in his dreams.

"Cliff is alive," Aidan told her.

Tears spilled over her lashes as her chest rose and fell with harsh breaths taken to hold back sobs. "I thought you were going to tell me…" Shaking her head, she swallowed hard. "He's okay then?"

Aidan guided her over to a sofa. "Let's sit down, shall we?"

She nodded. Releasing him, she sank down on the soft cushions and swiped at her tears.

Aidan retrieved a wingback chair from one corner and plunked it down across from her so he could face her. Seating himself, he leaned forward and placed his elbows on his knees. "I tried something new yesterday that I hoped would help him. I teleported him to a sunny meadow on my estate in Scotland."

Her eyes flew wide. "You hurt him?" she demanded furiously. "How could you? He's been helping you— "

Aidan held up a palm. "I didn't hurt him. I'm a powerful healer and kept my hand on his shoulder the entire time, healing the damage the sun wrought so quickly that he didn't feel it."

Her brow furrowed. "You can do that?"

"Yes. I tried it first on Ethan, an immortal who is only a century old and can tolerate very little sun exposure, to confirm it would work."

She still looked skeptical. "So Cliff was able to stand in sunlight without it hurting him?"

Aidan smiled. "Yes. And we discovered that sunlight silences the voices as effectively as you do."

Hope brightened her features. "So he's better now?"

"He's better," Aidan confirmed.

She smiled. Reaching out, she took one of his hands. "Thank you."

"I was happy to do it."

"Do you think—if it gets bad again—that maybe you could do it again?"

Aidan patted her hand. "I've already told Cliff I'll take him into the sunlight every day he continues to fight."

Her eyes filled with hope. "Really? You would do that for him?"

"Of course." He had taken him into the sunlight a second time today. "He's my friend."

"But doesn't it hurt?" she asked, face pensive. "I thought immortals healed others by absorbing the damage into their own bodies."

Aidan shrugged. "I told Cliff it's a mild discomfort at most."

She smiled wryly. "It hurt like hell, didn't it?"

He laughed. "Yes. The longer we stood in the sunlight, the worse the pain grew. But I can tolerate it for Cliff. He's a good man, well worth saving."

Her lips turned up in a sad smile. "I wouldn't love him if he weren't."

Cliff had chosen well indeed.

"Did you know he saved my life?" she asked.

Surprised, Aidan shook his head. "No."

Her smile grew. "I work the day shift now but used to work nights at the network. And I was there when mercenaries bombed the original network headquarters just before dawn."

That had happened before Aidan had come to North Carolina. Apparently a mercenary group had learned of the virus that infected vampires and immortals and had decided to use it to create an army of supersoldiers they could hire out to the highest bidder. When they realized that vampires always descend into madness, they ferreted out the location of network headquarters and proceeded to bomb the hell out of it in an attempt to get their hands on an Immortal Guardian so they could find out why immortals *don't*.

The damage done had been so catastrophic that Reordon had had to abandon the site entirely and move all operations to a new building.

"I worked on Sublevel 1," she continued. "Part of the ground floor collapsed before I could evacuate. Something hit me on the head and knocked me unconscious. And when I woke up, I was buried beneath the rubble and couldn't move." She shook her head. "I didn't even have a chance to call for help before the concrete and whatever else above me began to shift and groan as someone lifted it away. The next thing I knew, Cliff was staring down at me, his eyes glowing bright amber while he told me not to be afraid, that he was there to help me."

"Did you know he was a vampire?" Aidan asked curiously.

"Not with certainty. But I had heard that one of the vampires housed on Sublevel 5 was a brother. And I figured he wouldn't keep telling me not to be afraid if he were an immortal."

Aidan peeked into her memories and saw Cliff repeatedly telling her not to be afraid, raising his voice so she could hear him over the barrage of explosions while he checked her for injuries. With preternatural speed, Cliff tore a strip of cloth from his shirt and tied it around her arm where it bled profusely. He then secured the broken arm with a makeshift sling and gently lifted her into his arms.

As Cliff sped over to the elevator shaft, preparing to leap down and take her to the doctors and the evacuation tunnel on Sublevel 5, Emma peered over his shoulder and saw mercenaries entering the building through one of the holes in the ceiling.

"I wouldn't have made it out of the building alive if Cliff hadn't saved me," she finished.

Those mercenaries had been merciless. If they had found her before Cliff had, they would have taken her, tortured her for information, then killed her.

"So *that's* how you two met." For some reason, he had thought the couple had met in the cafeteria at the network.

She grinned. "Yes, but he doesn't remember it. I was pretty unrecognizable when he found me."

And according to what Aidan had heard, Cliff had been captured by the mercenaries shortly thereafter and tortured badly enough to trigger his first psychotic break. Cliff had very little memory of that night or the days that followed.

Aidan drew a piece of paper from his front pocket and handed it to her along with a small box.

"What's this?" she asked as she took them.

"Cliff asked me to speak with you."

She frowned. "Why?"

"He's worried he's going to hurt you."

"He won't," she countered. "I've already told him he won't hurt me. I'm sure of it. But he— "

Aidan held up a hand. "You didn't see him yesterday, Emma. You didn't hear his thoughts. And you've never seen a vampire who has completely succumbed to the madness and lost all knowledge of right and wrong."

She shook her head. "Dr. Lipton told me that—even during psychotic breaks—the other vampires have never attacked her or Dr. Machen."

"Melanie knows about you?"

"Yes. Bastien told her Cliff and I were lovers. And she came to see me, afraid I might not understand the consequences of getting pregnant by him or that I might not understand fully what the virus will do to him."

"Did she try to talk you out of seeing him?"

"No. She loves Cliff and wants him to find whatever happiness he can. She just wanted me to be prepared."

Aidan sighed. "Well, Vince asked Bastien to end his life before the damage progressed too far, so we don't really know if he would've attacked Melanie eventually. Cliff has held out far longer than the others and, despite his valiant efforts, is beginning to lose the battle. His greatest fear now is that he may hurt you."

"He won't," she insisted.

Aidan pointed to the piece of paper she held. "That's my cell phone number." He pointed to the box. "And that is one of those cell phone wristwatch gadgets with voice activation. If you want to continue seeing Cliff, program my number into it and keep that watch on you at all times. And I mean *all* times. When the two of you are making love. When you take a shower. Never take it off."

Her brow crinkled. "Is it waterproof?"

"Yes. And if you have even the slightest fear that Cliff is about to have a break or that he may hurt you, call me immediately. I'm a teleporter, so I can be here in half a second to protect you and help Cliff."

Clearly she wasn't happy about it. "He'll stop coming here if I don't agree to this, won't he?"

"Yes. He loves you, Emma. If you love him as much as you appear to, then do this for him and ease his fears. He doesn't need those on top of everything else he's facing."

Nodding, she opened the box and fastened the watch to her wrist. It took a while and several consultations of the instruction manual for them to figure out how to add his number and achieve voice recognition. But they succeeded.

"Call Aidan," she said.

Aidan's cell phone chirped in his pocket.

Both grinned.

"Now," Aidan said, sobering, "here is something Cliff *doesn't* know about." Reaching into his coat, he withdrew two tranquilizer guns.

"Uh-uh," she said, eyeing them with belligerence. "No way. I am *not* going to shoot Cliff."

"These are tranquilizer guns, already armed with darts that can sedate Cliff should the need arise."

Shaking her head, she held up her wrist. "I don't need those. I have this."

"You need to have a defensive measure that Cliff doesn't know about, Emma. Once the brain damage progresses to a certain point, psychotic breaks can occur without warning. If Cliff flies into a rage and rips the watch off your arm, you'll have to go for one of these. They've been specially designed for vampire hunting by the network's weapons experts, so each can fire up to five darts. A single dart should calm him. Two will knock him out. Three will kill him. Avoid the last if at all possible." He placed the guns beside her on the sofa. "Hide these where they will be handy in an emergency but where Cliff won't accidentally happen upon them."

She eyed them with dread.

"If Cliff hurts you, Emma, it will kill him. He will end it himself in a heartbeat, even if the wound is so minor you shrug it off. If you want to hold on to him, you need to ensure he can't hurt you."

She nodded, disconsolate. "He said I quiet the voices," she murmured again.

Aidan nodded. "You do. But the voices are getting louder. And soon you will only dampen them a little." Returning his chair to the corner, he headed for the front door. As he reached for the doorknob, she spoke.

"Aidan?"

He turned.

She closed the distance between them. Rising onto her toes, she kissed his cheek, then hugged him hard. "Thank you for giving Cliff the sun again."

Aidan hugged her back. "Thank you for loving him and bringing him happiness."

She moved away.

"Are you going to see him tonight?" he asked.

"Yes. He's supposed to come over after he and Bastien finish hunting."

Aidan smiled. "Then you should shower and wash my scent off you. We don't want to tempt fate."

She laughed. "I'll go do it now."

Stepping outside, Aidan closed the door and waited for Emma to lock it. Seconds later, he heard a faucet squeak and water spray tiles as she turned on the shower.

As he strode down the front walk, a figure stepped from the shadows. Aidan halted as Bastien joined him.

"Thank you," the British immortal said. "Both for what you did yesterday and for this." He looked toward the house.

Aidan nodded. "Cliff is my friend. If all Melanie and the others need to save his sanity and his life is more time to understand the virus, I want to give them all we can."

Sighing wearily, Bastien rubbed his eyes. "I know I should've told Cliff not to see her, but..."

"She makes him happy."

Bastien nodded. "I love him like a brother. I can't take that away from him."

"You don't need to." He titled his head toward the house. "She's strong. A fighter. She knows what's coming and understands how rough things will get. But she loves Cliff and wants to have every moment — good or bad — that she can with him."

Bastien's Adam's apple rose and fell.

"Does Seth know?" Aidan asked curiously.

Bastien snorted and rolled his eyes. "I'm sure he does. That bastard knows *everything*."

Aidan laughed. Then an unsettling thought intruded.

In her vision, Dana had seen Seth and Aidan engaged in furious battle. It wouldn't be because of Cliff, would it?

Maybe Seth *didn't* know.

The Immortal Guardians' leader had a hell of a lot on his plate right now, trying to hunt down and destroy Gershom before he could trigger fucking Armageddon. Aidan would think it quite plausible that something like Cliff taking a lover could escape Seth's notice.

"What?" Bastien asked.

Aidan shook his head. If he told Bastien about Dana's vision, Seth might see it in Bastien's thoughts. "You should probably remove the weapons from Cliff's apartment."

The younger immortal stilled. "What weapons?"

Aidan arched a brow. "The large cache of hunting weapons you purchased for him and let him keep there."

He grimaced. "You know about that?"

"Of course I do. I know you gave them to him as a gift, but removing them will give the voices in his head less to blather on about. You'd be doing Cliff a favor. Just tell him Reordon found out and insisted they be removed. If he were well, Cliff would understand and forgive you the lie."

Bastien nodded.

Aidan tucked his hand in his pocket and drew out a pocket watch. "I have to go." Tucking the watch away, he smiled. "I have a date." And was damned eager for it to start.

Bastien's eyebrows flew up. "You do?"

"Yes. With a very lovely psychic. Any advice you'd care to offer?"

"Hell no. The closest thing to a date Melanie and I ever had was her going vampire hunting with me. And that nearly got her killed. I *still* don't know why she loves me."

Laughing, Aidan clapped him on the back. "The important thing is—she does."

He grinned. "I know. I'm a lucky bastard."

"That you are."

"You should ask Richart about dating. Judging by the nauseatingly sweet phone calls I overheard while we hunted together, he courted Jenna for quite some time before vampires outed him."

Unfortunately, Aidan didn't know the French immortal as well as he did Bastien. "I'll consider it. Good hunting tonight."

Bastien saluted him. "Enjoy your date."

Chapter Five

AIDAN JERKED AWAKE WHEN HIS phone rang. Glancing at the clock, he groaned.

He had been seeing Dana for two weeks. And after yet another fantastic date, he had hunted until dawn, then stumbled back to his apartment at network headquarters just as the sun peeked over the horizon. Cliff had been wandering the halls, unable to sleep, so Aidan had teleported him to Auckland, New Zealand, and taken him hunting. When hours of that hadn't helped, he'd taken Cliff into the sun again, then returned to the network and finally gone to bed. Two hours ago.

He fumbled for the phone. "Yes?" he answered, his voice gravelly from sleep.

"It's Seth. I'm in Chris's office and need to speak with you."

"Okay. Do you want me to come now?"

"Yes." The voice of the Immortal Guardians' leader lent Aidan no clue to his mood.

"All right. I'm on my way."

Aidan took a minute to shower and dress, then pocketed his phone and headed upstairs.

Kate, Chris Reordon's assistant, looked up when he entered the reception room outside his office. She nodded to the door. "They're waiting for you."

"Thank you."

Inside, Chris leaned back against his desk, arms crossed.

Seth stood patiently beside him, his expression telling Aidan no more than his voice had.

"What's up?" Aidan asked.

Seth motioned to a door. "Let's speak in there, shall we?"

"Okay." Aidan strode through the door and found himself in what appeared to be a large boardroom. A long wooden table, its surface as shiny as glass, dominated the room. At least thirty elegant black chairs on wheels surrounded it.

Seth entered, Chris on his heels.

"Have a seat, Aidan," Seth said.

While Chris closed the door, Aidan drew out a chair and sat down.

Seth took the chair across from him.

Chris sat at the head of the table.

Aidan had noticed over the years that—though Seth was always the most powerful man in the room—he never usurped another's place in that person's home or place of business. At David's home, Seth always reserved the seat at the head of the table for David. And here Seth left the seat at the head of the table for Chris. Aidan had always liked that about him. The best leaders were always those who didn't feel the need to flaunt their power.

Wondering what this was all about, Aidan studied the boardroom. Very posh. Very elegant. "Very nice," he commented.

Chris said nothing.

"Any particular reason we're talking in here instead of your office?" Aidan asked.

Seth answered. "This room is soundproof."

Aidan frowned. "It can't be. I can hear what's happening in the rest of the building."

Chris placed a laptop on the table. "There are mics in my office and speakers in here that let us hear what's happening out there without anyone out there hearing what's happening in here."

What exactly was about to happen that Chris and Seth didn't want Melanie, Bastien, and the vampires in residence to hear? "So what's this all about?"

Chris leaned back in his chair. "Do you know Veronica Becker?"

"I don't *know* her," Aidan said. "But I've met her."

"When?" Chris asked, his face stony.

"The night she got a flat tire and called you to say vampires were attacking her."

"That was the first time you'd talked to her?"

"Yes."

"What happened when you teleported there?"

Aidan frowned. "You know what happened. You heard most of it yourself over the phone, and I told you the rest when I returned to the network."

Chris crossed his arms over his chest. "Tell me again."

Aidan glanced at Seth.

Seth dipped his head in a nod.

Perhaps Seth hadn't heard it yet. "I teleported to the intersection of Saxapahaw-Bethlehem Church Road and Highway 54, then raced up Sax-Beth Road. When I found Veronica, she was standing beside her car, holding off two vampires with a tire iron and a can of pepper spray."

Seth's lips twitched. "Smart woman."

Aidan nodded. "I killed the vampires, then heard more coming. I told Veronica to get in the car. Then I met the other vampires some distance away and slew them all."

"How many were there?" Seth asked.

"Six, if I'm recalling correctly." Aidan frowned. "Do you think the vampires are amassing another army?" Usually vampires either hunted alone or traveled in twos or threes.

"It would appear so," Seth said. "Ethan and Heather killed a dozen last night. Roland and Sarah killed nine the night before. So clearly something is building."

Great. Was that the *something bad* Dana had seen coming?

Chris shifted, drawing his attention. "Did you kill all the vampires that night, Aidan?"

"Yes."

"You're sure?" he pressed. "None could've lingered downwind and escaped your notice?"

Aidan shook his head. "I don't see how. If there had been more lingering downwind, I might not have smelled them, but I would've heard their heartbeats and the slightest movements they made."

Chris nodded as though that was what he had expected to hear. "What happened next?"

Aidan shrugged. "I returned to Veronica and her son."

"Her son was with her?" Seth asked.

"Yes. He was sleeping in his car seat and, fortunately, didn't see a thing."

"Then what?" Chris asked.

"Veronica was pretty shaken up, so I escorted her home, waited until she and her boy were safely inside, then left."

Silence fell.

"What's this about, Seth?" Aidan asked when no one else jumped in to break it.

"Veronica Becker is missing," he responded.

Aidan straightened. "What?"

"She's missing," Seth repeated.

Alarm struck. "Since when?"

"Since the day after you rescued her."

She'd been missing for two weeks? "I don't understand. I was sure no more vampires lingered nearby, and I heard no signs of pursuit on the way to her home." His stomach sank. "Do you think more vampires went looking for their comrades and found the battle scene? Do you think they tracked us to her home? I didn't think vampires could do that. I would've thought they'd lose the scent as soon as we got in her car."

"If there was blood on one or more of the tires...," Seth speculated.

Aidan shook his head. "She lived a fair distance away. Blood on the tires wouldn't have lasted that long. And the scent of blood on the car would've faded too quickly on the breeze for them to track. I'm not even sure *I* could've tracked the car to her home, and you know how old and powerful I am. There's no way a vampire could've tracked her."

"And yet," Chris said, "she's missing."

"Is her boy missing, too?" Aidan asked, recalling the peacefully slumbering toddler.

If vampires had taken both mother and child, Veronica might still live, but the boy would have already been slain. Aidan had seen enough child victims of vampires to know that with certainty.

"Veronica's son is safe," Chris stated.

That was a relief. "Where is he?"

"At an undisclosed location."

Odd. Chris said it almost in challenge.

Aidan looked to Seth. "He's okay?"

Seth nodded. "He's well. He just misses his mother and doesn't understand why she hasn't come for him."

Poor little lad.

Chris cleared his throat. "Tell us what happened the next time you saw Veronica."

Aidan frowned. "There *was* no next time. I only saw her and spoke with her the once."

Chris sent Seth a pointed look.

Seth just stared at Aidan as though trying to read his thoughts.

But Aidan had spent many years strengthening the barriers in his mind. There was no way Seth—or Zach, or any other elder immortal telepath—could topple those barriers and read Aidan's mind without alerting him to their presence and causing him great pain.

"What?" Aidan asked, then frowned. "Wait. You don't believe *I've* done something to her, do you?"

Chris arched a brow. "Have you?"

Aidan resisted the urge to punch the human in the face. "Of course not. I've no reason to harm her."

"No, but everyone knows how *desperate*," Chris said with sarcasm, "you are to find a *gifted one* who can love you. Maybe you thought if you hid her away somewhere to give her time to get to know you, you could talk her around."

"That's bullshite and you know it," Aidan growled, tired of the other man's animosity. Chris could hold a grudge like no other. That crap grew tiresome after a while.

"Do I?" Chris replied. "What happened the next time you saw her?"

"I told you. There *was* no next time. I only spoke with her the once."

Chris turned to Seth. "I told you he'd lie."

Anger rose. "I'm not lying." Aidan met Seth's gaze. "You know I'd never hurt a woman. You know me better than that."

"Yes," Seth confirmed, "I do. Which is why we appear to have a serious problem."

Aidan shook his head. "Seth, whatever Chris has told you I've done… I didn't do it. I vow it."

Seth nodded to Chris's laptop. "Show him."

Chris leaned forward and typed something on the keyboard, then swung the laptop around so Aidan and Seth could both see the video that filled the screen.

It looked like footage from a security camera mounted on a pole outside a day care center.

Strange. Aidan had thought day care centers were usually located in town where parents could conveniently drop their children off on their way to and from work. But this place looked like it was out in the country with no other structures around it.

Playground equipment poked around one corner, indicating an outdoor play area behind the large house-like structure. The front lawn consisted mostly of a gravel drive and parking spaces.

"What is this?" Aidan asked as he studied the day care center.

"You don't recognize it?" Seth asked.

"No."

A car pulled into one of the spaces.

"That looks like Veronica's car," he mentioned and glanced at the date and time on the bottom right corner of the screen.

The morning after Aidan had seen her.

The driver's door opened. Veronica Becker stepped out. Pulling a purse onto her shoulder, she closed the door and smiled through the dusty car window before opening the back door and leaning in.

A minute later, she helped her boy out and handed him a colorful drink bottle.

The little boy stood beside her and chattered while she locked the door and closed it.

Veronica laughed and nodded. Taking her son's hand, she led him into the day care.

When Aidan looked away from the screen, he found Chris and Seth studying him closely. "I don't understand. Why are you showing me this?"

Seth nodded to the laptop. "Keep watching."

He did.

After a few minutes, Veronica emerged and strode toward her car, keys in hand, her pretty face wreathed in a smile.

She opened the driver's door and tossed her purse inside.

A tall, dark figure abruptly appeared behind her, his back to the camera.

Aidan rested his arm on the table and leaned in closer.

Judging by his clothes, the man was an Immortal Guardian. Black pants. Black boots. Long black coat. Short black hair.

But Aidan wasn't sure which one.

He had once heard Sarah tell her husband Roland that male Immortal Guardians looked so much alike they could pass for brothers, and he had to agree. All but the newest inductees had black hair, brown eyes, and were of a similar height and build.

Veronica spun around, a look of alarm on her face. Then she smiled up at the newcomer and pressed a hand to her chest. *Oh. Hi. You scared me.*

Even if Aidan weren't a passable lip reader, he could've guessed what she said.

The man took a step backward.

Nodding, Veronica leaned against the car. She said something else, but Aidan couldn't read it because of the camera angle.

The man reached out and rested a hand on the open driver's door, turning to the side to better face her.

Shock tore through Aidan. "What the hell?" he whispered.

The man talking to Veronica was… *him.*

As he watched, uncomprehending, Veronica tilted her head back and smiled up at a man who could easily pass for Aidan's twin.

Reaching out, Aidan gripped the laptop and slid it toward him. "What the hell is this?"

Over the dozens of questions that flooded his brain, Aidan heard Chris say, "Security footage recorded outside one of the network's day care centers."

It didn't surprise Aidan that the network provided day care for its employees. No doubt the service was free. But who the hell was that talking to Veronica? Because in profile, the man really did look like Aidan.

"Can you enlarge this? Or make it zoom in or whatever you call it?" Aidan murmured, wanting to get a closer look at the man's face.

Chris rose and moved to stand beside Aidan. Leaning down, he tapped several keys on the keyboard.

The screen changed, blurring for a moment before it provided an enlarged view of the two conversing by the car.

The man looked identical to Aidan.

"That's not possible," he murmured.

Veronica nodded and ducked into her car, settling herself behind the wheel.

The Aidan look-alike closed her door for her, then walked around to the passenger side, opened the door, and got in. A moment later, the brake lights came on. The car backed out of the parking space and drove out of view.

The image froze.

Aidan looked at Seth. "What the hell *is* this?" he repeated.

Chris spoke as he reclaimed his seat at the head of the table. "*This* is the last time anyone saw Veronica Becker. She never made it to work that day and never returned to the day care to pick up her son. You were the last one to see her."

Aidan shook his head and pointed at the laptop. "That isn't me."

"If the footage were blurry or pixilated and difficult to see," Chris countered, "I'd give you the benefit of the doubt. But we have high-def video that clearly shows you getting into the car with her and driving away."

"Play it again," Aidan demanded.

Chris did so. But Aidan could find nothing in the man's appearance to suggest it wasn't him.

He looked to Seth. "I don't understand. Seth, that's *not* me. I don't even know where that place is."

Seth turned to Chris. "I believe him. I don't think he has any memory of that place."

What? "I have no memory of that place because I was never there." Aidan swung on Chris. "Did you do this? Did you have one of your techno geeks fudge the footage because you're still pissed at me for breaking and entering two years ago?"

Chris's jaw clenched. "You know I didn't. You were there. The footage is clear."

"Fuck the footage! I'm telling you that's not me!"

"Then let Seth read your mind and confirm it."

And have Seth find the visions Dana had had of the two of them engaged in furious battle and of Roland doing his damnedest to kill Aidan, too? *Hell* no. That would just make him look even guiltier.

"Lower your barriers," Seth requested softly.

Aidan refused with a shake of his head. "You've known me for nearly three thousand years, Seth. My word should be enough."

Chris snorted. "If you weren't guilty, you wouldn't mind him reading your thoughts."

"Oh really?" Aidan delved into Chris's mind. "You wouldn't have a problem with Seth reading *your* thoughts?"

"Not if it would prove my innocence."

"So you're saying it wouldn't bother you in the least that Seth would see other things up there as well? Personal things you'd rather keep private? Things you never tell anyone about? Like the vivid sexual fantasies you weave around your assistant Kate whenever you have a spare moment to think?"

Fury flooded Reordon's face. "You stay the fuck out my head, Celt! That's none of your damned business!"

"And my private thoughts are none of Seth's, but he'll see them *all* if I lower my barriers and let him in."

"These are extenuating circumstances! You don't think that warrants a look?"

"No, I don't! Not when I've already told you I was never there!"

Seth held up a hand. "Gentlemen," he interjected softly.

Aidan didn't realize until then that he had risen and now stood nose to nose with Chris, exchanging shouts, ready to blacken the bastard's eyes.

Both men scowled and retook their seats.

Aidan studied the laptop screen again, then felt a surge of triumph. "You know damned well that wasn't me," he told Chris. "Look at the date and time on the video. I couldn't possibly have been there because I called you half an hour before that video was recorded and told you I was teleporting Cliff away." He turned to Seth. "Cliff was struggling. The voices in his head were so loud that morning that they woke me from a sound sleep. I knew Cliff was contemplating ending it, so I called Chris and told him I was going to teleport Cliff away for a distraction."

Seth frowned. "The voices were that loud?"

"Yes. Chris turned off the alarm here at the network so we could teleport out, and I took Cliff to a sunny vale in Scotland."

"What?" both men blurted.

Aidan waved off their alarm. "I kept my hand on his shoulder, healing him in real time, so he wasn't harmed. I'd hoped being able to stand in sunlight again would quiet the voices and give him a reprieve."

"Did it?" Seth asked.

"Yes. So I kept him there for an hour."

"That must have hurt like hell," Seth murmured.

"It did. But it was worth it. Cliff calmed. Then I called Chris to let him know we were on our way back. Chris turned off the alarm. And we returned." He looked at Chris. "So I *couldn't* have been at the day care. I was with Cliff."

Chris scowled. "How do we know you didn't drop Cliff off somewhere, abduct Veronica, then return to him?"

"Ask Cliff. He'll confirm I was with him the whole time."

Chris shook his head. "You could've mind-warped Cliff the way you did my guards here at the network, made him *think* you were with him the whole time, then left him in the shade somewhere and sought Veronica out."

Aidan ground his teeth and turned to Seth. "You can read Cliff's mind and confirm I'm not lying."

Seth sighed. "Actually, that's not precisely true."

Aidan frowned. "What do you mean? Cliff's thoughts will confirm I was with him the whole time. You'd see the telltale signs if I had used mind control instead."

Chris's face darkened with anger. "Because mind control causes brain damage."

"Yes, damn it," Aidan ground out. "But when I used mind control on the guards here at the network, I only erased a minute or two from their memories. The damage done was so minute that it didn't scar them. But if I had done what you claim I did, I would've had to erase half an hour or more from Cliff's memory, which would've caused more damage. Damage that Seth wouldn't miss if he read Cliff's mind. So Seth can confirm I wasn't at that day care center."

"No, I can't," Seth corrected.

Aidan stared at him. "What do you mean? Sure you can. Just read Cliff's mind and you'll find his memory intact and undamaged and you'll know I was with him while this video was recorded."

Seth sighed. "The brain damage the virus is causing in Cliff has begun to progress more quickly. Cliff's brain is so riddled with scar tissue now that I wouldn't be able to discern with certainty what damage was caused by the virus and what damage might have been caused by you *if*"—he held up a hand when Aidan started to interrupt him—"you did use mind control on him and erased the memory of it."

In other words, Aidan was screwed. He shook his head. "I didn't do this. I don't know how to convince you of that. I shouldn't *have* to convince you of it. But I did *not* do this." He pointed to the laptop. "I don't know who that man is, but it's not me."

Studying him thoughtfully, Seth drew his cell phone out and dialed a number.

"Hello?" a male voice answered. Ethan, the American immortal who had only been transformed a hundred years ago.

"Ethan, it's Seth. Have you got a moment?"

"Sure."

"Good. I need to borrow you for a few. Am I clear to teleport there?"

"Give us a minute first."

"Okay." Seth pocketed his phone. His lips curled up in a somewhat sheepish smile. "I teleported over once and caught him and Heather naked, so I always ask first now."

Under other circumstances, Aidan would've laughed.

A minute later, Seth vanished.

Quiet fell, thick with tension.

Aidan met Chris's hostile gaze. "In the two years I've been here in North Carolina, I've come to believe that you're as exceptional a leader in the mortal world as Seth is in ours. Don't let past grudges fuck that up and steer you in the wrong direction."

"I don't hold grudges. I learn from past mistakes."

"I freely admitted that I used mind control on the guards two years ago. Why would I lie about this?"

Chris shrugged. "Desperate times call for desperate measures."

"You're making a mistake, Chris."

"Time will tell."

"Waste too much of it on me and Veronica will pay the price."

"Is that a threat?"

"No. I'm worried about her. And I know we'll find her more quickly if you stop pissing away your time trying to persecute me and instead focus all your resources on trying to find the arsehole," Aidan ground out, pointing at the screen, "who took her."

Seth reappeared, his hand on Ethan's shoulder.

Aidan liked the young American immortal. Ethan had a friendly, easygoing nature and lacked the darkness that wove its way into older immortals who had seen too much of life. Aidan even felt protective toward the younger man since Aidan had transformed Ethan's wife for him.

Smiling, Ethan nodded a hello to Aidan and Chris. His smile died, however, as the tension in the room reached him.

Though Ethan was six foot four, he still had to look up at Seth, who towered over most of them at six foot eight. "What's up?" he asked.

Seth motioned to the laptop. "I'd like you to watch this video."

"Okay." Ethan leaned forward. Bracing his hands on the table, he stared at the screen as Chris set the video in motion.

After a moment, Ethan's eyes slid to Aidan. "Is that you?"

Aidan forced a tight smile. "That's the question of the day." And if anyone in this room could answer it without scouring Aidan's thoughts, Ethan could.

Frowning, Ethan again focused on the laptop.

Though Ethan often bemoaned the fact that he had been born with a "boring" gift, in moments like this his gift could be crucial. Ethan had what he often described as a photographic memory raised to the nth power. He remembered every second of every day he had lived. Everything he had seen, heard, smelled, tasted, and touched. And he remembered it all with crystal clarity.

Heather had even once told Aidan that Ethan remembered the day he had been born.

The video ended.

Ethan straightened.

Seth motioned to the video. "Is that Aidan?"

The American's brow furrowed. "I'm not sure. It's harder to tell in profile. Do you have any images of him head-on?"

Chris shook his head. "No. This is it."

Ethan watched the video again. "It looks like Aidan, but something's off."

"What is?" Seth asked.

Ethan motioned to the frozen image of the man speaking with Veronica. "His hair is about a quarter of an inch too long."

"Aidan could've gotten a haircut since then," Chris said.

"I haven't," Aidan told Seth.

"And his smile isn't quite right," Ethan continued. "When Aidan smiles, his eyes crinkle a little more in the corners. I wish I could see this guy from the front, because Aidan's smile is also a little crooked."

Aidan eyed him with surprise. "It is?"

"Yeah, one side goes up a tiny bit more than the other, but the difference is so minute that I doubt anyone else would notice."

"Anything else?" Seth asked.

"Well, this guy's boots are a size larger than Aidan's and less scuffed."

"He could've bought new ones," Chris pointed out.

"And his coat doesn't have that little string that pokes up from the shoulder seam of Aidan's coat."

Aidan glanced down at his shoulder.

"Not that one," Ethan said. "The other one."

Aidan looked at the other shoulder, the same one visible on the man in the video. Sure enough, a single black thread poked up from the seam, its frayed end about an inch long.

Seth and Chris leaned forward a bit and peered at the coat, then leaned back.

Chris frowned. "He could've been wearing a different coat."

"This is the only one I own," Aidan protested.

Ethan nodded. "And it's the only one I've ever seen him wear."

Aidan's Second, Brodie, was particularly talented at removing bloodstains, so Aidan didn't have to replace his clothing as often as other immortals did.

"All the more reason," Chris said, "for Aidan to buy another coat to wear when he kidnapped Veronica." The man was like a dog clinging tenaciously to a bone, damn it.

Ethan frowned. "The woman's missing?"

"Yes," the rest of them chorused.

"Why would you think Aidan took her?"

Chris pointed to the laptop. "Because we have visual confirmation that he did."

Ethan shook his head. "I don't think that's Aidan in the video. If I had to guess, I'd say it was his twin."

"I don't have a twin," Aidan said at the same time Seth said, "He doesn't have a twin."

Ethan shrugged. "Could Jared be up to something again?"

Jared was one of the Others, ancient immortals who were almost as powerful as Seth but believed that any interference in the fate of mankind would result in the world's destruction. Seth had defected from the Others' ranks millennia ago to marry a human woman and lead the Immortal Guardians. Zach had defected three years ago to marry Lisette.

Jared had secretly defected shortly after Zach when he'd had a vision that Gershom would succeed in his quest to launch Armageddon. But Jared had done so without the Others' knowledge and had since adopted something of a secret-agent role, working with the Immortal Guardians while maintaining the status quo with the Others.

Ethan looked at Seth. "Jared assumed Marcus's appearance once, and Ami said Jared looked exactly like him. Maybe he did the same this time with Aidan."

Seth shook his head. "Jared would have no reason to kidnap Veronica."

"Then maybe it's Gershom," Ethan countered.

Aidan looked to Seth. "Can Gershom assume the appearance of other men?"

Seth frowned. "I know he can shape-shift into animal forms, but the human body is more complex. Getting every facial expression, every freckle or wrinkle or even the walk and posture just right is exceptionally difficult. Jared can do it because he's particularly talented at such. But I don't know about Gershom."

Aidan curled one hand into a fist. "It *must* be Gershom." And the bastard had used Aidan's form to trick Veronica into trusting him.

Chris crossed his arms. "I'm still not convinced it wasn't you."

Aidan lunged to his feet.

Seth sped around the table and planted a hand in Aidan's chest before Aidan could kick Chris's ass. "Chris, stop provoking him."

"I'm not provoking him," Chris said, no anger in his voice. "I'm viewing the situation as objectively as I can and have what I believe are reasonable doubts. A haircut and a shopping spree could explain all but one of the differences Ethan spotted in the video. And *the smile being a little bit off* could be because it wasn't a genuine smile. Real smiles reach the eyes. Fake ones don't."

Seth reluctantly met Aidan's gaze. "He has a point."

Aidan's stomach knotted. "You don't really believe— "

"No, I don't." He turned to Chris. "Which is why I need your word that you will consider all possibilities while conducting your investigation. If Gershom is responsible, we need to discover what his endgame is and why he took Veronica."

Aidan shook his head. "Could he have done it just to fuck with you, Seth?"

Ethan nodded. "He knows how protective you are of immortals and *gifted ones*. It would be an easy way to get back at you for defeating him last time."

Seth swore.

Chris removed a small spiral notebook and a stubby number two pencil from his breast pocket and began to scribble down notes. "I'll look into Veronica's background and see if I can find a reason beyond her being a *gifted one* that would make her seem to be a valuable tool Gershom could use against you."

Ethan pursed his lips. "You didn't, by any chance, used to date her or anything like that, did you, Seth?"

Hell, that hadn't even occurred to Aidan.

Chris either, apparently.

All three stared at Seth expectantly.

"No," their leader answered.

They breathed sighs of relief.

"Did the woman work here at the network?" Ethan asked.

"Yes," Chris and Aidan answered in unison.

"Then perhaps that's why Gershom wanted her. We know he

was manipulating Dr. Whetsman and using him to sneak vials of the sedative out of the network. Whetsman's dead, right?"

Seth nodded. "The brain damage from Gershom's mind control combined with the damage that resulted from Cliff beating the crap out of him was too great. We couldn't save him."

Ethan nodded. "Then maybe Gershom is simply looking for a new puppet or a new source of intel. He may not have even known she's a *gifted one*."

Seth looked to Chris. "He has a valid point."

Chris scribbled some more. "I'll look into all the employees who have called in sick or missed work this month and double-check to ensure they're really sick and not missing like Veronica in case she wasn't the only target. It may also be a good idea, Seth, for you to read their minds once they're all accounted for and make sure Gershom didn't tamper with them."

"Give me their names and I'll do it."

"I'll also have my guys look up all the other *gifted ones* in the area, just in case that's the lure and not the network connection. Make sure they're okay."

"Sounds good."

Ethan glanced at Seth. "Is there anything *I* can do to help?"

"We'll let you know," Seth told him.

Chris handed Aidan a stack of papers.

"What's this?"

"The list of female *gifted ones* you stole. I want you to go over it and circle the names of every woman you've had contact with."

Aidan slammed the papers down on the table. "This is ridiculous! You make it sound like I'm the carrier of a contagious disease or something."

"I just want to make sure none of the others have been harmed in any way," Chris retorted, unperturbed by Aidan's anger.

Aidan swung on Seth. "Seth — "

Seth held up a hand. "Indulge him in this, Aidan. He isn't going to let it go. And the faster he can eliminate you as a suspect, the faster we'll determine what and whom we're dealing with."

"Fine," Aidan grumbled and retook his seat. Catching the pencil Chris tossed him, he swiftly scanned the list and circled the name of each woman he'd met.

When he reached Dana's name though, Aidan hesitated.

He'd seen her every night since their first date. He had taken her to dinner. She had cooked for him in her home above her shop. He had cooked for her at the country home he rarely used. They had slumped down, hip to hip, on her sofa and watched movies together, feet propped on her coffee table, hands brushing as they shared a big bowl of popcorn. They had walked along the stream behind her home, holding hands as the night serenaded them.

She was so warm and funny. So affectionate.

They had talked and laughed and kissed and touched and teased until his body burned.

And he had loved every minute of it.

It had been the best two weeks of his entire existence.

But they had not made love.

Though Aidan thought she was ready to take that next step, he hesitated.

Yes, they had learned a lot about each other. But she still didn't know that one oh-so-important fact: that he was immortal.

It just didn't seem right to make love to her without telling her first.

And he sure as hell didn't want Reordon to be the one to tell her. Chris might claim to lack bias, but he would always think the worst of Aidan.

Aidan wouldn't put it past Chris to sabotage his relationship with Dana out of pure spite.

"What's wrong?" Seth asked.

Glancing up, Aidan found the Immortal Guardians' leader studying him carefully.

Aidan shook his head. "Nothing. Just trying to puzzle it all out." Returning his attention to the papers on the table, Aidan skipped Dana's name without circling it and continued down the list.

Aidan spent damned near every spare minute he had with Dana. He didn't need Chris to confirm that she was all right. Aidan would keep her safe himself.

Besides, she didn't work for the network. And Aidan thought it likely that Veronica had been targeted for her network connections.

Why Gershom—and it *had* to have been Gershom—had chosen to adopt Aidan's appearance to abduct her, Aidan didn't know.

Hopefully Chris would get the bug out of his butt quickly enough to help them figure it out so they could find her.

Chapter Six

DANA GLANCED AT THE CLOCK. Aidan was due any minute. And she was eager to see him again. The day had been a long one, the visions she'd had compelling her to deliver more bad news than usual. The high point had been telling LeAnn, who had just discovered she was pregnant and didn't want to wait to hear it, that her baby was a girl. The midpoint—or the good news/bad news point—had been telling Connie that her husband wasn't cheating on her and spending their savings on a mistress, he was blowing it gambling. And the low point had been telling Ashley to stop procrastinating and see her doctor because the cancer was back.

The tinkling of the bell over her door alerted her to a new arrival. Turning, she watched Aidan duck inside. He was dressed casually tonight in black pants and a black button-down shirt with the collar open. They had decided not to venture out tonight and instead planned to order in from that fantastic restaurant he'd taken her to on their first date and watch a movie.

"Hi, handsome," she said with a smile. As always, the stress of the day fell away and her heart began to beat faster as he grinned down at her.

"Hi, yourself, beautiful."

Grabbing his tie, she tugged him down for a kiss.

Lightning struck at the first touch of his lips, sending heat coursing through her body.

Humming his approval, Aidan curled an arm around her waist and drew her up against him.

Dana rose onto her toes and wrapped her arms around his neck.

How he made her body burn. No man had ever made her feel the way Aidan did, so desperate for his touch.

Aidan wrapped his other arm around her, clutching a fistful of her hair and urging her closer. Her breasts pressed against his muscled chest, nipples hardening at the delicious contact. When he slid his other hand down over her bottom, urging her against his growing erection, she moaned.

It was getting harder and harder to resist the urge to make love with him.

Was fourteen dates long enough to wait? She had wanted to take things slowly and proceed with caution but really didn't think she could go another night without feeling his bare skin against hers.

He was so damned hot. And Dana had never felt happier than she had during the past two weeks. It felt almost as though she had been merely sleepwalking until Aidan had found her and woken her up. He made her laugh, made her heart light, and eradicated the loneliness that had begun to weigh on her as her damned gift ruined every relationship she tried. She had really begun to think she would never find that special someone, that she would spend the remainder of her life alone.

But Aidan wasn't threatened by her gift. He rarely even mentioned it. Visions still came to her. The same two of Aidan sword fighting with his reenactment buddies. She'd had more visions of them making love as well, which made it all the harder to resist temptation. But the other things she had seen had been pretty mundane. Him standing in a sunny meadow with his hand on a man's shoulder. Aidan had told her the African-American man was his friend Cliff, who was ill.

She also saw him singing a lullaby to a pretty redheaded baby. That, he had told her, had been a moment from his past. The child he'd sung to in a very appealing, deep voice was the little one for whom he had cleaned up his language and was now a toddler.

The fact that she caught glimpses of his past, present, and future didn't seem to bother him in the least. It was so nice to have the freedom to simply be herself around him. To be around someone who didn't care that she was different. And to have so much fun with him.

Aidan gave her something to look forward to every evening. Instead of dreading the quiet that would surround her the moment her last customer left, Dana now couldn't wait for the day to end and counted the minutes, knowing Aidan would arrive soon after and the two would spend hour after amazing hour together.

Life was good again, in a way it really hadn't been since her parents had died. All because of the man in her arms.

Dana combed her fingers through his hair, arched her hips into his.

Groaning, Aidan rocked against her.

Sparks of heat shot through her as she broke the kiss on a gasp.

Aidan ducked his head, burying his face in the crook of her neck. "Damn, you feel good," he whispered, his deep voice hoarse with need.

It only excited her more. "What do you say we forget dinner and the movie?" she whispered, her breath shortening.

"How you tempt me," he rumbled, tightening his hold.

"If I tempted you as much as you tempt me," she pronounced boldly, "we would both be naked right now."

He growled—actually *growled*—as his hands roved her back.

His phone chirped in his pocket.

Aidan swore and loosened his hold.

Dana groaned.

"I'm sorry," he said gruffly. "I have to take this. I told Cliff and his friends to call me if he should need anything, so I want to make sure he isn't worsening."

"Of course," she said, understanding. But she couldn't help but feel disappointed as she lowered her heels to the floor, slid her hands down his chest, and released him.

Aidan kept his eyes closed as though savoring her touch while he tugged his phone out of his pocket. "*So* tempting."

She chuckled.

Turning away, he answered the call. "Yes?"

Dana's body tingled as she watched him pace away a couple of steps.

"Yes," he said again. "Why? Do you need me?"

Say no, she mentally willed whoever had called. *Please, say no. Say you were just calling to shoot the breeze, because I really want this man naked in my bed tonight.* She smiled. *Even though he's so tall his feet will probably hang off the end by quite a bit.*

"Where?"

Her heart sank at Aidan's brusque tone.

"Okay. I'm on my way."

Tucking the phone in his pocket, he withdrew his keys and turned to face her. "I'm sorry. I have to go."

She bit her lip, reading the concern in his gaze. "Is it your friend? The one who's ill?"

He nodded. "And the matter is of some urgency." He backed toward the door, the bulge in his pants and the regret on his face indicating he would've much rather stayed and explored every inch of her body. "Forgive me?"

"Absolutely." Smiling, she closed the distance between them and gave him a quick kiss. "See you tomorrow?"

"Hell, yes," he said, giving her a heated look full of promise.

She grinned.

Hurrying out the door, Aidan jumped in his car and sped away.

"Damn," Dana said on a sigh as she watched him through the window.

The bell above the door dinged again as a woman entered, glancing back over her shoulder.

Marietta, Dana's next-door neighbor, arched a brow and eyed Dana speculatively as the door swung shut behind her. "Was that the handsome Scottish hunk you've been spending all your nights with?"

"That's him," Dana confirmed with a smile.

Marietta shook her head. "No wonder I hardly see you anymore. I'd spend every waking moment with him, too, if he were mine. He is freaking *hot*."

Dana laughed.

Marietta's smile dimmed a bit. "Nothing's wrong though, is it, hon? He left in an awful hurry."

She smiled wryly. "Nothing a cold shower won't fix."

Marietta laughed.

"Aidan got called away on an emergency, so we had to cancel our plans."

"That sucks."

"It really does."

Marietta had bought the store beside Dana's last year after going through a messy divorce with a philandering husband. Based on their conversations, Dana had concluded that Marietta was in her early forties. And though her relationship history had left her reluctant to test the waters again herself, Marietta frequently encouraged Dana to get out there and find a good guy who could make her happy.

Needless to say, she had been thrilled to hear about Aidan.

"Are you all packed for your trip?" Dana asked. Marietta was flying to California to see her son perform for the first time at UCLA.

"Yes. And I'm so nervous you'd think *I'm* the one who's going to be onstage."

"I'm sure he'll do fine."

"I know he will, although I have no idea how he ended up with so much talent. Neither his father nor I can dance. And thank *goodness* he didn't inherit my stage fright."

"Is Frank going to be there?" The last Dana had heard, Marietta's ex was dating a girl their son's age.

She rolled her eyes. "No. The bastard can't be bothered. Fortunately, Owen doesn't want him there anyway, so he won't be disappointed." Forcing a smile, she held up a set of keys and jangled them. "So, here are my keys. Thank you again for keeping an eye on the place while I'm gone."

"No thanks necessary," Dana replied cheerfully, taking the keys.

"You have my cell number. If anything comes up, just give me a ring."

"I will. Do you have any plants you want me to water while you're gone? Or fish that need feeding?"

"No fish. And I gave up on houseplants years ago because the damned things kept dying."

Dana laughed.

Marietta glanced at the clock. "I'd ask if you want to watch a movie or something since your man had to cancel, but I've got a six-o'clock flight in the morning."

"Ugh." Dana grimaced. "You're going to have to rise before the sun to make that one."

"I know. Hopefully the other passengers won't complain when I end up snoring on the plane." She winked. "So you go take your cold shower while I try to get some shut-eye."

Grinning, Dana followed her to the door. "I hope you'll have a nice trip and that Owen's performance will go well."

"Thanks, sweetie. Give that gorgeous Scot of yours a hug and a pat on the ass for me the next time you see him."

"I will," Dana promised with a laugh.

"Good night."

"Good night." Dana closed and locked the door.

Quiet settled upon the empty shop as she turned to face it.

Closing her eyes, she thought of Aidan, of the fervency of his kisses and the urgency in the hands that had roamed her and held her so tight.

"Yep," she murmured. "One cold shower, coming up."

Sighing, she headed for the stairs.

The moment Aidan was out of Dana's sight, he turned his car onto a deserted side street and hit the brakes.

The darkened businesses that bordered it vanished, as did the street as he teleported himself and the vehicle away. Grass replaced pavement beneath the car's tires. UNCW's campus appeared around him. As did a rather astonishing number of vampires.

In their midst, Bastien and Cliff stood back-to-back, sword blades winking beneath the campus lights as they did their damnedest to kill every vampire within reach.

One of the vampires noticed Aidan's abrupt appearance.

As Aidan stepped out of the car and drew on his coat, the vamp leapt onto the hood.

The vampire's hair hung in a limp, oily mess around his face. His fangs glinted in a sneer. And madness glinted in his glowing green eyes.

Scowling, Aidan drew his weapons. "Don't scratch the paint, you horse's arse!"

Several yards away, Bastien laughed.

The vampire actually looked down at his feet as though he had borrowed his father's car and just realized he was mucking it up.

Grinning, Aidan used telekinesis to pick the vamp up and hurl him at his cohorts. Then Aidan teleported right into the thick of things, swinging his swords in strong, broad arcs. He teleported again and impaled two vampires. Teleported again and beheaded another.

Utter panic infused the group as they realized Death was in their midst, appearing and disappearing like magic, swinging swords and culling souls.

Aidan smiled grimly, then felt a twinge of unease as he wondered what Dana would think if she could see him now. Would she fear him? Feel horror? Disgust?

The distraction cost him.

Pain cut through Aidan's side as a vampire's blade dug deep.

Swearing, he impaled the vampire who wielded it, then turned to the next combatant.

The vampires' numbers began to decrease. Then more arrived on the scene, eyes glowing blue, green, silver, or amber.

What the hell?

Aidan glanced over at his brothers-in-arms.

Bastien fought with smooth precision. Though he was a mere two and a half centuries old or thereabouts, Bastien's skill exceeded those of other immortals his age.

Aidan supposed the immortal would *have* to have been stronger and faster. He had, after all, once raised and commanded an army of vampires he had pitted against the Immortal Guardians. It would've been imbecilic to live in a lair with over a hundred psychotic vampires if he hadn't been capable of defeating any who rebelled against him.

Those years of command had also, Aidan guessed, made it harder for Bastien to bow to Seth's leadership and obey his orders. The younger immortal's induction into their ranks had not gone smoothly, according to Cliff.

Speaking of whom…

Aidan removed another vampire's head, then glanced over at Cliff.

Though his movements were as smooth and precise as Bastien's, Cliff exhibited none of the cool detachment found in Bastien's expression.

No, Cliff tore his opponents apart with a rage and ferocity that even Aidan found disturbing.

When the vampires' numbers dwindled to only five or six, Bastien backed away several steps and allowed Cliff to take on his opponents.

Aidan followed Bastien's example, confident Cliff could defeat those who remained.

Bastien cast Aidan a grim look.

Unspoken concern leapt back and forth between them.

The last vampire fell.

Aidan studied the dozens of vampire bodies that lay in various stages of decay around them.

"What the hell is going on?" Bastien asked, echoing Aidan's thoughts. "Why so many?"

"I don't know." Aidan looked to Cliff.

The vampire's chest rose and fell with rapid breaths as he stared down at his fallen foes. His eyes glowed not just with amber light but with the madness that fought so hard to consume him.

Cliff's hands fisted around the hilts of his short swords. His biceps—riddled with cuts and gashes—bulged as he fought an inner battle Aidan didn't have to hear to recognize. The voices in Cliff's young, damaged mind called for more blood. More violence. More death.

Bastien sheathed his weapons and looked to his friend. "Cliff?" he asked, voice gentle.

Cliff didn't respond.

Sheathing his own weapons, Aidan slowly approached Cliff and touched his shoulder. It took a lot of effort to keep those voices from invading his own mind, but Aidan managed to do it and focused his healing gift on sending warmth and soothing energy into his friend.

Gradually Cliff's breathing slowed. The muscles in his arms and shoulders relaxed.

The young vampire drew in a long deep breath, held it, then slowly released it. The glow in his eyes fading, he looked over his shoulder at Aidan. "Thank you."

Aidan gave his shoulder a squeeze, then released him. He met Bastien's gaze while Cliff bent and used the shirttail of one of the fallen vampires to wipe the blood from his weapons.

Dread filled the British immortal's eyes.

Cliff frowned as he straightened. "How many were there?"

Aidan glanced around. "Two dozen, give or take."

Bastien shook his head. "They're amassing again."

Aidan agreed. "But under whose leadership?"

"I don't know. Did you see anything in their thoughts?"

Aidan's phone rang. "I didn't have time to read them." Retrieving his phone, he glanced down to see who was calling. "It's Brodie." His Second. "Yes?" he answered as Bastien's phone rang.

The two immortals shared a concerned look.

"Chris has called a meeting," Brodie said.

Aidan heard Bastien's Second, Tanner, echo the news when Bastien answered.

"When?" Aidan asked.

"Tomorrow," Brodie responded. "Just after sunset. At David's place."

"Okay. Thanks." Aidan pocketed his phone.

Bastien did the same. "What do you think it's about?"

Aidan shook his head. "I don't know." But if it was about Veronica Becker, he hoped Chris would bring them good news.

Shortly after sunset the next day, Aidan and Brodie strolled up the walk to David's sprawling home. A cacophony of voices met Aidan's sensitive ears as friendly conversation ebbed and flowed within.

"We may be the last to arrive," he commented.

Brodie cast him an amused look. *Because you took too long prettying yourself up for you-know-who.*

Aidan laughed when he caught the thought. Perhaps he *had* spent an extra minute or two trying to tame his wavy hair. He would be seeing Dana later and would rather not look like Medusa when he did.

When he reached the front door, Aidan opened it without knocking and strode inside. Brodie entered behind him and closed the door.

Though it was only one story, David's house was large with

high ceilings and furnishings that were both modern and comfortable. It also boasted a basement that was even larger than the ground floor, providing his immortal family with multiple bedrooms and a large gym in which they could train and spar during the day.

Until Zach had joined their ranks, David had been the second oldest and most powerful Immortal Guardian in the world. He had lived so long that—like Seth—he had witnessed biblical events and was Seth's second-in-command. Though Zach exceeded David in age, Aidan really wasn't sure which one of them would win if those two ever fought. He saw little chance of that happening though. David was the most even-tempered Immortal Guardian Aidan knew and considered all immortals and their Seconds family. Treated them like family, too, opening the doors of all his homes to them, inviting them to come and go as they pleased, and providing them with a warm family atmosphere in which to decompress after a hunt.

Several men and women called a greeting to Aidan as they abandoned the sofas and love seats in the living room on the right and headed for the dining room on the left.

Aidan didn't bother to remove his coat as he and Brodie followed. He was hoping this would be a short meeting. And even if it wasn't, he didn't have to worry about becoming overheated since immortals could control their body temperature.

David nodded to Aidan and seated himself at the head of the table. His Second, Darnell, took the chair on his left. Chris Reordon brushed past Aidan and plunked a battered, soft leather briefcase down beside the chair to David's right.

Seth already occupied the seat at the foot of the table and spoke softly to Ami, who sat on his left. Her husband Marcus occupied the chair beside her, listening to Seth while he arranged construction paper and crayons on the table in front of him and balanced little Adira in his lap.

Roland Warbrook sat on Marcus's other side. He had long been deemed the most antisocial, untrusting immortal on the planet. Yet he smiled at Adira as she chattered away and waved a green crayon at him. Marcus had been like a brother to Roland for roughly eight hundred years. And Roland clearly adored his friend's toddler.

Seated beside him, Roland's wife Sarah leaned across him to take the crayon Adira handed her.

Richart d'Alençon claimed the chair on Sarah's other side after seating his wife Jenna beside him. Jenna's son John sank down beside her. If Aidan wasn't mistaken, John was a *gifted one* who was studying medicine at Duke University. He and his mother looked like brother and sister now that Jenna had transformed, something that always seemed to amuse Jenna.

Seconds Sheldon and Tracy sat beside John. Richart's twin, Étienne, and his wife Krysta chose the seats on the other side of the two. Then Krysta's brother Sean, and Nicole, his Second, took two of the last three seats on that side.

On the opposite side of the table, Zach lounged at Seth's elbow, the only man present who didn't wear a shirt. Shirts tended to get in the way of the huge dark wings he often bore, which were absent tonight, tucked away so he could lean back in his chair.

For the first time, Aidan found himself wondering if perhaps Seth had wings. Seth and Zach had both been Others, after all. So if Zach had wings, wouldn't it stand to reason that Seth did, too?

Or was Zach simply a shape-shifter who enjoyed manifesting wings?

Either way, if Seth had wings, Aidan had never seen them.

Lisette d'Alençon leaned into Zach's side and whispered something in his ear that made him smile and curl an arm around her. Though Aidan knew she had long been burdened with the guilt of accidentally transforming her brothers, he couldn't help but think how nice it must have been to have two loving members of her family with her for two centuries.

Ethan and his wife Heather sat beside Lisette.

Aidan took the empty chair next to them, returning the smile Heather gave him. She was the youngest immortal present, only turned the previous year.

Brodie sat with Ed, Ethan and Heather's Second, on Aidan's right. Then Bastien, Melanie, and their Second, Tanner, took the remaining chairs.

"Thank you all for coming," Seth said as soon as everyone was seated and conversations trailed away. "Chris has a matter he would like to discuss with us before you begin your hunt."

Everyone looked to Chris.

Leaning forward, Chris braced his elbows on the table. "Some of you may not know that the network provides our employees with free day care. We maintain over two dozen day care facilities in the area, all of which are distanced from network headquarters to ensure no children will be harmed if the network is attacked."

Dread seeped into Aidan as he listened. This was definitely going to be about Veronica. And Chris's grim expression squashed any hope Aidan had clung to that she had been found safe and well.

"A few days ago," Chris continued, "I received a call from one of the day care managers who was concerned because a network employee had failed to pick up her son on schedule. When I did a quick check, I discovered the *gifted one* had called in sick and hadn't made it to work but wasn't at her home. Nor did she see any of our doctors. Further investigation confirmed she was missing."

Rising, he bent and removed a stack of manila file folders from his briefcase, then circled the table, handing a folder to each immortal and Second he passed. "I spoke with Seth and Aidan about it. Both believed her absence might be related to her ties to the network."

Ethan cursed. "Don't tell me another mercenary group found out about us."

Chris shook his head. Distributing the last file, he retook his seat. "Not as far as we know. Personally, I think the fact that she's a *gifted one* was the lure. So I had my team check on every *gifted one* in North Carolina to see if hers was an isolated case."

"Was it?" Heather asked beside Aidan.

"No. Five other female *gifted ones* have gone missing during the past month."

Aidan stared at Chris as curses filled the air. Five more female *gifted ones* were missing?

"How did you not know they were missing before?" he asked.

Meeting his gaze, Chris folded his arms across his chest. "There were plausible explanations for every absence. Illness. A death in the family. Vacation time."

Chris's countenance confirmed that he thought Aidan was

responsible. He actually believed Aidan had abducted those women. Seth didn't, too, did he?

Aidan glanced at Seth but could glean nothing from his expression.

Unsettled, he opened the folder in front of him. Veronica's smiling face stared back at him from a photo that had probably been taken for her ID badge. He flipped the page. Dawn graced the next page. Dawn, whom Veronica had said gushed over him for days after he changed her flat tire.

He turned the page. Kimberly, who had also sung his praises to Veronica after he had changed a flat tire for her.

He turned another page. Sofia, whom he'd bumped into at the grocery store.

A chill slithered through him.

Roland frowned, fingering the edges of his file folder. "You said you talked with Seth and Aidan. Why Aidan?"

Aidan returned his attention to Chris and felt his hackles rise.

"Because," Chris said, directing an accusing glare at Aidan, "he's the only thing all six women have in common."

Shock tripped through him. What?

"Oh no," Heather whispered as she touched his arm. "You knew some of them?"

Chris removed a laptop from his briefcase and opened it on the table.

Several men and women shifted their chairs so they could better see the screen.

The security footage from the day care center began to play.

Aidan paid little attention as his heart thudded in his chest.

"Veronica Becker?" Roland said suddenly, sitting straighter. "One of the missing *gifted ones* is Veronica Becker?"

"Yes," Chris confirmed.

Veronica. Dawn. Kimberly. Sofia. Aidan turned the page. Nia. He turned another. Tiana.

All of the six missing women were *gifted ones* he had arranged *chance encounters* with prior to meeting Dana.

"You knew Veronica?" Roland asked him.

His heart thudding in his chest, Aidan didn't answer.

He had met dozens of female *gifted ones* in the past couple of years. But none of the women he had chatted with a year and a half ago, or a year ago, or even six months ago were missing. Only six of the last seven *gifted ones* were.

Chris turned his laptop around and typed on the keyboard. "We have video footage of Aidan meeting with three of the women shortly before they disappeared. As far as we can tell, he was the last one to see them all."

The last six *gifted ones* he had seen before meeting Dana had been taken.

Would Dana be the seventh?

Fear pounding through him, Aidan wanted to teleport to her shop and see with his own two eyes if she was okay, but she didn't know he could teleport and would expect him to arrive in a car.

Swearing, he leapt up—knocking his chair over in his haste—and raced out of the house.

Exclamations of surprise followed in his wake as he dove into his car, started the engine and tore away.

Please, let her be okay, he thought as he took the corner at the end of David's long drive way too quickly and nearly skidded off the road. He'd teleport himself and the car closer to her to shorten the drive but couldn't risk her neighbors seeing him appear out of nothingness.

Taking out his phone, he dialed her number. *Answer. Answer. Answer. Come on, sweetheart, answer.*

The call went to voice mail.

Aidan pressed the accelerator to the floor and dialed again.

Voice mail.

Speeding around an SUV that itself was exceeding the speed limit by ten miles per hour, Aidan swung back into his lane just in time to avoid a head-on collision with an oncoming truck. Several turns and near misses later, he pulled into the small parking lot in front of her shop and skidded to a stop.

Relief flooded him as he saw her through the window.

She was safe, singing under her breath as she restocked some shelves. The tips of her ears were pink. And some of the hair tucked behind them bore damp ends. She must have either been in the shower or blow-drying her hair when he'd called.

He stepped out of the car.

Dana glanced over and saw him through the window. Her lovely face lighting up, she waved.

Aidan waved back, wanting only to drag her into his arms and hold her close. But he hadn't taken the time to remove the multitude of weapons tucked inside his coat before he'd raced over.

As soon as she turned to put a book back on a shelf, he reached into his coat to disarm himself.

Car tires screeched behind him before he could. The scent of burning rubber filled the air.

Aidan turned as a car took the closest corner too quickly.

A sleek black Fisker Karma drifted sideways, then shot forward. Passing a stop sign without slowing, it hit a bump and flew into the parking lot.

Surprised, Aidan prepared to launch himself at the vehicle to shove it aside so it wouldn't crash headlong into Dana's store. But the tires locked suddenly as the driver hit the brakes.

Gravel struck Aidan like buckshot. Dust rose in a cloud that burned his eyes.

Before it could settle, the driver threw open the car door and leapt out.

Ah, hell. Roland Warbrook. This couldn't be good.

Aidan glanced at the shop and found Dana staring out at them with wide eyes, her face full of alarm. *Stay inside*, he counseled her telepathically, speaking directly into her mind.

If anything, her eyes grew wider.

It's okay, he told her. *I'm okay. Just stay inside.*

He'd tell her to look away, too, but thought that would just alarm her more.

"Did you think I wouldn't find you?" Roland roared.

Eyebrows flying up, Aidan watched the nearly-millennium-old immortal stalk toward him. "What?"

"Did you think I wouldn't make you pay?"

Aidan backed away from the shop, luring Roland after him so Roland's back would be to Dana.

The British immortal's eyes glowed bright amber with fury. The tendons in his neck stood out as Roland shouted at him and drew two short swords.

"Pay for what?" Aidan asked. He didn't know this particular immortal well. So he didn't know how he could have possibly wronged him.

"For Veronica!" Roland roared.

Shock halted Aidan's feet. "What?" It was the last thing he managed to say before Roland struck.

Aidan ducked the first swing of Roland's blade and drew his own swords.

Roland had been born in medieval England and had been an exceptional swordfighter long before a vampire had transformed him. So Aidan knew Roland would be a formidable opponent and wondered how the hell he was going to hold him off long enough to find out why he was so furious.

"Veronica," Roland roared, keeping Aidan on the defensive with swift, steady, powerful swings of his swords.

"Veronica Becker?"

"Yes!"

Aidan glanced at Dana's shop and saw her dive for the phone on the counter. A peek into her thoughts found her intent on calling 911. *Don't*, he told her.

She stopped short and looked at him through the glass.

I'm okay, he told her. *Don't call the police.*

The distraction cost him.

Aidan hissed in a breath as one of Roland's swords sliced through his coat and cut a deep furrow across his chest.

"Aidan!" Though Dana was inside with the door and windows shut, both immortals heard her clearly.

Roland spun around and glared.

Aidan swore. No way would she miss the other immortal's glowing eyes now.

It was a struggle to keep his own from glowing as Aidan began to simmer with anger.

Damn Roland for forcing his hand like this. Now he would have to either come up with some bullshit lie to explain Roland's eyes or tell Dana everything.

Aidan leapt forward, intending to lock Roland in a half nelson until the bastard would explain why he was trying to gut him.

Roland swiveled and struck before he could, his blade carving a gash in Aidan's arm.

Fury crashed through him. Aidan abandoned the plan to simply hold Roland off long enough to get an explanation and instead took the offensive, pounding the other immortal's swords with strike after strike after strike, driving him backward. "What the hell is this about?" he demanded, all patience gone. "What is Veronica to you?" He was surprised the reclusive immortal even knew her.

The heels of Roland's boots pushed up dirt and gravel as he dug in and met Aidan blow for blow. "She's my descendant!"

Hell. No wonder he was so pissed. "Roland— "

"You killed her, you bloody bastard!" he bellowed. "You killed her!"

And suddenly Dana's vision made sense. "If Chris told you that, he lied," Aidan growled, mentally cursing the human.

"Bullshit!"

"I'm telling you he lied!" Damn it, he'd lost sight of Dana.

Roland scored another hit.

Growling in frustration, Aidan scored four more.

A Tesla Roadster suddenly tore around the corner with a screech of tires, then flew into the parking lot and skidded to a halt inches from the Fisker Karma.

Sarah jumped out of the car.

At the same moment, the door to the shop flew open and Dana barreled out, carrying something in one hand.

"Roland, stop!" Sarah called.

"Stay back!" he commanded.

While Sarah tried to coax her irate husband back to sanity, Aidan glanced at Dana.

Striding forward with a look of grim determination, Dana raised a weapon of some sort and aimed it at Roland.

Was that a gun? "Dana, no!" he called. Gunshot wounds would just piss Roland off more.

Too late.

She squeezed the trigger.

Two small objects shot forth and embedded themselves in Roland's back.

The crackle of electricity filled the air.

Roland stiffened and jerked as Dana held the trigger down and

Tasered the hell out of him. But he didn't go down. Gritting his teeth, he dropped one sword, reached behind him and yanked the small metal probes out of his back. More curses spewed forth as he flung them to the ground.

Sarah gaped. "Roland?" she called with concern and took a hesitant step toward him. "Honey? Are you okay?"

Roland swung to face Dana. "That hurt, damn it!"

Dana's face lost all color.

Aidan shot forward in a blur and placed himself between them. "You stay the hell away from her, Roland." He'd slay the other immortal if necessary and damn the consequences to keep her safe. Aidan wasn't about to let Roland harm Dana, intentionally or not, because Chris Reordon had run his fucking mouth without thinking first.

"I'm not here to hurt her," Roland thundered. "I'm here to kill you."

And the battle began anew.

Behind Roland, Sarah yanked a phone out of her pocket and raised it to her ear. "Seth!" she cried.

Seth appeared beside her.

Dana gasped.

Aidan and Roland both swore.

Seth's eyes flashed a brilliant gold as fury darkened his features. Thunder split the night. Scowling, the powerful Immortal Guardians' leader waved a hand.

Aidan's and Roland's swords flew out of their hands and landed in the gravel somewhere on the other side of the cars.

Breathing hard, Aidan shook his head. "I wish to hell *I'd* thought of that." He'd been so concerned about Dana and her reaction to Roland's attack that using his telekinetic abilities hadn't even occurred to him.

Sarah rushed forward to grip Roland's shirt. "Honey, are you okay?"

"Yes," he grumbled, then glared at Seth. "I demand the right to seek retribution."

"*You*," Seth retorted, pointing at Roland, "need to rein in your fucking temper. You left before Chris could finish his report." He turned his glare on Aidan. "As did you. What the hell is wrong with you?"

"What's happening?" Dana whispered.

Seth frowned, noticing her for the first time. A long sigh escaped him. "I'll take care of this," he grumbled and started toward her, no doubt intending to bury her memories of the past several minutes.

Aidan caught his arm as Seth drew even with him. "Wait."

Seth halted.

"It's okay," Aidan told him, voice low. "I'll handle it."

The elder immortal tilted his head to one side. His glowing eyes narrowed. But Seth couldn't read Aidan's mind without tearing down his strong mental barriers. So of course the elder turned those narrowed eyes on Dana and read her mind instead.

Damn it.

A look of surprise washed over Seth's face. He glanced at Aidan. "You didn't circle her name."

"What?" It took Aidan a moment to figure out what Seth was talking about. "You mean on Chris's list?"

"Yes. You didn't circle her name."

"I know." Aidan gave a weak shrug, then winced as pain shot through his arm and chest. "I didn't want Chris to muck things up."

Seth looked over Aidan's shoulder at Dana, then motioned to Roland, whom Sarah now examined for wounds. "I think Roland may have done that for him."

Aidan could only nod, afraid to glimpse Dana's expression.

She had gone very quiet behind him.

Why did you flee the meeting? Seth asked telepathically. *Chris took it as an admission of guilt, as did Roland.*

I thought Veronica was the only one, Aidan responded, sending him the thought so Seth wouldn't need access to Aidan's mind to hear it. *I thought Veronica had been targeted for her connections to the network. But* five *of the other* gifted ones *I've encountered in recent months have been taken. The last five I saw before I met Dana and stopped looking.* He shook his head. *Once I heard that, I didn't really think at all. I just hauled arse over here to make sure she was safe.*

And you drove instead of teleporting because she doesn't know what you are, which allowed Roland to follow you. Releasing a weary sigh,

Seth rubbed his eyes, then drew his hand down his face. *All right. I'll see to Roland and Sarah. You see to Dana. Tell her what you will, then take her to David's place.*

Seth—

He held up a hand. *Do as I ask. I'll meet you there and we will discuss this more then.* "Roland," he commanded aloud, "get in your car and go back to David's."

Roland bit back whatever caustic rebuttal he wished to make and limped over to his car, Sarah at his side.

A common complaint Aidan had heard many an immortal mumble was that Seth, at times, had a way of making even those who were thousands of years old feel like teenagers being upbraided by a parent.

Sarah cast Seth a cautious look. "Can I ride with him, Seth?"

"Yes. I'll take Ami's car."

The immortal couple got in the Fisker Karma without another word and drove away.

Seth closed his eyes, his face a study in concentration.

Aidan remained silent until Seth opened his eyes once more. "What did you do?"

Seth nodded to the second story windows. "Made sure no neighbors saw or heard anything."

Aidan groaned. He had forgotten that Dana wasn't the only proprietor who lived above her shop.

"Don't worry," Seth said. "The woman next door is out of town and the couple down the street heard nothing. But you still fucked up."

"I know." And according to Dana's visions, he would do so again in a big enough way to make *Seth* want to kill him the next time.

After giving Aidan one last warning look, Seth folded himself into the Tesla Roadster Sarah had borrowed and drove away.

The immortal leader was so powerful he could have simply touched the car and teleported both himself and the vehicle wherever he wanted to go but drove instead, Aidan knew, in an attempt to minimize the damage with Dana.

Speaking of whom…

With great reluctance, Aidan turned around.

Chapter Seven

DANA STOOD SEVERAL YARDS AWAY, face pale, features pinched with shock and he wasn't sure what else.

Aidan wanted so badly to read her mind just then, to see how much damage had been done, if there was any way he could salvage their relationship. But he had promised he would only do so in an emergency.

Inwardly, he kicked himself. He should have told her. He should have told her *everything*. Before *this*. Before most of his secrets had been flung in her face in a few minutes' time span. Because this was a hell of a lot to take in all at once.

He took a hesitant step toward her.

She didn't back away. That was a good sign, wasn't it?

"Dana — "

"Your eyes are glowing," she interrupted. Though she said it matter-of-factly, he could hear her heart pummeling her rib cage.

Aidan reached up and rubbed his eyes. Of course they were. He was furious at Roland. Furious at himself. And terrified that Dana would not be able to accept this part of him. Or that she would not forgive him for keeping it from her.

Their relationship was new. Too new, perhaps, for them to work through this.

And the notion tore him up inside.

"I know," he responded softly. "I'm sorry. The stronger the emotion that grips me, the harder it is for me to control it."

He might have only known Dana for a couple of weeks, but he had never been this drawn to a woman before, had never been so captivated or craved a woman's company as much as he had Dana's. And it wasn't because of loneliness. It was because she made him happy. Made him feel normal... human... and had brought light back into his life.

Lowering his hand, he met her wide-eyed gaze.

"*Their* eyes were glowing, too," she said.

"Yes."

Her throat moved in a swallow. "And when you were fighting that guy..."

"Roland," he offered, providing the name of his opponent.

"You both moved as fast as the Flash," she continued.

Roland had given him little choice, damn him. "Yes."

Time ticked by, stretching his nerves taut.

She nodded slowly. And even from this distance, he could see her hands shaking. "You said you were different."

He had.

"On our first date, you told me you were different," she repeated.

"Yes, I did."

Glancing down, she considered the Taser in her hand, the probes Roland had removed with ease, the abandoned swords Seth had cast aside, then met his gaze once more. "You kind of downplayed it, huh?"

Under other circumstances, he might have laughed. But now the best he could do was muster a weak smile. "Yes, I did."

Insects hummed.

Frogs croaked.

And every second Dana didn't tell him to go to hell, Aidan felt a tiny spark of hope.

He motioned to the Taser. "Are you going to use that on me?"

She glanced at the weapon she held. "Would it do any good?"

He shrugged. "It might make you feel better."

Another nod. "Then I reserve the right to use it on you later. Right now..." Tears welled in her eyes as she swallowed hard once more. "Could you maybe just hold me for a minute?"

Heart aching, he closed the distance between them and pulled her into a tight embrace.

The Taser clattered to the ground as she dropped it and fisted her small hands in the back of his coat.

"I'm sorry, sweetheart." He pressed a kiss to her hair, then rested his cheek on top of her head. "I'm so sorry."

━━━◉◉◉◉◉━━━

Dana nearly burst into tears.

Those hoarsely uttered words carried such remorse.

"I thought he was going to kill you," she whispered, voice breaking. When she had seen Aidan and that other man hacking at each other with swords as they had in her vision...

"Roland?" he murmured.

She nodded against his chest, doing her damnedest to fight back the sobs that threatened to tumble forth. She had never been so afraid in her life. Her body still shook from it.

"I'm stronger than he is," Aidan said, his voice both gentle and full of regret. For the scare he had given her? Or for her finding out he'd been keeping such enormous secrets from her? "He wouldn't have bested me."

Aidan *had* fought fiercely, but...

"When that other guy appeared out of nowhere," she said, "the one I saw trying to kill you in the other vision..." The one who'd looked like he was damned near seven feet tall and had black hair down to his ass and eyes that glowed golden. "I thought..."

"It's okay," he murmured, stroking her back.

She had thought the taller man and Roland would join forces, that they would work together to kill Aidan. And utter terror had gripped her because she had known she couldn't do jack about it.

"I'm okay," he whispered. "We both are. I'll never let anyone harm you, Dana. I vow it. I'd give my life to protect you."

And despite everything, she believed him.

But hadn't *he* hurt her by not trusting her with whatever the hell all this meant?

"I'm so sorry," he said again.

Dana burrowed closer. "This doesn't mean I'm not pissed at you," she said in a broken whisper. She *was*. She just couldn't seem to let go.

"I know," he said with so much sorrow that she wanted to cry even more. "Let's go inside, shall we?" he suggested. "I can feel you trembling."

Her heart continued to pound erratically, too.

"Let's go inside," he urged again. "So you can be warm and comfortable while I try to explain all this and engage in what I imagine will be a fair amount of groveling and begging your forgiveness."

Dana couldn't imagine Aidan begging for anything, not after she'd seen him swing his swords with such precision. But she really did need to sit down. "Okay."

"Do you want me to carry you?"

"No," she told him. "I'm okay."

Shifting her to his side, he kept one arm around her shoulders as he escorted her into her shop and halted just inside the door. "I need to collect the weapons. It will only take a moment."

When she nodded, he stepped out into the night.

Moving over to the waiting area, she looked through the bay window.

Outside, Aidan bent down to retrieve her discarded Taser, then headed for the swords that had flown across the parking lot as though guided by an unseen hand.

He didn't zip around like the Flash this time. He moved at normal speeds, his lips clamped together in a grim line.

She supposed he did that for her benefit.

As she watched him, she became conscious of her reflection in the windowpanes.

The heartbeat that had begun to slow picked up speed once more as she stared.

Something red was smeared all over one side of her face and neck. The side she had pressed to Aidan's chest.

Holding out her arms, she looked down.

Blood—a lot of it—painted a sickening amount of skin on her arms and stained most of the front of her shirt. But she hadn't been wounded.

Dana recalled the vision that had struck her when Aidan had kissed her hand the first time they'd met. The one of him standing before her with blood streaking across his face and neck. Of a deep slash opening on his chest. Another opening on his left arm, then his right. Of his hand, curled around hers, growing wet with blood.

She gasped, realizing that—like the vision with Roland—the vision of Aidan wounded had shown her what would happen *tonight*. She had thought the vision a glimpse of Aidan's past. He had even implied it was by describing exactly where the wounds had been on his body. How could he have known that if it hadn't happened yet?

Oh. Right. He had read her mind.

A bell tinkled as the door opened and Aidan entered.

As Dana stared up at him, she registered all the things she had been too overcome with shock to notice a few minutes ago.

Blood splattered his face and neck. His shirt bore a long tear across his chest, the fabric parting enough for her to see jagged flesh covered with blood. Both his coat sleeves bore similar tears.

Aidan wiped the swords clean with his shirt, then tucked them into hidden sheaths sewn into his coat's inner lining.

Holy crap, there were a lot of weapons in there. Swords. Daggers. Throwing stars.

Did he always carry around that many weapons?

When he let the coat fall back into place, her scattered thoughts refocused on the tears that marred it.

Raising his head, he caught her look and froze. Dread crept into his somber expression. "Have you changed your mind? Am I not welcome?"

"You're hurt," she blurted. Badly. How was he even still standing?

Brow furrowing, he glanced down like someone who had stepped in dog doo and only just realized it. His gaze shifted to her, skimming her face and bloody arms. "Oh." He winced. "Sorry about that." Crossing to stand in front of her, he reached into a back pocket and drew out a startlingly white handkerchief.

Cupping her chin in one warm, wet hand, he began to wipe the blood from her face.

"Are you serious?" she exclaimed. He thought she was upset about his getting blood on her? What the hell?

Swatting his hands away, she gripped one of his wrists, turned, and headed resolutely past the reading room.

"Dana?"

Upon reaching the door to the stairwell, she hurried up the steps to her apartment and drew him after her through the first doorway on the left.

What she had always considered a roomy bathroom felt almost cramped with Aidan in it. Releasing him, she opened the largest cabinet and took down the basket that held her first aid supplies.

"Dana?" he asked again, his voice both hesitant and concerned.

Slamming the door shut, she snagged Aidan's wrist again and pulled him across the hallway to her bedroom.

"Dana— "

"Sit down," she ordered, nodding toward her bed.

He cast it an uncertain look. "I can't. I'll stain the covers."

She stared at him. "You're kidding, right?" He sported deep wounds that bled profusely and he was concerned about staining her bedding?

"Perhaps if I cleaned up a wee bit— "

"Sit your ass down," she ordered, pointing at the queen-sized bed.

Eyebrows flying up, he sat so swiftly she almost laughed.

The firm mattress bounced as the old wooden bed frame creaked beneath his weight.

Setting the basket on the bed beside him, Dana moved to stand before him and began to help him out of his coat.

Every movement must be incredibly painful for him. His shoulders moved back, stretching the skin of his chest and parting the edges of that ghastly wound. The heavy fabric abraded the cuts on his arms as she carefully drew the coat down and, once it was free of his hands, let it fall to the covers behind him.

"Dana," he murmured.

"Please don't say anything," she implored softly. She needed quiet. Needed to focus on just tending his wounds so her mind could have a chance to catch up and process everything.

He nodded, watching her warily.

"Now your shirt," she said and bent to grab the hem of his T-shirt.

Without a word, he raised his arms so she could tug the sodden black material over his head and drop it atop his coat.

The hard, muscled chest she had snuggled against and run her hands over and fantasized about so much bore a deeper gash than she had anticipated. The cuts on his arms were pretty scary, too. Surely such wounds required more than butterfly closures and bandages. He needed stitches.

She raised her eyes and met his. "Any chance I can talk you into letting me take you to the emergency room?"

He shook his head.

She had thought as much.

Spinning around, she left the room and ducked into the bathroom again. It only took her a moment to grab a couple of towels and wet them. Then she returned to the bedroom. Tossing one towel onto the bed, she knelt in front of Aidan. "I could lie and say we were in a car accident." If he was worried about the hospital calling the police...

"I can't go to the hospital," he told her softly.

As gently as possible, she drew one of the wet towels across his chest, removing the blood so she could better view the damage. The wound she revealed was nauseatingly deep, but—much to her surprise—seemed to have stopped bleeding.

Dana frowned as she dabbed the edges with the towel. "Because you're wanted by the police?" He had been adamant earlier that she not call 911.

He covered her hand with his to halt her ministrations. "Because I heal quickly."

She steadfastly kept her eyes focused on his chest. "Aidan, these wounds are serious. I'm not going to just sit here and watch you die."

"I'm not going to die," he promised. Taking the towel from her, he grasped her hand and drew her up. "Sit with me for a moment and you'll see."

Dana stared at him. Inconceivable though it might be, he seemed okay. Except... "Your eyes are glowing," she whispered, mesmerized by the amber light.

The corners of his lips turned up in a sad smile. "I won't die. But the wounds do hurt." Still holding her hand, he urged her to sit beside him on the bed. "And right now my emotions are too tumultuous for me to make my eyes stop glowing."

She frowned as she perched on the edge of the bed. "Strong emotion makes them glow?" He had already told her that, hadn't he, when they were outside?

"Yes. That and pain."

Reclaiming the towel, she gently drew it down his arm, starting at his shoulder.

"Dana—"

"Just let me do this, okay?"

He clamped his lips shut.

"I have a lot of restless energy right now," she explained, "so it's either this or pacing, because I need to do something while my mind tries to catch up with things."

A moment passed.

"As you will," he acceded.

The silence that descended then was painful.

One of the things she had liked about Aidan from the beginning was that there had never been any awkward or uncomfortable silences when they were together. She didn't think she had ever experienced that with a man before. Especially when she was initially getting to know one. With other men, there had always been those instances in which she wasn't sure what to say or if she should say anything at all. Moments when the silence seemed to stretch a little too long.

But with Aidan, she had felt so comfortable around him from the beginning that their time together had always felt refreshingly natural, as though they had known each other since childhood and were merely reacquainting themselves with one another after several years of being apart.

This silence, however, was heavy with words unspoken, thick with concern and other emotions she didn't want to examine too closely.

Fear, perhaps, that everything would be different now.

Fear that they had lost what they had only just found.

She cleaned both of his arms, the white towels turning pink and red from the blood. Setting them aside, she glanced at her first aid basket, then finally met his eyes.

They still bore the faint remnants of that surreal glow.

She supposed it should scare the hell out of her because it clearly indicated he was something more than human. Yet the amber light peeking out from his dark brown irises fascinated her.

"Thank you," he murmured.

"I know they aren't bleeding anymore, but I feel like I should at least put a Band-Aid on them. Or maybe fifty."

He shook his head. "They're already healing."

She frowned. "What do you mean?" Dana lowered her gaze to his chest. Her heart jumped as shock rippled through her.

The edges of the wide-open gash that had spanned his chest, cutting deeply into his pectoral muscles, had drawn together while she'd tended his arms.

Her pulse picked up. "That's not possible," she whispered, barely able to produce a sound.

"Keep watching," he instructed softly.

Was that sadness she heard in his voice? Resignation? Something else?

Dana didn't ask, her eyes glued to that angry red slash.

She didn't know how much time passed. How many minutes. A few or a lot. But beneath her astonished gaze, the deep laceration sealed, healed, formed scar tissue, then faded away until his chest was once more unmarred.

Dana reached out and touched his warm skin, smoothed her hand across his muscles where the wound had been, and found no evidence that it had ever existed. When she ran her fingers up and down his biceps, she discovered that they, too, had healed completely.

She looked up.

Aidan's eyes were closed, his brow furrowed.

When she withdrew her hands and clasped them in her lap, his lids lifted.

"Your eyes are really bright," she murmured. He had said such resulted from pain and strong emotion. Since his wounds had healed, she didn't think pain still plagued him. So that left emotion. "What are you thinking?"

Shaking his head, he forced a smile. "Just hoping and praying that won't be the last time I ever feel your touch."

She didn't doubt his sincerity. His beautiful eyes were full of dread and sorrow.

"You're different," she whispered.

He nodded. "Yes, I am."

"You should have told me *how* different."

A mirthless laugh escaped him. "When?" he asked helplessly. "On our first date, when you expressed such unease upon discovering I'm telepathic?"

She bit her lip, feeling a tad guilty over that. She knew firsthand how hard it was to tell people you were different, the negative reactions that usually resulted, and how crappy it could make you feel.

"Or during that first reading you gave me?" he continued before she could respond. "When you told me my lifeline was the longest you'd ever seen, should I have told you it's because I've lived far longer than anyone else you've met?"

She stared at him. "How long *have* you lived?"

Reaching up, he rubbed his forehead as though an ache slowly built there. "Please, don't make me answer that. Not now. Not yet. It will only make this more difficult."

Really? How old was he?

He had said he'd lived far longer than anyone else she'd met. She assumed that included grandparents. So how long had he lived? A hundred years? A hundred and fifty? Two hundred? How was that possible? And how could he look so young and heal at such an astounding rate?

"What are you, Aidan?" she forced herself to ask. *Please say human.*

Sighing, he lowered his hand. "We call ourselves immortals."

Crap.

"But we aren't truly immortal. We just"—he shrugged—"don't age and are very hard to kill."

With his rapid healing ability, she would imagine so. "Are you an alien?" She felt ridiculous asking it, but he clearly wasn't human. "I mean, how did you come to be like this?" She motioned to his smooth chest.

"I'm not an alien. I began my life the same way you did. I was born a *gifted one*."

"What's a *gifted one*?"

"Someone who is born with advanced DNA that lends them special talents ordinary humans lack. Your psychic abilities are a result of the advanced DNA with which you were born. And that

DNA was passed to you from your parents. Much like mine was by my mother."

"I don't have advanced DNA."

"Yes, you do. All *gifted ones* have advanced DNA. It's the source of our gifts."

"Gifted *ones*?" she repeated, stressing the *s*. "Are you saying there are more people out there with special gifts?"

"Yes. Many more. All my brethren possess them. And there are thousands of others."

Every time she thought he couldn't confound her more, he did. "Wait. Are you saying Sheldon and Tracy—the couple I met on our first date—have special gifts? Is that why your telepathy was no big deal to them?"

He shook his head. "Neither Sheldon nor Tracy are *gifted ones*, but the men and women they work with are. Or *were*, before they became immortal."

"What about the others you introduced me to?"

"Martin and Evie are *gifted ones*. Martin is like you and can see the future. Evie is an empath and can feel others' emotions."

"And the rest?"

"Étienne, Krysta, and Sean are *gifted ones* who have become immortals."

"They've *become* immortals? How does one *become* immortal?"

"By being infected with a very rare symbiotic virus that behaves like no other on the planet. When one is infected with it on a large enough scale, the virus conquers, then replaces, the immune system, giving one the speed, strength, and healing abilities that will enable it—and its host—to survive as long as possible."

She grimaced. "It isn't like those snake things in *Stargate* that live in their host's stomach, is it?" *Gross.*

"No. It's nothing like that. It really is a virus. It just behaves unlike any other we've seen."

"Why?"

"Our doctors and scientists are still trying to puzzle that out."

Dana pondered his words. "So Étienne, Krysta, and Sean are like you? They heal superfast, can outrun the Flash, and have glowing eyes?"

"Yes. Étienne is telepathic. He has fewer scruples than I do and can be a nosy bastard. So whenever you're in the same room with him, you can pretty much count on him reading your thoughts."

"You say that as though you think I *will* be in the same room with him again at some point."

"Krysta can see auras," he continued. And Dana found the evasion unsettling.

"Wait." She frowned. "Auras? You mean those glowy things some people claim surround the body? Those are real?"

"Apparently so. And her brother Sean can heal with his hands."

"Seriously?"

"Yes."

"So he can just lay hands on a wound and heal it?"

"Yes."

Okay. That was actually kind of cool.

Aidan's look turned guilty.

Or guilti*er.*

"What?" she asked, already dreading whatever he would say.

"Now might be a good time for me to tell you that I can heal with my hands, too."

Again she stared at him.

"I *did* tell you," he hastened to add, "the night of our first date that I had more than one gift."

She thought back to that night. Had he?

I'm not pretending. I do have a special gift. More than one, if you're to know the truth of it.

Yes, he had. But Tracy and Sheldon had come up then. And Dana had been so surprised by their casual acceptance of his telepathy that she had forgotten.

"You did," she confirmed.

He seemed only slightly relieved to hear it.

"So you can heal with your hands?" she asked. Why, she wondered, did that seem less believable than the other revelations he had made?

He nodded.

Leaning over, Dana reached behind him and rummaged through his coat. When her hand found the hilt of a dagger, she curled her fingers around it and removed it from its sheath.

Aidan eyed her warily when he saw it. "What do you plan to do with that?"

She drew the sharp blade across her palm, cutting a deeper gash than she had intended. "Ow! Shit!" she cried, dropping the dagger. "That hurt more than I thought it would."

Aidan's eyes flashed bright amber. "Are you mad, woman?" Reaching for her wounded hand, he cupped it in one of his and turned it up so he could examine the damage.

Blood spilled out of the deep cut and filled her palm.

Swearing, he pressed the palm of his free hand to hers.

"Seriously," she gritted, "how the hell could you act like your chest and arms didn't hurt? Your cuts were way deeper than this one, and this hurts like hell." It really did.

Aidan's hand heated, becoming as warm as a hot-water bottle.

The pain in her palm decreased, then vanished altogether.

"I'm used to it," he commented absently as he lifted his hand and peered down at her palm.

Dana did, too, and couldn't believe her eyes. The wound was gone.

Grabbing one of the damp towels she had used on Aidan, she wiped her palm clean.

No wound. No scar. Nothing.

"Holy crap," she whispered and stared at him with no little awe. "You can heal with your hands."

He shrugged, his lips turning up in an adorably sheepish smile. "Amongst other things."

She groaned. "Ai*dan!*" she complained. "You can't *do* that!"

"Do what?" he asked, all innocence.

"Tell me you can read minds and don't age and heal quickly and can heal *me*, then—just as I'm beginning to process all of *that*—imply there's more."

He winced. "There *is* more. Quite a bit, I'm sorry to say."

She sighed. "It's times like this I wish I were a heavy drinker."

He laughed. "Shall I pop over to the liquor store and fetch you some scotch?"

Amazingly, amusement flitted through her. "No, thank you." Then she frowned as she recalled the ultra-tall, scary guy with the long hair appearing out of thin air earlier. "When you say pop over there, you don't mean— "

"I can teleport," he announced matter-of-factly.

Her mind went blank. "Oh, *come* on!" she nearly shouted.

Aidan laughed.

And she had to admit, despite everything, that it was good to see his handsome features lighten and his eyes lose some of their sobriety.

"Please, tell me you're joking," she begged, "and that teleportation only happens in sci-fi movies."

"I'm not and it doesn't. You saw Seth teleport earlier tonight."

"Seth was the giant with the long hair?"

He grinned. "Yes. He's our leader or commanding officer."

"And he can do magical stuff, too?"

"There's actually very little Seth *can't* do."

"What about Roland and the woman? They were immortals?"

"Yes. Roland can heal with his hands. And his wife Sarah has prophetic dreams."

She sighed. "This is a lot to take in."

"I know."

"Too much for you to mention on a first date," she admitted now that her brain was starting to process everything. "Or a second. Or even a third."

"Such was my thought." Slowly, as though he expected her to jerk away, he reached over and covered one of her hands with his. "It's also a lot for me to trust you with, Dana. These secrets are not solely my own to share. We've worked hard to keep knowledge of our existence—of *your* existence, of *gifted ones*, immortals, and our advanced DNA and abilities—a closely guarded secret. Our lives and the lives of many others depend upon it. And each time one of us trusts someone with that knowledge, we make our brothers more vulnerable."

She could see the truth in that. Society had always, it seemed, been dominated by people who would rather hate, harm, kill, or exploit those who were different from them than seek to learn from them and live in peace. "But you're immortal. How vulnerable could you be?"

He squeezed her hand. "Remember, I said we're *mostly* immortal. We can still be killed. Two of my brothers were slain not long ago when our secret was shared with the wrong people. A third immortal nearly lost her life as well."

"I'm sorry."

"And I'm sorry I didn't find a way to tell you all this sooner."

"I guess I can understand why you didn't. But I can't help feeling a little hurt that you didn't trust me with it."

"Had it only been my secret to share..." Brow furrowing, he combed the fingers of his free hand through his hair. "Hell, I probably still wouldn't have told you. I care about you, Dana. More than I was beginning to think I could, if you're to know the truth. I've enjoyed so much our time together. Every minute we've shared. And I feared losing that if I told you and you found it all to be too much."

Drawing in a deep breath, she let it out in a long sigh, then turned her hand over and twined her fingers through his. "Okay. You can read minds, heal superfast, teleport, don't age, can heal other people with your hands, run superfast, are superstrong and can make your eyes glow."

"The last is more of an involuntary response."

"Is there anything else you can do?"

His face crinkled up in a *Welllllllllll, now that you mention it* expression.

She groaned. "Just tell me."

"Are you sure you don't want me to fetch you that scotch first?"

She laughed. "No, thank you." His reluctance to confide more didn't anger her. Oddly, it made her feel better, because she believed him when he said it didn't stem from distrust but from a fear that she wouldn't want him anymore if she knew it all.

"I have telekinetic abilities, too," he confessed. "I just don't use them very often."

"You can move things with your mind?"

"Yes."

"Will you show me?"

A pillow suddenly leapt up and hovered a couple of feet from her face.

Dana gaped. "*What?*" Even though she had expected something of the sort, it still shocked her.

Aidan's look turned mischievous a second before the pillow flew forward and gently bounced off her face.

Dana burst out laughing and caught the fluffy projectile as it fell to her lap. Slinging it playfully at Aidan, she hit *him* in the face.

Aidan grinned, fell backward as if she had hit him with a fist instead, then sat up again.

"That is *so* cool." Much cooler than prophetic visions.

He shrugged modestly.

"Can you only move little things? Or can you move bigger things, too?" she asked.

Turning toward her dresser, he stretched a hand out toward it dramatically.

Dana watched the dresser. After a second or two, it began to vibrate.

She sent Aidan an encouraging smile.

He winked.

Then *Dana* rose into the air.

Shrieking in surprise, she threw out her arms but found nothing to grab.

Aidan laughed.

When she looked down at him, he twirled his index finger.

Dana laughed as she spun in a circle, then floated down onto his lap.

He wrapped his arms around her.

Still smiling, she slid her own around his neck.

"Still like me?" he asked softly, the glow in his eyes failing to hide the vulnerability that lurked there.

She nodded.

"You're not afraid of me?"

"No." Whatever his abilities, he was still Aidan.

Her Aidan.

Closing his eyes, he hugged her tight and buried his face in her hair. "Thank you."

Chapter Eight

SETH DROVE ONLY FAR ENOUGH away from Dana's shop to leave the sight of any late-nighters. Stopping the car, he closed his eyes and teleported himself and the vehicle to the barn behind David's home, which served as a huge garage. Parking the car in Ami's spot, he cut the engine, got out, and left the keys above the visor.

By the sounds of it, the Immortal Guardians and Seconds who had assembled at David's home for the meeting remained where he had left them—at the dining room table. Voices overlapped as everyone speculated over what might be happening with Seth, Roland, and Aidan.

Seth strode down the drive and around to the front of the house, taking a couple of minutes to dampen his anger and gather his thoughts.

He'd had no idea Aidan was seeing someone.

Aidan had said nothing. And, contrary to popular belief, Seth didn't *like* intruding on his friends' thoughts, seeing all their secrets and private moments, so he didn't do so nearly as often as most assumed he did.

Joy crept in. Aidan had found someone. After seemingly endless lonely centuries, he had found a woman he loved who was also falling in love with him. Or who *had* been before Roland had mucked it all up.

Bitterness invaded. Why did all hell have to break loose whenever an immortal found love? Couldn't one damned courtship go smoothly?

Grinding his teeth, Seth opened the front door and closed it behind him with a little more force than he'd intended.

All conversation ceased.

Entering the dining room, he crossed to the foot of the table and retook his seat.

A long minute passed.

"Seth," Ami said tentatively, "are you okay?"

"Yes," he gritted, though anger continued to pummel him.

The men and women seated at the table exchanged uncertain looks.

"Are you sure?" she asked. "Because your eyes are really bright. And I'm pretty sure I just heard thunder."

He swore, then muttered, "Give me a minute." But when he closed his eyes, he saw again the dread that had darkened Aidan's features. The fear that he would lose Dana. The dying hope.

Thunder rumbled outside, louder this time.

Opening his eyes, Seth pointed at Chris. "You need to get your shit together and stop persecuting Aidan. From now on, when you come to this table, you will damned well leave all bias at the door."

Chris stiffened and held up a sheaf of papers. "This isn't bias," he insisted.

"Bullshit," Seth countered. "You're holding a grudge."

"I don't hold grudges."

Laughter erupted around the table.

Some of his anger easing just a bit, Seth arched a brow.

"Okay, okay," Chris ground out when the laughter was slow to die down. "I get it. You all think I hold grudges."

"Hell yes you do," Bastien uttered.

Chris shot him a scowl, then met Seth's irate gaze. "But, Seth, when it comes to Aidan, can you really blame me?" He motioned to their audience. "You consider all the immortals and Seconds at this table—as well as the immortals and Seconds who *aren't* at this table—members of your family. And you worry about them and protect them accordingly. Well, that's how I feel about the network employees. I think of them as my family. And Aidan erased the memories and damaged the brains of several of them."

Eyes widened.

"What?" Marcus murmured. "Aidan did that? Why?"

Seth shook his head. "I won't go into that right now."

Bastien cleared his throat. "In his defense, Aidan only erased a minute or two of their memories, so the damage done was negligible."

"Only a minute or two?" Sheldon snorted and waved a hand. "Hell, I probably damaged my brain more than that binge drinking with my buds in high school."

Étienne eyed him curiously. "Is *that* why you're the way you are?"

Sheldon and Tracy both laughed.

Chris clenched his teeth. "*Any* damage is unacceptable."

Seth held up a hand. "I have no problem with your being pissed about that. But I *do* object to your letting it cloud your judgment."

Chris sent him an incredulous look. "How is it clouding my judgment? We know for a fact that Aidan was the last person to see the six women who have disappeared. We even now have three of those encounters on video."

"Yes," Seth said. "But those aren't the only *gifted ones* who have gone missing. You conveniently left out the fact that three men have disappeared as well. And there is no evidence whatsoever that Aidan had any contact with them."

Everyone looked at Chris, awaiting his rebuttal.

Chris frowned. "I just hadn't gotten to that part yet."

David spoke up. "Because you were focusing all your suspicion on Aidan."

Seth nodded. "I know you dislike him, Chris. I know he gave you reason to. But you need to get past that now. If all I knew of this matter was what you told us right before Aidan left, I would believe Aidan guilty of harming those women."

Sheldon nodded. "You did kinda make Aidan sound like a serial killer."

More nods.

"Had you instead," Seth continued, "begun your presentation by saying that nine *gifted ones* have gone missing, three males and six females, then explained that we have strong reason to believe that someone bearing Aidan's appearance was seen with several of them shortly before they vanished — "

"Not someone bearing Aidan's appearance," Chris corrected.

"*Aidan.*"

Ethan spoke up. "I still don't think it was him. I think it was someone else. One of the Others maybe."

Chris rolled his eyes. "You're biased and don't want to believe he could do anything bad because he transformed Heather for you."

Heather huffed a laugh. "And you *aren't* biased?"

"I have three videos that say I'm not," he countered.

Heather raised her eyebrows. "Really? And if the man in the videos appeared to be Seth or David, would you still be so quick to disregard Ethan's input?"

That actually seemed to give Chris pause. "I trust Seth and David."

Ami leaned forward. "Then trust Seth's judgment. When Gershom hit us on multiple fronts last year, we trusted Aidan to keep Adira safe and he did."

All eyes went to the redheaded toddler who slept in Marcus's arms.

Marcus nodded. "Aidan risked his life to protect her. He knew there was a good chance Gershom would follow him. He knew he couldn't outrun Gershom or beat him in a fight. Yet he still didn't hesitate to put his life on the line, whisk her away, and do everything he could to keep her safe."

Heather spoke once more. "Ethan remembers every tiny, insignificant detail he sees. If he says he doesn't think the man in the video is Aidan, then I believe him. And I think you would, too, if that man looked like anyone else here."

Chris ground his teeth for a full minute, then sighed and sank back in his seat. "You're right. I fucked up."

One might think that would assuage Seth's anger, but it didn't. "Yes, you did. And *because* you did, Roland followed Aidan, attacked him, and did his damnedest to kill him."

Gasps of dismay.

Marcus scowled. "Are they okay?"

In the rare instances in which immortals fought each other, the elder immortal almost always emerged the victor.

"They each suffered a few deep gashes," Seth disclosed. Gashes he supposed he should have healed for them, but he had been too pissed to think of that at the time.

"Why was Roland so upset?" Marcus asked, his voice reflecting puzzlement.

Sheldon nodded. "Yeah. Did Roland used to date Veronica or something?"

Seth almost laughed over that. Sarah was the first woman in whom Roland had shown an interest in centuries. "Veronica is his descendant."

Every eye widened.

Sheldon looked at the faces around the table. "So she's like his great-great-great-et-cetera-granddaughter?"

"Yes." Seth shook his head. "Roland didn't move to America a century ago just for the hell of it. Or to disappear, as some believe. He came because the bulk of his descendants migrated here. And a large portion of those now reside in North Carolina and surrounding states." He motioned to Jenna. "Jenna is his descendant."

Heather gaped at Jenna. "You are?"

She smiled. "Yes."

"Veronica is Roland's descendant, too," Seth continued. "And when Chris stopped just short of telling us Aidan had killed her..."

Marcus swore. "Roland was understandably furious."

Chris shook his head. "If Aidan is innocent and didn't harm those women or — at the very least — abduct them, then why did he flee the meeting?"

Seth didn't see much reason to withhold the information. "Aidan has been seeing a mortal woman. A *gifted one* by the name of Dana Pembroke. When he heard that the last six female *gifted ones* he'd met had disappeared shortly thereafter, he feared Dana was in danger and wanted to ensure she was safe."

"*Was* she safe?" Brodie asked.

"Yes."

Sheldon's brow creased. "Why didn't Aidan just teleport over there? Why drive?"

Seth glared at Chris. "Because Dana doesn't know he's immortal and can teleport. Or at least she *didn't* until Roland followed Aidan to her home and outed him."

Groans all around.

Chris frowned. "Aidan didn't circle her name on the list."

"No, he didn't. Because he didn't want you to fuck things up," Seth ground out, "which you managed to do quite efficiently anyway. Roland attacked Aidan and was doing his damnedest to kill him—with glowing eyes and at preternatural speeds—when Sarah called me."

Brodie slammed a fist down on the table. "Damn it, Reordon!"

Little Adira jumped. Cracking open sleepy eyes, she peered at the faces around the table, then snuggled back against her daddy's chest and let slumber claim her once more.

Brodie sent Marcus and Ami an apologetic look, then glared at Chris. "Aidan has waited three thousand years to find a woman he loves, a *gifted one* who might love him enough to transform for him the way Sarah did for Roland. And when he finally finds her, or thinks he has, you go and fuck it all up?"

The anger and belligerence in Chris's expression gave way to guilt.

Ami turned to Seth. "What about Dana? Is she okay?"

"Yes. But she Tasered Roland."

Jaws dropped.

"That is *awesome!*" Sheldon declared.

Brodie grinned. "I knew it. She's a fighter."

Seth agreed. It had taken a hell of a lot of guts for her to grab that Taser and rush outside when she saw Roland and Aidan zipping around at preternatural speeds, trying to slay each other. "She's understandably shaken up though. Angry. And afraid." He shook his head. "We may have just blown Aidan's shot at finding a woman he can spend the rest of his immortal life with by robbing him of the opportunity to share the reality of his existence with her and reveal the truth himself in his own time."

Bastien swore. "Three thousand years alone and he's going to miss out on love because Chris had his head up his ass?"

Seth shook his head "It's not definite yet. He's talking to her now."

Chris frowned. "You left him alone with her?"

"Yes, Chris," Seth gritted. "I left him alone with her to try to undo the damage you've wrought. And before you object, let me remind you that I've known Aidan for a hell of a long time. I made a colossal mistake two years ago when I falsely accused him of working against us — based on video footage you provided, I might add. I won't make the same mistake twice without having more conclusive evidence than you've shown us tonight."

Chris dragged both hands down his face. "Okay. You're right. I fucked up." Leaning forward, he braced his elbows on the table. "And I don't mean in a small way. I mean in a huge, Sheldon kind of way."

Sheldon sent him a disgruntled frown. "Come on, man."

Everyone chuckled.

The tension in the room eased.

Chris flipped through the papers in front of him. "From this point on, I'll pour more time and effort into considering the options I shoved aside because I believed Aidan was guilty."

Seth nodded his approval. Chris was a good man, unafraid of admitting when he was wrong. He'd find a way to make amends.

Chris folded his hands on top of the papers and addressed them all. "Aidan swears the man in the videos isn't him. And most of you want to believe that, so this won't be a popular supposition, but what if it *is* him and he just doesn't remember it? We all know Gershom is fond of mind control. What if Gershom has stepped up his game and, instead of using mortals, is now using Aidan as his puppet?"

Seth looked at David. "I think Aidan's mind is too strong for that, don't you?"

David nodded. "Yes. His mental barriers are nearly impenetrable. I don't think Gershom could plant commands or tamper with Aidan's memories without him knowing it."

Seth looked to Zach.

"I agree," Zach said. "I had to constantly enforce a command to sleep the one time I tried to read his mind. His mental barriers are, in fact, so strong that I failed to topple them. His nose and ears bled. And even though he slept through it all, he still knew when he awoke that someone had been in his head."

Chris's brow furrowed. "If Zach could command him to sleep, couldn't Gershom command him to forget?"

"Theoretically," Seth admitted. "I'll try to convince Aidan to lower his barriers enough for me to look for signs of such. I believe he wouldn't do so before because he didn't want me to know about Dana. But now that I do…"

Melanie bit her lip. "Seth, even if Gershom *did* manipulate Aidan's mind, I don't know that you would find any evidence of it. In humans, you would see scar tissue and other signs of the damage that causes. But immortals have incredible regenerative capabilities. If Gershom planted commands in Aidan's mind to make him abduct the *gifted ones*, then returned after the fact and erased those commands—along with all of Aidan's memories of the events—the virus could conceivably have healed the scarring that would've resulted and left no traces of tampering in Aidan's brain."

David frowned. "So we can't clear Aidan simply by reading his mind?"

"I doubt it," she confirmed with regret.

Seth shook his head. "Then our problems have just multiplied."

Ethan frowned. "I still don't think that was Aidan in the video. I think it was Gershom or someone else who can shape-shift."

Brodie braced his elbows on the table. "If it's Gershom, why assume another's appearance at all? I don't see the purpose of it."

"Plausible deniability?" Zach suggested. "As long as no one actually sees him do it, he can deny it."

"Or," Bastien proposed, "perhaps he just likes to fuck with us. He's tried once before to turn us against each other."

Seth hid his pleasure over Bastien's use of the word *us*. It had taken the immortal black sheep a long damned time to truly become one of them.

David made a sound of agreement. "We know Gershom holds a great deal of animosity toward Seth. What better way to strike at him than to the make Seth strike at one of his beloved Immortal Guardians, only to discover too late that he was wrong?"

Which was why Seth was loath to believe Aidan guilty.

Bastien shook his head. "Vampires appear to be amassing again, too. I think we also need to consider what, if any, role they may be playing in all this."

Ethan nodded. "Heather and I killed a dozen in just one night. Then killed a dozen more a few nights later."

Marcus spoke softly so as not to wake the toddler he held.

"Roland and Sarah have been encountering such numbers as well, killing nine one night, eleven the next. I took out seven myself last night."

Étienne frowned and leaned forward. "Krysta and I just took out ten. But I didn't have time to explore their thoughts and look for signs of manipulation."

Krysta snorted. "You would've had plenty of time if you hadn't been killing them as fast as you could so I wouldn't have to kill as many myself."

He looked down at his wife. "I don't like your taking on such numbers."

She gave his cheek a little pat. "I was killing vampires long before I met you and transformed, sweetie. I can take care of myself."

Sheldon grinned. "She sure as hell can. Strong women are so hot."

Tracy scowled and hit him on the shoulder. "Hey!"

"What?" Sheldon asked with a wince.

"I'm sitting right here," she protested.

"And you're strong," he retorted. "What do you think drew me to you in the first place?"

Her eyes narrowed, then her lips twitched. "I believe you once told me it was my breasts."

Grinning, he sent her a wink. "Those did, too."

Seth felt his ire recede and leaned back in his chair. "All right. Let's get back to business and see if we can't figure this out. Chris, redirect your efforts toward proving that the man in the video is *not* Aidan."

Chris removed a small notepad from his breast pocket, along with a stubby number two pencil, and began to scribble notes.

David spoke next. "You might also consider having your special ops men surveil the other women on Aidan's list of female *gifted ones* to ensure no more are taken."

Chris nodded, still writing. "I'll give them all pictures of Aidan and have them call you directly, Seth, if they see someone matching his description approach any of the women."

David glanced around the table. "The rest of you keep an eye out as well. We don't know yet who is guiding the vampires, but

Gershom is likely responsible for both the abductions and the sharp increase in vampire population."

Seth nodded. "Telepaths, read the thoughts of as many vampires as you can without endangering yourselves unduly and search for anything else that may help us identify their leader and learn his goals."

Lisette spoke. "Should we start carrying tranquilizer guns with us and tranq those we think may possess useful intel?"

"Yes." Seth consulted his pocket watch. "We should end the meeting early. I asked Aidan to bring Dana here after they talked, and I don't want her to have to deal with a house full of powerful immortals on top of everything else."

Heather regarded the Immortal Guardians gathered around the table. "You *are* kind of a lot to take in all at once."

They smiled.

Seth tucked his watch away. "David, Darnell, Marcus, Ami, Ethan, and Heather, you may stay. The rest of you, make yourselves scarce."

Those who hadn't been named all rose and swiftly exited.

The house quieted.

Seth turned to Ethan and Heather. "Ethan, we have already ascertained that you are impervious to mind control. And I believe your gift can be particularly useful to us, so I would like your aid in this."

"I'll do everything I can," Ethan said without hesitation.

Heather nodded. "Me, too."

"Good. I'm going to ask Aidan and Dana to stay at your house until we get to the bottom of this. I'd ask them to stay here but…"

Ethan glanced at Ami and Adira. "You're reluctant to put Ami and Adira in danger?"

"Yes."

Ami was like a daughter to Seth. Adira like a granddaughter. He couldn't bear the thought of anything happening to them.

Ami bit her lip. "Seth, I can be just as useful as Ethan when it comes to discerning the difference between Aidan and an imposter. I think they should stay here."

Ami had come to them from another world. And though she wasn't immortal and couldn't transform (none of them were sure what the vampiric virus would do to her), her race was very long-lived, had incredible regenerative abilities, and possessed special gifts of their own.

One of Ami's was the ability to feel individual energy signatures.

Apparently every living person boasted an energy signature that was as unique as his or her thumbprint. Once Ami was in the presence of someone like Aidan, she would always be able to identify him again—even while blindfolded—just by sensing his energy signature. So if Ami were in the presence of the man in the video, she would be able to tell them with absolute certainty if the man was Aidan, Gershom, or someone else.

"No," Seth and Marcus said simultaneously.

Ami frowned at them. "Why not?"

"It's too dangerous," Marcus protested.

"With all of you here to protect us?" she countered incredulously.

Seth shook his head. "Gershom has not yet dared to breach these walls. But if he wants Dana and can get you and Adira, as well, in one fell swoop, that may tempt him into trying it."

"I agree," Marcus said.

"Also," Seth added, "David's home sees too much traffic." Ami and Marcus had moved in with David when she had been targeted by mercenaries. And since Ami had been the first woman in history to bear an immortal's child, the Immortal Guardians in the area all felt very protective of her and had begun to spend most of their downtime at David's to ensure her safety and Adira's. "Dana is new to our world and may find it more difficult to accept if she can't turn around without bumping into another immortal."

"Oh." Ami nodded. "I guess you're right."

Heather smiled. "I'm the youngest immortal around and still fairly new to the game. Do you want me to see if I can help ease her into things?"

Seth smiled. "I would appreciate that, Heather. Thank you. Ethan, you keep a close eye on Aidan. Keep him in your sight as often as possible. And in the instances that you can't, keep your ears tuned to him. If another woman goes missing and Chris gets another video that implicates Aidan, I want you to be able to confirm with absolute certainty that Aidan was with you when it happened."

Unease crept into Ethan's expression. "That could get awkward, couldn't it? I mean, if Aidan and Dana work things out, they'll probably want to *make up*, if you know what I mean."

Heather's brow furrowed "So?"

"So," her husband told her, "if I keep my preternatural hearing attuned to him, I'll hear everything."

"Oh." Her brow cleared. "Ohhhhhh. Yeah. That *would* be awkward."

Seth shrugged. "Zach did it for you, Ethan. You can do it for Aidan."

Heather looked from Ethan to Seth and back again. "What do you mean Zach did it for Ethan?"

Ethan shot Seth a narrow-eyed look, then sighed and turned back to his wife. "When vampires kept attacking you and someone was messing with your mind last year, we stayed with Zach and Lisette to ensure your safety and…"

Her eyes widened. Then her face scrunched up. "Oh. Ew. Zach was listening to us when we made love?"

Ethan winced. "Not by choice. He *had* to, honey. He couldn't risk tuning us out and missing it if Gershom were to pop in and do whatever he wanted to do."

Heather didn't look appeased. "Did Lisette listen, too?"

"No. She put on headphones and blasted music."

Heather's face flamed with color. Covering it with both hands, she moaned with embarrassment. "Do you know how many times we made love while we were staying with them?" she cried in dismay.

Ethan rested a hand on her back. "Yes. But— "

"We did it like *all day* that one time!"

"I know, but— "

Heather dropped her hands and looked at Seth. "Why did you tell me that?"

Seth sent her what he hoped was a look of apology. "I was merely trying to reassure Ethan that— "

"Erase my memory," she blurted, interrupting him.

Seth stared at her in surprise. "What?"

"Erase that from my memory. Quick. Before it does too much damage. I like Zach and want to keep being friends with him and Lisette, but I won't be able to if every time I see Zach I think about him listening to us humping our brains out."

Marcus burst into laughter.

Ami elbowed him but looked as though she wanted to laugh, too.

"Honey," Ethan said, his face full of concern, "erasing that from your memory would cause brain damage."

"I'm immortal," Heather said. "I'll heal."

"We *think* you'll heal," Ethan qualified.

"You healed when Seth tried to see if you could be mind-controlled and did enough damage to make your ears and nose bleed."

"True. But just to be on the safe side, I don't think we should risk it."

Heather met her husband's earnest gaze. "Ethan, if Seth doesn't get this out of my head, then every time we make love from this point on, instead of thoroughly enjoying it, I'm going to be fixating on all the sounds Zach heard when we made love at their place."

Eyes widening, Ethan swung to Seth. "Do it. Erase it. Melanie said she'd recover, right?"

Seth laughed. "I can bury it instead. That will cause no lasting damage."

Heather smiled with relief. "Thank you."

Ami cleared her throat. "Even if you bury the memories, won't Heather figure it out if she hears Aidan and Dana make love?"

Heather looked at Ethan. "If I do, just tell me Lisette's basement bedrooms were soundproofed. I was still mortal then, so I won't know it isn't true."

Ethan frowned. "I don't want to lie to you."

Heather arched a brow. "The vigorous sex life we'll enjoy for the rest of eternity is worth one lie, don't you think?"

He grinned. "Well, when you put it like that..."

Heather looked at Seth expectantly.

Seth delved into her thoughts, found her memories of the past few minutes, and buried them. He looked at Ethan. "It's done."

"What is?" Heather asked.

Seth smiled at her. "Heather, I'm going to ask Aidan and Dana to stay with you and Ethan until we can get to the bottom of this."

She smiled. "Oh. Okay. I'm the youngest immortal around and still fairly new to the game. Maybe I can help ease her into things."

The others all shared a glance.

"Thank you. I would appreciate that." Seth looked at Ethan, who watched his wife from the corner of his eye, and repeated his instructions for Heather's benefit.

As he wrapped up the meeting, Seth fervently hoped such precautions would prove unnecessary. But none of them knew if or when another *gifted one* might go missing.

Chapter Nine

DANA WASN'T SURE HOW LONG Aidan held her, his arms tight enough to make her wonder if he feared she would run away if he loosened his grip.

But it helped. It really did.

He still felt like Aidan to her. Still smelled like Aidan. Still made her laugh like Aidan.

He was just so much more than she had realized.

Snuggling against him as she had each time they'd parked their butts on her sofa and watched a movie helped quiet her tumultuous thoughts. He didn't feel like the stranger the past half hour had made him seem. He felt familiar. Good. *Hers*.

He had also held her like this after good-night kisses had spiraled out of control, leading him to run those big hands of his over her body and heat her blood.

She frowned. "Is all this why you haven't made love with me yet?" Several times he had kissed her and stroked her until she had orgasmed. But he had never peeled away her clothes, torn off his own, and buried his body in hers the way she had wanted him to.

No. He had always called a halt to things before she could get naked and straddle him.

"Yes." He loosened his hold enough for her to lean back and look at him. "I thought it would be wrong to make love with you before you knew what I am. I thought you should know all of it"—he shrugged—"before you knew all of *me*."

And she really wanted to *know* all of him.

But she supposed she would've felt betrayed if he had made

love with her first, *then* told her, as if he were trying to trick her into accepting him or something. "You didn't tell me how you went from being a *gifted one* to becoming immortal."

He shifted her on his lap, inadvertently making her aware of his erection.

Glancing down, she arched a brow.

"Sorry about that," he said with a sheepish smile. "It's just what you do to me. I've been walking around in a state of near-constant arousal ever since you put your hands on me during that first reading."

She had, too, but didn't admit it.

He gave her a cautious look. "Let me just preface this by saying that I never planned to drop this on you all at once. I was going to ease you into things a little bit at a time."

"How exactly were you going to do that?" she asked skeptically.

"I hadn't figured that part out yet but obsessed over it constantly." He smiled. "When I wasn't fantasizing about making love with you, that is."

Yes, he was still her Aidan. So likable she just couldn't stay mad at him. "I'm guessing that—since you had to preface it—you think the way you became immortal is going to freak me out?"

"Yes."

"All right. Let's hear it." How bad could it be, considering everything else she had learned tonight?

He drew in a deep breath. "I became immortal after a vampire bit me and infected me with the vampiric virus."

Dana stared at him as long minutes ticked past.

"Dana?" he asked finally.

"I'm sorry. I was trying to find a nice way to tell you how utterly ridiculous that sounds but couldn't come up with anything that isn't insulting."

He smiled. "I understand. I know it sounds fantastical, but... don't be afraid."

"I'm not." It was too ridiculous to scare her.

"No. I mean, don't be afraid of this." He parted his lips enough for her to see the tips of his straight white teeth.

As she watched, two fangs descended from the gums above his canines.

Two *long* fangs.

⬥⬥⬥

Aidan's heart sank as Dana leapt off his lap and backed all the way to the doorway, gripping the frame on either side with white-knuckled fists.

He held up both hands. "It's okay," he assured her. "It's okay. I'm still Aidan. I still suck at dating. I just have weird teeth on top of everything else."

He could hear her heart pounding in her breast.

"You're a vampire?" she demanded incredulously.

"No," he swiftly denied. "I'm not a vampire. I'm an immortal."

"But you just said a vampire bit you and now you have fangs and you don't age and I can't believe I'm actually saying this as if vampires are real, because that's insane."

"They *are* real."

She shook her head. "Vampires are fictional. And even if they weren't, they're dead. Or undead. You aren't. You breathe. You have a heartbeat. You eat. You drink. You can go out in daylight. I've *seen* you in daylight. You aren't all gross like the vampires in *From Dusk till Dawn*. And you don't sparkle in sunlight like you're wearing glitter makeup."

He rose but didn't approach her. "I don't know anything about your last two references. But I can tell you that vampires and immortals are both very much alive. Vampires are humans who have been infected with the virus. Immortals are *gifted ones* who are infected with it."

Fear entered her pretty features. "How contagious is this virus?"

"You can't get it from kissing or making love," he reassured her, assuming that was direction her thoughts had taken. "You can only become infected through one of two means. If a vampire feeds from you— "

"*Feeds* from me? As in drinks my blood?"

He clamped his lips together. Judging by her appalled expression, she wasn't going to take his requiring periodic blood infusions well at all. "I'll get to that in a moment," he promised. "When you're exposed to the virus through a bite, your body can't create memory B cells to grant you immunity from it if you're exposed to it again in the future." At least, he thought that was how Melanie had explained it. "So when a vampire feeds from you, the virus compromises your immune system a bit. If you're not bitten again, you recover, like you would from a cold. But if the vampire bites you again in a short enough period of time, then does it again and again, the virus will eventually cripple your immune system enough to gain a foothold and replace it entirely. Then you will transform and become an immortal."

"And the other way?"

"If a vampire drains almost all your blood, then returns it to you after it's mingled with his own, you'll be infected on a massive scale and transform within days. That's the shorter way of doing it. And I can personally attest to the fact that it's less hard on you than the longer way." He shrugged. "At least the longer way was harder on *me*. But the vampire who infected me also tortured me a good long while, so that may have only made it seem worse."

She stared at him.

"Blink," he ordered.

She blinked. "I keep forgetting to do that."

"It's understandable."

"This is so unreal."

"I'm sorry to say it's very real indeed."

That didn't appear to make her feel better. "So the big difference between immortals and vampires is that immortals have gifts and vampires don't?"

"It's *one* of the differences. The other big one is that the virus causes progressive brain damage in humans who transform, so they rapidly descend into madness and prey upon innocents. But the advanced DNA in *gifted ones* shields us from the more corrosive aspects of the virus, so immortals don't."

Her grip on the doorframe didn't loosen. "You aren't in the private security business, are you?"

"No. I and my brethren hunt and slay vampires for a living. We call ourselves Immortal Guardians."

She offered no reply, just kept staring at him. And his teeth.

He shifted, uncomfortable beneath her regard. "I didn't think it a lie since we do ensure the safety of humans by slaying the vampires who would otherwise prey upon them. So it's a *kind* of private security business."

Again she said nothing.

"Dana?" he asked, wishing he could read her thoughts, but he didn't want to make things even worse by abusing her trust.

"Don't you think everyone would know if vampires really existed?" she asked him. "Wouldn't the vampires' victims—the ones who weren't killed—come forward?"

He shook his head. "When vampires and immortals transform, glands form above our fangs that release a chemical similar to GHB under the pressure of a bite. So those who are bitten retain no memory of it."

She frowned. "Even so, this is the information age. With the internet and cell phones that can record video and upload it instantly, don't you think everyone would know? I mean, someone had to have seen *something* by now and caught it on camera."

He didn't begrudge her the doubt. He hadn't wanted to believe it in the beginning either. "We've worked hard to ensure knowledge of vampires' existence—as well as knowledge of our own—never reaches the public."

"Why? I mean, if vampires are real, don't you think people should know? Forewarned is forearmed and all that."

He shook his head. "Do you remember my telling you that I lost two brothers not long ago because knowledge of us was leaked to the wrong ears?"

"Yes."

"Well, they were slain when a mercenary group learned of the virus and decided they'd use it to create an army of supersoldiers they could hire out to the highest bidder."

"Oh, crap," she whispered. "That's just what they'd do, isn't it?"

"It's what they *did*," he corrected. "They had already transformed dozens of their mercenaries, uncaring that the virus would drive the soldiers insane, and were all set to rake in billions of dollars when we discovered the truth. The two brothers I lost fell in battle when we descended upon the mercenaries' compound."

Her brow puckered. "I'm sorry to hear that."

He nodded. "We had to destroy the group to prevent them from unleashing their vampire mercenaries on the world. And, too, because they were intent on capturing immortals so they could study and dissect us and figure out how to keep their army from going insane so they wouldn't have to kill all the soldiers after a year and start over with a fresh batch."

"Seriously? They were just going to kill them all and rotate in new ones?" she asked in disbelief.

"Yes. A mad army is an uncontrollable one. So, of necessity, they would have to replace it every year unless they could get their hands on one of us immortals and figure out why we don't go insane like the vampires do."

"All in the name of money."

"Yes. They knew they would earn billions."

"At the very least."

"Yes."

"Well, crap," she said. "Now it all actually sounds believable."

Aidan didn't know what to say to that. "I'm sorry?" he offered lamely.

She nodded. "Vampires are real."

"Yes."

"And you *are* one. Sort of."

Aidan knew what she meant, so he didn't deny it. "Is it too much?" he asked softly, dreading her answer.

She sighed. "I'd be lying if I said, *No, not at all*, because my mind is just all over the place right now, Aidan."

He almost wished she *had* lied to him.

His phone rang.

Taking it out, he saw it was Seth calling. "I'm sorry. I have to take this."

Dana nodded.

"Yes?" he answered.

"I take it by the grim inflection in your voice that things are not going well," Seth said.

"Correct."

A long sigh. "Well, I believe I've succeeded in pulling Chris's head out of his ass and have asked him to look for anything he can find that will clear you."

"I appreciate that." But he still wanted to kick Reordon's arse.

"I'll deal with Roland as well."

Aidan didn't blame Roland for his anger. Roland had merely

feared for the life of one of his descendants. But Aidan wished like hell Roland had not confronted him in front of Dana.

"Until we have all this sorted out," Seth continued, "I want you and Dana to stay with Ethan and Heather."

Aidan glanced at Dana. "Why?"

"Because Ethan is impervious to mind control and we need him to help clear your name."

That gave him some hope. At least Seth didn't believe Aidan was guilty.

"I would offer to bury Dana's memories of tonight," Seth said, his voice gentling, "but you were going to have to tell her everything anyway. And she needs to know why the two of you will be staying with Ethan and Heather. She needs to know she's in danger."

"I suppose so."

"All right. Wrap things up as quickly as you can, then hie yourselves over to Ethan and Heather's house. They're expecting you."

"I will." Aidan ended the call.

So on top of everything else he had just dumped on Dana, he now had to tell her that one of the men he worked with thought Aidan was guilty of kidnapping six female *gifted ones* and that the only way to clear Aidan's name was to temporarily move in with two Immortal Guardians.

And he had to tell Dana that she was in danger because apparently women of his acquaintance were being targeted by someone who could pass for his identical twin.

Aidan stared at Dana, noted the new wariness in her gaze, and just didn't think he was up for that tonight.

"What's wrong?" she asked. "You look like you just got some bad news."

Shaking his head, he returned his attention to his cell phone and dialed Ethan's number.

"Yeah?" Ethan answered.

"Are you with Seth?"

"No. Heather and I are on our way home. Did Seth tell you he wants you and Dana to stay with us?"

"Yes." Aidan stared down at his big blood-speckled boots. "I've a boon to ask of you."

"Ask it," Ethan immediately responded.

Aidan had expected as much. Ethan was a real stand-up guy. "I need some time," he confessed.

Only the quiet rumble of a well-tuned car engine came over the line as Aidan imagined Ethan visually consulting his wife.

"Can we cover for him?" he heard Heather ask softly.

Since Heather was the only mortal Aidan had ever transformed, he had come to think of her a bit like a daughter and was touched by her desire to help him in this.

"As long as no more *gifted ones* go missing," Ethan returned, equally soft, "I don't think we'll have to."

That was Aidan's hope. "You know the risks. If you aren't comfortable with it— "

"Take what time you need," Ethan interrupted, his voice firm. "Chris may still have his doubts, but I don't. I know that wasn't you in the videos. So take your time, Aidan. We'll be here if you need us."

"Thank you." Aidan ended the call.

Weariness assailed him. He had lost quite a bit of blood, thanks to Roland.

Dana lowered her arms and leaned against the doorframe. "You look tired."

Was that concern he heard in her voice?

He rubbed his eyes. "I am."

"Do you need blood?" she asked tentatively. "It looked like you lost a lot earlier." And her expressive face revealed her unease with the notion of his *drinking* her own.

"No," he told her, returning his gaze to his boots. "I'm okay."

He wasn't really. But with someone out there mimicking his appearance, Aidan didn't want to teleport away and leave her alone even for the few minutes it would take him to pop home, grab a couple of bags of blood, and infuse himself with his fangs.

"Do you know what I *do* need?" he asked instead. "Or what I would like most in the world right now?"

"What?"

"To take one of those timeouts I've seen American football players do. Stop everything. Put it on hold for a moment and just…

lie down. Hold you in my arms. And rest for a bit."

When she made no response, he risked a glance at her.

"I'd like that, too," she said, surprising him. "I could use the time to assimilate all this."

Relief filled him as he rose. "I need to clean up first."

Her lips turned up in a smile that didn't reach her eyes. "Still worried about staining the bedding?"

He nodded. "I have a change of clothes in my car."

Stepping back, she let him pass into the hallway. "While you do that, I'm going to take a quick shower."

She *was* smeared and stained with a healthy amount of his blood.

That she didn't invite him to shower with her neither surprised nor upset him. "As you will."

While she ducked into the bathroom and turned on the shower, Aidan headed downstairs.

The scent of his and Roland's blood still tainted the air outside, thanks to the lack of a breeze.

Aidan kept his ears tuned to Dana as he opened his car's trunk and retrieved the duffel bag Brodie kept there for him. He didn't think he had ever used it before. Since he could teleport, a shower and clean clothes were always just a heartbeat away, but his Second insisted he keep it in the car just in case.

Closing the trunk, he headed back inside and locked the door behind him.

Dana's shower didn't last long.

Aidan waited in the hallway, so concerned about her that he didn't even ponder how alluring she must look, smoothing soapsuds all over her delectable body.

The bathroom door opened. Balmy, humid air wafted out and embraced him.

Dana stopped short when she saw him. Dark, wet hair bracketed a pretty face free of makeup. Her smooth, pale skin glistened with a hint of moisture, much of it exposed by the fluffy white towel she had wrapped around herself sarong style. The end was tucked between her breasts, drawing his gaze to her tempting cleavage. Most of her shapely legs were left bare by the towel, which barely covered her bottom.

Even as tired and anxious as he was, Aidan felt his body harden, which meant—

"Your eyes are glowing," she mentioned, voice hushed.

Damn it. Bending, he grabbed the handles of his duffel bag. "I'll only be a minute."

Nodding, she stepped aside.

Aidan felt her gaze as he entered the bathroom but didn't look at her again before he closed the door. Disrobing at preternatural speeds, he showered equally fast, then donned the black T-shirt, boxers, and cargo pants he found in the duffel bag. His feet he opted to leave bare for now. After taking a moment to drag his hands through his wet hair, he tucked all his bloodstained clothes in the duffel, zipped it, grabbed his boots and opened the bathroom door.

Dana swore softly, out of sight. A rustle of clothing ensued.

When Aidan entered the bedroom, Dana stood with her back to him, naked save for a pair of lavender-and-black plaid shorts.

Aidan's hand clenched around the duffel bag's handles as he stared at her back. Smooth and soft he knew from the times he had slipped his hands beneath her shirt, it tapered down from her shoulders to a narrow waist, the sides of her full breasts visible when she raised her arms and hastily tugged a lavender tank top over her head.

Pulling the hem down to meet the shorts, she turned to face him. "Wow. When you said you'd only be a minute, you weren't exaggerating."

Dana usually dressed conservatively compared to the young women Aidan saw on television and on college campuses who wore pants cut so low you could see their butt cracks, and shirts with necklines that dipped so low he was surprised their nipples didn't show.

To see Dana now in shorts so short they barely covered her lovely bottom and a tank top that clung to her form and revealed more cleavage than usual thoroughly scattered his thoughts.

"What?" he asked belatedly.

She pulled her damp hair out of the front of her tank top and flipped it around to settle against her back. "I said that was fast. It literally only took you a minute."

Wet splotches darkened her tank top in places. The hard beads of her nipples pressed against the light fabric. Sooooo tempting.

He forced his gaze up to her face. "I'm sorry, what?"

She grinned. "Thank you."

He raised his brows. "For what?"

"For making me feel normal again. For making *this*—you and me—feel normal again."

He lifted one shoulder in a shrug and sent her a rueful smile. "I can't help it. You take my breath away."

"I could say the same thing," she responded.

He glanced down, then up again. "I'm fully clothed, except for my bare feet."

"And even fully clothed, you take my breath away," she admitted with a smile.

Aidan relaxed.

The next several minutes were refreshingly domestic. Aidan plunked his bag and boots down on the far side of the bed and laid his coat over it, weapons exposed. Then he and Dana removed the bloodstained bedding and replaced it with fresh sheets and a pretty quilt she said her great-grandmother had made.

Aidan drew back the covers and motioned for her to lie down.

She did, curling up on her side.

After draping the covers over her, he walked around to the far side of the bed and slipped in beside her.

She started to turn toward him.

Aidan rested a hand on her shoulder, silently asking her to stay where she was.

She stilled.

Slowly, he eased forward and spooned up behind her. When she didn't protest, he slid one arm beneath her pillow, then curled the other around her waist and drew her against him, snuggling her close. Her back met his chest. Her full hips cradled his erection. The back of her lovely legs molded to the front of his.

Sighing, he buried his face in her cool, damp, fragrant hair.

He needed this so much.

He heard her heart rate increase and hoped it wasn't due to fear. "I tend to sleep deeply after I've been wounded," he murmured drowsily, fatigue pulling at him despite his desire to stay awake, "so if you want to stake me through the heart, that would be the best time to do it."

She rested her arm atop his and toyed with his fingers. "I'm not going to stake you," she whispered and pressed a kiss to his knuckles.

Nodding, Aidan clung to consciousness and savored the moment as long as he could.

<hr />

Dana's eyes flew open.

Aidan's big warm body still spooned around hers, his front glued to her back. The arm he had wrapped around her was heavy and relaxed. His muscled chest rose and fell with deep, even breaths.

She frowned. What had woken her?

The faint illumination that filtered in from the streetlight out front didn't allow her to see much farther than the bedside table.

Easing Aidan's arm off her, she sat up and reached for the cell phone she usually kept by the bed at night but didn't find it.

She must have left it downstairs.

Opening the top drawer in the table, she felt around until her fingers closed around her iPod. Pressing the power button, she slid her thumb across the screen to unlock it.

Pastel wallpaper lit up the screen, along with the time: 3:57.

Looked like they'd slept for several hours.

She glanced at the battery indicator. Red instead of white. Seven percent battery power left. That should be enough to help her fetch her cell phone.

Rising, she tiptoed out of the bedroom and into the hallway.

The house seemed to slumber, too, encapsulating her in quiet. Even the air conditioner made no sound.

Moving toward the stairs, she turned on the iPod's bright flashlight.

Much better. She hadn't wanted to turn it on in the bedroom and risk waking Aidan.

Descending the staircase, she passed the door she had forgotten to close earlier and entered her shop. All seemed quiet there, too.

Padding forward, toes curling against the cold wood floor, she found her cell phone where she had left it on the counter before all hell had broken loose.

No new calls or texts had come in.

Hmm. So what had awakened her? She was usually a pretty sound sleeper and had assumed her phone had chimed.

Perhaps Aidan had shifted and inadvertently nudged her awake?

Could be. She hadn't slept with anyone in quite a long time, so she wasn't used to having a big warm body in bed with her.

Glancing up, she froze.

Faces peered at her through the bay window.

Sneering, blood-splattered faces that housed long, sharp fangs and glowing eyes.

Oh, crap. Vampires. A *lot* of them.

They smiled in unison.

Spinning around, Dana raced for the stairwell. "Aidan!" she screamed.

Glass shattered behind her. Wood splintered. The front door burst inward and flew past her, one corner slamming into the back of her head.

Stumbling, she managed to remain on her feet as pain erupted behind her eyes. "Aidan!" she cried again, still moving forward, terror engulfing her.

A heavy weight slammed into her back, taking her down to the floor.

She threw her hands out to break her fall and ended up bruising her elbows and hitting her chin.

Her cell phone flew out of her hand and skidded into the stairwell.

The vampire who had tackled her wrapped a fist in her hair and jerked her head back.

Crying out, Dana struggled to throw him off, but he was strong. And heavy. And twice her weight.

His fangs pierced her neck.

Pain streaked through her as though someone had just stabbed her with two sharp knitting needles.

A second vampire yanked her left arm hard enough to pull it out of its socket and sank his fangs into her wrist.

Again she cried out, tears filling her eyes.

A third vampire did the same with her right.

They were so strong! Her struggles were nothing to them!

"Aidan!" she screeched.

Aidan appeared out of thin air just outside the door to the stairwell, his hair rumpled from sleep, his amber eyes as bright as candles. Anger darkened his features. The cords of his neck stood out as he roared his fury and leapt forward, swinging two swords.

The vampire at her neck lunged backward, tearing flesh and sending new agony through her. Those at her wrists did the same.

Movement blurred around her. Feet stumbled over her, kicking her in the ribs. Bodies fell. Men screamed. Weapons hit the floor with a clatter and skidded beneath boots and sneakers.

So terrified she couldn't make a sound, Dana brought a hand up to the gaping wound in her neck. Blood gushed from both it and her wrists, making her hands and the floor around her slick and warm.

A knife fell to the floor, inches away.

As lethargy pulled at her, Dana grabbed it with her free hand and rolled onto her back.

Cold seeped in. Breathing grew difficult as bodies and glowing eyes shifted and flowed above and around her in a blur of motion.

Dizziness assailed her.

Then Aidan crouched over her, fear in his glowing amber eyes. Moving her hand aside, he covered the wound in her neck with his hand. "It's okay," he said, his voice hoarse with emotion as he grabbed her wrist with his other hand. "You're going to be okay."

Both of his hands heated. Both also trembled.

Too late, she thought. It was too late. She had lost too much blood.

"Dana," he said, blinking back tears, "I can save you."

She shook her head, unable to speak. No, he couldn't.

"I can," he insisted, his beautiful face full of torment. "I can save you. If you'll just let me…"

His voice faded as unconsciousness beckoned.

Dimly, she became aware of a form rising up behind him. A vampire whose face twisted in a malevolent smile as he raised a machete in both hands.

Her eyes widened. She tried to speak and produced only a choking sound instead.

Aidan!

The vampire swung his blade in an arc that would cleave Aidan's head from his body.

No!

Dana jerked awake, breath hitching with a sob, her heart pounding in her breast.

Adrenaline swam through her veins. Her breath came in short gasps. Tears burned the backs of her eyes as she frantically searched her darkened bedroom.

Shifting onto her back, she looked at Aidan.

His head still shared her pillow. His eyes were closed, his face peaceful in slumber.

Easing his heavy arm off her, she slid out of bed and turned in a circle, trying to figure out what the hell had just happened.

All was dark. All was quiet.

No glowing eyes peered at her.

Trying to calm her racing heartbeat, she skimmed a hand across the surface of her bedside table but didn't find her cell phone. Yanking open the top drawer, she grabbed her iPod and turned it on. Tapping the flashlight symbol, she held the iPod out in front of her, directing bright white light all around the room.

Empty.

No vampires lurked in the shadows, flashing fangs, waiting to pounce.

Her fingers shaking, she touched her neck but found no gaping wound. Only smooth, unmarred skin.

She shone the light down on her pajamas.

No blood soaked her tank top. The flesh of her wrists wasn't torn open.

Had it really been a dream?

She remained motionless for several seconds, trying to calm her jagged breathing.

Lowering the iPod, she glanced at the screen. Seven percent battery life.

She checked the time: 3:57.

Oh, crap. It *hadn't* been a dream. It had been a vision.

Chapter Ten

SCRAMBLING BACK ONTO THE BED, she knelt beside Aidan and shook him. "Aidan."

He slumbered on.

Hadn't he said something about sleeping deeply after he'd been wounded?

She shook him harder, damned near shoving him off the bed. "Aidan!"

Eyes flying open, he jackknifed into an upright position and raised a sword. "What?"

Dana gaped at him. When had he hidden a sword in the bed?

He looked at her and blinked in confusion. "Dana? What is it?"

She shook her head, tears rising as fear pummeled her. "I just had a vision. Vampires attacked. A lot of them. They ripped my throat out and — "

Eyes flashing amber, he dropped the sword and drew her into a tight hug. "It's okay. It's okay. Where will they attack?"

"Here."

Swearing, he released her, threw back the covers, and rose. "When?"

"Two minutes. Maybe three." Backing off the bed, she watched him yank on his weapons-filled coat. "In the vision, I went downstairs to get my cell phone and they burst through the windows, knocked down the door, and attacked me. They bit me on the neck, and my wrists, and I couldn't get to you, so I yelled and — "

"That isn't going to happen," he declared grimly. "I'm going to teleport you to Ethan and Heather's house. They'll keep you safe while I come back and fight the vampires."

"They're immortal?"

"Yes."

"Oh hell no!" she blurted, her voice a bit strident. "After what I just saw in that vision, the only person with fangs I trust is you. I'm staying here." Just the *idea* of being alone with someone else who had fangs terrified her. She'd much rather stay here and take her chances with Aidan. He was the only one she trusted not to kill her. "Or better yet. Why don't we just get the hell out of here?"

He shook his head. "They'll move on to your neighbors down the street and kill them if I don't stop them."

Damn it. She couldn't let them kill Mr. and Mrs. Crimshaw. Both were in their eighties and had never once complained about Dana running a business out of her home or looked down their noses at her because she claimed to be psychic.

Turning back to her bedside table, Dana yanked open the second drawer and drew out a 9mm and spare magazine.

Aidan cursed. He must have read her thoughts and her fears though, because he didn't try to change her mind.

Reaching into his coat, he drew out a gun. "Take this."

She did, then frowned down at it. "What is it?"

"A tranq gun. It's point and shoot just like your 9mm and will drop any vampire in his tracks." He drew out his cell phone and dialed. A second passed. "Ethan. Are you at home?" He looked at Dana. "I'll be right back."

Before she could blink, he vanished.

Her mouth fell open.

Aidan reappeared, his hand on the shoulder of a man who looked enough like him to pass for his brother. Dana guessed the man was about six foot four inches tall with short black hair and brown eyes like Aidan's. He wore black cargo pants, combat boots, and a black T-shirt that hugged muscles as huge as a professional bodybuilder's.

"What the hell?" the man demanded in an American accent.

"Vampires will attack in one minute," Aidan told him. "I've weapons in my bag. Arm up." Then he vanished again.

The man's eyes flashed amber.

Fear rising, Dana backed away from him.

"Where's his bag?" he asked.

She pointed to the duffel.

The man blurred. When he stilled, he held two shoto swords and had several daggers and throwing stars strapped to his body.

Aidan reappeared, his hand on the shoulder of a woman.

The woman was about Dana's height with longish brown hair. She, too, wore black cargo pants, heavy boots, and a black T-shirt. But her shirt hugged a narrow waist and full breasts.

She smiled up at Aidan. "That is *so* cool!" She also was American by the sound of it. Then she saw Ethan and Dana. "Oh shit. What's wrong?"

"Arm up," Aidan told her. "Vampires will attack any minute."

The woman blurred. When she stilled, she bore as many weapons as the men.

Aidan crossed to Dana and touched her arm. "Dana, this is Ethan and Heather. I trust them absolutely."

Both nodded and said, "Hi, Dana."

Aidan turned away so he could strap on more weapons. "Tell them what you saw in your vision, sweetheart."

Dana glanced at the others. "I went downstairs. Vampires attacked, crashing through the door and the bay window. They tackled me and bit my neck and wrists."

Ethan swore.

"I yelled for Aidan. He appeared and started fighting them. The ones who were biting me tore open my neck and wrists."

More curses.

"Aidan knelt over me and started healing my wounds. A vampire came up behind him. I tried to warn him but couldn't. Then the vampire swung a machete and decapitated him."

Aidan spun around to look at her. "What?"

"I'm sorry," she said. "You didn't let me finish earlier."

Heather swung her swords with a flourish, anger sparking in her pretty features as her eyes began to glow with amber light. "Well, *that's* sure as hell not going to happen."

"You're damned right it isn't," Ethan seconded.

"No, it isn't," Aidan added and headed for the hallway. "Heather, you stay with Dana and keep her safe. Ethan, you're with me."

Dana stared at him. "What?"

Heather turned to Ethan. Rising onto her toes, she wrapped her arms around his neck, her hands still clutching weapons, and pressed her lips to his.

Ethan closed his arms around her and deepened the kiss.

Glass shattered downstairs.

The kiss ended. "Be careful," they said simultaneously.

Then Ethan and Aidan blurred and disappeared down the hallway.

Heather glanced around. "Is there a room up here that doesn't have any windows?"

"Yes," Dana said numbly. "The bathroom."

Heather motioned to the doorway. "Let's go."

Thuds and crashes sounded downstairs as Dana led the immortal woman to the bathroom and ducked inside.

Heather nodded. "This'll do." She stationed herself in the doorway, facing outward.

Dana's nerves jangled as she listened to the sounds of violence below.

"I know you're scared, Dana," Heather said over her shoulder. "I sure as hell was the first time I encountered vampires and immortals a year ago. But don't worry. We've got this."

"Upstairs!" a male bellowed outside.

More glass shattered, this time on the second floor.

Heather stepped out into the hallway, then left Dana's line of sight.

Blades clashed with metallic *shicks* and *tings*. Thuds sounded. Grunts of pain and curses filled the air, all masculine.

Dana cautiously approached the doorway and peered out.

Heather fought two vampires that had apparently crashed through Dana's bedroom window.

Had they jumped that high? Could vampires do that?

Yes, Aidan said in her head. *Stay vigilant. More intend to follow those. If they overwhelm Heather, call or think my name.*

Okay. As Dana watched, three more vampires entered the hallway from the guest bedroom beyond Heather and the vampires she fought.

Two of the newcomers were blond. One was brunet. The first two had eyes that glowed a vibrant blue. The eyes of the third glowed silver. All flashed fangs and grinned with glee when they saw their friends fighting a woman.

Raising her 9mm before they could do that blurry-fast-motion thing, Dana fired multiple shots, hoping Heather wouldn't inadvertently jump in front of the bullets. The first blond vampire's head snapped back as a hole appeared between his eyebrows. The second blond's head did the same. Neither went down though. So as their brunet friend gaped at them, she shot both in the head again.

The arteries, Aidan said in her head. *Hit the major arteries.*

Oh. She fired again and thought she managed to hit the first two in the carotid arteries, because they collapsed.

Their friend turned a look of outrage on her and roared as he streaked toward her in a blur.

Panic flaring, she fired at what she thought was his chest.

One of the vampires Heather fought grunted as he leapt away and inadvertently took the bullet.

Dana fired again. And again.

The brunet vampire racing toward her stumbled, slowing enough for her to see him better. As he leapt past Heather and her foes, his eyes still on Dana, Heather spun and swung her sword. The vampire's body dropped to the floor as his head flew through the hair and landed at Dana's feet.

Dana jumped away from it as it rolled past, then looked up in time to see Heather step back as the two vampires she fought dropped, lifeless, to the ground.

Heather grinned at Dana, her face splattered with blood. "Excellent shooting."

More vampires exited Dana's bedroom as two more raced out of the guest bedroom.

"Really?" Heather said, the word rife with exasperation. She nodded to Dana. "You get the two at the end of the hallway. I'll take these clowns."

Dana raised her 9mm but hesitated as Heather and the vampires she fought leapt into preternatural motion.

All were a blur. What if she hit Heather by mistake?

I'll keep to the right, Heather told her telepathically.

Surprised by the woman's voice in her head, Dana moved to the left and started firing.

She ran out of bullets before she could drop the vampires.

Ducking back into the bathroom, she ejected the empty magazine and slammed the full one home. Backing away, she advanced the first bullet into the chamber and aimed at the doorway.

A blur filled it and solidified into the form of a vampire.

Dana fired three times, hitting him in the head, the carotid, and his chest, inches away from his heart.

Eyes widening, the vampire raised a hand to the blood gushing from his neck and staggered backward.

Another vampire filled the doorway.

This one didn't slow until Dana shot him four times in the chest. He was only a few feet away when she shot him in the head and the neck. And he *still* reached for her, spewing curses and blood as he dropped to his knees, then finally pitched forward.

Her heart slammed against her rib cage.

That had been close.

Aidan spoke in her head. *I wouldn't have let him reach you, sweetheart.*

The vampire on the floor breathed his last breath.

You just concentrate on what you're doing down there, Dana thought back to Aidan, *and make sure your head stays on your shoulders.*

Dana inched past the dead vampire.

The flesh of the vampire's exposed arm began to shrivel up as though he were being mummified.

Creepy.

More grunts and thuds filled the hallway.

"Okay," Heather growled, "now you're starting to piss me off."

Dana saw the tranq gun Aidan had given her on the counter beside the sink. She had been so rattled earlier that she didn't even remember placing it there.

Grabbing it, she tucked it in the waistband of her shorts and poked her head out into the hallway.

Heather was surrounded by vampires.

Don't do it, Aidan said.

Ignoring him, Dana yelled, "Hey, numbnuts!"

The blur of motion ceased.

Half a dozen vampires stopped battling Heather and looked at Dana.

Heather laughed. "Looks like they *all* answer to that. Next time see if they'll answer to dumbass." Swinging her short swords, she opened the arteries of the two vampires closest to her.

Two of the remaining vampires darted in Dana's direction.

Ducking back into the bathroom, she backed toward the far wall and aimed her 9mm at the doorway.

As soon as it darkened, she fired three bullets. The first vampire stopped, grimacing in pain as he pressed a hand to the holes in his chest. Dana fired again and ended up hitting the vampire behind him as the first dodged to the side.

Both snarled in anger.

Dana fired multiple times until a *click* warned her she'd emptied her last magazine, but she'd hit enough arteries for the first vampire to drop.

The second vampire kept coming, stumbling over the bodies of his friends.

Oh crap.

Aidan appeared behind the vampire, yanked the man's head back, and slit his throat. "Call me if you need me, damn it," he grumbled, then vanished again.

Dana pulled the tranq gun. She didn't even bother to leave the bathroom this time. When Heather's grunts and curses reached her ears, Dana just yelled, "Hey, dumbass! In here!"

Sure enough, a vampire filled the doorway. "You're the human," he sneered. "This is gonna be fun."

Dana fired the tranq gun.

The vamp looked down at the dart sticking out of his chest and started to smile. Then his knees buckled. A look of surprise crossed his face as his eyes rolled back in his head and he collapsed to the floor atop his friends.

A blurred form appeared in the doorway.

Dana fired again.

Heather ducked the dart, then stilled and held up her weapons. "It's okay. It's just me." Remaining in the doorway, she looked this way and that. "I think that's all of them up here."

By the sound of things, Aidan and Ethan had nearly defeated the vampires below. At least Dana hoped that was what the dwindling noise indicated.

Heather casually leaned one shoulder against the doorframe. Her clothing was torn in several places, revealing jagged wounds. She had a nasty gash on one arm. Her face, neck, and pale arms were splotched and smeared with blood. "So," she said, giving Dana a friendly smile, "you like Aidan?"

Dana stared at her. *Really? There are three dead vampires shriveling up at my feet. A fourth is passed out on top of them. A dozen or so more are lying dead in the hallway. I'm still breathing hard and trying to get my hands to stop shaking. And she wants to engage in a little girl talk?*

Aidan appeared in the hallway just behind Heather and frowned down at the female immortal. "Don't be impertinent."

Grinning unrepentantly, she looked beyond him as Ethan appeared. "All done?"

Ethan nodded. "You okay? Any wounds?"

Heather wrinkled her nose. "A few. They hurt like hell, but I'm trying to be tough like you guys and not let it show."

Ethan frowned. "It isn't that we're tough, honey. We've just had more time to get used to it."

Aidan raked his gaze over Dana. "Are you okay?"

"Yes."

He looked as though he would've hugged her if his clothes weren't saturated with blood.

"Are *you* okay?" she countered.

He nodded and turned to Heather. "Where are you injured?"

Setting her weapons on the counter beside the sink, she pulled her right sleeve up over her shoulder to expose the deep gash in her arm.

Aidan added his slick weapons to the countertop, then curled his hands around Heather's biceps.

As Dana watched, the wound on Heather's arm closed and healed.

Aidan did the same with additional wounds on her side, then on the back of her thigh. "Ethan?" he said when he was finished.

Ethan shook his head. "I'm good."

"You're favoring your right side and your breath is short."

"It's just some broken ribs. I'll be fine."

"No," Aidan said. "I owe you." Grabbing Ethan by the left shoulder, he held him still and rested a hand on Ethan's right side.

After a minute, Ethan drew in a deep breath. The tension in his face eased. "Thank you."

Aidan nodded, then healed a deep slash in Ethan's back. Another on his arm.

Dana watched it all in awe as her hands finally stopped shaking.

Aidan frowned and nudged Ethan's chin up. Yet another slash scored his jawline. "What did he do, try to decapitate you and miss?"

Ethan laughed. "I think so."

Shaking his head, Aidan covered Ethan's jaw with one hand.

Seconds later, a deep cut opened along *Aidan's* jawline.

Dana gasped and took a step forward.

Ethan swore and slapped Aidan's hand away. "You didn't tell me you were low on— "

Aidan shot Ethan a quelling look.

"Energy," Ethan finished with a glance at Dana. "You didn't tell me you were low on energy."

But Dana was pretty sure he had intended to say blood. "Aidan?" she asked, picking her way over the vampires' bodies. "Are you okay?"

"I'm fine," he said with a faint smile.

Clearly he *wasn't* fine. But she forgave him the lie. He was trying to ease her fears.

Heather offered Dana a hand to steady her as she stepped over the splayed legs of the vampires. "Immortals like Aidan heal others by taking the wounds into their own bodies, which heal at an amazingly accelerated rate. When Aidan is at full strength and does that, he heals so swiftly that the wounds don't have time to afflict him. But when he pushes himself and his gift too far, whatever wound he's attempting to heal on the other person will open on his own body."

Dana stared up at him. Aidan had healed her hand earlier by taking the wound into himself? She had caused him physical pain?

Aidan glared at Heather. "Why did you tell her that? Now she won't want me to heal her if she's injured."

Heather shrugged. "Well, that's kind of a good thing, right? I mean, if she cares about you enough that she doesn't want to cause you pain, then maybe she'll be able to get past all of this." She motioned to the corpses and the blood-splattered walls and floor.

Aidan sighed.

Ethan sent him a look of sympathy. "Been a hell of a night, hasn't it?"

He nodded.

Heather squeezed Dana's hand. "Why don't we go sit in your bedroom for a bit and catch our breath while the boys clean up this mess?"

Dana nodded but pulled her hand from Heather's as they came abreast of Aidan. Wrapping her arms around him, she hugged him tight.

"Dana," he protested, holding his arms away from her.

"I don't care about the blood," she mumbled into his cold, damp shirt, fighting tears all of a sudden.

Her visions had always come true before. And Aidan had been decapitated in the last one. Seeing that cut open along his jawline had reminded her that he could've died tonight, that he *would've* died if—

"It's okay." Aidan closed his arms around her and rested his chin on her hair. "I'm okay, Dana. We both are."

She nodded, probably smearing blood all over her face, but she didn't care. She had come very close to losing him tonight.

"And I you," he murmured, his voice hoarse.

⇒◈◈◈⇐

Aidan gave Dana a last squeeze, then gently set her away from him.

Her hazel eyes held tears when she raised them to meet his.

How he loved her. He had been reading her thoughts ever since the battle had begun. And when she had recalled her vision just now, she hadn't been relieved upon realizing she had survived the battle herself. She had been relieved that *he* had survived, that he had not been decapitated, that he hadn't been taken from her.

He looked to Heather. He didn't know what Heather saw in his face. But she nodded. Moving forward, she wrapped an arm around Dana's shoulders.

"Did I mention that the vampires all responded to dumbass, too?" she asked conversationally.

"No."

"Every single one of them," Heather told her as she guided her out of the bathroom.

"Next time I'll have to try knucklehead," Dana joked wearily.

Heather gave her shoulders a squeeze and lowered her voice. "I know this is a lot to take in, Dana. I just learned about all this myself last year and totally freaked when I found out."

"You did?" Dana asked.

Heather nodded. "But immortals are good guys. And Aidan is one of the best. He wouldn't hesitate to give his life to protect his brethren. And he wouldn't hesitate to give his life to protect you."

Dana motioned to the carnage marring her hallway. "Is that a possibility? I mean, does this sort of thing happen often?"

"No, of course not," Heather countered, then winced. "Well… Okay. I don't want to lie to you. It's been happening more than usual in recent years. There's kind of been a lot going on in the Immortal Guardians' world lately. Mercenaries trying to create a race of supersoldiers. Gershom's evil ass sending vampires to attack military bases. And—"

"Heather." Ethan interrupted his wife. "I don't think you're helping, honey."

She grimaced. "Well, I'm *trying*. I love Aidan. He's been good to us. And I like Dana."

"You just met me," Dana pointed out.

"Yes, but you're smart."

She raised a brow. "And you know that because…?"

Heather grinned. "Because you care about Aidan. And you're brave, too. When all hell broke loose, you didn't scream and pee your pants or curl up in a ball and whimper."

Dana's lips twitched. "Or run two steps, then trip and fall down like women do in horror movies?"

Heather laughed. "Exactly. Instead, you kicked ass and took names."

Dana smiled. "Those names being numbnuts and dumbass?"

Aidan laughed, as did the others.

The two women entered Dana's bedroom.

"Wow," Heather said. "Vampires sure can make a mess, can't they?"

"Yes," Dana agreed morosely.

"Don't worry. It'll all be as good as new soon."

"I can't stop shaking," Dana confessed in a hushed voice.

"That's normal," Heather assured her. "I used to shake after every battle when I first started hunting vampires, but I eventually got used to it. When I saw how close a vamp had come to cutting Ethan's throat though..."

"Wow. You're shaking as badly as I am."

"Yeah. Don't tell Ethan."

"Can't he pretty much hear everything we're saying?"

"Yes. But he loves me, so he's going to pretend he can't. Right, sweetie?"

"Right," Ethan said with a smile as he examined the bodies shriveling up in the bathroom and out in the hallway. "Should I call Chris?"

Aidan sighed. "Yes. Only he can clean up a mess this big. And I want Dana's home and business to be exactly the way they were before the vampires attacked."

"What about her neighbors?"

Aidan took a moment to listen. "The woman next door is out of town. And the elderly couple down the street fell asleep with their TV blaring and didn't hear a thing."

Ethan took out his cell phone and dialed network headquarters.

"Reordon," Aidan heard Chris answer.

"It's Ethan. We need you to send a cleanup crew over to Dana's home."

As Ethan gave Chris an abbreviated breakdown of the battle they had just fought, Aidan crouched down beside the sedated vamp and touched his temple.

The vamp's thoughts and memories were cloudy from the drug and jumbled up by madness. It took Aidan several minutes to sort through it all and find the information he sought.

When he did, he swore.

Ethan ended the call and pocketed his phone. "What?"

We have a problem, Aidan told Ethan telepathically so Heather wouldn't hear him.

Ethan's glance went to the doorway, then returned to Aidan. He raised his eyebrows in a *What's up?* expression.

Ethan's mind was wired differently than that of humans and other immortals, leaving it mostly inaccessible to telepaths. Seth, Zach, and David could all read Ethan's mind if they forced it, but all Aidan and other younger telepaths could do was send thoughts his way. They couldn't read any he sent back.

I read the vampire's mind and scoured his memories, Aidan told him, *trying to ferret out who sicced him and the others on Dana.*

Ethan nodded.

According to his memories, which appear to be real and not planted, Aidan told him, *the vampires met with* me *two hours ago, at which time I instructed them to attack. Contrary to Dana's vision, they were supposed to only scare the bejesus out of her until I gallantly showed up to rescue her.*

Taking out his cell phone again, Ethan typed something on it with his thumbs and turned the screen so Aidan could read it.

Aidan smiled at the foul epithet that stood out in bold type. *That's how I feel about it, too.*

Again Ethan typed, then showed Aidan the screen.

That makes you look guilty as hell.

Yes, it does. It makes it look as though I've upped my game, as Chris accused, to try to get a female gifted one *to fall for me.*

Ethan typed some more, then showed Aidan the screen.

Especially after what happened with Veronica.

Yes. And since I wasn't where I was supposed to be tonight — with you and Heather — you can't confirm it wasn't me. Chris will say I could have met with the vampires as soon as Dana fell asleep.

Frustration darkened Ethan's features. Pacing away a couple of steps, he rubbed his stubbled jaw, then stared down at the unconscious vampire.

After a moment, Ethan picked up the discarded tranq gun and opened the cartridge.

Most tranquilizer guns only held one dart, but when Melanie had begun reproducing the sedative for use against vampires,

Chris's weapons experts had created tranq guns that could hold and fire multiple darts that were also smaller than the norm.

Removing a dart, Ethan closed the cartridge and set the tranq gun back on the counter.

What are you doing? Aidan asked.

Ethan typed his response, then showed it to him.

> Buying us time to prove you're innocent.

Kneeling, he jammed the dart into the unconscious vampire an inch from the other one.

Aidan stared. On top of the other wounds the vamp had suffered, the dose delivered by the second dart would prove lethal.

As if to confirm his thought, the vampire began to shrivel up as the virus inside him devoured him from the inside out.

Ethan rose and typed some more.

> If Dana says she only tranqed him once, Chris and the others will assume she was rattled by the battle and just isn't remembering it correctly. And Seth won't see the damning memory of you and think you're guilty.

Which explained why Ethan was typing his responses instead of speaking them aloud—so Heather wouldn't hear them and be forced to either lie for Aidan (something Seth would see if he read her thoughts) or tell the truth and condemn him.

Why would you do this for me? Aidan asked, astonished that Ethan would risk Seth's wrath for him like this.

Ethan typed again, then showed Aidan the screen.

> You gave me Heather.

Thank you, Aidan said, touched that the younger immortal would risk so much for him.

Smiling, Ethan nodded.

A ripple of power made the hair on the back of Aidan's neck stand up. "Up here, Seth," he directed the Immortal Guardians' leader who was down on the first floor.

Ethan blanked the screen of his phone and tucked it back in his pocket.

Seth's heavy boots sounded on the stairs and heralded his appearance in the hallway outside the bathroom. "Well," he said, looking all around. "This is going to throw a wrench into the works. Is Dana all right?"

"Yes," Aidan, Ethan, and Heather all chorused.

"That isn't the giant with the really long hair, is it?" Dana whispered.

"If you mean Seth," Heather answered, amusement entering her voice, "the leader of the Immortal Guardians, then yes."

"Crap."

Seth smiled. "I suppose I did make a rather bad impression earlier." He looked to Aidan. "I'm guessing you ignored my orders and remained here alone with her?"

"Yes. While Dana and I were sleeping, she had a vision that vampires were about to attack. I didn't want the vampires to prey upon her neighbors, so I teleported to Ethan's and brought him and Heather here to help us defeat them."

Seth looked toward the bedroom for a long moment.

Long enough for Aidan to guess he was reading the minds of both Dana and Heather.

Seth's eyes flashed golden. "Had Ethan and Heather not joined you, the vamps would've taken your head."

"Apparently."

Seth nodded to the vampire shriveling up on the floor. "That's the vamp she tranqed?"

Aidan nodded.

Seth sighed. "It would've been nice to have read his thoughts and found out who is behind all this."

Not so much, in this instance, since those thoughts would've implicated Aidan.

"Did you read the thoughts of the other vampires?" Seth asked.

Aidan shook his head. "My attention was already divided between killing as many vampires as I could and reading Dana's mind so I'd know if she needed my help up here."

"Heather, did you read any of the vampires' minds?" he asked, looking toward the bedroom.

"No. I was too busy fighting them."

Seth accepted the bad news with a nod. "Well, let's hope no more *gifted ones* disappeared while you were unsupervised, Aidan. Your openly defying my orders, combined with another *gifted one*'s disappearance, would instantly reinstate Chris's original assumptions."

Guilt suffused Aidan. Seth had defended his credibility and Aidan was repaying him with lies. "I'm sorry I defied you, Seth."

He shrugged. "I defied the Others to be with the woman I loved. I won't fault you for doing the same." He cast Aidan a warning look. "*This* time."

Message received: don't fuck up again.

Seth turned away.

Aidan glanced at Ethan, the gravity of their deception weighing on him.

Chapter Eleven

SEATED ON THE BED BESIDE Heather, Dana congratulated herself on finally getting her hands to stop shaking.

Until Seth entered the room.

Her heart thumping with nerves, she rose.

Heather rose as well and stood shoulder to shoulder with her, the light contact comforting even though Dana scarcely knew her.

Dana guessed Seth must be at least six feet eight inches tall. He was garbed in the same clothing he'd worn earlier: black pants, a black shirt, and a long black coat. Hair, equally dark, was pulled back with a leather tie, the thick mass dangling down his back to his hips in a ponytail.

Aidan and Ethan entered behind him.

Dana eyed Seth with dread. This man would one day try to kill Aidan. She had seen as much in her vision and was *not* comfortable having him in her home.

Seth offered her a smile that was startlingly kind. "Hello, Dana. I'm Seth, leader of the Immortal Guardians." He spoke with an accent that sounded almost British but had a hint of something else in there, too. "I'm sorry we keep meeting under such unpleasant circumstances. I'm sorry, too, that your entrance into our world has been fraught with violence. The difficulties we immortals and our colleagues are currently facing are unprecedented. And it appears you've been caught in the middle of it."

Dana didn't know how to respond to that, so she opted to remain silent.

Aidan sidestepped Seth and crossed to stand beside her. Giving her a reassuring smile, he wrapped an arm around her shoulders.

Dana curled an arm around his waist and leaned into his side.

Ethan moved to stand beside Heather.

Seth kept his gaze on Dana. "We're still trying to understand the most recent problems that have arisen. Until we have sorted things out, I would like you and Aidan to stay with Ethan and Heather."

Dana straightened. "What?"

Seth motioned to the disintegrating vampires in the hallway. "These vampires targeted you for a reason. Until we determine what that reason may be and eliminate the threat, we must operate on the assumption that more attacks will follow. You and Aidan will not be safe on your own. Your vision showed you as much. Had Ethan and Heather not aided you tonight, you both would've been slain. So I've asked them to serve as your guard until all is resolved."

They wanted her to leave her home? Her business?

Dana glanced around. Both were currently riddled with carnage and might have sustained structural damage. Still… "I really have to leave?"

"You don't *have* to," Aidan said gently. "But it would be best if you did. You'll be safer if we stay with Ethan and Heather." He brushed her disheveled hair back from her face. "And I need you to be safe, Dana."

She didn't doubt his concern for her.

"Please, sweetheart," he continued. "It's just temporary until we can defeat the one stirring up all this trouble."

Nodding slowly, she turned back to Seth. "All right."

He smiled. "Thank you."

It was weird. Seth seemed almost nice. Trustworthy. Not at all like someone who would one day try to kill Aidan. She would have to keep her guard up around him.

Then another thought occurred. "Oh crap," she blurted.

Aidan frowned. "What?"

Heat crept into her cheeks. "I just realized I'm standing here in front of all of you, practically naked."

Seth and Ethan dropped their gazes to her thin tank top that revealed a lot of cleavage and molded itself to hardened nipples, her short shorts, then hastily looked up at the ceiling.

Aidan stepped in front of her, blocking their view. "Heather, would you grab her something to wear, please?"

Heather dashed over to Dana's closet, then returned with a button-down shirt and a pair of jeans.

Once Dana finished donning them, she stepped to Aidan's side and took his hand.

Seth motioned to the broken glass, splintered furniture, and damage around them. "The network of humans who aid us will clean this up and restore your home and business to their original state while you're away. The network will also compensate you for whatever financial losses you will face by not being able to conduct business until you can return. Whatever you expect to earn during that time, we will pay you tenfold to make up for the inconvenience and for any difficulties you may face in pacifying your customers."

Dana stared at him. "Seriously?"

He nodded.

Skillet's "Monster" suddenly began to play. Seth dug a cell phone out of his pocket and raised it to his ear. Dana didn't recognize the language he spoke before he tucked the phone away again.

"I have to go," he said, striding forward. "I'm needed in Zimbabwe."

Dana tightened her hold on Aidan's hand, still not trusting Seth.

"You'll have to release him for a moment," Seth informed her gently.

When Aidan nodded for her to let him go, she did so with great reluctance.

Seth rested a hand on Aidan's chest.

Aidan hissed in a breath.

Dana frowned as the moment stretched.

Then Seth withdrew his touch and stepped back.

"Thank you," Aidan said.

Seth nodded with a faint smile. "Don't drive to Ethan and Heather's place. Teleport. And do so as soon as Dana finishes packing a bag."

"We will."

Seth vanished.

Dana gasped.

"I *so* wish I could do that," Heather proclaimed with a broad grin.

Ethan smiled. "Me, too."

Dana turned to Aidan. "What did he do to you when he put his hand on you?"

"He healed my wounds and infused me with energy so I'll be able to teleport you all to Ethan's without difficulty."

"So your wounds are gone now?"

"Yes."

She eyed him curiously and noted the gash along his jawline had disappeared. "What does the energy part feel like?"

Aidan looked thoughtful for a moment. "I suppose it's similar to a mortal downing a hell of a lot of caffeine."

Unbelievably, amusement trickled through her. "So you're going to start bouncing off the walls now?" She glanced around and grimaced. "Or what's left of them."

"I'm sorry, Dana."

She shook her head, not liking the remorse that haunted his features. "It wasn't your fault. You didn't tell them to attack. And you saved my life." She glanced at the others. "You *all* did. Thank you."

Heather smiled. "Why don't I help you get some things together to take to our place?"

Dana liked Heather and was a little surprised that the woman being an immortal didn't bother her anymore. She just seemed so normal. Except for the killing-vampires thing. "Thank you. I'd appreciate that. My mind is all over the place right now, so I'll probably forget something if I pack alone."

Aidan touched her arm. "Don't forget your computer or whatever you store your client information and schedule on. You'll have to cancel all your upcoming appointments and reschedule them later."

Great. "I should call Marietta, too."

"Your neighbor?"

"Yes. She's going to freak out when she gets back and sees the damage done over here. I was actually supposed to be watching her place." Eyes widening, she looked up at Aidan. "Oh crap. Did the vampires trash her place, too?"

"No. Just yours. But don't worry. Everything will be repaired by week's end and I'll have the network guards watch both places for you."

"Thank you."

It didn't take long for Dana and Heather to pack a bag. The immortals seemed to harbor some doubt that all this would be resolved swiftly. So Dana packed a week's worth of clothes, her laptop, cell phone, iPad, iPod, toothbrush, hairbrush, and comb.

"I don't know what else to take," she admitted. "I'm not sure what I'll be doing there."

Heather smiled and motioned to the bag. "This is fine. If you need anything we don't have at our place, Ed can get it for you." She turned to Aidan. "Will Brodie be joining us?"

"Most likely," Aidan replied.

Dana zipped the bag closed. "Who are Ed and Brodie?"

"Our Seconds," Aidan explained. "Seth assigns every Immortal Guardian a Second, or human guard, to protect him or her during the day and lend some semblance of normalcy so nosy neighbors won't ask too many questions when they only see us at night."

Dana studied him. "So Seconds are like Dracula's Renfield or Blade's Whistler?"

He smiled. "Yes."

Heather grimaced. "Only they don't eat bugs."

Aidan regarded her with surprise. "What?"

Heather shrugged. "In some of the Dracula movies I've seen, the Renfields were rancid guys who ate bugs."

Aidan looked at Dana with something akin to alarm. "Brodie isn't like that," he insisted, as though he feared she'd think the worst. "Ed isn't either. They're like Sheldon."

Ethan laughed. "Only older, wiser and much more competent."

Heather grinned. "In other words, they're like Tracy."

The immortals all laughed.

Dana smiled. "Well, I guess I'm ready then."

Aidan grasped the handle of her bag, then wrapped his arm around her and drew her up against his side.

Ethan did the same with Heather.

Then Aidan rested his free hand on Ethan's shoulder.

Dana looked up at him, a little nervous about the whole

teleportation thing. What exactly did that entail? Disassembling all their molecules, then reassembling them somewhere else?

That sounded pretty terrifying.

Aidan dipped his head and pressed a kiss to her forehead. "Teleportation is fun. Once you get used to it, I think you'll like it."

"If you say so," she responded and forced a smile.

His eyes crinkled at the corners.

Darkness abruptly swallowed her. The floor seemed to fall away beneath her feet as an odd feeling of weightlessness struck, much like that she sometimes experienced in an elevator. A second later, she found herself standing in a large, brightly lit, tastefully decorated living room.

Gaping at her new surroundings, she tightened her hold on Aidan. Excitement filled her. Elation, too.

Tilting her head back, she grinned up at him. "That is *so* cool!"

His face brightened with a grin. "I'm glad you like it."

"Can we do it again?" she asked, as eager as a child wanting another piggyback ride.

He chuckled. "Maybe later, when I'm at full strength."

A man entered the room from the adjoining kitchen. "Glad to see you all survived the battle." He glared at Aidan. "Next time you can damned well take me, too. My job is to protect Ethan and Heather. I can't do that if you leave my ass behind."

Aidan nodded. "My apologies, Ed. Time was short and I was low on energy."

He nodded. "I'm guessing that wasn't all you were low on."

Dana dropped her gaze to the dark bags he carried. The excitement tingling in her belly sank like a stone. "Is that blood?"

Ed glanced over at her, seeming to notice her for the first time. Dismay flashed across his handsome features. "Oh, shit." He tucked the blood bags behind his back. His gaze flew to Aidan. "I was so worried about Ethan and Heather that I forgot…"

Beside her, Aidan loosed a long sigh.

She glanced up at him. "It *is* blood, isn't it?"

"Yes."

She tried to school her face into an expressionless mask so he wouldn't see her disgust. "And you drink it?" *Gross*. "Immortals drink blood like vampires?"

"No. We don't drink it," he corrected. "Our fangs behave like needles and siphon the blood directly into our veins."

"Oh." That was less gross. "I thought you said you didn't need blood." She had asked him as much before they fell asleep earlier.

"I lied," he admitted.

"Because you didn't want to scare me?" she guessed.

"And because you were the only source available to me at the time."

Dana opted to forgive him the lie. She didn't know what she would've done if he had told her yes, he needed blood and would like to partake of some of hers. "Does blood loss weaken you?"

"Yes."

From the corner of her eye, she saw the others share an uneasy look and understood better why he had not revealed all this sooner. By answering her honestly, he had just revealed a vulnerability that could be used against every immortal in this room, not just himself.

But if blood loss left him weaker…

She frowned. "You weren't at full strength when you fought the vampires?"

"I was strong enough."

"But you weren't at *full* strength," she pressed.

A muscled jumped in his jaw. "No."

The knowledge chilled her. He could have lost his life, simply because he hadn't wanted to frighten her by taking her blood.

She motioned to Ed. "Give him the blood." She looked up at Aidan. "And you do whatever you have to do to restore your strength." And stay alive. She didn't want to lose him.

He shook his head. "I'll do it later."

"Do it now," she insisted. "You want me to know everything, don't you? You want me to see it all?"

Clamping his teeth together, he nodded.

"Then show me."

Without another word, Aidan set her bag down and crossed to Ed.

Ed brought his hands out from behind his back and offered Aidan one of the blood bags. "Sorry, man. I wasn't thinking."

"No worries," Aidan murmured.

While Dana watched, Aidan parted his lips. Just as they had at her place, two long fangs descended.

His eyes on hers, Aidan raised the bag and pressed his fangs into the plastic. Almost immediately, the bag began to lose its fullness, sinking in on itself as the blood it contained found its way into Aidan's veins.

When the bag was empty, he handed it to Ed.

Ed gave him a second bag.

Dana looked at Ethan and Heather, both of whom watched her warily. "You, too."

The couple joined Aidan and sank their teeth into bags of blood Ed handed them.

After two battles—the first with Roland, then the second with vampires—Aidan must have been dangerously low on blood, because he consumed more bags than the others.

No. Not consumed. Infused himself with?

Dana wasn't sure. But the unease that painted every expression save her own gradually began to amuse her. "You all look like you're waiting for me to faint or something."

Aidan handed Ed an empty bag. "You Tasered Roland. You're not the fainting type."

Ed laughed. "Everyone is going to love you for that one."

"Why?" she asked. "Is Roland a bad guy?"

"Nah." Ed chuckled. "He's not a bad guy. He's just not a very *likable* guy."

"*I* sure as hell don't like him," she muttered. The man had tried to kill Aidan.

Aidan laughed, his fangs retreating and leaving straight white teeth that bore no bloodstains. "Let's go ahead and get settled, shall we?" he suggested, picking up her bag. "Ed, did you call Brodie?"

He nodded. "He'll be here any minute."

"Good."

Heather started down a hallway. "You can stay in one of our guest rooms." She stopped beside an open door. "This one is the largest."

Dana peered inside. She had feared they would end up sleeping in a cold dark basement like the vampires in movies did. But this bedroom was on the ground floor and large enough to encompass most of the first floor of Dana's duplex. Beautifully decorated, it reminded her of something she might find in a high-end hotel and had windows with curtains and everything.

"Is this okay?" Heather asked them. "We have another one if you'd prefer it."

"This is fine," Aidan assured her, following Dana inside.

Heather smiled. "Good. Just let us know if you need anything."

"Thank you, Heather. We will." Aidan closed the door.

Dana looked at the king-sized bed, the bedside tables, the plush chairs and large-screen television, and realized this was where her vision had shown her they would make love.

Warmth unexpectedly unfurled inside her as she recalled the feel of Aidan's mouth on her breast.

Turning, she found him studying her.

He tilted his head to one side. "Tonight? Or ever?"

She raised her eyebrows. "What?"

His lips turned up in a faint smile. "I thought you were going to tell me you're not having sex with me, like you did on our first date."

Smiling, she motioned to the bed. "You recognize this place?"

He nodded, his eyes acquiring an amber glow. "This is where we made love in your vision."

Her pulse picked up. "So it is." What the hell was wrong with her? She had just had the scare of a lifetime—two actually—but suddenly could think of nothing but the feel of Aidan's hands on her, tugging her shirt over her head so he could touch bare skin, teasing her nipples and tantalizing her with his tongue.

Heat flashed through her.

"Shall I tell Heather we'd like another room?" he asked.

Dana shook her head.

He took a step toward her. "Do you want me to sleep on the floor?"

Again she wagged her head from side to side, staggered by the desire that suddenly coursed through her.

Aidan slowly approached her. "What *do* you want?" he asked softly.

"Honestly?"

"Honestly."

"I want *you*," she stated boldly. "Naked. I want to feel your bare body against mine."

His eyes brightened with amber light. "Dana," he whispered, his voice deepening as he drew close enough to touch.

"I think," she said breathlessly as she tilted her head back to look up at him, "that I'm doing that thing where—after narrowly escaping death—you feel a sudden, driving need to reaffirm life."

He settled his hands on her hips and squeezed as though he wanted desperately to let those hands go exploring and was barely keeping them in check. "Don't tempt me, sweetheart."

Easing forward, she leaned her body into his. "I'll tempt you and more," she promised, sucking in a breath when he slid his large hands around and down to cup her ass.

Both moaned when she rose onto her toes and arched against the hard length behind his fly.

"I don't want you to do anything you'll regret tomorrow," he said, though his body was clearly more than eager to play with hers.

"I don't care about tomorrow." Reaching up, she cradled his face in her hands. "I thought you were going to die tonight, Aidan. *Twice*, I thought you were going to die. And we *both* died in my vision."

"Dana— "

"I don't care about our differences. I don't care that you're immortal and I'm mortal. I care about *you*. When I awoke from that vision… The grief I felt in the seconds before I realized you hadn't died, that you were still sleeping beside me, made that abundantly clear to me." She drew her thumbs across his beard stubble, enjoying the prickly feel of it. "I care about you," she whispered, pressing a kiss to his lips. "I'm falling in love with you." She tasted his warm, soft lips again. "I want you."

Groaning, he lowered his head and claimed her lips in a long, deep, pulse-spiking kiss. Heat seared her as his tongue slid inside to dance with her own. Every tantalizing stroke made her body burn.

She moved her hips. He was so hard for her. And it felt so good to rub against him while he did such wicked things with his tongue. *Never* had a kiss aroused her so thoroughly.

Still cupping her ass with one hand, he slipped the other beneath the hem of her button-down shirt and smoothed it up her side to palm her breast. Her breath caught as he drew a thumb across the taut peak. She hadn't taken the time to don a bra earlier, so only the soft, thin material of her tank top separated them as he teased her, toyed with her, then delivered a sharp pinch.

Lightning shot through her.

Dana buried her fingers in his hair. Sliding one leg up his, she hooked her knee over his hip and opened herself to him. A low growl of approval rumbled in his chest as he ground his erection against her core. So good. She wanted more.

Without warning, Aidan lifted her and spun in a blur to press her up against the nearest wall. Dana gasped, wrapping her legs around his waist and holding on tight.

His lips left hers, trailing a fiery path down her neck. "I'm sorry," he whispered. "Did I scare you?"

He *had* moved preternaturally fast, but…

"No." She moaned as he began to rock against her. "Don't stop."

His hands grew more aggressive, his rough touch increasing the pleasure while his thrusts continued to build the pressure, making her frantic for more. She gave his hair a tug.

Another rumble of approval.

She stroked his back, loving the heavy muscles that moved and flexed as he drove her wild. She gripped his tight, muscled ass and urged him on. "Why aren't we naked?" she complained on another moan. If they were naked he would already be inside her, driving into her with deep powerful thrusts and assuaging this burning need.

A sound of protest escaped her when he released her breast. He fumbled with the tiny buttons on the front of her shirt. "Why did you have to go and put more clothes on?" he grumbled, his voice raspy with arousal.

She laughed.

He sent her a boyish smile, holding her up with his hips while he worked the buttons with his fingers. When he looked down again, he froze. "Shite. I forgot."

"Forgot what?" she asked, squirming against him and delighting in every dart of pleasure it inspired.

Aidan abandoned her buttons. Wrapping his arms around her,

he stepped back. "Let go for a moment," he murmured.

Frowning, she lowered her feet to the floor.

Cool air rushed between them when he released her and moved away. But it didn't dim her desire in the least.

Dana looked up at him in confusion. "Aidan?"

He held up an index finger as he backed away. "Hold that thought."

A breeze whipped her as he darted into the bathroom at preternatural speeds.

Swaying drunkenly, she stared after him as he closed the door behind him. Her thoughts scattered. Her body hummed with desire.

A thunk sounded, followed by a squeak. Water splashed.

What was he doing in there?

The bathroom door opened.

Dana's eyes widened. Her already pounding heart went into overtime, slamming against her ribs as Aidan strode out, naked save for a white towel wrapped around his hips.

"Holy crap," she whispered.

He was beautiful. His body rippled with muscle as he prowled toward her as smoothly as a lion. His eyes still glowed. A sensual smile tilted his lips.

"I'm sorry," he said as he stopped before her. "I forgot I was covered in blood."

Blinking, Dana glanced down. Red splotches marred her shirt where the blood that hadn't dried on his clothes had rubbed off on hers. "Oh."

Taking her chin in one hand, he produced a damp white washcloth and gently drew it across her cheek and down her neck. "I didn't mean to sully you."

Dana ogled his bare shoulders and chest, wanting badly to tell him to just drop the towel and take her. "Do you, um...?" What were they talking about? "Do you want me to shower?"

If he did, she was damned well going to drag him in there with her, because she couldn't wait that long for him to touch her again.

He shook his head. "The rest is just on your shirt." Tossing the cloth into the bathroom, he eyed her speculatively. "How angry would you be if I tore your clothes in my haste to remove them?"

She nodded to the plush white cloth wrapped around his hips. "Depends on how fast you ditch the towel."

Grinning, he dropped the towel.

Dana sucked in a breath. Aidan was perfect. Broad, muscled shoulders. Well-developed pecs. Washboard abs. She had never been with a man who had such a superbly sculpted body. Her gaze dropped to the erection jutting toward her.

And *all* of him was perfect.

She felt a tug on her shirt. Something clickety-clacked on the floor like a string of pearls falling. Glancing down, she gaped.

In less than a heartbeat, without even moving her, Aidan had stripped her bare except for her shoes.

Looking up, she met his brilliant amber eyes and breathed one word. "Finally." As quickly as she could, she toed off her shoes, then bent to remove her socks.

Aidan backed away toward the bed, his hands curling into fists. "You're beautiful," he said, his voice rough with need as his heated gaze roved her like a pair of hands.

How did he do that? How could he sharpen her arousal with just a look?

"*You're* beautiful," she said, closing the distance between them. At the last minute, she veered around him and knelt on the mattress. Turning to face him, she moved back in invitation.

The mattress dipped beneath his weight as Aidan knelt before her on the bed.

She stilled, her pulse fluttering wildly at the heat in those glowing eyes.

Cupping her shoulder, he slid his hand down to clasp her breast. Her breath caught as he teased the tight peak with thumb and fingers, tweaking the sensitive bud.

Her body went liquid.

Aidan curled his arm around her and drew her up against him, trapping his erection between them. He lowered his lips to her other breast, drew the hard pink nipple into his mouth and stroked it with his tongue.

Burying her fingers in his hair, she moaned. "That feels so good."

Leaning into her, he urged her back against the pillows.

Dana shifted her legs restlessly as he transferred his attention to her other breast, laving and sucking and nipping. The ache within her grew, rapidly becoming unbearable. She wanted him to lower his body to hers, wanted to feel all of that delicious weight pressing down on her as he plunged inside. But Aidan had other ideas.

Abandoning her breasts, he kissed a path down her stomach, dipped his tongue in her navel, then moved on.

Excitement built.

His warm breath brushed her clit just before he lowered his head and delivered a long, slow lick. A throaty sound of desire, unlike any she had ever made before, escaped her as she fisted her hands in his hair.

Another lick followed, then another and another, ratcheting up her need. He closed his lips around the sensitive nub, flicking it with his tongue. That oh so wicked tongue. She arched against him, breath shortening, muscles tightening as the pleasure built and built until she threw back her head and cried out as an orgasm swept through her. Ripples of pleasure rocked her, going on and on and on as Aidan continued to work her with his mouth. And just as the tingles were fading, he did something preternaturally fast that sent a second orgasm careening through her.

Dana cried out in surprise as ecstasy whipped through her anew.

At last she collapsed against the pillows, her breath coming in quick gasps.

<hr>

Aidan kissed his way up Dana's lovely form, wanting her so badly he nearly shook with it. His heart raced. His pulse pounded in his ears. And he was so hard for her he didn't think he could wait much longer to be inside her. She was so beautiful. So passionate. Her taste titillated him. Her scent intoxicated him.

Her breath emerged in short pants as he pressed kisses to her delicate rib cage and caressed her breasts.

Reaching up, she cupped his face in her hands. How he loved that, those small soft hands stroking his rough cheeks as her eyes met and held his.

Aidan settled himself between her thighs, his cock teasing her slick entrance.

Dana leaned up and delivered a long, slow kiss. "Now you," she murmured with a siren's smile.

Sliding her hands down his neck, she smoothed them across his shoulders then fondled her way to his chest. Her fingers brushed his nipples, toyed with them, pinched them as she rolled her hips.

Never had he wanted a woman more.

She burned a path down his stomach with one small hand and curled her fingers around his erection. "I want to taste you," she whispered.

The image of her kneeling before him and taking his cock in her mouth damned near sundered his tenuous hold on control. "Taste me later," he ground out. "I need to be inside you." He sucked in a breath when her fingers tightened around him, her thumb circling the sensitive crown. "I want to feel you clamp down around me and squeeze me tight when you come for me again," he told her, every muscle tense.

Her face flushed with renewed desire as her throat moved in a swallow. "I can go with that."

Aidan laughed. And realized he had never laughed during sex before.

But all humor faded once she guided him to her entrance.

His eyes met and held hers as he slid inside. So warm. And wet. And tight.

She slid her arms around him as he buried himself to the hilt. "So good," she moaned.

Drawing back, he plunged inside again. And again. Driving into her with deep, hard, powerful strokes, angling his body to bring her the most pleasure.

Dana lowered her hands to his ass, her nails digging in as she urged him on, her breath coming in gasps as she arched up to meet him thrust for thrust. "Harder," she begged.

Hell, yeah.

The headboard of the bed began to strike the wall with rhythmic thumps, but Aidan didn't care. He found her breast with his hand. Tried not to be too rough. But the pressure was mounting and the little cries emerging from her lips as her muscles tightened around him drove him wild.

Flinging her head back, she called his name as she came. Her inner walls clamped down around him, pulsing and squeezing him tight. Aidan shouted with his own release as an orgasm rocked him, pleasure streaking through him and turning his blood to fire.

Breathing hard, he wrapped his arms around her and held her tight.

When he rolled them to their sides, Dana slid one leg up his and draped her knee across his hip, holding him inside her body. Damp tendrils of hair clung to the sides of her pretty, flushed face. Her lovely hazel eyes held so much emotion as they met his.

Aidan smoothed her hair back from her face and felt such love for her. How she'd changed his world, his very existence.

She smiled.

Did she see it? All the things he wanted to say to her but feared it might be too soon?

Leaning forward, she pressed a light kiss to his lips, then closed her eyes and snuggled against him.

A contentment Aidan hadn't experienced in almost three thousand years stole over him, swiftly lulling him into sleep.

Chapter Twelve

AIDAN AWOKE WITH A START, instantly alert, senses tingling. No sunlight filtered in through the drapes, letting him know it was night. They must have slept the day away… when they hadn't been making love, that is.

He frowned.

Something was wrong. He could feel it.

Careful not to wake Dana, he sat up.

Despite the darkness, Aidan had little difficulty seeing the room around him. But nothing appeared to be out of place.

No intruders lurked in the shadows. No hearts beat in the room, aside from his own and Dana's.

So what was raising the hairs on the back of his neck?

He sent his senses exploring.

Heather slept. Ethan slouched beside her on their bed, watching a movie, the sound turned down low. Ed was tapping away on a computer keyboard somewhere. Brodie was with him and sounded as though he was ensuring Chris had sent enough network employees over to Dana's home to make the necessary repairs.

The rest of the house was quiet.

Rising, Aidan crossed to the window. Careful not to make a sound, he unlatched it and raised it enough to allow a gentle breeze to waft inside.

Closing his eyes, he let the sounds of the night tease his ears while his nose sorted through the plethora of scents that floated on the wind.

His eyes flew open.

Emitting a snarl of frustration, he swung around and grabbed his discarded pants.

Wake up Heather, he ordered Ethan telepathically as he dressed at preternatural speeds. *Roland Warbrook is coming.*

"Shit!" Ethan spat in the other room.

Exactly.

With everything else going on, did they really need another go-around with the irascible immortal?

Aidan leaned over the bed and drew a hand over Dana's mussed hair. "Dana? Wake up, sweetheart."

She slept so deeply he had to call her name a couple more times before her eyes slowly opened to half-mast. Her lips curled into a soft smile. "Hmm?"

"I need you to wake up, sweetheart," he urged. "Quickly now."

That reached her.

Swiftly rolling onto her back, she looked up at him with alarm. "What is it? Are vampires attacking again?"

"No. Roland is coming."

Her brows slammed together. "The Roland who wants you dead?"

"Yes. He'll be here momentarily."

She sat up, face darkening with aggravation. "Well, shit. We just can't *get* a break, can we?" she grumbled, throwing the covers back and rising.

Aidan laughed.

Dana sent him a smile full of chagrin. "I'm sorry. Now might be a good time to tell you I'm not a morning person."

"Nor am I," he said with a grin. Damn, he loved her. She even appealed to him when she was grumpy. "And it isn't morning. It's night. Get dressed, love."

Dana hurried over to her bag and began yanking out clothing while Aidan tried not to let her nudity distract him.

"Don't worry," he said, refocusing his attention too late to keep his body from responding. "I'm at full strength now and will have Heather and Ethan at my back. Heather matches me in both speed and strength, so Roland poses no real threat to us."

"You say that, but I know you and can tell you're uneasy about his coming here."

"Only because — if he intends to try to kill me again — I'll have to find a way to stop him without inflicting so much damage that it will piss off Seth."

"Great," she groused as she stomped into the bathroom with a pile of clothes tucked under one arm. "Don't worry about the nutcase who's trying to kill you. Worry about pissing off the great and powerful Oz." She slammed the door behind her.

Laughing, Aidan grabbed a couple of katanas.

The bathroom door eased open enough for Dana to poke her head out. She sent him a rueful smile. "Sorry. The whole *I'm not a morning person* thing might have been a bit of an understatement."

Closing the distance between them, he pressed a quick kiss to her lips. "You've gotten very little sleep in the past forty-eight hours. And I think you're cute when you're cranky."

She laughed. "Then maybe *you're* the nutcase."

Aidan chuckled. "Get dressed. If Roland sees you looking so enchantingly disheveled, *I'll* end up wanting to kill *him*."

All concern and crankiness leaving her expression, she ducked back into the bathroom.

Still smiling, Aidan crossed to the bedroom door and opened it.

Ethan and Heather waited in the hallway, already dressed and armed.

Heather grinned. "I like her," she whispered.

"Me, too," Ethan seconded.

Aidan shook his head. "I'm a bit fond of her myself."

Heather laughed. "Just a bit, huh?"

The three headed toward the front of the house.

"So what do you think this is?" Ethan asked. "Is he going to try to kill you again?'

"I have no idea, but I think it a distinct possibility."

"You know we have your back, right?" Ethan said.

Heather nodded.

Aidan smiled. "I appreciate that. But you should know that Sarah is with him."

Heather's brow furrowed as she glanced at her husband.

Ethan's look turned uneasy. "I wouldn't feel comfortable fighting Sarah. Roland may be an irascible pain in everyone's ass, but Sarah is a real sweetheart."

Heather nodded. "And Seth does *not* like fighting among the ranks."

Ed strolled into the room, garbed in black jeans, a black T-shirt, and scuffed black boots.

Brodie followed in similar garb.

"Roland and Sarah are on their way," Aidan informed them.

"We heard," they said, unconcerned.

Dana entered.

Aidan motioned to the Seconds. "Dana, this is Brodie, my Second. You met Ed when we arrived."

The three exchanged hi, nice-to-meet-ya's.

Dana eyed the two men curiously. "You aren't worried?"

"Nope." Brodie motioned to the immortals in their midst. "These guys tend to overthink things." So saying, he held something up in one hand. An EpiPen-like auto-injector, no doubt loaded with a strong enough sedative to drop Roland in his tracks.

Ed held up several more.

"Oh," Heather said. "Right. Duh."

When Dana opened her mouth to ask what it was, Aidan shook his head to silence her. *It's a sedative*, he explained telepathically. *The only one on the planet that affects us. Don't say anything aloud so Roland won't be forewarned.*

Ed gave each immortal two auto-injectors. One for Roland and one for Sarah.

Aidan hoped they wouldn't need them. Like the others, he didn't feel comfortable fighting or tranqing Sarah.

The immortals pocketed the auto-injectors.

Ed turned to Dana. Reaching behind him, he produced a tranq gun. Pressing a finger to his lips to indicate a desire for silence, he moved to stand behind her and tucked the gun in the back waist of her jeans.

She looked up at Aidan and raised her brows.

Aidan ground his teeth and fought back… what? Jealousy?

He did *not* like seeing another man touch her but supposed he would have to get used to it. If, by some miracle, all this ended well and Dana agreed to transform for him, Brodie would become her Second, too, and would touch her every time he helped her arm up for a night of hunting.

The doorbell rang.

All regarded each other with surprise.

"Interesting approach," Ethan mumbled, then opened the door.

Roland and Sarah stood on the front porch.

Roland looked grim as usual.

Sarah held his hand and looked anxious.

"Hi, guys," Ethan greeted them cautiously. "What can I do for you?"

"I'm here to speak with Aidan," Roland announced, his tone revealing nothing.

Ethan glanced over his shoulder at Aidan, then looked around the room. "Yeah. Why don't we take this outside?"

Probably hoping to save the furniture.

Roland and Sarah backed away, down the front steps and onto the neatly mown lawn, allowing Ethan, Heather, and Ed to exit.

Aidan turned to Dana. "Wait here."

"I don't think so," she said with a definite *hell no* inflection.

Sighing, he exited with her, his Second following. "Brodie?"

Brodie nodded, needing no further words, and moved to stand beside Dana.

Aidan walked several yards away to draw Roland away from the mortals.

Ethan and Heather moved to stand on either side of him. And damned if that didn't make him feel all warm and fuzzy inside.

"So?" Aidan asked, no aggression in his tone. He had no beef with Roland and would prefer to keep the peace.

"Seth doesn't believe you had anything to do with Veronica's disappearance," Roland pronounced.

"Because I didn't."

"Reordon believes otherwise," Roland continued, "and has video evidence to back up his suspicions, but…" He looked down at his wife, who nodded her support. Roland met Aidan's gaze. "I trust Seth's judgment. So I'm here to apologize and see if I can make amends."

Aidan could not have been more shocked.

Nor could Ethan, Heather, Ed, and Brodie, whose jaws dropped in astonishment.

Dana continued to eye Roland with distrust.

Roland glanced at Dana, then strolled over to Aidan and motioned to the long drive with a tilt of his head. "Walk with me?"

Curious, Aidan accompanied the taciturn immortal down the driveway.

"Stay within my sight," Ethan ordered behind them.

Roland sent Aidan a look of inquiry. "Because he thinks I'll try to kill you?"

Aidan shook his head. "Ethan is impervious to mind control and remembers every detail he sees, hears, smells, et cetera. So Seth has assigned him to be my babysitter. If I'm always within Ethan's sight or hearing, then he can prove absolutely that it wasn't me if another *gifted one* goes missing."

Roland nodded, his brow furrowed.

Minutes passed as the two continued their slow stroll down the gravel driveway until they were out of earshot of Dana, Brodie, and Ed.

"I didn't know you were seeing someone," Roland said, his voice low from either a reluctance to speak or a reluctance to be overheard, Aidan guessed.

"Very few did."

Roland studied the landscape around them. Nothing but field and trees as far as the eye could see. "I lived alone for nine hundred years before I met Sarah."

Aidan nodded. He'd heard as much. Roland had lived in almost total isolation, refusing even the company and protection of a Second, having been betrayed too often in the past by those he loved and trusted most.

"I know how wretched it can be to live that long without love and affection," he continued. "And from what I understand, you've lived without it far longer."

Again Aidan nodded. "I have."

Roland shook his head. "I'm not as cold and heartless as they say I am."

"I know." Aidan had seen how the dour immortal had opened his heart to Sarah and Adira and had witnessed his fierce determination to protect Sarah, Adira, Marcus, and Ami at all costs.

Roland's Adam's apple rose and fell with a swallow. "I was

furious when I thought you'd harmed my descendant. It took Seth a while to calm my arse down after I got back to David's. But when he did and told me that Reordon had skewed the information because he was pissed at you about something… When Seth told me he believes you had no role in Veronica's disappearance and that I had just outed you in front of the mortal woman you love…" He shook his head. "I felt sick."

Surprise stole any response Aidan would've made.

"What, I asked myself, if someone had done that to me?" Roland continued. "What if Reordon or… hell, almost anyone else who knows what a surly pain in the arse I am… had scared the hell out of Sarah and turned her away from me?" He shook his head. "What if I didn't have Sarah in my life today? What if she hadn't chipped away at my distrust, stolen my heart, and helped me grow closer to Marcus and Ami and beautiful little Adira? What if she hadn't made my life so much fuller in every way? What if someone had taken all that from me by frightening her away?"

Silence reigned, broken only by the nocturnal creatures that foraged for late-night snacks.

When Roland next looked at Aidan, remorse and self-recrimination filled his eyes. "Have I done that?" he asked with dread. "Have I stolen that from you?"

"Roland — "

"You put your life on the line to protect Adira last year, and now I've wronged you so sorely that I don't even know how to *begin* to make amends."

Aidan sighed. "I would've had to tell her the truth eventually."

"*Telling* her is one thing. Shoving it in her face all at once is another."

It was indeed. "Didn't Bastien pretty much shove it all in Sarah's face?"

Roland released a mirthless chuckle. "Yes, he did, the bastard. I believe I had one afternoon with her before he and his vampire army attacked."

Aidan sighed and sheathed the weapons he only then realized he still held. "Maybe that's the way it always is for us. No slow and easy breaking of the truth. No long courtship and slow getting to know one another. Look what happened with Richart."

Roland nodded. "That doesn't change the fact that I've wronged you." He glanced over at Dana, who stood beside Ed, arms crossed, eyes squinted as she scowled at them through the darkness. "Dana is here with you now. Does that mean she hasn't turned away from you?"

"She's here because Seth mandated it. Had he not and did a threat not remain that compels me to watch over her..." Aidan shook his head. "I don't know what she would've done." She might have instead sent him on his way, gone to bed alone and—having missed out on the hours they had just spent making love—opted to not see him again.

"She looks pissed."

Aidan smiled. "Actually, that's all for you. She's angry about your trying to kill me and fears you may attempt to do so again."

Roland regarded him with something akin to hope. "Well, that's a good sign, isn't it? If she wanted nothing more to do with you, she wouldn't care if I killed you."

Aidan nodded. "She seems to be accepting it all. Accepting me. I just don't know if she's willing to..."

"Accept it all—and you—on a permanent basis?" Roland finished for him.

"Aye."

"Is there anything I can do?"

"No, but I thank you for offering."

"It's because I'm antisocial, isn't it? You think I'll make things worse."

"No, I don't think things can get much worse than they are now. At this point, I just have to wait and see and hope that it won't all prove to be too much for her."

"Then at least let Sarah and me remain here and help guard her," Roland insisted.

He really did seem to want to make amends. The other immortals would be shocked.

"As you will," Aidan agreed.

Roland thrust a hand toward Aidan.

Before Aidan could shake it, a dart struck Roland in the chest.

Roland frowned down at it. Then his eyes rolled back in his head, his knees buckled, and he sank to the ground.

Aidan turned to the small group watching them.

Ethan, Heather, Brodie, and Ed all gaped at Dana, who aimed a tranquilizer gun in Aidan and Roland's direction.

"Roland!" Sarah cried and started forward.

Dana fired the tranq gun again.

Sarah stumbled to a halt, then sank to the ground, unconscious.

Aidan stared. "What the hell are you doing, woman?" he called loud enough for Dana to hear him. "Why did you tranq Roland?"

"It looked like he was going to stab you!" she called back.

Since she didn't have the preternaturally sharp vision of Ethan, Sarah, and Heather, he supposed it could have.

"He was apologizing," he called with exasperation, "and wanted to shake my hand!"

"Oh!" she yelled. "My bad!"

Her companions burst into laughter.

Shaking his head in amusement, Aidan tossed Roland over one shoulder and rejoined the others. "Why did you tranq Sarah?"

Dana shrugged. "I thought she was going to rush over there and try to finish what Roland had started."

Ethan knelt beside Sarah and gently lifted her into his arms. "Ed, do we have any of the antidote on hand?"

"Yeah." Ed headed inside. "I'll get it."

Aidan nodded toward the open front door. "Let's go."

<hr />

Dana chewed her lower lip as Ethan carried Sarah inside. The unconscious immortal's long brown hair flowed over his biceps, dancing with every movement.

Aidan followed with Roland draped over one shoulder, the surly immortal's arms dangling down his back and swaying back and forth.

"Will they be okay?" she asked anxiously. She really *had* thought Roland was going to hurt Aidan. Sarah, too. It had just been so dark. Unable to see them clearly, she had caught the quick movement and figured *better safe than sorry.*

"They'll be fine," Aidan assured her.

"Fine, but pissed," Heather corrected with a wry smile as she followed them inside and closed the door.

Ethan lowered Sarah to the sofa.

Aidan seated Roland beside her and stepped back.

The couple looked as though they had fallen asleep while watching television, shoulders brushing, heads lolling back against the cushions.

Dana, Aidan, Ethan, and Heather stood in a semicircle, staring down at them as they waited for Ed and Brodie to reappear.

"I can't believe he said that," Heather whispered, her eyes on Roland.

"Which part?" her husband asked.

"All of it."

Dana looked at Heather and the others. "What did he say?" They seemed stunned, as if whatever Roland had told Aidan had made them completely rethink everything they knew about him.

"I feel sort of bad now," Heather admitted in lieu of answering. "I really did think of him as being kind of…"

"Cold and heartless?" her husband offered.

"Well, not heartless," she qualified. "No one who has seen how he is with Sarah and Adira can call him heartless."

Aidan and Ethan nodded their agreement.

"But cold?" Heather went on. "Yeah. I mean, he's always so—I don't know—unapproachable. So closed off to the rest of us. But now? After this? After what he said to Aidan? And the emotion I heard in his voice?" She shook her head. "I gotta admit, I teared up a little."

Dana looked up at Aidan. "What did he say?"

Aidan shifted his weight from one foot to the other, unease creeping into his handsome features. "He apologized."

Dana waited for him to say more, but he opted not to elaborate.

Heather frowned up at him. "There was a little more to it than that, Aidan. You should tell her. Or, better yet, show her. All of it. You can do that, right?"

Dana looked to Aidan. Show her? How?

"Yes," he admitted with obvious reluctance.

"Then you should," Heather urged him. "Let her see it all. Because it sounds like Roland intends to stick around. And the last thing Dana needs on top of everything else is to worry about him attacking you again or not being fully on your side."

Dana turned a doubtful gaze on Roland.

"See?" Heather pointed to her. "She doesn't believe he can be trusted."

All eyes turned to Dana.

She shrugged. "Of course I don't. He tried to kill Aidan."

And still Aidan looked reluctant to comply. But he did, nevertheless.

Turning toward her, he touched the tip of one finger to her temple.

The living room around her vanished, replaced by Ethan and Heather's front yard. Aidan's stroll with Roland and the words they spoke played out before her as clearly as a movie on a big-screen, hi-def television. Except Dana was *in* the movie, seeing everything from Aidan's point of view.

Soooo cool.

And she didn't just hear the words and see the images. She *felt* what Aidan had felt, because all of that was part of the memory he retained.

Her breath caught.

Aidan withdrew his touch.

The memory dissolved.

Ed and Brodie entered the living room.

Dana barely noticed as she stared up at Aidan, her heart beating faster.

Aidan met her gaze, his handsome face somber, his brown eyes unreadable.

Again she heard Roland's voice in his memory. *When Seth told me he believes you had no role in Veronica's disappearance and that I had just outed you in front of the mortal woman you love… I felt sick.*

Ed leaned over Roland.

"No." Ethan stopped him. "Wake Sarah first. Roland may not blame Dana for tranqing *him*, but if he sees she tranqed Sarah, too, he'll be pissed."

Nodding, Ed moved to stand over Sarah and leaned down.

Dana is here with you now, Roland had said. *Does that mean she hasn't turned away from you?*

She's here because Seth mandated it, Aidan had responded, so much emotion buffeting him.

Did he really believe that? That she wouldn't be with him tonight if Seth hadn't forced her hand?

Ed pressed an EpiPen-like thing against Sarah's neck.

Sarah's hazel eyes opened, then flared bright green as she sat up straight and looked around for her husband, almost bumping heads with Ed.

Dana didn't hear whatever Ethan and the others told her. Didn't really care, truth be told.

She seems to be accepting it all. Accepting me. I just don't know if she's willing to...

Accept it all — and you — on a permanent basis?

Aye.

Aidan loved her.

Deeply.

He wanted to spend the rest of eternity with her. And — even after the amazing day they had just spent together making love — feared she either didn't or couldn't feel the same way.

"Aidan," she whispered.

Face somber, he cupped her face in one hand. "You still have choice," he murmured, stroking her cheek with his thumb.

Because he would always place her needs and desires above his own. No matter how much he dreaded the centuries of loneliness and regret he believed would follow if she walked away, he wouldn't press her.

Tears welled in her eyes. Emotion suffusing her, she moved forward, buried her face in his chest, and hugged him tight.

Aidan said nothing, just closed his arms around her and rested his chin atop her head.

"Roland?" Sarah said.

"What the hell happened?" the British immortal replied groggily.

"Dana tranqed you," his wife told him. "She couldn't see clearly in the dark. So when you went to shake Aidan's hand, she thought you were trying to stab him and tranqed you to protect him."

Dana couldn't help but notice that Sarah didn't mention being tranqed herself.

"She did?" Roland asked, his voice lightening with amusement. "First she Tasers me, then she tranqs me." He chuckled. "I like her.

She reminds me of you."

Laughter filled the room.

A chuckle rumbled through Aidan's chest beneath Dana's ear. Tilting her head back, she smiled up at him, and his answering smile bore a hesitance that twisted her heart. She lifted her lips, inviting a kiss.

Smile broadening, he started to lower his head to comply but stopped just short of making contact. He frowned, then turned to look at the front door.

Releasing her, he drew his swords.

The other immortals all followed suit as Aidan stepped around Dana and placed himself between her and the door.

Ed and Brodie both drew what appeared to be 9mms.

"What is it?" Dana asked, wondering if the tranq gun she'd tucked back in her pants still held any darts.

Aidan answered telepathically. *Someone just teleported onto the front porch.*

All shared an intense look, so Dana assumed he had told everyone, not just her.

Hell. Was it Seth? The other vision wasn't about to come true, was it? Had Seth returned to kill Aidan?

The doorbell rang.

Heather's eyebrows rose. "Really?" She took a step toward the door.

Ethan blurred and got there first.

Heather frowned as she moved to stand beside him.

Unperturbed, Ethan opened the door.

Dana's jaw dropped.

The tallest man she had ever seen in person—even taller than Seth—stood on the front porch beside an absolutely gorgeous woman. The male was only an inch or two shy of seven feet, the woman about five foot six. Both had black hair. The man's fell below his shoulders. The woman's was pulled back in a long braid. Both also wore the clothing Dana was coming to associate with just about everyone in the Immortal Guardians world: black pants, black shirts, black boots, and long black coats.

Did the black clothing help them blend into the night better? Or did they wear it to conceal the bloodstains they accrued on their nightly hunts?

She suspected the latter and found the idea unsettling.

Ethan smiled as everyone sheathed and holstered their weapons. "Zach. Lisette. What are you two doing here?"

"Defying Seth's orders," Zach muttered with what sounded like a British accent.

Lisette elbowed him, never losing her smile. "There was a game on earlier." *Her* voice carried a lilting French accent. "I was hoping Ed recorded it so we could watch it together."

Ethan laughed. "Bullshit. You're here to check up on me."

Her smile turned sheepish. "Mmmmaybe I was a little worried after hearing what happened last night."

Ethan motioned for them to enter and closed the door behind them. "Dana, this is Lisette and her husband Zach. Both are immortal."

Lisette strode forward with a big smile, offering her hand. "It's a pleasure to meet you, Dana."

Returning her smile, Dana shook her hand. "Nice to meet you, too." At least she hoped it was. Lisette seemed friendly. But Zach gave off kind of a scary *don't-fuck-with-me-or-I'll-kill-you* vibe and seemed to exude almost as much power as Seth.

Patting their clasped hands, Lisette slid Zach a glance. "I know some find my husband intimidating because of his dark and brooding nature, but I assure you, he's as gentle as a kitten."

Everyone snorted in disagreement, even her husband.

Lisette frowned. "He *is*."

Zach's lips curled up in a sardonic smile. "I don't think that one's going to fly, love. They know me too well."

Lisette started to reply, then paused and turned a frown on Aidan. "I wasn't."

"Yes, you were." Aidan's brows lowered. "Don't do it again."

Dana glanced at Zach, expecting the warning in Aidan's voice to anger him.

But Zach merely chuckled. "Looks like he caught you."

Lisette wrinkled her nose as she released Dana's hand. "I'm sorry. I won't do it again."

"Do what again?" Dana asked, wondering what she'd missed.

Aidan curled an arm around her shoulders. "Read your

thoughts."

Dana looked at Lisette, anger rising over the intrusion. "You're a telepath?"

"Yes," the woman confirmed. "And I'm sorry. I won't read your thoughts again unless a dire emergency compels me to. I just did it this time— "

"Because you're nosy?" Ethan suggested with a grin.

She laughed. "Sometimes, yes," she admitted, then turned back to Dana. "But I really just wanted to know how you were faring." Her smile gentled as she reached out to touch Aidan's arm. "Aidan is precious to us."

Dana glanced up.

Aidan seemed surprised by the pronouncement.

"He gave me a very special gift," Lisette continued.

"I did?" Aidan asked.

Lisette's smile widened. "You told how to me how to strengthen my mental barriers so I can know all of Zach's secrets without you and the others ferreting them out."

Aidan smiled. "So I did. And it's working, by the way. Your mental barriers are already so much stronger that I couldn't breach them. I just *assumed* you were reading Dana's thoughts."

Lisette laughed. "You assumed correctly." She turned back to Dana. "As I said, he's precious to us. And you're clearly precious to *him*. So I wanted to take a little peek and see if you were finding our world too overwhelming." Stepping back, she grinned up at her husband. "Clearly not, because she Tasered Roland *and* tranqed him."

Zach laughed. "The other immortals are going to love her."

Even Roland laughed at that.

Then all levity died as the immortals looked toward the front of the house. Again.

"Seriously?" Heather blurted in disbelief.

Dana consulted Aidan. "What is it?"

"Marcus, Ami, and their daughter Adira."

Roland swore.

As did Zach. "Seth will be furious."

Nodding, Heather turned to her Second. "Hey, Ed?"

"Yeah?"

"It looks like we're going to need a bigger house. You can tack on a few extra rooms, right?"

He laughed. "That's a little outside my job description."

The crunch of gravel under tires intruded upon the night, accompanied by the low rumble of a well-tuned engine.

Seconds later, both sounds ended. Doors opened and closed. Then the doorbell rang.

Ethan opened the door.

A man and a woman stood on the porch.

Dana recognized the woman. Ami was the redhead she had seen in her vision. The one with the Chuck Taylor high-top sneakers. Although tonight she wore heavy boots.

Marcus, the man at her side, held a beautiful redheaded toddler in his arms and had a large bag looped over one shoulder. Like all of the other males present, he bore black hair and brown eyes. But his hair fell a few inches below his shoulders like Zach's.

Both newcomers wore all black like their brethren, so Dana assumed they were immortal.

Although maybe not. They *did* have a baby.

She frowned. Could immortals have children? She hadn't thought to ask Aidan.

Ethan shook his head at the couple. "Seth is going to be furious."

Ami thrust her chin out stubbornly but didn't deny it as she stepped inside. Marcus followed.

The baby grinned when she saw the gathering and bounced in her daddy's arms. "Unca Wowand! Unca Wowand!"

As Ethan closed the door, Marcus bent and lowered the little girl's feet to the floor.

"Dana," Aidan said, "this is Marcus and his wife Ami."

The little girl beelined over to Roland, who bent and scooped her up into his arms, giving her an affectionate grin and a peck on the cheek.

"And that's their daughter Adira."

Seth abruptly appeared just inside the front door. When his gaze alighted upon the large group in the living room, his eyes lit with golden fire.

Chapter Thirteen

"SERIOUSLY?" SETH ROARED.

The world beyond the windows brightened for an instant with a flash of lightning.

Thunder followed, so loud that Dana felt the vibrations in her chest.

Everyone quieted.

"Was I unclear in my instructions?" Seth demanded. "When I said I wanted Aidan and Dana to stay with Ethan and Heather instead of at David's place so Dana wouldn't have to bump into powerful immortals every time she turned around and perhaps might have an easier time adjusting, did I muddle my words or speak in a language you failed to comprehend?"

Seth had wanted them to stay away so she could have some time and space to come to terms with all this?

That was kind of nice. And really didn't gel with Dana's knowledge that Seth would soon want Aidan dead.

Roland stepped forward, Adira cradled in his arms. "I screwed up, Seth, and wanted to make amends. *I'm* the reason Dana has to deal with all of this at once. I pretty much threw it in her face."

Sarah nodded. "We wanted to see if there was anything we could do to mitigate the damage and — if not — thought the least we could do was guard Aidan and Dana and keep them safe."

The fury that blazed in Seth's eyes didn't dim when he turned his gaze upon Ami.

Thunder rumbled again at the same time lightning brightened the windows.

"I told you I didn't want you in the same home as Aidan and Dana," Seth bit out. "It's too dangerous. We believe the vampire attack last night confirms Gershom's interest in Dana and—as I said earlier—I believe the chance of getting you, Adira, *and* Dana all in one fell swoop might prove a great enough lure for him to risk *anything*."

Ami looked both defiant and nervous.

Hell, they all looked nervous. Except for Zach. Seth was emitting so much power that the hair on Dana's arms stood up. And Dana was pretty sure Seth was responsible for the sudden storm brewing overhead. The skies had been clear when she, Aidan, and the others had been outside.

"Seth," Ami said, "I would know it if Gershom were nearby. I would feel it. You know I would. And as soon as I did, I would call you."

Seth vanished and reappeared in front of Ami, the long fingers of one hand wrapped around her throat.

Dana gasped.

Marcus emitted a shout of protest and lunged forward, then stopped short about the same time Dana realized the powerful immortal leader was exerting no pressure with his hold.

"A second to you," Seth growled, "is half an hour to one with my power. Gershom could silence you before you even had time to recognize his presence. And he could take you and Adira beyond my reach without your ever having made a sound." The Immortal Guardians' leader sounded tormented by the thought. "Do you know how hard it would be for me to find you? How long it might take?" he rasped.

Too long, his tone implied.

Remorse filled Ami's green gaze. "You're right. I'm sorry."

Lowering his hand, Seth stepped back and turned his eyes, still bright with anger, on Marcus. "What the hell is wrong with you, letting them come here?"

Marcus scowled. "*Let?* You know how hard her head is," he said in his own defense. "I can only bang mine against it for so long before I end up caving. Besides, I knew you'd follow as soon as you realized where we'd gone."

Zach laughed.

But Dana remained on edge. The danger had not yet passed. Seth looked the way he had in her vision. And she feared it might be coming to pass, that Seth would turn that wrath upon Aidan and attack.

Seth swung on Lisette. "Why are *you* here?"

Lisette gave him a penitent shrug and looked to Dana like a child being chastised by a parent. "Aidan has been good to me. I wanted to make sure they were okay."

Grumbling something under his breath, Seth shifted his gaze to Zach. "Et tu, Brute?" he said, sarcasm creeping into his deep voice.

But his glowing eyes, Dana noted, didn't dim.

Zach smiled and nodded toward Lisette. "I go where she goes."

Seth grunted and turned those eyes, still blazing with fury, on Aidan.

Dana didn't think, she just reacted, her vision strong in her mind.

Raising the tranq gun, she fired.

A dart lodged itself in Seth's chest.

All around the room, mouths fell open as eyes widened. More than one person gasped.

Seth frowned down at the dart, then looked at Dana.

He didn't pass out.

"Oh crap." Dana fired again.

The second dart impaled him an inch or so from the first.

Aidan swung on her. "Are you mad, woman?" He eyed her with what could only be described as appalled astonishment.

She looked around.

All of them eyed her with appalled astonishment.

Except for Zach, who burst out laughing, and little Adira, who just looked puzzled.

Dana frowned up at Aidan. "I thought he was going to attack you." Her visions always came true. She had foreseen Roland attacking Aidan, and Roland had attacked Aidan. She had foreseen vampires attacking them at her home, and vampires had attacked them at her home. And she had foreseen Seth hacking away at Aidan with a sword, his eyes glowing and fury painting his face as it did now. So a preemptive strike had seemed like the way to go.

No one responded. They all just continued to gape at her.

"Well," she complained as the silence stretched and frustration rose, "if you didn't want me to tranq anyone, you shouldn't have given me the damned gun."

Zach, who had managed to corral his mirth, burst into laughter again.

Seth's lips twitched. He looked at Aidan, the bright golden light in his eyes fading. "I like her."

Aidan chuckled. "Aye. She's a fighter."

Around the room, tight expressions lightened with amusement. Shoulders and stances relaxed. And, most important, Seth didn't attack.

Dana lowered the tranq gun and leaned into Aidan's side as he wrapped an arm around her.

Seth looked toward the front windows and scowled, his anger resurfacing. "Oh, for fuck's sake! Are you kidding me?"

A moment later, Dana heard a vehicle approach. A thud sounded as someone exited the vehicle.

Seth crossed to the front door and yanked it open.

The man on the porch raised his eyebrows and eyed Seth's furious expression with surprise but no real concern, it seemed to Dana. He was about six feet tall with black hair that fell almost to his waist, brown eyes, broad shoulders, and plenty of muscle.

Seth looked at those gathered in the living room and pointed to the newcomer. "Okay, I admit it. This surprised me."

Nods all around.

Ami offered the newcomer a hesitant smile. "Hi, Bastien."

Bastien nodded to her, then studied Seth. Backing up a couple of steps, he looked up at the stormy sky, then over his shoulder at the trees that swayed in a rough wind, before arching a brow at Seth. "Did I come at a bad time?"

Seth sighed. "Just get your ass in here."

Dana looked up at Aidan as Bastien entered and Seth closed the door behind him.

Why did everyone seem so shocked to see this particular immortal?

Aidan glanced down at her. *Bastien is the black sheep of the Immortal Guardians family. He once raised an army of vampires in an attempt to defeat us all and is not well liked by some as a result. Roland, in particular, bears him a great deal of animosity because Bastien once kidnapped Sarah.*

Dana slid Roland and Sarah a look.

Both seemed more concerned about Seth's anger than Bastien's appearance.

She returned her gaze to Aidan's. *So no one likes him?* she thought. *That's why they all look so shocked?*

Zach likes him, he clarified. *Those two are birds of a feather. And the others present have gradually come to accept him. But the shocker is that Bastien rarely concerns himself with the lives of other immortals. So his coming here is…* He frowned. *Actually, I'm not sure why he's here.*

Seth scowled at Bastien. "If the others defied me, I don't know why it surprises me so much that you did, too. Why are you here?"

Bastien motioned to Aidan. "Aidan has been good to me."

Surprise lit Aidan's features. "I have?"

Bastien nodded. "You've gone out of your way to help Cliff. And Cliff is like a brother to me. So I'm here to have your back."

Love and pride filled Dana as she looked up at Aidan. These men and women, his brethren, all loved him so much for the things he had done for them in the past that they had risked Seth's wrath to be here for him, which apparently was pretty ballsy.

How could she not love him, too?

He glanced down at her.

Her eyes widened. "Don't read my thoughts," she blurted.

His forehead crinkled. "I'm not. I only read the others because you sent them to me."

"Oh." Good. Now did *not* seem like the most appropriate time for declarations of love.

Bastien motioned to Seth's chest. "What's with the darts?"

Glancing down, Seth plucked them from his chest and tucked them in a pocket. "Dana tried to tranq me."

Bastien's eyes widened as a startled laugh escaped him. Clamping his lips together, he turned to look at her. "You're the psychic?"

Dana nodded.

Smiling, he strode forward and offered her his hand. "Sebastien Newcombe. Pleasure to meet you."

Shifting the tranq gun to her left hand, Dana shook his hand.

"Nice to meet you, too."

Bastien covered their clasped hands. "If you or Aidan ever need anything, large or small, don't hesitate to call me. Aidan has my number."

She returned his smile. "Thank you. That's very kind of you."

Someone—Ed, she thought—whispered, "Did Dana tranq Bastien and I just didn't see it? Because he is *not* acting like himself."

Muffled laughter.

The amusement that rose within Dana died a swift death as the comfy living room faded away, replaced by a stark white room littered with splintered furniture. In the vision, a young man gripped the front of her shirt as he stared up at her with eyes that glowed orange and sparkled with tears.

She clasped his shoulders with Bastien's large hands and gave them a squeeze.

The young man mouthed something she didn't hear and released her shirt. Naked joy blossomed on his face.

Then, in the blink of an eye, she drew a sword and severed his head.

A scream sounded beside her as anguish filled her.

Her eyes welled with tears.

Bastien released her hand.

Dana returned to the present, to the living room full of immortals. But that lump of grief remained lodged in her chest.

Bastien stared down at her uneasily, then looked to Aidan. "Did I say something wrong?"

Dana hastily blinked back tears.

Aidan smiled. "No. She's just touched by your show of support. As am I." *Don't mention what you saw*, he murmured in her mind. *It was a moment from his past that still causes him great pain and sorrow.*

Dana forced a smile. "And the past forty-eight hours have been pretty exhausting."

Bastien's smile returned. "I imagine they have." He glanced around. "So," he said to no one in particular as he tucked his hands in his pockets, "should we order pizza?"

"No," Seth declared with exasperation. "The whole point of lodging Aidan and Dana here was to keep her from bumping into all of *you* every time she turned around."

Bastien pursed his lips. "Well, that plan sort of backfired, didn't it?"

Seth loosed a growl of frustration that Dana found more amusing now than scary. "Just get your ass back to the network, Bastien. Roland, Sarah," he ordered, turning to the couple, "begin the night's hunt. Marcus, you do the same." He turned to the tallest man in the room. "Zach, you take Ami and Adira to David's place. Then you and Lisette can begin your hunt."

Zach offered him a cocky salute.

Since every immortal who had come to visit had apparently defied Seth's wishes to do so, Dana was a little surprised by how quickly they jumped to do his bidding now.

Bastien offered Dana a goodbye, then left with Roland and Sarah right behind him.

Marcus kissed his wife and daughter, then headed outside after the others.

Cars rumbled to life and drove away.

Ami carried Adira over to Zach, who touched her shoulder, then curled an arm around Lisette. A second later, the small group vanished, leaving only Dana, Aidan, Ethan, Heather, Ed, Brodie, and Seth.

Seth gave Ed and Brodie a pointed look.

Without a word, the human males turned and headed down the hallway into another room. A door quietly closed behind them.

Seth turned his gaze upon Ethan and Heather. "Go get some rest. And by rest I mean *sleep*," he stressed. "I'll wake you when I leave."

Nodding, Ethan took Heather's hand.

Seth sank down in a big cushioned chair while the couple strolled down the hallway and disappeared through another doorway.

⟶◈◈◈⟵

Aidan touched the small of Dana's back and motioned to the closer of two sofas. Once she seated herself, he sank down beside her. Offering her a smile, he extended his hand in front of her, palm up, silently asking her to relinquish her weapon.

He still couldn't believe she had tried to tranq Seth.

Narrowing her eyes in displeasure, she handed him the tranquilizer gun.

Damn, he loved her. There really didn't seem to be anything she wouldn't do or anyone she wouldn't take on to protect him. That was actually a little terrifying.

Setting the tranquilizer gun on the somewhat battered coffee table, he leaned back into the soft cushions. Her hip pressed against his. When he stretched an arm across the back of the sofa, she leaned into him and settled a hand on his thigh.

His whole being warmed at the casual contact.

"I take it the darts don't work on you?" Dana asked Seth, breaking the silence.

Seth shook his head. "I'm an ancient. Zach is, too. *No* drugs affect us." Closing his eyes, he rested his head against the chair.

When Dana sent Aidan a questioning glance, he touched a fingertip to his lips.

Nodding, she waited.

After a moment, the rustle of leaves outside ceased as the harsh breeze stirred up by Seth's fury diminished. Lightning stopped flashing. No thunder rumbled.

The night creatures that had quieted resumed their chorus.

Raising his head, Seth opened his eyes. The glow was gone, leaving them so dark a brown they almost appeared black. "I really did try to give the two of you some privacy," he said, his voice carrying apology now rather than anger.

"I know you did," Aidan told him. "And I appreciate it." Especially since Seth was *really* giving him the benefit of the doubt after seeing Reordon's incriminating video.

Seth's lips tilted up in a faint smile. "Did Roland really apologize?"

"Very nicely," Aidan replied.

Seth shook his head. "Will wonders never cease?"

He laughed.

"So," Seth asked, "how does it feel to be so beloved by your brethren that they will defy me and risk my wrath to come to your defense?"

Aidan thought about it for a moment. "I find it both humbling and frightening. I don't want to put any of them in danger."

"Gershom is proving to be annoyingly adept at sowing dissent and dividing loyalties," Seth grumbled.

Dana's eyes widened. "Divided loyalties," she repeated.

Seth's eyebrows rose. "What?"

Aidan covered Dana's hand with his as realization dawned. "When Dana scried my future with her tarot cards, she foresaw danger, conflict, and divided loyalties. I thought the divided loyalty referred to me because I was hiding my relationship with her." Amongst other things.

"Divided loyalties," Seth murmured. "An abundance of that was demonstrated tonight."

Unease and guilt suffused Aidan as he thought of Dana's visions. "We can't let Gershom come between us, Seth. We can't let him pit us all against each other."

Though Gershom already had. More than once. First Roland had attacked Aidan. Then Ethan and Heather had been prepared to fight Roland on Aidan's behalf. And he and Ethan were *both* keeping secrets from Seth.

"No, we can't," Seth agreed.

"So what's the solution?"

Seth drummed his fingers on the chair's arms. "Take tonight off. No hunting. For you or for Ethan and Heather. As Dana mentioned, the past forty-eight hours have been tough ones. So I want the two of you to have tonight off to rest and regroup and…" He shrugged. "Hell, I don't know. Have a date night or something. Anything that will restore a little normalcy." He looked to Dana. "Again, I must apologize for your turbulent entrance into our world."

Much to Aidan's surprise, Dana offered Seth a hesitant smile. "Actually all of this"—she waved to the room around them that had previously been filled with immortals—"kind of helped. You guys really do seem like a family, willing to risk all to have each other's backs, bickering among yourselves and"—she motioned to Seth—"standing up to the patriarch."

Seth laughed. "The last, I hope, will remain a rarity."

Again, Aidan felt guilty for withholding information from Seth. The silence that descended then was a comfortable one.

"Dana," Seth said, seeming to choose his words carefully, "I know that, despite your words, you are still wary of us. We have certainly given you reason to be, what with Roland's attack on Aidan and then my show of temper tonight. But I stayed behind because I think it's time you knew about our enemy. And I believe it would be best if you heard it from me rather than Aidan."

Ah, hell. Seth was going to tell her all of it.

Dana looked up at him, a question in her gaze. "You look worried."

"I am," he admitted.

She squeezed his thigh. "After everything you've already told me, do you really think there's anything that could turn me away from you?"

A couple of things actually.

Returning her gaze to Seth, she said, "Okay. Who is your enemy?"

"We believe Gershom is the one causing our current troubles. He's most likely the one who sent the vampires to attack you and Aidan."

Aidan watched Dana carefully, noting the faint furrow that formed in her brow.

"And who is Gershom exactly?" she asked. "Is he a vampire leader or something?"

Seth shook his head. "Until recently, vampires have always been very solitary creatures. For thousands of years, they lived or traveled alone or only in pairs. Even seeing three together was a rarity."

"Why?"

"Because their insanity drives them to attack each other. The madness that afflicts them is often accompanied by paranoia and inevitably compels them to commit and *relish* committing violence. But in recent years, vampires have banded together in unprecedented numbers, first under Bastien before he joined our ranks, then under a vampire who declared himself their king, then with mercenaries. And it has escalated over the years until today, when we suspect Gershom is now leading them. Gershom is not a vampire. He also is not an Immortal Guardian. He is what we call an Other."

Dana frowned. "Another what?"

"Not *another*. But *an Other*," Seth clarified, enunciating the difference. "He is an ancient. Many of the immortals you saw here today are quite young by our standards. Ethan is a mere century old." He glanced at Aidan. *Have you told her your age?*

No.

Seth returned his attention to Dana. "Heather and Sarah have only recently transformed and are considered youngsters. Aidan is considered an elder because he is somewhat older than most of those you've met."

Dana slid him a look. And Aidan didn't have to read her mind to know she was trying to guess how *much* older.

"I," Seth continued, "and Zach are Others. Or we were once. We are ancients, too, though the rest of the immortals kindly call us elders. We were amongst the very first immortals in the world. We have in fact, been around since shortly after the Great Flood."

Dana stared at him. "You're not talking about the one in the Old Testament, are you? The one in the book of Genesis?"

"I am."

"The same one mentioned in ancient Egyptian, Greek, Mesopotamian, Hindu, and Mayan mythology?"

"Yes."

Her eyes widened. "You've lived thousands of years?"

"Yes. Millennia ago, the Others decided to withdraw from humanity. They decided they would not interact with mortals or do anything that would alter the natural progression or fate of humanity."

"Why?" Dana asked. "I don't understand. I've seen the wondrous things Aidan can do. And he said you can do even more. Why would you withhold that? Why would you not use those gifts to aid humanity and advance our society?"

"We had good reason," Seth answered, "to believe that if we tampered with humanity, if we altered mankind's fate in any way, if we *interfered* in any way, Armageddon would unfold."

Dana turned to Aidan. "Seriously?"

Aidan nodded. He didn't know what "good reason" Seth and the Others possessed, but he trusted Seth's judgment. "I've heard David compare it to the hypotheses that are often put forth in time-travel movies in which the men and women who go back in time are told that if they alter anything, if they so much as kill a butterfly or step on a bug, they could change the present in disastrous ways."

"Who is David?" she asked.

Seth answered. "My second-in-command."

Confusion clouded Dana's pretty features as she turned back to Seth. "But you're here. How is that not interference? Doesn't that contradict what you're telling me?"

Seth nodded. "I'm here now because I defected from the Others a long time ago. I deviated from the path. The Others did not. They steadfastly clung to it, believed in it, and — for several years after I left their ranks — wanted to kill me for abandoning it."

She shook her head. "If you really had reason to think tampering with mortals would spark Armageddon, why did you deviate from the path?"

Seth gave her a faint smile. "Because I fell in love with a mortal. A human woman. And I gladly risked everything to be with her. To this day I do not regret it."

Aidan could relate. He would risk anything to be with Dana.

Seth lowered his gaze for a moment. "After I lost my wife..."

Dana glanced up at Aidan. *Because she was human?*

He caught the thought clearly. *Yes.*

A human whose daughter had trusted the wrong person with their secret. Seth's wife and both his children had been slain as a result. But Aidan wouldn't tell Dana as much unless Seth wished it. That was Seth's story to share, not his own.

"I needed a new path," Seth finished his thought. "I needed something to..." He hesitated, then shook his head. "I needed a new path." He met Dana's gaze once more. "So I took it upon myself to lead the Immortal Guardians. To guide them. I was older, wiser, had seen more of the world, had learned from past mistakes. And when vampires began to prey upon humans and roamed unchecked, I believed that pitting the Immortal Guardians against them would *balance* the scales, not tip them. The Others objected. But, unbeknownst to them, I had begun building and increasing my power, so they could not stop me. I took the risk. And, thus far, it has paid off.

"The Others still tread the same path they always have. They watch. They do not participate. They do not interfere. And they disapprove of my own interference. Zach was also an Other. He is an ancient like myself. He steadfastly clung to the path of the Others until he met and fell in love with Lisette a couple of years ago. Then he, too, defected, which caused some upheaval."

A bit of an understatement.

"But we soon discovered that Zach was not the only Other to abandon the path. Gershom deviated as well. But Gershom did not deviate for the same reason Zach and I did. There is no love in Gershom. Quite the contrary. We believe he has slowly, without the Others realizing it, been descending into madness, much like the vampires Aidan and the Immortal Guardians hunt."

Dana scowled. "Well, that's just great. A madman who is as powerful as you are running around out there?"

Aidan nodded. "I'm afraid so."

Seth leaned forward, bracing his elbows on his knees. "Gershom apparently wants to kick-start Armageddon. He wants to watch the world burn and delights in sparking chaos."

"Wonderful," Dana muttered.

Aidan squeezed her hand. "But we're doing everything we can to stop him."

Seth nodded. "In his first attempt, Gershom did his damnedest to sow dissent amongst our ranks and did succeed for a time. Much to my regret, I briefly believed Aidan was working against us."

Dana cut Aidan a look. *Was the vision I saw of Seth trying to kill you showing me the past?*

Again, he heard the thought clearly. *No.*

Damn. She frowned at Seth. "How could you believe Aidan would betray you? Why *would* you believe it? Aren't you friends?"

Aidan saw guilt enter his leader's countenance and sought to erase it. "We are," he told Dana. "But there was compelling evidence. Had Seth and I not been as close as we are, I don't know what would've happened."

She didn't seem to like that.

Seth sighed. "We weren't able to defeat Gershom. And we have not been able capture him. Although we *did* manage to foil his attempt to start a third World War last year."

Dana's mouth fell open. "What?"

"But Gershom has not abandoned his quest," Seth went on. "And he is once more attempting to sow dissent amongst us."

A short laugh containing no mirth escaped Dana. "Well, he seems to be succeeding."

Seth nodded. "Whatever new plan he has hatched is more complex than the last. He knows Immortal Guardians and the vast network of humans that aid us watch over *gifted ones*. We have been watching over *you*, Dana, since your birth, as we do all others."

Her brow furrowed. "That's kind of creepy."

Seth smiled. "Not really. We do it so that—if your advanced DNA should ever be discovered or come to the attention of those who may want to hurt you or exploit you for your differences or even dissect you to seek their source—we can protect you."

Her frown deepened. "Okay. That's even creepier."

Again, Seth nodded. "It seems that someone has begun abducting *gifted ones* in North Carolina. Six women and three men have gone missing thus far."

"Are they still alive?" she asked.

"We don't know... in part because of the circumstances surrounding some of the abductions."

Aidan shifted, uneasiness rising.

Dana noticed and gave his thigh another affectionate squeeze. "Now you look *really* nervous."

"I am," Aidan admitted.

"Dana," Seth said, reclaiming her attention, "the six female *gifted ones* all went missing after having contact with Aidan."

She narrowed her eyes at Aidan. "What kind of contact?"

"Casual," he hastened to clarify. "I bumped into two at the grocery store. Changed a flat tire for another. Or for a couple. Ah, hell." He rubbed his forehead. "Truth be told, I stole a list of *gifted ones* from the network and arranged to bump into them so I could strike up a conversation with them and see if, perhaps..."

She cocked a brow. "You might hit it off with one of them?"

"Yes."

"Only *gifted ones*?"

"Yes."

"Was *I* on that list?" she asked, a distinct edge entering her voice.

"Yes. But none of the others interested me," he vowed. "Only you. I stopped looking once I met you."

When Dana opened her mouth to say Aidan-didn't-know-what, Seth interrupted.

"If you think about it, Dana, it wasn't that different from trying an online dating service or letting a friend set you up with a blind date. Aidan did what most men and women do. He narrowed the field to *gifted ones* in hopes of finding someone he had something in common with, someone who was more likely to understand his differences, and instead of dying in a few decades and leaving him alone again would eventually trans— "

Aidan shook his head quickly. He did *not* want any of his brethren to start pressuring Dana into transforming for him.

Seth clamped his lips shut. "I'm sorry. I don't think I'm helping this situation very much. So, back to the problem at hand."

Dana looked from Seth to Aidan and back again with suspicion.

"It appears as though Aidan was the last person to see the missing women," Seth informed her. "And three of those encounters were caught on video by security cameras that showed the women getting into vehicles with Aidan. They have not been seen since."

Dana eyed Aidan with concern. "Were you trying to help them? Taking them to a safe house or something?"

That her mind would go there first and not jump to the conclusion that he was the villain who had abducted them made Aidan rejoice inside. "The man in the video wasn't me," he explained. "I didn't know six *gifted ones* I'd spoken with were missing. I knew *one* woman was missing, but thought Gershom had taken her because of her connections to the network. I didn't learn that five others I'd spoken with had also gone missing until last night. As soon as I did, I panicked and raced to your place to ensure you were safe."

Seth shifted, drawing Dana's confused gaze. "We believe the man in the video abducted those women. But we don't think that man was Aidan. We believe it was Gershom."

She shot Aidan a glance. "Gershom looks like you? I mean, all of you Immortal Guardians seem to look so much alike that you could be brothers, but does Gershom look enough like you to actually *pass* as you?"

"No," Aidan corrected. "Gershom doesn't resemble me. But he can shape-shift and make himself look like my twin."

She stared at him a long moment. "Really?"

He didn't blame her for her skepticism. None of the gifts she had witnessed thus far had altered one's physical traits aside from healing wounds.

He looked to Seth. "A demonstration, please?"

Dana followed his gaze.

Seth's form abruptly shrank. His long dark hair shortened, curled, and turned red. His masculine features softened into a pretty feminine face. His broad shoulders narrowed. Then Ami sat where Seth had previously been.

"Hooooooooooly crap!" Dana exclaimed.

Ami morphed into Seth once more.

"Holy crap!" Dana repeated. Her head snapped around. Wide hazel eyes met Aidan's. "Can *you* do that?"

"No."

"Most shape-shifting immortals," Seth told her, "can only shift into the shapes of animals. Generic creatures, large or small. Changing one's appearance to mimic that of a specific person requires enormous power and concentration. It's very difficult because of the many unique nuances that must be perfected. Posture. Movement. Mannerisms. Tiny changes in facial expressions. I can do it. Zach can, too. But for the Others, it poses a greater challenge because they have kept their distance from humanity for so long that mastering all those little nuances... Well, I had not thought any of them capable of it until recently. And Gershom appears to have mastered it."

She frowned. "So you're telling me that there is an immortal out there who is as old and powerful as you are, can make himself look exactly like Aidan, and is abducting *gifted ones*? Is that why vampires attacked us at my home? Did Gershom send them to abduct me?"

"Yes," Seth answered. "I believe so."

"And I somehow fit in with whatever wild plan he's hatched to end the world?"

"Essentially."

Swiveling to face Aidan, she threw up her hands. "Well, shit. I kind of understated it when I said we couldn't catch a break. This is bad, Aidan. This is really, really bad."

He grinned, so damned relieved he wanted to throw his head back and laugh.

Dana eyed him with disbelief. "What the hell are you smiling about? This is not good news."

"I'm smiling because you don't believe I'm guilty."

"Well, of course I don't think you're guilty, honey. Why would I?"

Aidan hugged her tight.

"Wait." Dana drew back and looked at both men. "Do the other immortals know about this? Do Ethan and Heather and Roland and the rest know that someone is mimicking Aidan's appearance to make him look guilty?"

"Yes," Seth answered.

"And they trust Aidan so much that even if their eyes tell them he's guilty, they know he's innocent?"

"Yes," Seth replied again. "Well, except for Roland. One of the missing women is his descendant, so he didn't wait around long enough to hear us dispute the evidence, but he's come around now. And Chris Reordon, the head of the East Coast division of the network, has some doubts. That's why I've told Ethan not to let Aidan out of his sight. Ethan has what he likes to call a photographic memory raised to the nth power and notices all the little details that tend to escape the rest of us. He has viewed the video footage and is convinced that the man in the video was not Aidan. So if he keeps Aidan close and another *gifted one* should go missing, then Ethan will be able to confirm without a doubt that Aidan was not responsible and lay Reordon's suspicions to rest."

Nodding, Dana seemed to mull over Seth's words for a moment. "So is it the old divide-and-conquer thing? Is Gershom trying to pit you guys against each other so he can defeat you more easily or do whatever he intends to do while you're distracted, fighting each other?"

"In part," Seth agreed. "But Gershom also bears a hell of a lot of animosity toward me. I'm still not sure why. But he knows how precious my Immortal Guardians are to me and knows he can strike at me through them."

"And through Ami and her daughter?" Dana added.

Seth's brows drew down in a frown. "How did you know that?"

Dana shrugged. "They clearly mean a lot to you."

Seth sighed. "Ami is like a daughter to me, her child like a granddaughter. I love them both dearly and fear they have also become targets of Gershom."

"This Gershom sounds like a real asshole."

Aidan laughed.

Seth did, too. "An insane one, apparently. Anyway, I'd rather not have a repeat performance, so after tonight I'd like you both to stay at David's place. David is nearly as old and powerful as I am and opens his homes to all immortals and the mortals who aid us. He is, in large part, the reason we've become such a close family."

Aidan frowned. "I don't want to place Ami and Adira in danger."

Dana shook her head. "I don't either."

Seth smiled. "I appreciate that, but my immortals seem to be leaving me little choice in the matter." He smiled wryly. "If you omit Zach and Bastien, Immortal Guardians very rarely defy me. The job I have assigned myself is to keep them all safe, so when they make that harder for me to do, I tend to not react well."

Aidan snorted. "A bit of an understatement. Unlike the youngsters, I've seen you fully unleash your anger." Which was another reason he hoped like hell that Dana's vision of Seth wanting him dead wouldn't come to pass.

"So their defiance tonight," Seth continued, "was quite telling."

Dana patted Aidan's thigh. "If defying Seth is such a big deal, they must really love you." *Almost as much as I do.*

His breath caught.

Had she meant to send him that thought?

Skillet's "Monster" began to play.

Seth drew out his cell phone and glanced at it. His lips quirked up as he answered. "Yes, David?"

"Everyone still alive and breathing over there?" Aidan heard the elder immortal ask.

Seth's smile widened. "Yes."

"No injuries?"

"Aside from Dana trying to tranq me twice? None."

David's startled laughter floated over the line.

Aidan glanced down at Dana.

"I'm going to be hearing about that a lot, aren't I?" she mumbled.

"Yes." Laughing, he gave her shoulders a squeeze. "They'll cheer you for tranqing Roland and revere you for trying to tranq Seth." And his heart did a little leap, because it sounded like she didn't mind sticking around.

"I'm going to stay for an hour or two and let Ethan and Heather get some sleep," Seth continued. "Can you and Darnell field my calls?"

"Of course," David promised.

"After tonight, Aidan and Dana will stay at your place until all is resolved."

"I'll have a room ready for them when they arrive. I thought I would also have Richart fetch Imhotep and Chaak for added protection."

"Good idea."

Seth pocketed his phone, then frowned. "I guess you can't really have a date night with me hanging around. But if you need an alibi, Chris would never doubt my word, so I shall remain here until Ethan has gotten some rest. "

Dana sent Aidan an apologetic smile. "I don't think I'm up for a date night anyway. I may not be a morning person, but I do usually go to bed before midnight and get up early for my clients. So the abrupt change to the night shift is taking its toll."

Aidan didn't think lack of sleep was the only thing taking its toll. Throw in several adrenaline rushes, a few brushes with death, and the reality of his world being dumped on her, and he was surprised she still had enough energy to stand, let alone stand up to Seth.

Seth gave her a kind smile. "Why don't you two get some sleep as well? I'll wake Ethan and Heather before I leave."

Nodding, Aidan rose and crossed to Seth. When he offered Seth his hand, Seth stood and clasped it.

"We can't let Gershom come between us, Seth," Aidan said

again. "We've been friends... family... for too long to let that bastard win."

Seth dipped his chin in a nod. "He won't." Pulling him into a man-hug, Seth clapped him hard on the back, then released him. "Go get some rest."

Chapter Fourteen

SETH LET THE YOUNGER IMMORTALS sleep for a couple of hours before waking them so he could teleport to David's study.

David sat behind his desk, speaking to an Australian immortal on the phone.

Darnell was seated at Ami's desk, fielding the calls Seth received that bore no urgency.

Both men nodded at Seth's appearance, then ended their conversations.

"Have Zach and Lisette returned from their hunt?" Seth asked.

Both nodded.

Zach? Seth called telepathically.

Yes? Zach responded from the bedroom he and Lisette shared below.

Join me in David's study. There's something I'd like to discuss.

I'm on my way.

Darnell grinned. "Did Dana really shoot you with a tranquilizer dart?"

"Twice," Seth replied, amused despite his worries.

Darnell shook his head. "That was gutsy as hell. I can't wait to meet her."

"Well, they'll be here by morning, so you'll have your chance then."

Zach entered, clad only in black pants and black boots. He had worn a shirt to Ethan's home in deference to Dana. But tonight his chest was bare, and large dark wings graced his back. "What's up?"

David rose, circling the desk to join them by the door.

Seth looked to Darnell. "Can you field my calls for a little while longer? Reordon can help you if you need him."

"Sure."

Without another word, Seth touched David's shoulder and teleported away.

A moonlit meadow replaced David's study. Long grasses and weeds swayed in a gentle breeze and brushed their knees.

The ground around them gradually sloped upward on all sides, as though he and David stood in the bottom of a massive salad bowl. At the top, verdant grasses gave way to a forest so dark and dense that even Seth's eyes couldn't penetrate it.

Stars winked above them in a cloudless sky.

Zach appeared beside them.

"We have a problem," Seth announced without preamble.

David's brow furrowed. "Aside from the missing *gifted ones*, the gathering vampires, our waiting to see if Aidan is being mind-controlled, and several immortals going astray?"

"Not to mention Chris Reordon's vendetta," Zach mumbled.

"Yes," Seth responded.

Zach grunted. "What now?"

Seth recalled his search of Dana's mind. "You know the woman Aidan is seeing is psychic."

"I assume," David said, "her gift is stronger than that of most other *gifted ones* of her generation, since she is able to earn a living with it."

Most *gifted ones* born in recent decades had gifts so mild that they weren't even aware of them. Melanie was psychic, too, but her gifts had been so dampened by centuries of human DNA winding its way through her family tree that she only got what she called *feelings* now. She might know the phone was about to ring. Or if something bad were about to happen she might feel a sense of foreboding.

"Dana's gift is surprisingly strong," Seth confirmed. "Even stronger when it comes to Aidan. I don't know if it's because he's a *gifted one*, too, or perhaps a result of the bond growing between them, but she's been seeing his future in brief, vivid visions since the day they met."

"And you saw her visions when you read her mind," David

guessed.

"Not the first time, when Roland attacked Aidan and brought her to my attention. Her thoughts were too chaotic and time was short. The same held true at her home after the vampires struck."

Zach frowned. "Wait. If she saw Aidan's future in visions, how did she not know what he is?"

"Most of her visions were of an intimate nature." Seth smiled. "There have been more of those than Aidan knows about."

David's lips twitched. "Good for him."

Zach laughed. "Clearly those need no explanation. And I see no problem with that."

"Nor do I," Seth agreed. "But I performed a more thorough search of Dana's mind after you"—Seth scowled at Zach—"and the others left a few hours ago and was able to access more of her visions."

"What did she see?" David asked curiosity lighting his dark features.

"Roland doing his damnedest to kill Aidan. She foresaw the battle that outed Aidan as an immortal."

Zach grunted. "And she didn't think that odd?"

"She did," Seth said, "but Aidan told her he was a member of a reenactment group."

"Smart thinking," David said. "What else did you see?"

"Me, doing the same."

Zach frowned. "She foresaw you trying to kill Aidan?"

Seth nodded. "Or maim him at the very least. We were both wielding swords with sharpened blades, and I looked furious. That's why she tried to tranq me earlier. She thought the vision was about to come true, that I was there to kill Aidan."

Zach sighed. "That's a damned shame. I had actually begun to like Aidan."

David looked at Zach in surprise. "Really?"

Seth did, too. He hadn't realized Zach liked *any* of the other immortals aside from Bastien. He had thought Zach just tolerated them all for Lisette's benefit.

Zach shrugged. "When I thought he was in league with the men who had nearly killed Lisette, I kicked Aidan's ass. I mean, I really beat the shit out of him. And Aidan has never held it against me.

Nor did he hold Seth's actions against him. Kind of hard to dislike the poor bastard when he's been so understanding." He looked to Seth. "If you're going to want to kill him, I guess that means Reordon was right. Aidan really *did* abduct those women. Gershom must be mind-controlling him."

"Not necessarily," David said. "If Ethan is right, it could've been Gershom posing as Aidan in the visions."

Zach shook his head. "If Dana was seeing Aidan's future, the Aidan in the vision would have to have been him, not someone posing as him."

"True," Seth said.

"Then perhaps," David inserted, "Gershom *is* using mind control to have Aidan do his bidding. Has Aidan let you read his thoughts yet?"

"I haven't asked him," Seth admitted. "But I doubt he will agree, because he probably doesn't want me to see Dana's vision."

Zach grunted. "Can't really blame him there."

"There's another option," David pointed out.

Seth nodded. "We know Gershom has assumed your appearance in the past, Zach. If he is assuming Aidan's as well, then there's no reason for us to believe he can't assume mine, too. What if the Seth in Dana's vision isn't me?"

Both men swore.

Seth himself had mixed reactions to the notion. On the one hand, it would be a relief to know that he wouldn't want to kill Aidan in the future. But the idea that Gershom might be moving about the immortals' ranks, pretending to be Seth, was disturbing as hell.

Zach's brow furrowed with doubt. "You had no difficulty determining that the man who met with the mercenaries two years ago wasn't me, that it was one of the Others. If the man in Dana's vision wasn't you, I would think you'd be able to tell."

"Not," David interjected, "if Gershom has been practicing and honing his shape-shifting skills."

"Such is my fear," Seth told them. "So I've called in a little backup."

Zach frowned suddenly and tilted his head as though listening to something.

Jared, one of the Others, abruptly appeared a few yards away.

Like Zach, he wore no shirt. Just black leather pants and boots. He was less lean and more muscled than he had been when Seth had last seen him. Seth guessed the Other was strengthening himself for battle now that visions of Armageddon had scared the hell out of him.

Huge wings spread behind Jared, the semitranslucent feathers that graced them the same tan of his skin at their base and darkening to black at their tips. Folding the wings in against his back, he strolled over to join them.

Seth smiled. "Just in time."

Zach drew back an arm and slammed his fist into Jared's face.

Bone cracked and blood spurted from Jared's nose as he flew backward and landed with a thud several yards away.

"Damn it!" Seth, David, and Jared all ground out.

Zach managed to look both innocent and wickedly satisfied at the same time. "What? The bastard tortured me."

Jared's eyes glowed golden as he sat up. Cupping his nose, he glowered at Zach. "How long are you going to keep punishing me for that?"

Zach's features hardened. "Until I've repaid you wound for wound."

Seth wouldn't admit it out loud, but he kind of sided with Zach on that.

Rising, Jared strode toward them, eyes still glowing golden from either pain or anger as the bones in his nose and face slipped back into place and healed. "Why did you summon me?" he asked Seth.

"Have you been posing as Immortal Guardians and tampering in their affairs again?" Seth didn't think he had, but thought it worth asking.

Jared's face lit with surprise. "No. I've been toeing the line and staying on the straight and narrow so the Others won't realize I've defected."

Instead of following Zach's lead and fully joining the ranks of the Immortal Guardians, Jared had become something of a double agent, living life as usual with the Others to avoid suspicion while helping Seth and feeding him information.

Jared studied them. "Why? What's going on?"

Seth smiled. "I'd like to conduct a little experiment."

Aidan opened his eyes. He lay on his back, Dana's head on his shoulder, her arm resting upon his chest, her thigh draped across his groin.

No sun shone behind the curtains, so it must still be night.

He sighed. While he had slept a deep healing sleep at Dana's, now that he was at full strength, he was having little luck getting any rest. He hadn't slept beside a woman since his days as a mortal and—much to his dismay—woke at Dana's every movement, no matter how slight. Dana sometimes talked in her sleep (mostly incoherent mumbles he found amusing), and that woke him as well.

With a mental shrug, he cuddled her closer. It was worth it. He didn't mind being a little tired if losing sleep enabled him to enjoy her warm body nestled up against his.

She shifted, tightening her hold on him. Tilting her head back, she raised her eyelids to half-mast and offered him a sleepy smile. "Hi, handsome."

"Hi, yourself," he returned with a grin. He loved seeing her like this. One cheek pink from resting on his shoulder. Her hair mussed and tangled.

She squinted at the window. "Did we sleep all day again?"

"No. We only slept three or four hours."

"Hmm." She shifted again, her smooth thigh teasing his erection. Her smile grew. "Ooh. Is that for me?"

"Hell yes, if you want it."

Chuckling, she shook her head. "If I want it, he says." Rising onto an elbow, she slid her lower body over on top of his, then sat up.

Aidan hissed in pleasure as she straddled him, her core settling atop his arousal. Clamping his hands on her hips, he arched against her.

Dana moaned as her head dropped back. "I just woke up and I'm already wet for you. How do you do that?"

He slid his hands up her thighs, his thumbs stopping just short of the dark curls at their juncture. He had enjoyed learning her body yesterday. How and where she liked to be touched. What drew the most gasps from her. What made her moan and writhe and beg for more.

When he slid his hands back down to her knees, she moaned a protest. "Tease."

Smiling, he repeated the caress, coming just a bit closer to the heart of her, then withdrew. Again he smoothed his hands up her thighs, retreating without giving her what she wanted.

"Aidan," she said, her voice hoarse.

"You want my touch?" he asked innocently.

She met his gaze. "I want your touch."

Aidan caressed his way up her thighs again, this time giving her a light brush of his thumbs.

Dana hissed in pleasure.

Another light touch, just enough to tease and tantalize.

"More," she pleaded.

Aidan obeyed, stroking her until she moaned and rocked against him, sliding along his shaft.

Lust hit him hard as he watched her slip a hand up her side and cup her breast.

She met his gaze as she toyed with her nipple. "Your eyes are really bright," she whispered before another moan escaped her.

"They always will be with you," he told her gruffly. Leaning up, he closed his lips over the other taut peak, took it between his teeth and teased it with his tongue.

Dana buried her hands in his hair, urging him closer, still rocking against him.

Heat flooded him. He would never get enough of her. Sliding his arms around her, he rose onto his knees, then pressed her back onto the bed.

She smiled up at him as he leaned over her. "I love feeling your weight on me. All that delicious muscle." She practically purred with anticipation as she reached for him.

Aidan gave her a sensual smile. "Not yet." Grasping her ankles, he eased her legs farther apart.

Her heartbeat picked up as her breathing quickened.

Sliding his arms beneath her knees, Aidan lowered his head and took her with his mouth.

Dana moaned, fisting her hands in Aidan's hair.

He found her clit with his tongue, stealing her breath with licks and flicks and undulations.

So good.

He slid a finger inside her slick entrance, then added another. Curling them upward, he stroked her while applying more pressure with his tongue.

She bucked against him, crying out as she came hard, her inner walls clenching and unclenching around his fingers.

Aidan lunged up over her.

Her heart jackhammering in her chest, she met his intense, glowing gaze. How she loved seeing him like this, so hungry for her.

She slipped a hand down between them and curled it around his erection.

He groaned as she gave him a squeeze and teased the tip with her thumb. "You're killing me, sweetheart," he said, voice gravelly with need.

Grinning unrepentantly, she guided him to her entrance and arched up to embrace him.

He was so big, stretching her and sparking new heat as he sank deep inside her.

He lowered his lips to hers, took her mouth in a devouring kiss as he withdrew almost to the crown and thrust again. He slid a hand up to her breast. His touch grew rough as he drove inside her again and again, but she voiced no complaint. She liked it. Wanted more. Loved that she could make him lose control like this. So the rougher he got, pounding into her, the more she moaned and urged him on.

Aidan gladly delivered, quickly driving her to another climax but holding back his own.

Sparks of pleasure still dancing through her, Dana reared up suddenly and shoved him off her and onto his back.

He stared up at her in surprise, his erection jutting toward her.

Dana swiftly straddled him, curling a hand around his cock and taking him inside her again.

Groaning, he clamped his hands on her hips and arched up against her as she rode him.

Resting her hands on his chest, she gave his nipples a hard pinch as she circled her hips.

He groaned.

"You're mine," she told him.

He smoothed his hands up her sides to tease her breasts. "And you're mine."

Again she rotated her hips in a way that made him groan and sent sharp darts of pleasure through her. "No one else's," she breathed, her body on fire.

"No one else's," he rasped, tweaking her nipples.

Dana cried out as a third orgasm rocked her.

As her inner muscles clamped down around him, Aidan growled her name and stiffened as he finally allowed himself to climax and came inside her.

Breathless, Dana slumped down on top of him.

Aidan closed his arms around her, his heart pounding a rapid beat beneath her ear.

"Damn, you're good," she mumbled. No man had ever pleased her more.

Aidan laughed, rolling them onto their sides.

Settling her head on the pillow beside his, Dana smiled as she tried to catch her breath.

His own smile tender, Aidan brushed her tangled hair back from her face and pressed a lingering kiss to her lips. "I love you."

Her heart skipped a beat.

"You don't have to say it back," he said softly. "I just wanted you to know. Because I do. I love you, Dana."

She touched a hand to his stubbled cheek. "I love you, too."

A shiver shook her as her passion-warmed skin began to cool beneath the gentle breeze of the air conditioner.

Aidan released her long enough to draw the sheet up over them both, then slid his arms around her beneath it. "I'm sorry our courtship was interrupted. I'm sorry I couldn't spend months wooing you as an ordinary man."

Amusement sifted through her. "But you *aren't* an ordinary man, Aidan. Even if you hadn't been born a *gifted one*, you still wouldn't have been an ordinary man."

Silence enfolded them.

Dana would've thought sleep would claim her pretty quickly after their fabulous lovemaking. But it didn't.

Aidan arched a brow.

She grinned. "I don't know about you, but I'm wide-awake now."

He laughed. "Me, too."

"Do you want to watch a movie or something?"

"As much as I would love to…," he murmured with regret.

Her smile faded. "What?"

"With vampire numbers increasing the way they are, I don't feel right about not hunting tonight."

She frowned. "I thought Seth told you to take the night off."

"He only said that as a kindness. He's trying to limit your exposure to the harsher aspects of our reality. But vampires are amassing again, which means they're preying upon more humans every night."

Sitting up, Dana tucked the sheet beneath her arms. "And you don't like the idea of staying home and watching a movie when you could be out there, protecting innocents."

"Yes," he reluctantly confessed. He said it as though he expected it to upset her.

"That's a good thing, Aidan," she said. "A noble thing. Why do you look so grim?"

"Because if I hunt tonight, you'll have to accompany me."

She had thought as much. "And?" Did he think she would hinder him in some way?

He sat up, the sheet falling to his lap and leaving his muscled chest bare. "Ethan and Heather would accompany us, so we'd have safety in numbers."

She had assumed that as well. "What aren't you saying?"

He ran his fingers through his mussed hair. "*Knowing* I hunt vampires and *seeing* me hunt vampires are two very different things."

And he looked as though he thought the latter would drive her away from him. "I've seen you kill vampires before," she reminded him. "You killed one right in front of me at my place."

"That was different," he said with a shake of his head. "They attacked us. You haven't seen me hunt and kill vampires who *haven't* attacked us."

She studied him. "And you think I'll leave you once I do."

"I hope like hell you won't," he admitted. "But you do have choice, Dana. And I love you enough to want you to know *everything* about my life before you make that choice."

Taking his hand, she raised it to her lips and pressed a kiss to his knuckles. "Which just makes me love you even more."

An amber glow entered his eyes. "I don't like the idea of exposing you to more violence after you've seen so much in the past couple of nights."

"But more humans may die if you don't hunt tonight," she finished for him.

"Yes." He gave her hand a squeeze. "Are you up for it? Will you go hunting with me?"

She smiled. "Yes."

He brought her palm to his lips for a kiss. "Is there anything you *won't* do for me?" he whispered.

Schooling her features into a somber mask, she nodded. "Yes."

His brow furrowed.

Leaning in close, Dana held his worried gaze. "I will *never*," she intoned, "wear thong underwear for you."

He laughed, his eyes sparkling with amusement. "I'd rather you not wear any at all," he said with a wink. Tossing back the sheet, he rose. "Let's take a quick shower, then I'll let Ethan and Heather know our plans and find you some hunting clothes."

⟶⟶◈◈◈⟵

Had Dana not been so deliciously sated, she would've wanted to spend more time in the shower with Aidan. She had learned yesterday that one of the perks of Aidan's being immortal was that he didn't need to recharge after having an orgasm. He could go again immediately and have as many orgasms as she did.

Dana had also learned, much to Aidan's amusement, that multiple orgasms left her too tired to move. So they rushed through their shower and donned hunting togs.

Heather's clothes ended up fitting Dana just fine, though the boots were a little snug. Judging by the faint glow in Aidan's eyes, he liked seeing her in the black cargo pants, long-sleeved black shirt, and boots.

Ethan, Heather, Brodie, and Ed all smiled when she and Aidan joined them in the living room.

Brodie crossed to Dana. "I don't know how much you know about Seconds, but our job is to arm and protect the immortals we serve. In this instance, that job extends to protecting you, so if you don't mind?" He held up a shoulder holster and weapons.

"Oh." She had thought she would just be observing. "Okay." While she held out her arms, Brodie fitted her for a shoulder holster he packed with 9mms.

Aidan's brows drew down as he watched them.

"Is he not supposed to arm me?" she asked. "You look a little pissed."

Heather laughed. "He just doesn't like Brodie touching you."

When Aidan didn't dispute it, Dana smiled at him. "It's not like he's trying to feel me up or anything."

Aidan's frown deepened. "He'd lose a hand if he did."

His Second laughed, unperturbed by the threat.

When Brodie reached both arms around Dana to secure a belt with a thigh holster around her waist, Aidan strode forward and elbowed him aside. "Let *me* do that," he grumbled, taking the belt.

Brodie stepped back with a good-natured grin. "Yes, sir."

Dana watched Aidan as he buckled the belt around her waist, then knelt and went to work, tying the bottom of the holster around her thigh.

He was jealous and didn't like that he was jealous. Dana didn't need be telepathic to glean that or to suspect that that was why he wouldn't meet her eyes.

When at last he did, she grinned. "You are too adorable."

His soft lips turned up in a sheepish smile. "Sorry about that. Jealousy is new to me. I vow I'll work on it."

Dana combed her fingers through his soft, thick, wavy hair. "I don't mind. I think it's cute."

Tucking a tranquilizer gun into the thigh holster, Aidan started to fill her pockets with extra ammo and darts.

Dana toyed with his silky hair.

The room around them changed, transforming from a living room into what looked like a huge walk-in closet. A *his and hers* closet with masculine black clothes on one side and feminine black clothes on the other. Long black coats hung beside each other on the wall behind him, one small, one large. Weapons and ammo adorned another wall.

In the vision, Aidan knelt before her, tying a thigh holster. When he smiled up at her, Dana saw her reflection in his deep brown eyes and sucked in a breath.

Her eyes glowed amber.

"How is that?" Aidan asked, dispelling the vision and plunking her back down in Ethan and Heather's living room. "Too heavy?"

Her heart hammered against her rib cage as he rose.

Concern entering his dark brown eyes, he stroked her arms. "Dana? What is it?"

She shook her head. "Just nerves, I guess."

It wasn't entirely a lie. She had just foreseen herself arming up as an Immortal Guardian. How could that *not* fray her nerves a bit? As Aidan had pointed out, *knowing* she might one day become immortal and *seeing* it were two very different things.

"We can stay home if you'd prefer."

"No." She produced a smile. "I'm fine. It was just a momentary aberration." Rising onto her toes, she gave him a quick kiss, then stepped back and accepted the long coat Brodie offered her. It, too, fit her well, the hem falling to her knees.

"Ready?" Aidan asked, his face still registering doubt.

She nodded. "Let's go hunt some vampires," she proclaimed cheerfully, then grimaced and shook her head. "I can't believe those words just came out of my mouth."

Heather laughed. "I know. It's weird, right?"

"Definitely."

But hunt vampires they did.

They didn't take a car. Aidan just touched their shoulders and teleported them to their hunting destination.

Dana examined their surroundings with some confusion. They were on the roof of a building. Beyond it lay what appeared to be a college campus. "Where are we?"

"Duke," Aidan replied, resting a hand on her lower back.

Music pulsed somewhere in the distance.

Dana wasn't familiar with Duke University's campus, but the

buildings around her did kind of scream money. "And we're here because...?"

"College campuses are prime vampire hunting grounds," he explained.

Heather grinned. "It's Friday night. Do you have any idea how many students are getting high or drunk off their asses tonight?"

Ethan nodded. "Easy pickings for vampires."

Dana looked up at Aidan.

He shrugged. "Vampires are lazy that way. And too, vampires who have fully lost their sanity tend to migrate toward places that were familiar to them in their mortal life."

"Like zombies in a horror movie?" That was a little freaky.

Heather pointed at her. "Exactly. We can almost always find vampires hunting on campuses like this."

Dana supposed so, because not more than fifteen minutes passed before Aidan and Heather suddenly looked toward the west. Both inhaled deeply.

"How many?" Aidan asked softly.

Heather drew in another deep breath. "Twelve."

"Thirteen," Aidan corrected.

Heather swore.

He smiled. "Don't be so hard on yourself. You're getting more accurate every day. This time you didn't let the scents of their victims distract you."

Ethan nodded and touched Heather's back. "I can't even smell them yet." He grimaced. "Wait. Yes, I can. I see they've already been hunting."

Dana saw nothing at all. Nor did she smell anything. How far away *were* the vampires?

And how cool was it that the immortals could scent them on the breeze like wolves?

"Heather," Aidan murmured, "I'd like you to remain here on the roof with Dana while Ethan and I take care of the vampires."

Heather's face darkened with a belligerent frown. "Are you ordering me to stay here because I'm a girl?"

Aidan's eyebrows flew up. "No," he responded with obvious surprise. "I want you to stay here and guard Dana because you match me in strength and speed. She'll be safer with you."

Ethan nodded. "And I need to keep Aidan in my sight during the battle so Chris can't say Aidan teleported away while I was distracted."

"Oh." Heather sent Aidan an apologetic smile. "Sorry. Force of habit. I have to deal with a lot of good ol' boys in law enforcement agencies and that *run along and play, little girl, while the* men *take care of business* attitude has gotten old."

Ethan grinned. "I keep trying to tell you, honey, immortal males aren't stupid. We *love* strong women."

Aidan smiled at Dana. "We really do." And the affection that accompanied his words as he stared down at her made warmth unfurl inside her.

"All right, all right," Heather said, waving her hands at Aidan. "Don't get all goo-goo eyed. You boys have work to do. Get moving."

Laughing, Aidan leaned down and brushed a quick kiss against Dana's lips. "I'll be back in a minute."

Turning away, he joined Ethan at the edge of the roof. Then the two just stepped off and dropped out of sight.

Gasping, Dana hurried forward and cautiously peered over the edge.

Down below, Ethan and Aidan strolled away as casually as if they had just jumped off a front porch instead of a three-story building.

Heather joined Dana, a smile gracing her pretty features. "That's nothing," she whispered. "I jumped off a ten-story building once."

Dana stared at her in wonder.

"I know, right? Being immortal is so cool. I can even lift and throw a car."

Seriously? Heather was Dana's size. Had transforming given her *that* much strength?

Dana returned her attention to the men. The powerful immortals' smooth gait revealed nothing of their purpose. Anyone who saw them and didn't know better would think they were just out for a stroll and shooting the breeze instead of preparing to slay over a dozen psychotic vampires. Their shoulders were relaxed, their hands nowhere near the weapons that lined the interior of their coats. Dana even caught the sound of them chuckling on the breeze.

A couple of male students, young and staggeringly drunk, stumbled onto the sidewalk, their laughter loud and obnoxious.

Aidan made a slight motion with his hand.

Without missing a step, the college boys turned and stumbled back the way they had come.

"Aidan guided them away," Heather whispered.

"Telepathically?"

She nodded, drawing two short swords.

Dana strained to make out the words of the men she couldn't see but failed. Thirteen figures entered her view, no longer cloaked by the trees that lined the path. As she studied them, Dana couldn't find anything remarkable about their appearance. Their eyes didn't glow like those of the vampires who had attacked her home. Their lips weren't peeled back to expose glinting fangs. Their features didn't contort with malevolent smiles.

And they were young. College aged. The lot of them could easily pass for students of the university if one failed to notice the blood that stained their clothing.

"Fuckers," Heather muttered, her hands tightening on the hilts of her weapons. Her jaw tightened. Her eyes flashed bright amber.

Dana caught her attention and tapped a temple. *Are you reading their thoughts?* she asked, trying to think the thought loudly, whatever that meant.

Yes, Heather replied. *And they made those girls scream.*

The group of vampires halted.

Words passed between the vampires and immortals.

"Oh, shit," Heather whispered.

"What?" Dana asked.

Heather looked stunned. Or maybe scared. Or worried?

Dana didn't have time to ask before Aidan and Ethan drew swords and leapt forward.

The vampires' eyes flashed as bright as Christmas lights — blue, green, silver, amber — as they drew weapons and blurred.

Over the faint booming of a party raging elsewhere on campus, Dana heard the clash of weapons and the spewing of vile epithets.

Once more, she didn't think. She just reacted. As soon as a vampire slowed down enough for her to be sure she wouldn't hit

Aidan or Ethan, Dana drew her tranq gun and fired three darts.

Three vampires sank, unconscious, to the ground.

"Wait!" Heather stopped Dana before she could tranq another vamp.

"Why?"

Heather shook her head, her gaze on the tempest below as she prevented Dana from raising her weapon once more.

The fighting took place at such speeds that Dana had difficulty following it. Aidan and Ethan seemed to remain in constant motion as bodies fell around them.

Dana swallowed hard. It *was* different from the last time she had seen Aidan kill vampires. If Heather hadn't told her the vampires had made their victims scream, Dana would've found it a lot harder to watch.

When the last vampire fell, Aidan and Ethan stood back-to-back, bodies scattered at their feet. All but three of the vampires began to shrivel up.

Though blood splattered their faces and dampened their clothing, the immortal males didn't appear to be breathing hard. Both warriors, however, looked grim rather than triumphant.

Chapter Fifteen

Heather sheathed her weapons, then turned and lifted Dana into her arms as though Dana were as light as an infant. "Hold on tight."

Dana barely had time to wrap her arms around Heather before the woman stepped off the roof. Fear whipped Dana alongside the wind as she tightened her hold.

Heather landed nimbly on her feet and lowered Dana to the ground.

Dana swayed a little. Not from dizziness but from shock. She had *not* expected that.

When Heather strode toward the men with urgency and concern, Dana hurried after her.

"I'm sorry," Heather blurted. "I didn't know she was going to tranq them. After reading their thoughts, I would've stopped her sooner, but..."

His brow furrowed, Aidan sheathed his weapons and moved forward to block Dana's view of the carnage. "Dana— "

She shook her head and stepped around him.

Seeing blood and guts in a movie was a hell of a lot different from seeing *and* smelling it in person.

Dana wanted to look away but refused to let herself. If she transformed and became immortal so she could be with Aidan, she would see this every night for the rest of her life. She needed to know if she would be able to handle it.

"I'm sorry," Heather said again, her voice tormented.

"It's okay," Aidan murmured.

"No, it isn't," Heather exclaimed, so agitated she couldn't seem to stand still and constantly shifted her weight. "I read their thoughts. What are we going to do?"

"What was in their thoughts?" Ethan asked while Dana continued to stare at the bodies.

"I was," Aidan told him. "The vampires believe I'm leading them."

"That's bullshit!" Ethan sputtered.

Heather bit her lip. "But Seth and Chris may not think so. Not after Seth reads the unconscious vamps' thoughts."

Aidan nodded. "The vampires' thoughts indicate that I've been coming to them during my afternoons with Cliff. And Chris and Seth have both already shot Cliff down as an alibi."

Understanding began to dawn as Dana listened. Dragging her gaze away from the bloody, deteriorating corpses, she looked at Aidan. "Seth will think you're guilty when he reads the vampires' minds? He'll think you've turned against him? Against your immortal family?"

No one answered her.

Horror filled her. "What have I done?" She had been trying to *help* Aidan but instead had pretty much ensured her vision of Seth attacking him would come true and signed his death warrant.

"Nothing," Aidan said, wiping his hands on his coat before he moved forward to grip her arms. "You've done nothing, Dana. This isn't your fault."

"Bullshit!" she said, echoing Ethan. "I tranqed the damned vampires, and now their thoughts will implicate you!"

"I say we kill them," Ethan said, his hands tightening on the hilts of his swords.

Aidan stayed him. "It will do no good. Seth will still read the truth in Heather's thoughts the next time he sees her."

Dismay and regret filled the other woman's features as tears welled in her eyes. "Aidan, I'm so sorry. I wish now that I hadn't read their thoughts."

Ethan sheathed his weapons. "Seth didn't believe you were guilty before. We can— "

"When Seth reads the vampires' minds," Aidan interrupted, "he will see me instructing them to turn more humans and to continue to increase their numbers. He'll see me order them to travel in packs and attack Immortal Guardians in large groups, to attack *us* and Dana again and again until Dana believes that the only way she can survive is to transform for me. And in return, they believe I will reward them with more *gifted ones*."

Silence fell, disturbed only by that distant booming music.

"Aidan," Dana said but could find no other words.

"That was not me, Dana," he told her earnestly "I vow it. I am *not* the man leading the vampires or abducting the *gifted ones*."

"I know. But my vision. Seth is going to try to kill you when he hears this."

Ethan took a step forward. "You saw Seth trying to kill Aidan in a vision?"

"Yes."

He and Heather both swore.

"Erase my memory," Heather blurted.

Aidan immediately refused. "No."

Heather shook her head. "If you erase my memory and slay the vampires, Seth won't— "

"He'll see the same thing in the mind of any vampire the other immortals capture. And if he fights vampires himself here in North Carolina, he'll see the same thing Lisette and Étienne will see in the vampires' minds: Me leading them. Me guiding them. Me promising them the *gifted ones* who rebuffed me. Erasing your memory and slaying these vampires will only delay the inevitable."

"If the inevitable," Heather insisted, "is Seth killing you, then I say we delay it until we can prove you're innocent! *You* gave me this life, Aidan. *You* made me as strong as I am. *You* ensured I wouldn't have to give up sunlight for the rest of eternity. I'm not going to just stand by and let Gershom make you look so guilty that Seth will execute you."

The fact that Aidan looked as though there were no point in fighting it anymore scared the hell out of Dana. "Can't we convince Seth that the man in the vampires' memories is Gershom?"

Aidan shook his head. "Your vision was clear. Seth will want to kill me. And, after everything he's overlooked thus far, this will give him good reason."

Ethan stepped forward. "But you don't even know that it was Seth in Dana's vision. What if it was Gershom?"

"It wasn't Gershom," Aidan responded.

"But you don't know that!" Ethan retorted. "Not with any certainty."

"Yes, I *do* know it," Aidan said, a sharp edge entering his voice.

"Bullshit," Ethan barked. "If Gershom can imitate you, then he can just as easily imitate Seth."

Aidan shook his head as anger darkened his features. "You aren't thinking clearly," he bit out. "You're only seeing what you want to see."

Dana looked at the others.

Both Ethan and Heather radiated frustration.

"Why do you think Gershom chose to mimic me in the first place?" Aidan asked them. "Because I'm the new guy. And the first thing I did when I came here was defy Seth."

Heather frowned. "You're not the new guy. *I* am. I just transformed last year."

Aidan shook his head. "But you're already a cherished member of the family. You have close friendships with many of the others stationed here. You spend a lot of time with them. They've all welcomed you and Krysta and Sarah with open arms and fall all over themselves to ensure you feel welcome. But *I* linger on the outskirts. I'm just an acquaintance. I'm not really part of the family. I'm just… along for the ride. And temporarily at that. I'm just backup. None of you really know me well."

Heather and Ethan shared an uncertain look.

"I don't think that's true," Heather said, her words hesitant.

"Most of you rarely see me outside of meetings at David's home. I've spent more time with Cliff than with any of you. And even when I do spend downtime at David's with the rest of you, your attention is usually focused on each other. Or on Adira. You haven't known me long enough and don't know me well enough to notice little alterations in my appearance or mannerisms that may be present when Gershom takes on my form." He looked to Ethan. "Only Ethan can spot those."

Confusion flooded Dana. They had all been so eager to defend Aidan. Did they really not know him well enough to see the difference if someone tried to mimic him?

"But you *all* know Seth," Aidan continued. "And you all know him well. Every one of us does. We know how he speaks… when he's angry, when he's tired, when he's amused or exasperated. We know his laugh. His growls of aggravation. We know how he moves. How he fights. How he reacts to just about everything. Because so many of us, upon transforming, admired him so much that we wanted to be just like him. Do you really think Gershom could convince any of us that he was Seth? Do you really think he could fool us? That we wouldn't know the difference even without Ethan's gift?"

Silence descended, the music still booming in the distance like a struggling heartbeat.

Neither Ethan nor Heather refuted his words.

Guilt crashed down on Dana's shoulders, so heavy she wanted to sink to her knees and weep with it.

If she hadn't tranqed the damned vampires…

If she had just thought before she acted…

"It would've only delayed the inevitable," Aidan told her gently as he drew out his cell phone.

Heather looked to her husband, tears in her eyes as Aidan dialed a number. "Ethan."

He shook his head. "Maybe Gershom abducted another *gifted one* while Aidan was with us. That's all the proof we would need to dispute this latest evidence."

Unconsoled, Heather nodded and sheathed her weapons.

"Chris," Aidan said. "It's Aidan. Ethan and I just fought thirteen vampires at Duke. We killed ten and tranqed three, so we could use a cleanup."

Dana's stomach knotted as he narrowed down their location on campus for the network leader.

How long would they have before Seth found out?

⁂

Ten hours.

Ten excruciatingly tense hours passed.

Aidan sat with Dana on a sofa across from Ethan and Heather in the couple's living room. Dana had pretty much glued herself to his side ever since they had returned home, not letting him out of her sight, which was fine by Aidan. Things were looking pretty grim, so he wanted to keep her as close as he could for as long as he could before whatever confrontation came.

She was wedged in against his side so tightly now that she might as well have sat on his lap. Aidan thought she probably *would* have if the other couple weren't present.

He wished he could tell her everything would be all right. But the grave looks on Ethan's and Heather's faces told him they feared the same thing he did — that his long-standing friendship with Seth wouldn't stop the Immortal Guardians' leader from doing what he felt he had to do in order to protect the other immortals as well as the *gifted ones*. If that meant executing Aidan, Seth would do it.

And Dana's vision would come true.

A program played on the television, but none of them watched it.

All stiffened when Aidan's phone vibrated on the table beside him.

Dana's hand tightened around his.

Giving it a squeeze, Aidan took the call. "Yes?"

"Aidan. It's Chris Reordon. Are you still with Ethan?"

"Yes. We're at his and Heather's home."

"That's what I thought. Listen, Seth needs to see you and Ethan for a minute. He could use your help with something."

Ethan and Heather, who had no difficulty hearing both sides of the conversation, shared a look.

Chris was all business, his voice lacking the dislike for Aidan that it usually carried whenever the two spoke. And nothing in his tone indicated that an ax would soon fall.

"Sure," Aidan said. "Everything okay?"

"Yeah, everything's fine."

Aidan actually felt a twinge of hope. Had Seth disregarded the captured vampires' memories after all and given Aidan the benefit of the doubt?

"Since the sun's up and Ethan is young, you'll have to teleport over," Chris went on. "We don't want Heather to be left alone guarding Dana, so we'd like you to bring them, too."

"Okay."

"Seth is worried that you might not be infusing yourself now that Dana is with you all the time. How's your strength? Would you like Richart to help you teleport the three of them over?"

"Is he there with you now?" Aidan asked.

"Yeah."

"Then yes, I would appreciate the help."

"Okay. He'll be there in a minute."

Aidan returned his phone to his pocket.

"What is it?" Dana asked.

"Seth wants to see me and Ethan down at network headquarters."

She bit her lip.

Heather leaned forward. "Aidan, do you need blood?"

He shook his head. "I'm at full strength."

Ethan shared a look with his wife. "Then why did you tell Chris you need Richart's help?"

"Because Richart is there with them now. If Seth is calling for my head, Heather and I will see it in Richart's thoughts."

"And if you don't?" Ethan asked.

Aidan forced a smile. "Then Richart teleporting you two will keep me from expending unnecessary energy." And help him remain at full strength in case Seth had *not* opted to disregard the vampires' memories.

He stood.

Dana rose beside him, clinging to his hand and curling her other hand around his biceps.

Ethan and Heather rose, too.

Richart appeared just inside the front door. When he saw them, he strolled over to join them and offered Dana a smile. "You must be Dana."

She nodded and forced a smile but failed to erase the pensive look from her pretty face.

"I'm Richart d'Alençon. I believe you've met my sister Lisette." He extended his hand, palm up. "It's a pleasure to meet you." When Dana placed her hand in his, Richart carried it to his lips and pressed a kiss to her knuckles.

"Nice to meet you, too."

Giving her a friendly smile, Richart released her hand and met

Aidan's gaze. "If you're conserving energy, I can take all three of them but will have to make two trips."

Richart was only a couple of centuries old, so teleporting more than one or two people at a time was difficult for him.

Aidan gave the young French immortal's mind a quick scan and found nothing to indicate they were about to face Seth's wrath.

He glanced at Heather, whose face lit with hope. "If you take Ethan and Heather, I can take Dana."

Richart nodded. "Shall we go then? Seth wants us to teleport directly to Chris's office."

Ethan and Heather clasped hands and moved to stand beside Richart. The French immortal touched Ethan's shoulder, then looked to Aidan.

Aidan glanced down at Dana and murmured, "Here we go."

When she gave him a silent nod, he teleported to Chris's office.

Richart, Ethan, and Heather appeared beside them just as Chris entered through the boardroom doorway.

He dipped his chin in a brief nod of greeting as he set some papers on his cluttered desk. "Thanks for coming. This shouldn't take long, then you can go back home and get some rest."

Well, hell. That sounded good. Had Aidan been wrong? Had Seth seen through the vampires' bullshit memories? Could Dana's vision of Seth trying to kill him be wrong?

Or had they, perhaps, managed to alter the course of events so it would never come to pass?

She had dreamed the vampires who attacked them in her home would kill both her and Aidan. But they had survived.

Chris strode toward them and offered Dana his hand. "You must be Dana. I'm Chris Reordon, head of the East Coast division of the network that aids Immortal Guardians."

Dana started to take his hand but jerked her own back at the last minute. "Wait. Did you say Chris Reordon?"

"Yes."

She narrowed her eyes as her brows drew down in a disapproving scowl. "Are you the asshole who keeps trying to make Aidan out to be the bad guy?"

Ethan barked out a laugh, then caught himself.

Aidan struggled to contain his own amusement as Heather

grinned and masculine laughter floated out of the boardroom.

Much to Aidan's surprise, Chris took no offense.

Smiling, Chris said, "I *used* to be the asshole who was trying to make Aidan out to be the bad guy. *But*," he hastened to add when Dana opened her mouth, ready to verbally lambaste him, "I'm now the guy who is trying to help everyone else prove that Aidan is *not* the bad guy."

Her expression still unwelcome, Dana grudgingly shook his hand.

Unperturbed, Chris got down to business. "Aidan, would you join us in the boardroom? Richart, you can come, too. Heather, Dana, Ethan, please make yourselves comfortable. If you need anything, my assistant is right outside that door." He pointed.

Aidan gently disentangled himself from Dana's grip. "I'll be back in a minute." Dipping his head, he gave her a swift kiss, then followed Chris into the boardroom.

Richart entered behind them.

The door snicked shut.

Seth, Zach, and a man Aidan didn't recognize stood on the opposite side of the room.

The third man was garbed much like Zach usually was. Black pants, black boots and nothing else. Like Zach, he apparently didn't wear a shirt so it wouldn't restrict the huge dark wings that peeked over the man's shoulders.

Fury filled Aidan. Was this Gershom? Had they caught him?

"You son of a bitch," Aidan growled and lunged forward.

Richart grabbed him by the arm and struggled to hold him back.

Seth threw up a hand and stepped in front of the Other. "This isn't Gershom."

Aidan stilled. "What?"

"This isn't Gershom," Seth repeated.

Confusion filled him. "But he's an Other." Seth, Zach, and Gershom were the only Others who had strayed from the path.

Weren't they?

"Jared has been working with us in secret for about a year now," Seth said, moving aside so Aidan could examine the newcomer. "The Others don't know it. Nor do most of the immortals in the area."

Aidan stared at the Other.

Jared was playing both sides, pretending to walk the line with the Others while aiding the Immortal Guardians? That was pretty damned ballsy. Zach had once been tortured by the Others just for telling Seth his phone wasn't working when the immortals in North Carolina had needed him. What the hell would the Others do if they found out Jared was actually *working* with them?

"Why take the risk?" Aidan couldn't resist asking.

Jared's lips turned up in a grim smile. "A prophetic vision showed me Gershom succeeding in launching Armageddon. In the vision, no one survived. Humans, *gifted ones*, immortals, vampires, and Others all perished."

Hell. Aidan looked to Seth. "Isn't Jared being here with us dangerous?"

"Yes," Seth answered. "But we want to confirm something and could use his aid."

Confirm what? "Is this about the vampires we captured?" May as well put it right out there.

Seth shook his head. "They're being held at another location. I haven't had a chance to see them yet."

Damn. There went the hope that Seth had read their minds and seen past the bullshit.

"This is about the surveillance videos," Seth explained.

"The ones that showed my doppelgänger with the *gifted ones*?"

"Yes. I'd like to try something."

As Aidan watched, Seth's shape changed.

Zach and Jared's forms shifted as well.

When the three finished transforming, Aidan smiled.

Maybe all hope *wasn't* lost.

<hr />

Ethan watched Dana's knee bob up and down, her teeth nibble her lower lip, and wished he could reassure her, but he felt as anxious as she looked.

She sat in one of the chairs by Chris's desk.

Ethan and Heather shared a nearby sofa that was so long Ethan guessed Chris probably slept on it on occasion.

The door to the boardroom opened.

Chris leaned out. "Ethan, will you join us?"

Ethan squeezed Heather's hand, then rose and crossed to the boardroom.

Richart stood just inside, arms crossed, a look of amusement on his face.

Chris closed the door.

Somewhat reassured by Richart's relaxed demeanor, Ethan glanced around.

Aidan stood at the other end of the room, beyond the long oak table, staring back.

Ethan took in the figures to either side of him.

Four Aidans stared back, to be precise.

"Okay," he said, eyeing the quadruplets, "this is weird."

Richart laughed.

"All right," Chris said. "Let's do this."

Ethan looked from Chris to the Aidans. "Do what?"

Chris motioned to the Scottish immortals. "Can you tell which one is the real Aidan?"

"Yeah." Ethan pointed. "That one. Second from the left."

The other three swore.

Ethan didn't ask if he was right. He already knew it.

Chris gaped at him. "How did you know that? And so quickly? You didn't even hear them talk."

Ethan shrugged. "I didn't have to. There are little things, like— "

"Don't tell us," the Aidan on the far right cut him off in what Ethan thought was an impressively close imitation of Aidan's brogue. "We have to figure it out ourselves."

"Hey, not bad," Ethan said. "You sound a lot like him, Seth."

Seth swore. "Turn your back."

Laughing, Ethan did so.

This was good. This was *very* good. If Seth had seen the vampires' memories, they clearly hadn't fooled him.

Seth wanted Aidan to be innocent.

This was definitely good.

Aidan stood still while Seth, Zach, and Jared—all of whom had shape-shifted into mirror images of him—walked around him in slow circles, scrutinizing him from head to toe.

Minutes passed.

"Frown," one of his look-alikes ordered.

He did so.

"Smile," another commanded.

He did.

"Squint your eyes," the third said.

It was like taking orders from himself.

He'd seen his own reflection in calm waters, looking glasses, and mirrors for millennia, yet even *he* thought they all looked exactly like him. Sounded like him, too.

Aidan cleared his throat. "I have to say I agree with Ethan. This is weird."

Ethan laughed, his back still to them. And Aidan could hear relief in his laugh, so Ethan must be thinking the same thing he was: this was good.

Aidan's three carbon copies lined up again.

"Okay," Chris told Ethan, "let's try this again."

Ethan turned around.

Chris nodded to them. "Which one is the real Aidan?"

Ethan pointed at Aidan. "Him. Still the second from the left."

The other three swore.

Chris looked astounded. "He was right?"

Aidan grinned. "Yes."

"That's amazing," Richart mumbled. "I can discern no difference between them."

Chris turned to Ethan. "What gave it away?"

One of the imitators held up a hand. "Don't answer that," Seth said in his usual voice. "If he tells you, Gershom will be able to read it in your thoughts."

"Oh." Chris grimaced. "Right. Yeah, don't tell me."

Ethan smiled. "Want to try again?"

Seth-Aidan shook his head. "Now we need to see if Dana can tell us apart."

Surprised, Aidan turned to him. "Why?" Then he frowned. *Is that how I look when I'm exasperated?*

"So we'll know," Seth explained, "whether or not she'll be able to recognize that he isn't you if Gershom comes to her in your form as we believe he did with Veronica and the others."

"Oh." Damn, that was disconcerting. Aidan would like to think Dana would be able to tell the difference, but even Chris and Richart couldn't tell them apart, and he'd known them a lot longer than he had Dana.

Aidan zipped over to the door when Chris opened it. "Dana," he said, leaning out.

Relief blanketed her features when she saw he was all right. "Yes?"

He smiled to let her know all was well. "Would you join us, please?"

"Sure."

Heather rose. "Can I come, too?"

Chris nudged Aidan back inside and motioned for him to hurry and rejoin the look-alikes. "Sure."

Aidan dashed back to the others and stilled before the women entered.

Dana didn't know what to expect when she passed through the doorway but ended up in a very large, swanky boardroom.

Wow. These Immortal Guardians and their network had money. A lot of it, by the looks of things.

Richart smiled at her and nodded toward the other end of the room.

Dana swiveled around, started to smile, then froze. "Whoa!" Her eyes widened. Her mouth fell open.

Four Aidans stood on the opposite side of the room.

Not four men who *resembled* Aidan, but four Aidans.

Slowly, she walked around the long table and stared at them.

The moment stretched.

They sent her encouraging smiles.

"Okay," she announced, "I'm not gonna lie. This is freaking me out a little."

Richart laughed.

Chris moved to stand beside her. "Can you tell which one is the real Aidan?"

She moved to stand in front of the Aidan on the far left.

He had the right height. The right build. Same hair. Same handsome-as-hell face.

When she had learned someone was posing as Aidan, she had thought—if no other way—she would see something in his eyes that would tip her off and help her discern whether it was *her* Aidan or a faker, but…

She moved on to the second one. Then the third. And the last.

She just wasn't *seeing* anything. "Can I talk to them?" she asked Chris.

"Of course," the Aidan before her responded. "We want you to be certain."

The third Aidan repeated the response. Then the second. And the first.

They even sounded like him.

So how else could she tell the difference?

An idea occurred. One she didn't particularly like.

"Aidan," she murmured, "don't be mad, okay?"

All four chorused, "Okay."

Drawing in a deep breath, she rose onto her toes, reached up, cupped the back of the fourth Aidan's head, and drew him down for a kiss.

His lips were soft like Aidan's. After a moment's hesitation, those soft lips parted. And like Aidan, he slid one arm around her waist and pulled her up against him as he deepened the contact.

Holy hell, he could kiss, teasing her as skillfully as Aidan did, his mouth moving on hers in a way that should have made her heart pound, but—

She jerked away and took a step back. "You're not Aidan."

"No," the other Aidans all growled in unison, "he isn't."

Then their eyes flashed bright.

Ethan gaped. "Holy crap. Dana just kissed Seth."

Heather gasped as her mouth fell open. "That's *Seth*?"

The eyes of three of the Aidans faded to a dark brown color.

The *real* Aidan's eyes remained bright as he glowered. "Yes. And Seth kissed her back."

The Aidan on the right shifted into Seth's taller form and held up both hands. "I was trying to convince her I was you," he said, his voice low and calming. "If I hadn't, we wouldn't know that she *does* have a way of identifying which one is you."

"By *kissing* him?" Aidan growled.

Dana scowled and propped her hands on her hips. "Okay. If you do this again, I am *not* going to kiss all of you. Especially since I now know I have *another* means of figuring out who is who."

Seth turned to her with interest. "What other means?"

Chris opened his mouth.

Dana held up a hand to silence him and arched a brow at Seth in challenge. "Care to test me again?"

He nodded. "Turn your back, please."

Dana gave them her back.

The scuffling of shoes filled the air, followed by silence.

Chris nodded to Dana. "Okay, you can turn around."

Dana swiveled around and faced them. Pursing her lips, she tilted her head to one side, then the other.

None of the men's eyes glowed. And the four of them really did look identical.

Walking up to the Aidan on the far right, she studied him closely. "You suck at dating," she announced, deadpan.

He grinned, his brown eyes sparkling with amusement. "Yes, I do."

She moved on to the next one. "You suck at dating."

Aidan Number Two grinned, his brown eyes sparkling with amusement. "Yes, I do."

She could identify no difference between them.

It was very unsettling.

Dana said the same to the next Aidan and the last, both of whom imitated the other Aidans' responses.

She moved closer to the last and rested her hand on his shoulder. Then, without warning, she rammed her knee up into his groin.

Groaning, the man's eyes flashed golden as he slammed his knees together and folded over.

Stepping back, she smiled. "One down. Three to go."

The Aidan beside him burst into guffaws as he shifted into Zach's form.

The Aidan beside *him* shifted into Seth.

The Aidan on the end—*her* Aidan—remained unchanged as he laughed in delight.

Dismay filled Dana as she turned to the Aidan who groaned as he shifted into the form of a tall man with no shirt and… wings? "Oh! I'm sorry. I'm so sorry." She looked at Seth with a wince. "I hate to admit this, but I was kind of hoping that was you."

Far from being offended, Seth laughed. "Had it been me, I would've deserved it. I hope you will forgive me for kissing you."

Relieved, she sent him a wry smile. "Since it tipped me off to your eyes, you're forgiven."

Seth brows flew up. "My eyes?"

She nodded. "When I kissed you, Aidan's eyes flared bright amber. Yours"—she looked at Zach and the recovering man—"all glowed golden."

Frowning, Seth looked at Ethan and the others.

They nodded.

"Hmm." The Immortal Guardians' leader closed his eyes.

Still grinning, Aidan crossed to Dana and wrapped an arm around her waist.

Rising onto her toes, she kissed him. Thoroughly. Then lowered her heels to the floor and gave him a grin. "Just making sure you're you."

He laughed.

Seth opened his eyes. "What about now?"

Aidan shook his head. "Still golden."

All three of the elder immortals then tried to alter the color their eyes glowed. Multiple times. None succeeded.

"That's interesting to know," Seth concluded. "Even when we aren't gripped by strong emotion, we can't control what color our eyes glow. And Gershom's eyes glow golden like ours."

Dana winked up at Aidan. "So all I have to do to make sure you're you is either kiss the stuffing out of you or piss you off."

Smiling, he pressed a kiss to her forehead. "Piss me off. If it's me, you can always make it up to me later."

She laughed.

"Well," Seth said. "I should go see the vampires you captured last night."

Dread pooled in Dana's stomach. He hadn't seen the vampires yet?

Seth turned to the unfamiliar man with wings. "Jared, you

should leave before your absence is noted."

Nodding, Jared vanished without another word.

Seth drew out a pocket watch, flipped it open, and glanced at the time. "The head of the West Coast division of the network wants to see me. It shouldn't take too long, then I'll pop over to speak with the vampires and read their minds." Tucking the watch away again, he looked to Chris. "They're in the missile silo you refurbished?"

"Yeah," Chris confirmed. "The guards there are expecting you."

"Good."

"Seth?" Aidan said.

"Yes?"

"I need to take Cliff into the sunlight for an hour. I didn't do it yesterday and don't want to miss another."

Seth hesitated. "Is it that bad?"

Aidan nodded. "Have you not read his thoughts?"

"Not in a while." A moment passed while Seth tilted his head as though listening. His brow furrowed. "All right. But take Ethan, Heather, and Dana with you and make sure Ethan has ample shade."

"I will."

Seth vanished.

Zach dipped his chin in an abrupt nod, then vanished, too.

Richart yawned. "Do you want me to help you teleport Ethan and Heather?"

Aidan smiled. "No. I've got it. Go home and get some rest."

The French immortal nodded. "Call me if you need me." In the next instant, he disappeared.

"Who is Cliff?" Dana asked. She'd learned so many new names in the last few days that she couldn't remember.

"My friend who is ill," Aidan told her.

Oh. Right. The one with the brain injury or brain-related illness.

"He's a vampire, Dana," Aidan admitted.

She stared at him. "I thought vampires were the bad guys." According to her gift, the man Aidan worried over was a friend, not an enemy.

"They usually are. But Cliff surrendered to us in battle a few years ago, hoping we'd be able to help him hold off the insanity —

or cure it altogether. He's been living here at the network ever since."

She didn't ask if they'd succeeded in helping Cliff. The concern she had felt when she touched Aidan during his second reading told her they had not and that his condition was worsening.

"He's become a strong ally to us. And a good friend to me. He's an honorable man. He's just…"

"Infected with a virus that is slowly robbing him of his sanity?" she finished for him.

"Yes."

That was messed up.

"We discovered that the sun silences the voices in his head. So I've been taking him into sunlight every day and healing him in real time to keep it from harming him."

Dana's admiration for Aidan soared. "Is he dangerous?"

"Not to you. I vow it."

And she trusted Aidan implicitly. "Okay."

Aidan dipped his head and gave her a brief kiss, then drew her into his arms for a hug. "Thank you."

She patted his back. "Let's go help your friend."

Chapter Sixteen

CHRIS OPENED THE BOARDROOM DOOR and led them into his office. "I'll turn the alarm off for ten minutes to give you time to teleport out. Call me when you're ready to bring him back and I'll turn it off again and alert the guards."

Aidan nodded as he took Dana's hand and led her out of Chris's office. Ethan and Heather followed. An attractive brunette sat at a large desk in an outer office. Dana smiled at her.

The woman smiled back and gave them a nod as she rose, picked up a stack of folders, and headed into Chris's office.

Dana accompanied Aidan down one hallway then another until they came to a pair of elevators. Men garbed in black cargo pants, black boots, and black shirts stood sentry on either side of the elevator doors, clutching automatic weapons.

Dana thought they stood a little straighter when they spied the immortals approaching them.

"Sirs," one of them said with a respectful nod to both men. "Ma'ams," he said to Heather and Dana with equal respect.

She smiled.

"Sublevel 5?" he asked.

"Yes," Aidan confirmed.

Turning to the elevators, the guard pressed a button. The doors swished open.

Aidan drew Dana inside. Once Ethan and Heather joined them, the guard stepped inside, too.

The doors swished closed.

As Dana watched curiously, the guard removed a plastic card

from his pocket and swiped it in what looked like one of those high-tech security gadgets she'd seen in movies.

He punched in a code, then pressed a button that said S5. A familiar weightlessness struck for a second as the elevator began to descend. The guard took up a position in front of the doors.

Dana eyed his weapon and the pockets that bulged with extra ammo. Were the guards at the network there to keep their enemies out or to keep the vampires in?

She glanced up at Aidan. "How many vampires live here?"

Aidan pursed his lips. "Seven, I think. Or is it eight now, Paul?"

"It's seven, sir," the guard replied.

Seven vampires with superstrength and speed who were afflicted with varying stages of insanity?

Yeah. The guards must be there to keep the vampires in.

The elevator eased to a halt. A bell dinged seconds before the doors swished open.

More guards—a *lot* more—clustered around a desk in front of the elevator and stood sentry before a door to a stairwell. Several more manned doors down a long white hallway.

One of the guards strode forward. "Sir."

"Todd," Aidan greeted him. "Is Cliff in his apartment?"

"No, sir. He's in the lab. The last I checked, he was running on one of the treadmills."

Aidan's look turned grim. "We'll be teleporting out with him shortly."

"Yes, sir. Mr. Reordon already informed us over the walkie."

Dana squeezed Aidan's hand as he led her down the hallway. *What is it?*

Vampires usually sleep all day, he told her telepathically. *If Cliff is on the treadmill, it means the voices are so loud he can't rest and needs something physically strenuous to do to help quash his desire to commit violence.*

That wasn't good.

Dana found her stomach fluttering a little with nerves as she followed Aidan inside the lab.

The huge room seemed to be divided into segments. A lot of medical instruments and gurneys occupied one area. Four desks, each boasting a computer, formed a square in another. A large shelving unit full of patient folders like those she saw in her doctor's office took up one wall while doorways provided glimpses of smaller rooms that boasted MRI machines, X-ray machines, and more. One room seemed only to house huge refrigerators that contained she didn't want to know what. Blood? Tissue samples?

Not snack foods, she would guess.

Treadmills, exercise bikes, and weight benches sporting more weights than she thought five Mr. Universes could lift took up one end of the room.

The lab was currently empty save one occupant. An African-American man ran on one of the treadmills, his legs and feet moving so swiftly that they were only a blur while his upper body remained mostly stationary.

It was a weird effect.

Upon seeing them, he stopped running.

Odd. He wasn't even sweating.

Dana studied him as he stepped off the treadmill.

Sadness filled her. He looked so young, like a junior or senior in college. His skin was smooth milk chocolate. Dark dreadlocks fell past his shoulders, tidy despite his run.

His handsome face did not lighten with welcome as he approached them. A muscle flexed in his strong jaw as though he was grinding his teeth. His eyes glowed bright amber as they met and clung to Aidan's.

He appeared to be exactly what he was: a man perched upon a precipice, trying like hell not to tumble over the edge.

Aidan tightened his grip on Dana's hand. *Huddle up*, he instructed mentally. *We need to go now.*

Ethan and Heather moved forward and placed their hands on Aidan's shoulders.

As soon as Cliff came within reach, Aidan gripped his arm and teleported them all away.

Blinding sunlight bathed them.

Ethan and Heather darted away.

Dana blinked against the sudden brightness and threw up a hand to shade her eyes as she glanced around.

She, Aidan, and Cliff stood on a neatly mown lawn about the

size of a football field. Tall evergreen trees rose around its edges, a playground for the birds she could hear but couldn't see.

Aidan released her hand. "Ethan, are you all right?"

"I'm fine," Ethan responded.

Dana swiveled around and spotted Ethan and Heather standing on the shaded back porch of a one-story house that was roughly thirty yards away. She thought Ethan's skin might be a little pink, but the extra color swiftly faded.

The house that sheltered them was pretty, painted a pale gray with white trim. The porch stretched the entire width of the home and boasted two comfy, cushioned chairs and a swing upon which the immortal couple soon settled.

She knew this place. Knew that swing. She and Aidan had curled up on it and enjoyed the evening breeze once after he had cooked dinner for her. This was Aidan's home.

Lowering her hand, she glanced at Aidan and Cliff as her eyes adjusted to the brightness.

All of Aidan's attention remained focused on the young vampire.

Dana wasn't sure if she should stay or go join his friends on the porch, but felt reluctant to leave him.

Cliff's tense shoulders slowly relaxed. The fingers he had curled into fists loosened and fell open. The tic in his jaw ceased. His eyes lost their amber glow and darkened to a warm brown as the crease between his brows smoothed.

A long sigh escaped him as he looked at Aidan. His lips curled up in a faint smile. "Thank you."

Aidan smiled back, keeping his hand on Cliff's arm. "Sorry I missed you yesterday."

Cliff shook his head, his manner almost easygoing now. "You have a lot on your plate." When he shifted his gaze to Dana, his smile grew. "Are you Dana?"

She nodded, her nerves settling now that he seemed less like someone who could attack at any moment.

He offered his hand. "It's really nice to meet you."

"It's nice to meet you, too." Returning his smile, she shook his hand... and had to fight not to recoil as images of violence filled her head. All took place at night, the shift from bright daylight to darkness and back to daylight making her dizzy. But she steadfastly kept her smile in place as she released his hand.

Had she not gone hunting with Aidan and his friends the previous night, she likely would have stumbled backward and freaked out the way she had the first couple of times she'd had visions of Aidan engaged in battle.

"Sorry about that," Cliff said, his smile shifting into an expression of regret. "I hope I didn't scare you."

"Not at all," she lied.

Aidan cut her a glance. Did he know her so well that he saw through the untruth?

"Yes, I did," Cliff responded, "but I appreciate your not wanting to hurt my feelings."

Cliff knew, too? How?

Oh. Right. Her heartbeat was racing. And everyone else could hear it.

"I forgot your visions are touch-sensitive," Cliff continued. "Had I remembered, I wouldn't have shaken your hand."

"I'm sorry," she returned, not knowing what else to say. "It kind of sucks that even when I keep a straight face, you guys can hear my heart race and know I'm unnerved."

Aidan's lips turned up. "Actually, your face is very expressive. We would've known even if we *hadn't* heard your heartbeat pick up."

"Really?"

Cliff nodded. "It was pretty obvious."

"Damn it," she grumbled. "I thought I was better than that."

Cliff grinned, his eyes twinkling with amusement. "You sound like Ami. Ami can't lie worth a damn and actually considers it a flaw."

Aidan laughed. "She really can't. It's an endless source of amusement for Marcus."

At last Dana relaxed.

"Gossip is flowing freely at the network," Cliff mentioned, his eyes still on Dana. "Did you really tranq Roland Warbrook?"

Dana smiled. "Yes."

"*And* Seth," Aidan added with what sounded oddly like pride.

Cliff's jaw dropped. "You tranqed Seth?"

"I *tried* to," she admitted with some disgruntlement, "but apparently the tranquilizer doesn't work on him."

Both men laughed.

In the next instant, as though summoned by their speech, Seth appeared.

Dana gasped.

Perhaps twenty yards away, the powerful Immortal Guardians' leader bent forward and braced his hands on his knees. Blood coated half his face and matted his hair on one side. His shirt and coat boasted dozens of holes torn by large caliber bullets. Blood saturated the shredded fabric, glistening beneath the sun's rays.

The porch swing squeaked as Ethan and Heather leapt to their feet.

Aidan took a step forward. "Seth?"

A low growl rumbled forth from Seth's chest, raising the hairs on the back of Dana's neck. Little lumps of metal fell from his clothing and hit the grass as the ground began to tremble.

Oh shit.

"Seth?" Aidan repeated, keeping his hand on Cliff's arm. "What happened? Are you all right?"

"What happened?" Seth snarled, then spat blood. "I teleported over to the missile silo to read the vampires' minds only to discover them wreaking fucking havoc as they attempted to make what was very nearly a successful escape." Reaching into his back pocket, he drew out a white handkerchief and wiped his blood-slick mouth.

"You caught them?" Aidan asked.

"Of course I caught them," Seth snapped. "*After* they killed or seriously injured most of the guards. I caught them, incapacitated them, read their fucking minds, then destroyed them."

Clouds began to gather overhead, fluffy white swiftly thickening and darkening to gray.

Thunder rumbled as a breeze picked up, tugging at Dana's hair.

"Oh shit," Cliff whispered, his hands once more curling into fists.

Dana's treacherous heart began to race again.

"Seth," Aidan said, his voice full of reason, "you know that wasn't me in their memories. Just like it wasn't me in the security footage. Even Ethan confirmed it wasn't me in the videos."

"I know that wasn't you in the videos," Seth said, tucking his handkerchief away. "It was Gershom."

Dana didn't breathe a sigh of relief though. Seth's words continued to resonate with fury.

"But that *was* you," he continued, "in the vampires' memories, taking advantage of Gershom's bullshit and telling the vampires to increase their numbers and attack your immortal brethren, to attack you and Dana so Dana would feel compelled to transform for you."

Reaching out with his free hand, Aidan settled it on Dana's hip and eased her behind him. *Heather*, she heard him instruct mentally, *get Dana to safety*.

"No," Dana blurted.

Heather zipped up beside her, picked her up, and zipped back to the porch. "Get inside," she ordered as soon as Dana regained her feet.

"No," Dana refused. "I'm not leaving him."

Aidan swore.

"Seth," Ethan said behind them, "that wasn't Aidan. It couldn't have been. He's been with us ever since the attack at Dana's home."

Dana glanced back at him just as Heather grabbed her husband's arm to keep him from stepping out of the shade of the porch. Was Ethan so photosensitive that even with clouds gathering and dampening the sun's rays, he couldn't go out without burning and blistering?

"*Aidan*," Seth growled, "is the one who *orchestrated* the attack at Dana's home."

The trees began to thrash and sway as though beaten by his anger.

Just teleport away, Dana thought desperately, hoping Aidan would hear her.

Instead, he took another step toward Seth.

Aidan stilled when Seth held up a hand, silently commanding him to halt.

Backing up a step, then another, Seth turned and paced away.

In an attempt to regain control over his temper?

"It doesn't make sense," Aidan said, keeping his voice calm. "I love Dana. Telling the vampires to attack her would've put her in danger. I would never do that. No more than I would put my fellow immortals in danger. You know that, Seth. Because you know *me*."

"Yes," Seth acknowledged. "I know you. Well enough to tell the difference between you and someone mimicking you."

Aidan frowned. "I thought... No. Even you couldn't tell that wasn't me in the videos. Not until Ethan confirmed it."

"I... *lied*!" he roared. "Of course I knew it wasn't you. I also knew Reordon wouldn't believe me, that he would assume I was just being cautious because I felt guilty for misjudging you once before. That's why I brought Ethan in. I wanted Reordon to think that whoever was mimicking you was so good that even *I* could be fooled! I was trying to *help* you!"

What? Aidan frowned. Seth had known that wasn't him in the videos?

"I didn't expect you to betray me!"

"I didn't," Aidan vowed.

Halting, Seth swiveled just enough for Aidan to view his bloody profile.

Beside Aidan, Cliff stiffened and began to strain against Aidan's hold. Violent thoughts slithered into Aidan's mind via his gift. Cliff's thoughts. His sudden, desperate need to rip Seth apart for threatening his friend.

Heather, Aidan warned telepathically, *I may need you to keep Cliff in check if this escalates. Don't let him attack Seth.*

Seth laughed, a chilling sound that held no mirth. Only anger and bitterness.

Even from this distance, with Seth not fully facing him, Aidan could read the hurt in his leader's—his friend's—glowing golden eyes and felt his stomach sink.

Seth shook his head. "Do you really think I don't know you as well as you know me? Do you really think I don't know *all* of you as well as you know me? I've watched over you all since your *births*. I watched over you when you were *gifted ones* and then I took you under my wing after you transformed and became immortals. I made you part of my family. Brought you into my world. Did every fucking thing I could think of to help you find happiness or at least some contentment in this existence. *I know you, Aidan!*"

"Then you know that wasn't me in *any* of the vampires' memories," Aidan repeated, frustration rising. How could Seth possibly believe otherwise?

"You think I'm mistaken?"

"I know you are."

Seth faced him. "Then let's see who's right, shall we?" His eyes flashed brighter.

Pain struck, as sharp as a knife stabbing Aidan in the eye, cutting through his skull and tearing its way through his mind.

Crying out, he released Cliff and gripped his head.

Cliff leapt forward with a snarl.

Someone swept past in a blur as Aidan staggered beneath the agony of Seth forcibly toppling his mental barriers and tearing though his memories.

Heather bumped into him as she dragged a struggling Cliff backward to the porch.

Something wet tickled Aidan's upper lip as he sank to his knees. His hearing wavered as blood filled his ears, then spilled out. The world around him went red as blood stung his eyes.

"Stop it!" Dana shouted. "You're killing him!"

Seth wasn't killing him. But any hope Aidan had held on to that this wasn't Seth — that it was Gershom instead — died a swift death as the pain peaked.

Gershom wouldn't have bothered to search Aidan's memories for something that would prove his innocence. But Seth *would*. Seth would explore every option, gather every piece of evidence he could before condemning Aidan.

The pain stopped abruptly.

Shaken, Aidan braced his hands on the grass and fought to catch his breath.

The sound of blades slipping from sheaths met his ears.

Wiping blood from his eyes, Aidan climbed to his feet and straightened.

Seth strode toward him, swords in hand, more menacing and terrifying than Aidan had ever seen him. "*How could you betray me like this?*" he roared in anguish.

Fear sliced through Aidan. Seth had read his thoughts and *still* thought him guilty?

He must have seen something. Must have found memories even Aidan couldn't access. Which meant Gershom *had* mind-controlled him. And Aidan *had* done the things he'd found in the vampires' memories. He had done them under Gershom's compulsion and just couldn't remember them. Aidan had sent those vampires to attack Dana in her home.

And those vampires would've killed her had her vision not forewarned them.

He staggered again, this time from shock.

How had Gershom mind-controlled him without Aidan knowing?

And how had he left so little trace of his influence that Seth believed Aidan the villain, not a victim? Was Gershom truly that powerful?

Seth blurred.

Aidan barely had time to drawn his own swords before Seth struck. Still thrown by the revelation that he had actually committed the crimes Seth thought him guilty of, Aidan incurred several wounds before he got his shit together and began to defend himself in earnest.

He had been sparring with Seth for nearly three thousand years. Seth had even told him that Aidan was one of only a handful of immortals who could still afford him a challenge. So once Aidan shook off the shock, he actually began to inflict a wound or two of his own.

The thoughts of everyone else present—excluding Ethan—clamored in his head. He couldn't focus on keeping Seth from killing him *and* shut off his telepathy.

Cliff wanted to kill Seth for hurting Aidan.

Heather was torn, wanting to defend Aidan but not wanting to betray Seth.

Dana was terrified, weeping as Ethan held her back.

Then Cliff broke loose. In the next instant, the young vampire appeared at Aidan's side. With astounding agility, he filched two blades from Aidan's coat and struck at Seth.

Shite!

Distracted, Aidan failed to fend off Seth's latest blow. Agony flashed through him as Seth's blade drove through his side. Stumbling backward, Aidan watched in horror as a furious Seth turned on Cliff, carving a path across the vamp's chest with his other blade. When Cliff didn't go down, Seth backhanded him so hard Aidan heard bone shatter.

Cliff flew through the air and crashed into a tree trunk, then fell thirty feet to land in a heap in the grass.

"No!" Aidan leapt forward and struck Seth once more.

"That's not Seth!" Ethan shouted abruptly. "That's not Seth! It's Gershom!"

Before Aidan could ask if he was sure, all hell broke loose.

Heather and Ethan leapt into the fray, blades gleaming.

Cliff lurched to his feet, reclaimed the weapons he'd dropped, then rejoined the battle.

Aidan didn't know where Dana was while the four of them fought Seth—or rather Gershom—but worried she, too, would enter to fight.

Seth! he bellowed mentally, losing strength and speed as he racked up wounds.

If he, Ethan, Heather, and Cliff could just hold Gershom until—

Seth appeared a few feet away.

Relief suffused Aidan, easing some of the pain. Despite Ethan's claim, Aidan hadn't been sure until then that the man they all fought really *wasn't* Seth.

Zach appeared beside Seth.

Seth's eyes flashed bright gold. Lightning streaked across the sky and struck a nearby tree.

Still bearing Seth's appearance, Gershom laughed, then vanished.

Caught midswing, Aidan, Ethan, Heather, and Cliff nearly fell on their asses.

"Zach!" Seth hissed, striding forward.

Zach vanished.

Breathing hard, Aidan shook his head as his leader approached. "You don't know how fucking glad I am that wasn't you."

Cliff bellowed in frustration when his prey disappeared. When he turned and noted Seth's presence, his lips curled up in a chilling smile as he lunged forward.

Seth held up a hand.

Cliff stopped short, held in place by telekinesis.

While the vampire struggled to free himself from the unseen force, Seth moved forward and touched his shoulder.

Cliff's struggles ceased. The anger and bloodlust fueling the fire in his eyes drained away as lucidity returned. His wounds and blistering skin healed.

"It wasn't me," Seth said, forcing calm tones despite the fury Aidan could feel riding him. "That was Gershom."

Cliff nodded.

A weight struck Aidan in the back, pushing him forward a startled step.

Dana hugged him with all her might, unintentionally doubling the pain of his wounds.

Dropping his weapons, Aidan reached behind him and shifted her around to his front. "It's okay, sweetheart. I'm okay."

His words did little to soothe her as she sobbed against his chest.

Seth gently touched her arm. "Step back a moment, please, and let me heal him."

Nodding, Dana allowed Seth to disentangle her from Aidan and stood staring up at them with tear-filled eyes.

Seth placed a hand on Aidan's chest. Healing energy swept through him, mending his wounds and erasing his pain.

"You didn't know he wasn't me?" Seth asked quietly.

"No. He was very convincing."

Seth turned to Heather and touched her shoulder, healing her wounds.

Guilt wormed its way through Aidan when he noticed the red splotches on her clothing as well as Ethan's. They had incurred those wounds trying to protect him.

Seth moved on to Ethan, healing both his wounds and his blistering skin. "You didn't know either?"

Ethan shook his head. "His wounds and the blood that poured from them explained away all the little differences I noticed. I had my suspicions, but wasn't sure until he hurt Cliff. I know you wouldn't do that, even when enraged."

Withdrawing his touch, Seth backed away. "Take Cliff to the

network, then go straight to David's. I need to help Zach track Gershom."

"Wait," Aidan blurted. "Gershom claimed he was wounded at the missile silo. He said the vampires had freed themselves and — "

Seth shook his head. "I was there when you summoned me. All is well."

Before any of them could reply, Seth vanished.

Aidan hastily grabbed Ethan and Cliff's shoulders and used his healing gift to keep them from blistering again as the clouds above dissipated, letting the sun fight its way through to them. "Call Chris," he told Ethan, "and tell him we're on our way."

Dana wrapped her arms around him, resting her face on his chest. "Do you think they'll catch him?"

"I sure as hell hope so," Aidan murmured.

<hr />

Dana's stomach burned with nerves as she stood in the shade of a huge barn that served as a garage for Immortal Guardians' vehicles.

"We're going to head inside now," Ethan said.

Aidan nodded.

Ethan took Heather's hand. The two blurred as they darted forward, their indistinct forms racing down the drive and around to the front of the house, disappearing from view.

Aidan had followed Seth's instructions and teleported them all to the network. While Dana had struggled to get her hands to stop shaking, the immortals and Cliff had availed themselves of bagged blood to replenish what they had lost in the battle with Seth.

Or rather Gershom.

Dana's stomach continued to tie itself up in a knot.

How could they defeat an enemy who was so good at camouflaging himself as someone else that he could stand right next to them and they wouldn't even know it?

Even after siphoning new blood into his veins, Aidan had admitted he wasn't at full strength and had borrowed a network car with dark-tinted windows to drive them all to David's home instead of teleporting them.

Aidan curled his fingers around hers.

Dana clutched his hand in a death grip. "Are you sure you're okay?"

He nodded. "I'm fine. I just need a deep, healing sleep. I'll be able to get one here without worrying over our safety."

She looked again at the sprawling house. Apparently this was the hub of the Immortal Guardians' world here in North Carolina, their favorite place to relax and unwind after a night of hunting and slaying vampires. So who knew how many of them were in there.

"It'll be all right," Aidan murmured, leaning down to press a kiss to her temple. "There's no reason to be nervous. They're all just like me."

Right. She was just rattled from the close call with Gershom.

"Ethan and Heather are already in there, though it sounds like they're retiring," Aidan murmured. "Since Seth and Zach are chasing down Gershom, we shouldn't have to worry about the bastard popping in and pretending to be me or anything like that. And even if he did, Ami would know it in an instant."

"Ami is in there, too?"

"Yes, as are her husband and daughter."

Aidan must have sensed her anxiety, because he seemed in no hurry to move despite his need of sleep.

But he *did* need sleep. His energy hadn't just been taxed by the wounds he'd incurred. It had been taxed by teleporting them to and from the network and by healing Ethan and Cliff in real time to keep the sunlight from harming them.

"Okay." She straightened her shoulders with determination. "I'm ready."

Aidan squeezed her hand, a warm smile lighting his handsome features. "I really do love you, you know."

She smiled. "I love you, too." The feeling was undeniable. And the two of them could very well be living on borrowed time, so she saw little reason to waste a minute of it playing the *Is-it-too-soon?* game.

The barn was located behind and to one side of the house. She and Aidan strolled down the shaded drive, then turned onto a sidewalk that led to a large front door.

Aidan didn't knock when they reached it. He just opened the

door and escorted her inside.

Unable to completely quash her nerves, Dana glanced over her shoulder and watched him enter behind her. The half dozen or so immortals who had made that impromptu appearance at Ethan and Heather's house hadn't unnerved her as much as she would've thought. But for all she knew, there could be dozens more here in David's home.

Smiling down at her, Aidan winked. "They're just like me," he mentioned again.

Was he reading her thoughts, or was her face really as expressive as he'd claimed?

Aidan looked over her shoulder. His eyes widened.

Dana swung around, followed his gaze, and gaped at the man who exited the kitchen.

"Okay," Aidan murmured. "Maybe they aren't *all* like me."

Chapter Seventeen

SHELDON LOOKED UP AT THE sound of Aidan's voice. "Hey, man. How's it goin'?"

Aidan dipped his chin in a nod and slowly approached the young Second. "Sheldon."

Balancing two substantial sandwiches on a plate, Sheldon shifted his gaze to Dana. "Hi, Dana. Great to see you again."

"Nice to see you, too." She tried not to stare. She really did. But failed miserably as her lips stretched into a broad grin.

The handsome redhead wore a tight black T-shirt that revealed muscled arms and a chest as broad as Aidan's. He also wore badly scuffed combat boots that were in dire need of replacement, worn black cargo shorts that ended just above his knees, and—atop the shorts—a fluffy pink tutu that began at his waist and fell almost to the hem of his shorts in delicate, filmy layers. A pretty yellow sunflower decorated the center of the waistband.

"I heard about the attack at your place," Sheldon said, his eyes on Dana. "That sucks. But from what I understand, you really kicked ass and took names."

That attack seemed so long ago now. "Those names being numbnuts and dumbass?" she asked, trying not to laugh.

He grinned. "Those would be the ones. I also heard you tranqed Roland. Well done. I wish I could've seen that."

"Sheldon?" Aidan said.

"Yeah?"

"What the hell are you wearing?"

Sheldon sighed. "Dude, don't dis my boots. I know I had to glue the soles back onto both shoes with superglue, but these are the most comfortable boots I've ever owned, so I don't want to replace them."

Dana glanced up at Aidan, whose expression remained deadpan.

"The tutu, Sheldon," Aidan said.

Sheldon glanced down. "Oh, that." He shrugged. "I thought Ami and Marcus could use some alone time and offered to take Adira to the playground. Adira didn't want to go without her mommy, so I promised her if she would let me take her she could go to my closet and choose what I would wear."

Aidan arched a brow. "And she chose a tutu?"

"Yeah."

"Do I even want to know why you happened to have an adult-sized pink tutu in your closet?"

Sheldon grinned. "Tracy ordered it online for Adira a couple of months ago, thinking it was child-sized, and didn't feel like returning it once she realized it wasn't."

"And you just… wore it to the park?" Aidan asked.

"Sure. A promise is a promise."

Dana smiled. "That was very sweet of you."

He shrugged. "Adira has me wrapped around her little finger."

Aidan grunted. "You and everyone else who frequents David's home. Didn't the other adults at the park find your attire odd?"

Sheldon laughed. "Are you kidding? The women loved it. Two moms and three nannies gave me their phone numbers."

"Hey!" a woman called from down the hallway. "I heard that!"

Grinning, Sheldon called back, "I only took their numbers in case Ami wanted to arrange a playdate or something."

The woman—Tracy?—grumbled something Dana couldn't hear clearly.

Sheldon held up his plate. "Are you two hungry? I saw Ethan and Heather pass by a minute ago and it looked like you guys might have had a long day." Word must not have gotten around yet about the battle with Gershom.

Aidan nodded. "I could use a bite." He looked down at Dana.

"I could eat," she said, only then realizing she hadn't had a meal in a while.

Sheldon handed her the plate. "I'm glad recent events haven't scared you away."

"Not yet," she said with a wry smile.

Sheldon waved a hand. "I wasn't worried about the violence. You kinda give off a Xena, Warrior Princess vibe, so I knew you could hold your own."

Dana looked up at Aidan. "Really?"

Aidan smiled. "I don't know who Xena is, but the term Warrior Princess suits you well."

"Oh." She couldn't help but feel pleased.

"Nah," Sheldon continued. "I figured if anything would send you fleeing to the hills, it would be Aidan's age."

She looked up at Aidan in time to catch him glaring at Sheldon.

That was the second time Aidan's age had come up, and he seemed no more interested in imparting it now than he had before.

She turned back to Sheldon. "Why? How old is he?"

Sheldon's features slipped into a comical *oops* expression. "Oh. He, uh… he hasn't told you yet?"

"No."

Recovering from his gaffe, Sheldon waved a hand. "You know what? It's not a big thing. It really isn't. Some people are just weirdly sensitive about their age. Hell, Tracy is only eight years older than me and she *still* freaks out about it."

"Nine," Tracy called from down the hallway. "I'm nine years older than you, loose lips."

Sheldon laughed. "See what I mean? She's only nine years older than me and still can't believe I'm not going to ditch her for a younger woman. But I keep telling her that I don't care how old she is. She could be a hundred years older than me, or a thousand years older, or even a million years older and I would still want to be with her."

Tracy entered with a smile. "Yeah, but what makes you think I'd still want *you* if I were a million years older than you?"

He grinned down at her. "All the wisdom you would've acquired over the ages would make you recognize my value."

She smirked. "And if it didn't?"

"Then vanity would make you want me for your boy toy."

Laughing, she curled a hand around the back of his neck and

drew him down for a quick kiss. "I'm sure it would." She turned to Dana. "Hi, Dana." She jerked a thumb toward Sheldon. "Ignore this one. He's still high from all the female attention he got at the park."

Aidan shook his head. "Who would've thought a man wearing a tutu would evoke such adoration."

Tracy rolled her eyes. "I know, right?"

"Unca Aidan!" a small voice cried with glee.

Aidan's face lit with a wide grin. "In here," he called.

The redheaded toddler Dana had seen briefly the previous night ran into the room on chubby legs. A fluffy pink tutu like Sheldon's covered pink shorts while matching pink fairy wings bounced on her back and a flower garland sporting a pink veil jounced on her curls.

"There's my lovely fairy princess," Aidan crooned, bending to scoop her into his arms.

Giggling, she wrapped adorably plump arms around his neck and gave him a hug.

She was beautiful. And Aidan looked damned appealing, hugging her and bussing her rosy cheek. This must be the little one for whom he had cleaned up his language.

"You did, did you?" he asked, his brown eyes alight with pleasure as he grinned at the little girl.

Nodding, she waved a glittery wand with a pink butterfly on the end.

"So he told me. And you had fun?" Aidan asked. A minute passed, then he laughed.

Dana looked to Tracy.

Tracy smiled. "Adira doesn't talk much yet, but she has strong telepathic abilities."

Dana looked at the child in surprise. Really? She couldn't be more than two years old.

The little girl turned her attention to Dana.

"Hi there," Dana said with a smile.

Giving her a grin that exposed little white teeth, the toddler lunged toward her.

Sheldon grabbed the plate of sandwiches while Dana scrambled to catch Adira and wrapped her arms securely around the little beauty.

Adira raised bright green eyes to meet hers and touched her cheek. "Annie Dana," she said with a grin.

Tracy's eyebrows flew up. "I think she just called you Auntie Dana."

Adira rested her head on Dana's shoulder and snuggled against her with a happy sigh.

"Dude," Sheldon said, his eyes going from the toddler to Dana to Aidan. "Adira can see the future. I'm pretty sure that means you're in."

Dana glanced up at Aidan, who looked as surprised as she was.

After a moment, he smiled and touched her shoulder. "Don't worry. You still have choice."

She smiled back and rocked from side to side, enjoying the feel of the baby against her chest, all anxiety fleeing amidst the comfort the child brought and the light, family atmosphere that welcomed her. "I know." But she didn't really. At least not where Aidan was concerned. She was in love with him. And that made choosing anything other than a future with him impossible.

The hallway behind them darkened as a figure filled it, then moved forward to join them.

Dana's eyes widened as she tilted her head back and stared up at him.

Wow.

Tracy laughed. "I bet I had that same expression on my face the first time I saw him. He's a handsome devil, isn't he?"

Chuckling, the man met Dana's gaze with dark brown eyes that infused her with as much warmth and comfort as the child did. "I'm David," he said, offering her a slight bow. "Welcome to my home, Dana."

"Thank you," she managed to say.

She estimated his height to be about six feet seven inches. His smooth, flawless skin was as dark as midnight. Pencil-thin dreadlocks—pulled back from his face with a leather tie—fell all the way down to his hips. Like the other immortals, he wore all black and wore it well. His shoulders were as broad and his body as muscular as Aidan's.

David nodded to the toddler she held. "I see you've already

made a new friend."

"Yes. She's beautiful." As with Seth, there was just something about this man that screamed power. Dana actually found herself a little tongue-tied around him.

"And as happy to have you here as the rest of us are. Seth has informed me of this afternoon's events."

Aidan's expression sobered. "Have they caught Gershom?"

"Not yet. They're pursuing him now."

Tracy and Sheldon exchanged a look.

"Seth got a lead on Gershom?" Sheldon asked, all business now.

David nodded. "Gershom posed as Seth and attacked Aidan this afternoon."

Sheldon's eyes widened. "Shit!"

Tracy popped him on the back of the head.

He glanced at Adira. "I mean shoot!"

David held up a hand to halt the questions that otherwise would've poured forth. "We'll discuss it later. Right now Aidan needs a healing sleep."

Sheldon nodded. "Of course." He handed Aidan the plate of sandwiches. "Let us know if you two need anything." Taking Tracy's hand, he headed down the hallway.

"With all that's happening," Aidan said, lowering his voice, "I'm surprised you let Sheldon take Adira to the park."

David's lips turned up in a wry smile. "I followed and watched over them in the form of a crow."

He could shape-shift? "That is so cool," Dana murmured.

David's smile broadened. "Fun, too." He turned his gaze to Adira. "Come here, sweetheart. Uncle Aidan and Auntie Dana need to get some rest."

"You heard that, did you?" Aidan asked.

"The Auntie Dana? Yes, I did."

Adira smiled and let Dana transfer her to David's arms. Reaching over his shoulder, Adira pulled one of his dreadlocks forward and began to play with it.

"I hope you will enjoy your stay in my home, Dana. I've had a room prepared for you both. Would you like to see it?" he asked.

"Yes, please."

Aidan nodded. "Thank you, David. I appreciate it."

David motioned for them to accompany him down the hallway. "This way."

Dana glanced curiously into the rooms they passed. A bathroom. A huge study/library. What appeared to be a medical facility of some sort. Perhaps an infirmary?

When David passed through a doorway and led them down a flight of stairs, disappointment threatened. They would be sleeping in the basement?

Her eyebrows rose though when they reached the foot of the stairs.

On their left, a pair of open double doors revealed a gym or training room roughly the size of a high school gymnasium with a padded floor, a wall of mirrors and a lot of exercise equipment.

That must be for the Seconds, since immortals were already superstrong.

On the right, a long, elegant hallway with at least a dozen doors stretched before them. Lovely dark wood floors. Earth-toned walls adorned with modern paintings. A high white ceiling with recessed lighting. Wingback chairs stationed in twos. Plant stands supporting plants that somehow thrived without any sun exposure.

Very nice.

Aidan nudged her shoulder, amusement dancing in his eyes. *You were expecting something cold and damp and crypt-like?*

She grinned. *Maybe.*

David led them down the hallway, stopping in front of the next-to-last door on the right. Opening it, he motioned for them to enter.

Dana stepped inside a large, sumptuous bedroom with an adjoining bathroom.

Aidan followed. "Thank you again, David."

Smiling, he turned to Dana. "My home is your home, Dana. You are welcome to explore it as you will. Grab a snack from the kitchen. A book from my study. Whatever will make you comfortable. I only ask that you knock first before entering any of the rooms down here, save the training room, because they are bedrooms and most are occupied."

"Thank you. That's very kind of you."

He clapped Aidan on the shoulder. "Get some rest."

David turned and headed back down the hallway, Adira waving at them over his shoulder. Aidan waved to the little cutie, then closed the door.

"He's so nice," Dana said.

Nodding, Aidan shrugged off his coat and tossed it over the wooden back of a nearby chair. "Go ahead and ask me."

She tilted her head to one side. "Ask you what?"

"The question you've been wanting to ask ever since Sheldon opened his yap upstairs. He's bound to blurt it out eventually, so I'd just as soon get it out of the way."

"Are you sure?" Dana saw the way his shoulders slumped with weariness. And David had said he needed a healing sleep. "It can wait."

"I'm sure." Sinking down in the chair, he began to tug on the laces of one boot.

She drew in a deep breath. "How old are you?"

Pulling the boot off, he set it aside. "I've lived just shy of three thousand years."

She stared at him. She had heard *thousand*, but he must have said *hundred*, right? "I'm sorry. I don't think I heard that correctly."

He went to work on his other boot. "You heard it right."

Shock and dismay warred within her. "You're three thousand years old?"

He winced, his expression almost apologetic. "Almost."

A heavy silence enveloped them as he removed the second boot and set it beside the first.

"Dana?" He seemed to be waiting for a comment, but…

"I don't know how to respond to that."

Leaning forward, he braced his elbows on his knees and clasped his hands between them. "If it helps, I look and feel a lot younger than that. *Far* younger since I met you and you breathed light and life back into my world."

"You're three thousand years old," she whispered, not really hearing him. He was *three thousand* years old. And she was *thirty*. "Why are you even with me?" she blurted, insecurity rising.

His features filled with dread. "What?"

"Why are you even with me?" she repeated. "I mean, all the things you must have learned and the wisdom you must have accrued in three thousand years… I just don't know what the hell about me would even appeal to you. I must seem so young and naïve and-and-and lacking in knowledge and experience. I must seem like an adolescent to you."

Her words seemed to take him aback. "What? No. Not at all."

"Oh come on, Aidan," she retorted, unable to believe him.

"Clearly I haven't acquired as much wisdom as you think I have, because the reason I avoided telling you my age is I thought it would repel you or—how would Sheldon put it—creep you out." He frowned. "Wait. Is that a saying? It sounds odd."

"It's a saying," she confirmed, her dismay lightening a little with amusement.

"How long have you lived in North Carolina?" he asked.

She frowned at the change in subject. "Twelve years."

"Where did you live before that?"

"Oklahoma."

"In all my time on earth, I've never been to Oklahoma," he told her. "Does my lack of knowledge regarding that state make you think less of me?"

"No, but that isn't the same thing."

"If the two of us went to Oklahoma, would showing me around seem like a chore to you?"

"Of course not. But that isn't— "

"It *is* the same thing," he told her. "And the fact that you think the difference in our ages should bother *me* more than it does *you* is a clear indication that I haven't learned as much as you think I have. Because I thought the opposite would be true."

She bit her lip. "Our age difference really doesn't bother you?"

He smiled. "The only thing that ever bothered me about it was the fear that you might declare me a decrepit old geezer when you found out."

She laughed. "That is one thing you will never be, Aidan."

He grinned.

Three thousand years. Sorrow filled her as she recalled something she'd learned the first time she had read his palm. "You've lived almost three thousand years and you've never married?"

He shrugged. "I never found a woman I felt comfortable sharing my differences with. Never found anyone I loved enough to risk it.

Not until I met you."

Her heart ached for him. "So you've been alone all this time?"

"I've had Seconds and my immortal brethren."

It wasn't enough.

Closing the distance between them, she brushed his hands aside so she could stand between his thighs, wrap her arms around him, and hold him close. "I'm so glad my name was on that list you stole."

Releasing a contented sigh, he slid his arms around her and buried his face in the crook of her neck. "I am, too."

<hr />

Branches snapped and fallen leaves crackled beneath David's big boots as he strode through dense forest.

The usual night sounds serenaded him. Insects buzzed. Frogs croaked and twanged, sounding alternately like growling belches and plucked guitar strings. Wings flapped far above him as an owl rode the breeze, seeking prey to fill its belly. And somewhere off to his left, a large opossum foraged through the brush.

The trees thinned ahead of David.

Stepping out of the forest, he crossed a paved road that no longer saw traffic. Two years of inactivity and no care had evoked quite a change in it. Weeds grew out of cracks in the pavement. Others thrived along the road's edge, obscuring the border as they crept toward the road's center, attempting to rendezvous with the weeds on the other side.

The twisted, rusted remains of a gate folded outward in a permanent bow, courtesy of the grenades that had blown it open.

David passed between the two sides, noting the No Trespassing sign each now boasted.

The signs themselves might not discourage curious ne'er-do-wells from exploring the former mercenary compound, but the network guards who monitored the place via hidden surveillance cameras would.

He walked past the remains of buildings that bore scorch marks and jagged holes between the vines that slithered up their walls. Broken windows watched like vacant eyes that revealed interiors damaged by the elements.

In the distance, a lone, dark figure stood in the center of a slab of blackened, weed-strewn asphalt that marked the place where an armory had once stood.

David had known he would find Seth there. The Immortal Guardians' leader often came to this place of loss when he was troubled. And after the day he'd had, Seth no doubt needed a moment to gather his thoughts.

Head bowed, Seth said nothing when David joined him.

Minutes passed.

"Anything?" David asked softly, referring not to Seth's hunt for Gershom but to what Seth sought every time he came here.

Seth shook his head. "Nothing."

David had known it would be thus. The loss of Yuri and Stanislav had hit Seth hard.

It had hit them *all* hard.

But for Seth, the uncertainty — the not knowing absolutely what had happened to Stanislav, not seeing him fall, never encountering his spirit — had made the loss all the worse because Seth couldn't quite abandon hope that Stanislav had somehow survived.

"How long to you intend to search for him?" David asked, no criticism in the question.

Seth turned his gaze to the decimated compound around them. "Until I know for certain he is gone."

David offered no objection. "Gershom eluded you and Zach again."

"Yes."

Gershom was proving to be a far more formidable foe than they had anticipated, which made him wonder just how long the Other had been plotting and planning and building his strength.

Far longer than his brethren realized, it would seem.

"The Others tried to aid us in our pursuit," Seth said.

David had hoped they would. Even the Others couldn't ignore the chaos Gershom was breeding and wanted him brought to heel as much as the Immortal Guardians did.

"They followed the same pattern they did before," Seth went on, "scattering themselves around the globe and teleporting from place to place, hoping they would land in Gershom's general vicinity and be able to hold him until Zach and I could get there.

But Gershom was expecting as much and used it against us."

"How so?"

"He teleported to the Others' home."

Surprise gripped David. And very little surprised him after such a lengthy life. "He did? Were any of the Others still there?"

"One, who was caught off guard and easily defeated."

"Defeated, but not killed?"

"Yes."

At least Gershom hadn't lost *all* his sanity.

"Gershom was already gone when Zach and I tracked him there. But there were so many energy trails leading from the place as a result of the Others teleporting out to try to help us that we couldn't discern which one was his and lost him despite trying all damned day and most of tonight to locate him."

"That was ingenious."

"And unexpected. The Others have vowed they won't make the same mistake again."

"At least there is that." But David knew such provided Seth with little solace.

"The bastard posed as *me*, David."

"I know."

"And he did it so well that even Ethan didn't know it wasn't me until Gershom made the mistake of harming Cliff."

David nodded, finding the news beyond troubling. "He must have been studying you for years. Every movement. Every mannerism. Every inflection in your voice."

"As Étienne would say, that shit is creepy."

David laughed. "Very much so."

"I just wish I understood why he hates me so much," Seth proclaimed with a sort of helpless bafflement.

"Perhaps Jared was right. Perhaps Gershom simply resents the fact that, while the Others have been merely observing life for thousands of years, you've been living it."

"Well, if that's the case, I wish to hell he had just defected like me and Zach."

David shrugged. "Or perhaps he's insane."

"I'm not sure which would be worse."

Frogs continued to croak and twang. Crickets chirped. Insects hummed.

"You need to talk to Aidan," David offered softly.

"I know. I want him to get some rest first. He isn't hunting tonight, is he?"

"No. He and Dana are both sleeping. And I ordered all the other immortals in the area to stand down and take the night off."

"Good. You called a meeting?"

"Sunset."

Seth nodded. "I'll be sure to talk to Aidan before then."

David locked his hands behind his back as the sky began to brighten with approaching dawn. "The day was a long one. The night, too."

Seth sent him a wry smile, at last meeting his gaze. "Yes, it was."

"According to Darnell, the internet is all abuzz."

Seth sighed. "Full of exclamations of dismay upon discovering that Gershom may be as powerful as I am? Whispered fears that he may triumph?"

David waved a hand in dismissal. "No. They're all confident you will defeat him."

Seth's face lit with surprise. "Really?"

"Of course."

"Then what's all the chatter about?"

Amusement stole away some of David's concern. "Every Immortal Guardian on the planet is sharing the jaw-dropping news that Aidan's woman kissed their illustrious leader."

His friend's face acquired a comical, pained look. "Seriously?"

"Yes."

"Even the men?"

"Even the men."

Seth shook his head. "With everything that's happened in the past few days, you'd think *that* wouldn't have even made the headlines."

David laughed. "Of course it made the headlines. You're not just their leader, their commanding officer. You're a father figure to them. And they just found out that their *daddy* kissed a woman."

Seth groaned. "No wonder my phone has gone silent. I thought they were all just dismayed over my having failed to capture Gershom again."

David grinned. "Your phone hasn't gone silent. I asked Chris to divert your calls to Zach after he returned. If anyone can quash their curiosity and get them to leave you alone, *he* can. Particularly since he's cranky over Gershom slipping away."

Seth's lips curled up in a wry smile. "I'm sure he can."

"And will enjoy doing so far too much," David guessed. "But at least it will give you some quiet time."

"Thank you."

"Dana may not fare so well though," David said. "I'm sure the female immortals and Seconds will pepper her with questions at the earliest opportunity."

Again Seth groaned. "Poor woman. You see now why I don't date."

David knew well why Seth didn't date. And it had nothing to do with Immortal Guardian family gossip.

The owl David had heard earlier abruptly dove down and plucked a field mouse from the weeds near the abandoned airplane hangar.

David cast Seth a sidelong glance. "So?"

He didn't have to say more for Seth to know what he wondered.

Seth looked up at the sky. "Thousands of years, and I still can't kiss another woman without feeling as though I'm betraying her."

That came as no surprise. David knew Seth still mourned the death of his wife and the deaths of their children.

"You know she wouldn't have wanted this," he said gently.

That sparked another wry smile. "I'm not so sure. She was a jealous woman."

David chuckled. "And you weren't a jealous husband?"

Seth's smile widened.

David shook his head. "She loved you, Seth. She wouldn't have wanted you to be alone all this time."

Seth shrugged. "I'm *not* alone."

David opted to let that pass, recognizing it as the evasion it was. In the thousands of years since his wife had been slain, Seth had taken no wives, had no girlfriends, no one-night stands, no intimacy of any kind with a woman.

Having experienced such a loss himself, David couldn't really blame him.

"So you felt nothing then," he asked Seth curiously, "when Dana kissed you?"

Seth snorted. "I felt guilty as hell for kissing Aidan's woman right in front of him, I can tell you that."

David laughed. "After what she did to Jared, I think you'd best mind your manners around her in the future."

Seth laughed. "She's a fighter. Zach is still chuckling over that."

"I'm sure he is."

A breeze set the weeds and grasses around them into motion. The trees beyond the perimeter fence swayed, their leaves brushing together and creating soothing swishing sounds.

"When will it be time to move on, Seth?"

Seth returned his stare to the blackened asphalt beneath his boots.

"How many more years of mourning will be enough?" And how long would the thought of being with another woman fill the Immortal Guardians' leader with guilt?

Seth responded with a slow shake of his head. "I don't know."

It was the same answer he always gave when David broached the subject.

"You were wed once, too," Seth murmured. "How long did it take *you* to get past losing your wife?"

Pain pierced David. "I'll let you know when that day comes." As in so many ways, he and Seth were the same in this. "I still think of her every day."

"As do I."

David tucked his hands in his pockets and sighed. "Well, I guess for a while longer then we shall remain what Chris has deemed us."

Seth's face lightened with a smile. "A couple of old farts who would rather read a good book than learn how to troll the internet for women?"

David laughed. "Just so."

Skillet's "Monster" blared from Seth's pocket.

David felt a stab of concern as he watched him retrieve his phone. The only calls that should be coming through now were those that could not be ignored and couldn't be handled by Zach.

"Yes?" Seth answered.

"Seth, it's Alena Moreno." Head of the West Coast division of the network. "I need to see you again. I have some new information, and it's disturbing."

Seth met David's gaze. "I shall be there shortly."

He ended the call and returned his phone to his pocket. "Monster" again disturbed the quiet.

His brow furrowing, Seth answered the call. "Yes?"

"Seth. Scott Henderson." Head of the Midwest division of the network. "I need to see you. The sooner the better."

This couldn't be good.

"I'll be there as soon as I can," Seth told him and slid his phone back into his pocket. "Good thing you called a meeting."

David nodded. "Looks like we'll have more to discuss than I'd thought."

Chapter Eighteen

*A*IDAN.
Aidan's eyes flew open.

Dana slept peacefully, curled up against his side with her head resting on his shoulder. She had slung one arm across his chest and draped a knee across his groin, effectively locking him in place.

A very happy place.

He loved having Dana's small, warm body snuggled up to him. It made him never want to get out of bed.

But something *had* awoken him.

He examined the dim bedroom. He had turned the light on in the bathroom prior to retiring and had left the door cracked so Dana would be able to find her way around if she awoke before him. Even had he not, his eyes would've had no difficulty piercing the darkness.

The bedroom was empty save for themselves. His and Dana's clothes still decorated the floor where they had dropped them wearily on their way to the shower.

Aidan.

His gaze slid to the bedroom door.

Careful not to wake her, he slowly eased out from beneath Dana and slipped from the bed.

Murmuring something in her sleep, she rolled onto her other side.

Aidan drew the covers up to her chin, then dressed at preternatural speed. Tossing their dirty clothing in the bathroom, he headed for the door.

Light bathed him as he opened it, only partially blocked by the figures in the hallway.

Seth stared down at him, Ami at his side.

Aidan eyed them both, dread and frustration filling him because he could guess why Ami was there. "You didn't catch Gershom."

"No," Seth confirmed, then nodded to Ami. "I thought you might be more at ease if Ami confirmed that I'm me."

Ami offered Aidan a smile. "He's Seth."

"Thank you," Aidan said, failing to muster up a smile in return. That bastard Gershom was still on the loose, which meant this wasn't over. Dana was still in danger. They were *all* still in danger.

Seth's smile didn't quite reach his eyes as Ami touched his arm, then left them.

Aidan stepped back, opening the door wider in silent invitation. "I don't want to leave Dana alone."

Nodding, Seth entered.

Aidan closed the door and faced his leader. His friend.

"You thought he was me," Seth said.

"I did."

"You thought I wanted to kill you."

"I did." And Aidan's stomach knotted up when he thought about it.

Seth offered his hand. When Aidan clasped it, Seth pulled him into a rough hug. "I'm sorry."

"It wasn't you." But damned if it didn't make him feel better to have Seth reinforce that fact. He had known Seth longer than he had known anyone else still living. They had been through a hell of a lot together. The knowledge that Gershom had nearly fucked all that up…

Releasing him, Seth stepped back. "Tell me what happened."

Aidan nodded. Picking up the large storage ottoman at the foot of the bed, he placed it against the wall and sat down.

Seth sank down beside him.

"He got into my head, Seth."

Seth shot him a sharp glance. "Literally or figuratively?"

"Both," Aidan confessed with a touch of despair. "He knew just what to say to make me think he was you. Knew what to do, how to behave, what I would expect. He even mimicked your temper perfectly. When I said he was very convincing earlier, I meant he was *terrifyingly* convincing."

Seth's eyes began to glow with renewed anger. "Tell me everything."

Aidan shook his head. "I want you to see it for yourself. I'm afraid I'll leave something out if I do the telling." And he wanted Seth to have every tiny shred of information in his arsenal. So Aidan tapped his temple. "Go ahead and have a look."

Seth shifted his gaze to Aidan's forehead.

Quiet engulfed them, broken only by the faint sounds of Dana's breathing that Aidan's preternatural hearing caught as she slumbered on, oblivious to their presence. This bedroom, like many others here at David's place, was soundproofed. David had enlisted the network's aid in accomplishing such when immortals began to marry, wishing to afford the couples more privacy so they could spend the night whenever they wanted to without worrying about the other immortals hearing them make love.

Seth's eyes grew brighter as he reviewed the confrontation with Gershom, the gold light a sharp contrast to the darkness of the bedroom.

The floor beneath Aidan's feet began to vibrate ever so slightly as Seth's fury rose in response to the memories he scoured.

If Aidan were to open the door of the soundproof bedroom, he likely would hear thunder rumbling outside as rain beat the grass and trees.

The rumbling vibrations increased.

Dana shifted beneath the covers, the quaking luring her toward consciousness.

Aidan touched a hand to Seth's arm and tried to infuse him with calm. Seth blinked, and the ground stopped shaking.

Dana stilled, sighing in her sleep.

But the bright golden light in Seth's eyes was slow to fade as they met Aidan's.

"What did you see?" Aidan asked.

"Everything that transpired in your backyard."

"Just that? Nothing else?"

"Yes." Rising, Seth paced away, his movements the same as those Gershom had demonstrated earlier.

It was eerie how identical the two appeared.

"The bastard made you doubt yourself," Seth growled in fury.

Aidan tried to shrug it off but couldn't. "I'm still doubting myself," he admitted softly.

Seth ceased his restless movements. "He was lying, Aidan."

"You don't know that. Not for sure. You only read my memories of the confrontation."

"As strong as your mental barriers are, I'm convinced he could not possibly topple them without your knowing."

"I've known you for three thousand years, Seth. Until yesterday, I was convinced no one could possibly trick me into believing he was you. And yet Gershom succeeded."

Silence.

"I need you to be sure," Aidan continued. "*I* need to be sure that Gershom isn't mind-controlling me."

"Aidan— "

"I know you don't want to. I know that, contrary to popular opinion, you don't like sneaking into people's minds and nosing about in their private business. But I need you to do it. I need you to comb every nook and cranny of my mind and tell me with absolute certainty that Gershom hasn't planted any commands up there."

Seth hesitated.

"Please," Aidan added as he glanced at the bed. "I need to know I'm not a danger to Dana and the others. That I'm not a danger to you," he said, meeting his friend's gaze. "I need to know that Gershom is full of shite."

A long sigh escaped Seth.

Aidan smiled. "Thank you."

Seth reclaimed his seat beside Aidan. "You've lowered the rest of your barriers?"

"Yes."

"As you will." Seth closed his eyes.

Aidan sat quietly, watching Dana slumber.

Minutes passed.

Many long minutes. The brain's capacity for storing information seemed limitless. And a brain could accrue a hell of a lot of information over the course of three thousand years. Since the virus that infected immortals protected their minds from the degeneration often caused by aging, Aidan had retained much of what he had experienced over time.

Not as much as Ethan, of course. Ethan's memory was phenomenal.

But there was enough crammed up inside Aidan's brain that it took Seth a good long while to sort through it all.

When Seth opened his eyes, the golden glow had left them, returning them to a brown so dark it was almost black.

"Well?" Aidan asked, almost afraid of the answer Seth would give.

"You're good," Seth said. "Gershom was bullshitting you."

Aidan let out the breath he hadn't realized he'd been holding. "You don't know how happy I am to hear it."

Seth offered him a wry smile. "Yes, I do."

Aidan laughed.

Seth glanced at the bed. "I can't believe Dana was more worried that you might think she was too young for *you* than she was about you being too old for *her*."

"I know." Aidan smiled. "It's kind of nice that people can still surprise us after all this time."

Seth rose. "I only wish Gershom weren't one of those people."

Aidan stood. "We'll stop him, Seth. I know we will."

Seth drew out a pocket watch out and consulted it. "Yes, but he's been up to more than you know."

That was unsettling. "What do you mean?"

"You'll hear it all at the meeting." Seth tucked the watch away and headed for the door. "Darnell, Tracy, and Sheldon have cooked dinner. You should probably wake Dana and partake before the meeting."

"Okay." When Seth opened the door, Aidan stopped him. "Seth?"

Seth paused and glanced over at him. "Yes?"

"We're good, right?"

Seth smiled. "We're good."

Aidan motioned to his head. "You didn't find anything up there that was as weird as the shite I find in Sheldon's mind, did you?"

Seth laughed. "No, I didn't."

Aidan grinned, happy to have made his friend laugh after such a stressful day. "Happy to hear it."

"I'll see you at the meeting." Stepping out into the hallway, Seth closed the door.

Aidan lost his smile.

What more had Gershom been up to?

He almost dreaded finding out.

Dana stood beside Aidan, her hand tucked in his while they watched Darnell and Sheldon add two new leaves to the already long table in David's dining room. The house had a fairly open floor plan with a huge living room—sporting a surprisingly modern décor, multiple sofas, love seats, scuffed-up coffee tables, and chairs—blending into a dining room. A bar separated the dining room from a kitchen that boasted two gargantuan refrigerators and so much cooking equipment that Dana didn't even know how to use half of it.

She thought it was very sweet of David to open his homes (apparently this was just one of many) to immortals and their Seconds and provide them with a gathering place. They really did seem like a family. She wasn't sure why that continued to surprise her, but it did.

Cheers erupted when the table slid back together.

She smiled.

The table must have sat at least twenty beforehand. Now she watched as they produced extra chairs and slid them up to the table, enabling—wow—thirty-one people to sit at it under Darnell's direction.

Dana was an only child. Both parents had also been only children, so she'd had no aunts or uncles and no cousins to play with when she was growing up. Her grandparents had passed away so early that she barely remembered them. And now her parents were gone.

What must it be like, she wondered as she watched the men and women around her smile and chat despite the gravity of recent events, to have a family this large? To have this many people you loved and cared about?

I guess I'm about to find out, she thought.

David claimed the seat at the head of the table with Darnell sitting to his left.

Exiting the kitchen, Seth strode over and seated himself at the foot of the table.

Ami smiled and said something to Seth as she sat down catercorner to him. Taking the seat next to her, Marcus scooted it back so his daughter, whom Dana hadn't noticed until then, could climb up onto his lap.

Roland leaned over Marcus's shoulder and held a thick coloring book boasting colorful cartoon animals in front of Adira. As her eyes lit up, he seated himself beside Marcus, then opened the book on the table while Sarah produced a box of crayons.

As the other immortals and Seconds converged on the table, Aidan guided Dana to a couple of seats on the side opposite Roland and Sarah.

Wood scuffed across wood as chairs were claimed and bodies filled seats.

As Dana scooted her own chair closer to the table, her gaze touched upon David.

He smiled. "Are you settling in okay?" he asked, raising his voice a bit so she could hear him over the rumblings of the rest.

"Yes, thank you," she said with a smile. After Aidan had disclosed his age, the two of them had taken a shower together, devoured Sheldon's sandwiches, then slept deeply. They'd been so tired that they hadn't even made love. As soon as their heads had hit the pillow, both had fallen into an exhausted slumber.

David nodded, then turned to speak with Darnell.

The seat beside Darnell was empty. Two very imposing immortals claimed the next two seats.

Dana squeezed Aidan's hand. "Read my thoughts," she whispered.

Okay.

Who are those two?

Imhotep and Chaak. They are elders like me who have been brought in as backup.

The front door opened and closed. Chris Reordon headed for the table and plunked a battered briefcase down on the seat to

David's right. After returning the greetings offered him, he nodded to Seth.

Seth rose and vanished.

Dana smiled up at Aidan. "I still think that's cool."

Across the table, Tracy leaned forward with a smile. "I know, right? When I first started serving as Lisette's Second, she almost ditched me because every time Richart would come over, I'd pester him into teleporting me to foreign countries."

Richart grinned. "You *still* try to pester me into teleporting you to other countries."

Tracy wrinkled her nose. "Yeah, but you stopped taking me because I started making you take Sheldon, too, and you're afraid he's going to spark an international incident."

"Oh, come on, guys," Sheldon protested with a grin. "I'm not *that* bad."

Everyone laughed.

Seth reappeared with two companions.

One was a slender woman with long, silky black hair and light brown skin, clad in a black business suit that showcased every curve and managed to appear both alluring and all business at the same time.

The other was a man with sandy brown hair who was dressed similarly to Chris in dark slacks and a white dress shirt that was open at the collar and had the sleeves rolled up almost to his elbows.

Both carried battered briefcases similar to Chris's.

Chris headed down the table with a smile. "Nice to see you again, Alena." He shook her hand, then shook the man's. "Scott, good to see you."

"Good to see you, too, Chris."

"If you'll both have a seat, we'll go ahead and get started."

Scott followed Chris to David's end of the table where they sank into the last two chairs on David's right.

Alena headed for the empty chair across from them, between Darnell and Imhotep. Darnell rose and drew the chair out as she approached. Smiling, she thanked him and set her briefcase on the table as she sat down.

Once Seth reclaimed his seat at the foot of the table, all

conversation ceased and everyone looked to him to begin the meeting.

"Thank you all for joining us," Seth began. "I assume you've all heard by now that Gershom escaped us once again."

Somber nods all around.

"Then you also know that the only reason we had this latest chance to play cat and mouse with him is because he posed as me and attacked Aidan."

The Immortal Guardians all exchanged uncomfortable looks.

"Gershom has upped his game," Seth began. "Even more so than we first believed. He is telling the vampires in our area to increase their numbers and travel in larger packs. And he poses as Aidan when he directs them. Apparently he has become very adept at shape-shifting and is using that talent to once more try to pit us against each other and sow dissent amongst our ranks."

"He's doing a hell of a job," Roland murmured.

Seth dipped his chin in acknowledgment. "There's more. Chris?"

Leaning forward, Chris braced his elbows on the table. "I'd like to begin by introducing our guests." He gestured to the woman. "This is Alena Moreno, the head of the West Coast division of the network here in the United States."

Dana nodded a greeting with the others.

He motioned to the man beside him. "And this is Scott Henderson, head of the Midwest division of the network."

More nods and greetings.

"Once you all not so subtly pointed out that I had my head up my ass and was fixating on proving that Aidan was the guilty party instead of proving him innocent," Chris said, "I took my investigation in a different direction."

Rising, he picked up a large stack of manila file folders and slowly circled the table, handing one to each person he passed. "The *gifted ones* Gershom abducted failed to come to my attention immediately because the abductions were all readily explainable. They were sick with the flu. Or on cruise. There had been a death in the family. You get the picture."

Nods all around.

"We had what appeared to be Aidan on video absconding with

three of the six women who went missing here in North Carolina. Then I discovered three men had also gone missing. I had my team at the network check up on every other *gifted one* who resides in North Carolina, as well as the rest of the East Coast that falls under my purview. Just to make sure all bases were covered, I also contacted Alena and Scott to inform them of recent events and ask them if they had encountered similar disappearances. They had not, but agreed to conduct their own investigations to be certain."

Dana's eyebrows shot up when Chris came abreast of her and handed Aidan a folder, then held one out to her, too. They really were treating her as if she were one of them.

Releasing Aidan's hand, she took the folder and set it on the table in front of her.

"What did you learn?" Aidan asked.

Chris distributed the rest of the folders, then retook his seat. "Seth and I both received calls from Alena. Alena did, in fact, come across a *gifted one* who was missing, a man who was supposed to be on a cruise. Seth met with her. Several hours later, after doing more investigating, Alena called him back. I also got a call from Scott about the same time."

When Aidan opened his file, Dana opened hers. The first in a stack of loose pages boasted a black-and-white map of the United States. Little red dots decorated the map like confetti, the largest group of them in North Carolina.

"When my East Coast team dug deeper," Chris announced, his face grim, "we discovered that a dozen more *gifted ones* who were believed to be on sick leave or on vacation, et cetera, have in fact gone missing in other states in my domain."

Dana stared at the map. Was that what the red dots represented? Missing *gifted ones*?

"Alena and Scott discovered that some of the *gifted ones* whose absences had previously been accounted for in the rest of the states were likewise not where they were supposed to be. All told, almost a hundred *gifted ones* have gone missing across the country in less than a month."

Exclamations of disbelief erupted.

Dana set the map aside. On the second page in the stack, a black-and-white picture of a woman stared up at her. The woman's name, age, and physical description were printed beneath the photo, as were her occupation and the details of her disappearance. According to her employer, she had contracted pneumonia and was supposed to have been home recovering. But the network was unable to locate her.

Dana turned the page. A man stared up at her. When his father had died, he had told his employer that he needed to fly to Dallas for the burial and would have to stay for a time to handle estate business. The network had confirmed that his father had indeed died and the man had flown to Dallas, but he had disappeared shortly after attending the funeral.

"Gershom was clever," Chris told them, answering the question that Dana thought must be hovering on a lot of lips: How could all of these abductions have gone unnoticed? "Except for here in North Carolina, he only took one or two *gifted ones* from each state."

Aidan looked at Scott and Alena. "Was I implicated in any of the other disappearances?"

Alena nodded. "We have video footage, taken from security cameras, of you"—frowning, she shook her head—"or someone who looks exactly like you, conversing with the women who went missing, getting into cars with them, then driving away. No one has seen them since."

"What about the men who went missing?" Ethan asked.

Alena shook her head. "We only saw Aidan with the women. We found no video record of the men's abductions."

When Aidan's eyes began to glow, Dana rested a hand on his arm and gave it a reassuring caress.

⇒●●●⇐

Aidan tried to keep his fury in check. But damn it, knowing that Gershom was posing as him while he kidnapped women and—for all they knew—harmed or killed them was beyond fucked up. His pulling that shite here had been bad enough. Knowing he was doing it all around the country...

"Is he doing it overseas as well?" he ground out.

"No," Chris reassured him. "Only here in the States."

Small comfort.

As Dana stroked his arm, Aidan forced his hands to relax their crushing grip on the edges of the file folder and leaned back in his seat.

Seth spoke into the leaden silence. "When Scott and Alena both informed me that an immortal might be implicated in the abductions, I assured them of your innocence, Aidan."

Alena's lips turned up in a faint smile. "By showing us that he himself can appear as you."

Sheldon snorted. "So he's a magician now."

"Who?" Tracy asked beside him. "Seth or Gershom?"

"Gershom," Sheldon said. "What do all magicians do?" He reached a hand out to his right in front of Jenna and waved it in a circle. "They do bullshit that's guaranteed to hold your attention here…" He thrust his other hand out to his left in front of Tracy. "While they do the *real* shit over here."

Ethan nodded. "He implicated Aidan here in a way we were guaranteed to notice and raised a vampire army so we'd be so busy fighting amongst ourselves, trying to clear Aidan's name, and addressing the new vampire threat that we wouldn't notice that he was quietly acquiring his own little collection of *gifted ones*."

Sheldon lowered his hands. "Exactly. The question is—why is he taking the *gifted ones*?"

"He isn't just taking them," Chris inserted. "As of this morning, six of them have been found dead."

Aidan's stomach sank.

"What?" Ami whispered, horror stamped across her pretty features.

"And Scott's team found three more an hour ago. All dead."

Curses filled the air.

Marcus glanced down at his daughter in reflex, but she appeared to be concentrating wholly on the picture she was coloring.

Nine dead.

"Why?" Aidan asked, frustration beating him. "What's his goal? What's his endgame?"

"To strike at Seth," Lisette proposed.

Zach draped an arm across the back of her chair. "What do little asshole schoolyard bullies do? They take away the other children's toys. They *break* the other children's toys and get off on the misery such spawns." He cast Seth a look of regret. "Gershom has already managed to break two of your toys."

Lisette swallowed hard, grief entering her eyes. "Yuri and Stanislav."

Seth's gaze dropped to the table, but not before Aidan caught the golden glow that entered them.

"Everyone knows," Zach continued, "how important immortals and *gifted ones* are to Seth. And we've all come to the conclusion that—for whatever reason—Gershom *hates* Seth's ass. Yuri and Stanislav were a heavy blow. But both of those immortals at least had a fighting chance. How much harsher will the blow be if *gifted ones* who can't fight back are slain this time?"

Aidan ground his teeth. "*Gifted ones* are so much weaker than Gershom that it would be like slaying children. What the hell is the appeal in that?"

Zach waved a hand in dismissal. "Bullies are all pussies deep down. They only pick fights with those who can't fight back or those who can't win if they *do* fight back. So instead of manning up and fighting *Seth* one on one—we all know Seth would defeat the fucker if he did—Gershom is choosing easier targets that will cut Seth deeply when slain."

When grumbled protests rose in volume, Seth held up a hand.

All quieted.

"The problem is," Seth announced, his gaze circling the table, "we don't know where Gershom is taking the *gifted ones*. Where he's keeping them."

Roland scowled. "How do you know he's keeping them at all? Are you sure they aren't all dead?"

Seth looked to Chris.

Chris shook his head. "He's definitely keeping them somewhere. All the bodies we've recovered were dressed the same way and looked as though they had been killed while trying to escape. And we believe humans killed them—not Gershom or vampires—because they were shot. All except one, whose neck was broken."

Silence.

"So what do we do?" Aidan asked when he couldn't take it anymore. "How do we find them? How do we stop him?"

Seth glanced around the table. "Any ideas?"

No one spoke as they exchanged troubled glances.

Dana cleared her throat. "Use me as bait."

Aidan's neck popped his head snapped around so quickly. "What?" he demanded incredulously.

She swallowed hard, dread clouding her features. "Use me as bait."

Chapter Nineteen

"**H**ELL NO!" AIDAN BLURTED. "ARE you mad, woman?"

"No," Dana said and looked around the table. "What other option is there?"

"That's not an option," he retorted. "That's not even *close* to the table, let alone *on* it. We are not using you as bait. Absolutely not." What was she thinking?

"Look," she said, her face and voice sober as she addressed them all, "I'm not real keen on the idea either. But we already know that in North Carolina, Gershom has been targeting female *gifted ones* who have been in direct contact with Aidan. We know he has ordered vampires to attack me in the past. I assume he knows Aidan and I are lovers. And since he's been sticking his nose into everybody's business, he probably also knows that you've all taken me under your wing and are trying to protect me. What better target could he have?"

"Ami," Marcus offered. "Or Adira."

Adira looked up at the sound of her name and tilted her head back to smile up at her father. Marcus kissed the top of her head.

"All the more reason to use me as bait," Dana said, "and direct his attention away from them."

"No," Aidan said again, still having difficulty believing she would even contemplate such a thing. Hadn't she heard Chris tell them that several of the *gifted ones* had been found dead?

Roland caught Dana's gaze. "The immortals present can all hear your heart racing with fear at just the idea of baiting a trap for Gershom. Why would you do this for us?"

She looked around the table. "Because I love Aidan. And you all stood up for him when Gershom made him look guilty as hell. You all broke the rules to stand by his side and try to help him. To help us both. To keep us safe." She shook her head. "I don't have a family of my own. I haven't in a long time. And three days ago, having never laid eyes on me before, you all welcomed me into yours and showed me what it would be like to be one of you. To be part of this family."

Aidan's heart began to pound. "Dana…"

She held up a hand. "I know. I have choice. And that's what makes all of this mean so much more to me. None of you have placed any conditions on my being here. None of you have pressured me to transform for Aidan and become immortal. I honestly think that all of you would welcome me and let me be part of your family whether I transformed or remained as I am."

"We would," David interjected.

"We would," Seth agreed.

"Of course we would," Aidan told her.

Reaching up, she pressed a hand to his cheek. "You've been trying so hard to protect me, Aidan. Well, I want to protect you, too. I love you. I really do. And watching Gershom do his damnedest to kill you yesterday before Seth and Zach showed up…" Tears welled in her eyes.

Aidan covered her hand with his and held it to him.

"You're worth fighting for." She looked around the table. "You're *all* worth fighting for. And if the only way you can get a leg up on Gershom is by shoving me out there as bait, then I say do it." She forced a smile. "And do it quickly, before I change my mind."

A few chuckles lightened the heavy atmosphere.

Dana lowered her hand, taking Aidan's with it and linking their fingers as she rested them on her thigh.

Seth visually consulted David.

Aidan frowned at them. "You aren't actually considering it, are you?"

David never took his gaze from Seth. "He would read it in her memories."

"Such was my thought."

Aidan shook his head. "Even if he couldn't, it's out of the question."

Dana looked back and forth between the two elders. "Would it work better if I were immortal?"

Aidan's breath caught. "What?"

Dana winced. "Ow—ow—*ouch*! Honey, you're squeezing the crap out of my hand."

He swiftly relaxed his grip. "I'm sorry." Glancing down, he examined her hand and noted the pale marks he'd left that slowly regained their color. "I'm so sorry, sweetheart. I'd never hurt you on purpose. Are you okay?"

She nodded. "I'm fine. It was just a little tight. No worries."

Roland caught her attention. "Are you saying you would transform and become immortal?"

"Yes. Would that help? Would that make it harder for Gershom to read my thoughts and know I'm bait?"

Aidan stared at her, both elated and terrified. He wanted so badly for her to transform and spend the rest of eternity with him. But he didn't want her to feel forced into it. "Dana…"

"Don't say it again," she said, irritation creeping into her features. "You keep telling me I have choice as if you're trying to talk me out of it."

"I keep telling you you have choice because I can't bring myself to believe you'll make the one I'm hoping for." He shook his head. "And I don't want Gershom to force your hand. I don't want you to make a hasty decision you may come to regret. This isn't reversible."

She smiled, a soft curling up of her lips that warmed his insides and coaxed his racing heart into calming the hell down. "I'm not doing it because Gershom is forcing my hand. And I'm not doing it because I felt so helpless standing on your back porch, doing nothing while I watched you fight Gershom. Ethan and Heather both leapt to your side to help you. Cliff did, too. And all I could do was just stand there," she told him, her smile gone.

Aidan hadn't thought much about that aspect of things but felt her frustration.

"That was terrifying and horrible and I never want to feel that helpless again," she continued. "But that still isn't what's compelling me to transform."

"Then what is?" he asked.

Her smile returned. "You. I love you, Aidan. And the opportunity to have hundreds, if not thousands, of years together instead of a few decades is just too tempting to pass up."

There went his treacherous heart again, slamming against his rib cage. "You're sure? We've been seeing each other for less than a month."

"I'm sure." She shrugged. "And we aren't the first couple to fall in love so quickly."

Roland grunted. "Hell, it only took me twenty-four hours to fall for Sarah."

Sarah looked up at him in surprise. "Really?"

"You know you're irresistible," he countered.

Grinning, she leaned up and brushed a quick kiss across his lips.

Ethan glanced at Heather. "We fell for each other after only a couple of dates." He frowned. "Wait. Does fighting vampires together count as a date?"

Heather laughed.

Farther down the table, Krysta laughed, too. "It did for *us*. That's how Étienne and I met and fell in love."

Étienne smiled. "If memory serves, you tried to decapitate me the first time we met. The second, too. What kind of date is that?"

Krysta winked. "A fun-filled, flirtatious one?"

Laughter all around.

Aidan paid little attention. His eyes continued to cling to Dana's. "You're sure?" he murmured beneath the chuckles.

"I'm sure," she said.

"No doubts?" he pressed, elation beginning to overcome fear.

"None at all."

Wrapping his arms around her, he hugged her tight. "Thank you."

She nodded against his chest. "I didn't mean to tell you in front of everyone."

Aware of the quiet that had settled around them, Aidan released her but kept an arm around her shoulders.

A faint blush climbed her cheeks when she noticed everyone watching them. "But if now would be a better time for me to transform…"

Seth sent her a kind smile. "Becoming immortal wouldn't keep Gershom from reading your thoughts."

"Oh." Her brow furrowed as she looked from Seth to David and back again. "Then you can't use me as bait?"

"No," Seth said.

"We appreciate the offer though and admire the courage you showed in making it," David added.

Thank you, Aidan told both elders telepathically.

"Then what are you going to do?" Dana pressed.

Chris spoke. "My contacts are going to see if they can dig anything up."

Heather leaned forward. "Do you mean your contacts in government agencies?"

Chris nodded. "FBI, CIA, NSA, NRO and a few others. I want to ensure the military is not in any way involved."

Heather frowned. "Why would you think the military might be involved?"

"Because my forensics team said the weapons used to kill the *gifted ones* we found are commonly employed by the military. The grouping of the gunshot wounds also pointed toward someone with military training."

Heather looked at Seth and David, then returned her gaze to Chris. "One of your contacts wouldn't happen to be my father, would it?"

Chris hesitated. "Yes."

Heather swore.

Dana caught Heather's gaze. "Who's your father?"

"General Milton Lane."

Dana's eyes widened. "The one I see on the news sometimes?"

"Yes," Heather ground out, her eyes on Chris. "I thought we had agreed to keep him out of this."

"I agreed to *try* to keep him out of it *last* time. I made no such agreement this time. And he's in a position to access even more classified information than my other contacts, so I gave him a call."

Heather turned to Seth. "You knew about this?"

"Actually," Seth said, "this is my first time hearing about it."

"Then kick his ass," Heather demanded furiously. Clearly she didn't like the idea of her father taking dangerous risks to acquire information for them.

Seth's face reflected regret. "In this instance, I'm afraid the decision was your father's to make." He eyed Chris. "I assume you didn't pressure him?"

"I did not," Chris confirmed. "I merely informed him of the situation and asked if he thought he could be of some assistance. He said yes."

Heather's eyes flashed bright amber. "Of course, he did! He — "

Seth held up a hand, silencing Heather and catching Chris's eye. "Does General Lane have my number?"

"Yes," Chris said, then looked at Heather. "And I told him to call it if he feels even the tiniest hint that he may be in danger."

Heather sighed.

They all did as tempers calmed.

"So, what do we do now?" Krysta asked.

"Wait to see what Chris can find out," Seth said. "See what we can find out ourselves."

David nodded. "You should all hunt in groups now. Not pairs, but groups. If possible, it would be best to include a telepath in each group."

"I agree," Seth said. "Telepaths, read the mind of every vampire you encounter. We don't know if the vampires are congregating in the same place the *gifted ones* are being held, so look for any clues in their memories that may lead us to where they are staying."

"And carry the sedative with you," David added. "Seth, Zach, and I can examine the minds of any vampires you tranq to see if there's something buried that you couldn't see yourselves."

Alena closed her file folder. "Scott and I will continue to work on things from our end and see what we can ferret out since we don't even know in what state the *gifted ones* are being held."

Seth inclined his head. "Thank you."

Zach leaned back in his chair. "There's one problem we've yet to address."

All waited for him to continue.

"The fact that Gershom can pass himself off as Seth."

Uneasy glances slid Seth's way.

Seth sighed. "I don't know how to combat that."

David eyed those present. "You should all spend your days and downtime here until we sort this out. Ami has no difficulty telling Seth from Gershom. She doesn't even have to be in the same room with Gershom to know he's present. So she can set your minds at ease while you're here."

"And when we're not here?" Aidan asked, wanting to avoid a repeat of his battle with Gershom and the confusion that had thrown him.

Seth shook his head. "I don't know how to assure you I'm me when I see you. Or how to ensure Gershom won't fool you into believing *he* is me."

A thoughtful hush descended.

"What about a password?" Melanie suggested. "Something we would know ahead of time that you'll say to prove you're you. Like a PIN."

Seth shook his head. "Gershom could pluck it from your thoughts."

She frowned. "I keep forgetting that."

Chris straightened. "Wait a minute. A password may not work, but you may be on to something with the PIN."

Aidan glanced around. What the hell was a PIN?

"Let me consult my tech guys. They may be able to come up with something electronic Seth can carry on him that can identify him as the real deal. Something you can scan from a distance."

Seth tilted his head to one side. "Couldn't Gershom steal a duplicate from the network or compel one of your tech guys to make a duplicate?"

"Not without us knowing," Chris said. "And not if I keep my tech guys on site. If I lock down the network, no immortals can teleport in or out and no humans can enter or leave without triggering the alarm."

Seth shared a look with David. "Sounds good. Have your tech crew work as swiftly as they can."

"I'll let you know as soon as we have something."

"Thank you."

Krysta glanced around the table. "Are we hunting tonight?"

"Yes, you may hunt tonight," Seth said with obvious reluctance. "But do as David said and hunt in groups. I want a telepath in every group."

David eyed the gathering. "I shall remain here and hold down the fort, so to speak."

And protect Ami and Adira, Aidan thought. No doubt Marcus would remain behind as well, wanting to ensure Gershom didn't get his hands on his wife and daughter.

"Bastien and Melanie," Seth directed, "I want you to stay at the network and keep an eye on things there. As usual, if trouble arises and you need reinforcements, let the vampires out to play until the cavalry can arrive."

The couple nodded.

Seth studied those around the table. "If I show up unexpectedly while you're away from David's place, I want the telepaths to summon me immediately. And I want the rest of you to speed dial me on your cell phones. Just to be sure it's me." Though Seth spoke in even tones, he radiated anger that such action was necessary. "Anything else?"

No one spoke.

"Very well. Be safe."

Chairs scuffed the bamboo floor as those gathered around the table scooted them back and rose.

Seth stood and wove his way through the others to reach Aidan and Dana as they rose. "I heard what you wanted to ask," he told Dana.

Aidan glanced down at Dana. "You wanted to ask something?"

She nodded but seemed reluctant to speak.

Seth took one of her hands and held it between his. "If Aidan transforms you tonight, you will be very ill and weakened for three days or more and he will be distracted. I'm very happy you've decided to join the immortals' ranks, but I believe it would be best if you waited."

Dana had wanted Aidan to transform her tonight?

Though she appeared disappointed, Dana again nodded. "Okay."

Giving her hand a pat, Seth headed over to David.

Aidan saw the logic of it but would've felt a hell of a lot better going up against Gershom if Dana were immortal.

Bastien stepped around Brodie and Ed. "Aidan. Any chance I

could talk you into teleporting Melanie and me back to the network? I'd like to check on Cliff."

Guilt struck. Yet again, Aidan had failed to take Cliff into sunlight this afternoon. "How's he doing? I wasn't able to take him into the sun today."

"Not good. He's been very agitated since the fight with Gershom. Melanie has been giving him watered-down doses of the sedative to try to keep things in check."

Aidan nodded. "We can go now then." He looked around. "Ethan? Heather?"

"Yeah?" Ethan said as the couple joined them.

"I want to stop off at the network before we begin the night's hunt."

"Okay," they both agreed.

Aidan slid an arm around Dana's waist. "Everyone grab a shoulder."

Heather rested a hand on Dana's shoulder. Ethan and Bastien both gripped Aidan's. Melanie leaned into Bastien and wrapped an arm around his waist.

"Aidan!" Chris called over the conversations rumbling through the room. Shouldering his way through the crowd, he stopped beside Bastien. "Can I hitch a ride back to the network?"

Aidan nodded. "Grab a shoulder."

Clutching his briefcase with one hand, Chris drew out his cell phone and dialed. "John. Chris Reordon. Aidan is about to teleport me and five others into the network. Turn the alarm off." He rested the hand holding the phone on Bastien's shoulder, then nodded.

David's dining room darkened and disappeared, replaced by the lab Dana had visited once before at the network.

Chris returned the phone to his ear. "Okay. We're here. Turn it back on."

"Dana?"

Dana glanced at the pretty brunette who stood beside Bastien. Unlike the other immortals present, Melanie wore faded blue jeans, a Tar Heels T-shirt, and sneakers.

"Yes?"

Melanie smiled. "I don't think we've been introduced yet. I'm Melanie. I believe you've met my husband, Bastien?"

Returning her smile, Dana shook the hand she offered. "Yes. It's nice to meet you."

"Nice to meet you, too." Melanie drew her aside. "I know the past few days have been very trying. And I'm sorry you've had such a violent and terrifying entrance into our world, but I'd like to ask your help with something."

"Okay," Dana said, not knowing how else to respond. "What can I do for you?"

Looping her arm through Dana's, Melanie began to slowly steer her toward an area that resembled an exam room in a doctor's office. "My colleagues at the network who have been studying the virus with me have been puzzling over an anomaly we can't explain, and I think you could help us solve the mystery."

Dana glanced over her shoulder.

Aidan stood beside Bastien, his brow furrowed as though he wasn't sure he liked what he was hearing.

"To put it briefly," Melanie continued, "older immortals are always stronger and faster than younger immortals. It's been that way for thousands of years until the past decade. When Roland, who is nine hundred plus years old, transformed Sarah a few years ago, she ended up being as strong and powerful as he is. Roland then transformed me and Jenna, and the same thing happened. We ended up being far stronger and faster than we should be. We weren't sure if it was because we were transformed by an immortal or, perhaps, if it might be something unique with Roland."

Dana frowned. "Weren't there other immortals who were transformed by immortals?"

"No. Until Sarah, every immortal in existence had been transformed by a vampire." She paused. "Well, except for Richart and Étienne. Lisette accidentally transformed her brothers because none of them understood the nature of the virus at the time."

"Oh." That was messed up.

Dana didn't realize until then that she didn't know how Aidan had been transformed. So much had happened that she hadn't had a chance to get the details yet, but it sounded as though he had been transformed against his will.

"Then Étienne, a younger immortal," Melanie continued, "transformed Krysta. And Aidan transformed Heather."

Dana's stomach sank. She looked back at Aidan.

Heather jumped up and down behind him, trying to see over his shoulder, then ducked around to stand beside him. "Ethan and I asked him to do it so I'd be stronger and better able to fight Gershom. But just FYI, there wasn't anything romantic or sexual about it, and we aren't bonded or anything like in the movies."

"Oh." Relief dispelled the jealousy that had risen so swiftly. "Okay."

"Anyway," Melanie said, reclaiming her attention, "we all thought Krysta was as strong and fast as Étienne until she graciously allowed me to run some tests and we discovered that she isn't. While she's stronger than a vampire, she isn't as strong as the immortal who transformed her. So we've come to believe that something different happens when immortals like Roland and Aidan transform *gifted ones* because they're healers. We believe their healing ability alters the transformation process in some way and—since you're planning to have Aidan transform you—I was hoping you would be willing to help us solve the mystery."

"How?" Dana asked.

Melanie bit her lip. "By letting me take some samples and do some blood work, both before *and* after your transformation. And maybe during?"

Aidan stepped forward. "You only want blood samples?"

She hesitated. "Actually, blood *and* tissue samples would be best. But I would only need the tiniest— "

"Hell no," Aidan blurted.

Dana didn't like that sound of that either.

Melanie eyed Aidan warily but spoke to Dana. "It sounds worse than it is. The tissue samples are tiny. It would be no more painful or invasive than having a mole removed and tested by your dermatologist."

"Oh." Reassured, Dana nodded. She had actually had a freckle-like mole removed and tested three years ago. "Okay. Sure. If that would help you, I'm fine with it."

"Well, I'm not," Aidan protested.

Bastien clapped Aidan on the back. "It won't hurt. I've seen her do it to Cliff and the other vampires loads of times. It really isn't as bad as it sounds."

Melanie offered Dana a hopeful smile. "Could we maybe do it now?"

"Seriously?" Aidan protested.

She nodded. "We don't know what Gershom is going to do next or whether or not Dana will manage to come through it unscathed. If she's seriously injured, you'll go ahead and transform her ahead of schedule, so I'd really rather do it now, just to be safe."

Dana took Aidan's hand. "She's right. If she doesn't do it now, I may be immortal the next time she sees me. I'm fine with it. Really. Why don't you go check on Cliff while we take care of this?"

"No, I want to stay with you."

She grinned, both touched and amused by his concern for her. "I'm not having major surgery, Aidan. She's just going to take some blood and a couple of itty-bitty tissue samples. It's no big deal. My doctors have done it before. More than once, actually. You just go check on Cliff. We'll be done by the time you get back."

It took a little more coaxing, but Aidan finally agreed.

After he left with Bastien and Chris, Ethan turned to Melanie. "Do you mind if we grab some bags of blood? I want to tank up before our hunt tonight."

"Not at all," Melanie said and gestured to one of the small rooms that branched off the lab. "Employees just donated a fresh batch today. It's right through there."

Taking Heather's hand, Ethan led her into the other room.

Melanie pulled a privacy curtain around them and motioned for Dana to sit on the exam table. "Thank you again for doing this. Shall we get started?"

His ears attuned to the murmured conversation passing between Melanie and Dana, Aidan started down the hallway to Cliff's apartment.

"He isn't there," Chris said. "His behavior became too erratic after Melanie and Bastien left for the meeting, so I isolated him."

Bastien scowled. "Isolated him where? In a holding room?"

Though Chris shook his head in slow, deliberate movements, he said, "Yes. We had to sedate him, too. Follow me. I'll take you to him." Then he motioned to the doors of the other vampires' apartments and tapped his ear.

Aidan shared a puzzled glance with Bastien.

What didn't Chris want the other vampires to hear?

Following Chris to the elevator, he noticed one of the guards was missing. Todd.

Aidan remained quiet as the elevator carried them to the ground floor. But he exchanged another confused look with Bastien as they followed Chris down the hallway that led to his office.

A dozen guards manned the entrance of the reception room outside Chris's office. Inside the reception room, Kate—Chris's assistant—sat at a large desk situated in front of a row of file cabinets. Garbed in a formfitting business suit not unlike the one Alena Moreno had worn, she glanced up at their entrance.

"Any calls?" Chris asked, striding toward the door to his office.

"Nothing that can't wait," she replied. When she reached to one side to pick up a sheaf of papers, Aidan spotted a weapon housed in a shoulder holster under her jacket.

Todd and a dozen more guards bracketed the entrance to Chris's office.

What the hell? Aidan had never seen such before.

Chris nodded to the guards as he strode inside his office.

Aidan and Bastien followed.

Chris closed the door, crossed to his desk, and dropped his briefcase atop it.

Aidan glanced around. Something was different.

Chris's sofa was missing.

Facing them both, Chris pressed a finger to his lips, then guided them over to the boardroom. Opening the door, he motioned for them to enter.

Aidan followed Bastien inside and stopped short.

Chris nudged them forward enough for him to enter behind them, then closed the door. "I didn't want the vampires to find out."

At the other end of the boardroom, Cliff was curled up on Chris's sofa with Emma.

Both slept soundly.

Aidan gaped at Chris. "You knew?"

Chris arched a brow. "Of course I knew."

Bastien grunted. "The bastard knows everything. He's as bad as Seth."

Chris laughed. But his laughter died quickly as the three of them studied the couple.

Emma's face reflected the peace she had found in slumber.

Cliff was another matter. His brow furrowed, his muscles tense, he clutched Emma tightly, as though he feared his violent dreams would tear her from his arms.

But at least he slept.

"I'm surprised you didn't put a stop to it," Aidan murmured.

Chris shook his head. "I like Cliff. He's smart as hell. He's brave. He's honorable. If he were human, he'd be one of my higher-ups here at the network. I knew you didn't take him into the sun today and could see he was struggling. So I brought them both in here."

Bastien turned to the network leader. "Thank you."

Chris shrugged. "Who knows? Maybe whatever Melanie learns from Dana's transformation might also help Cliff."

Aidan sure as hell hoped it would.

Chapter Twenty

A COOL BREEZE RUFFLED AIDAN'S hair as he eyed the small bandage at the bend of Dana's arm. "Are you sure you don't want me to heal it?"

She laughed. "I'm sure. It was just a tiny needle prick, Aidan. Honestly, I would feel like a total wuss if you healed it for me."

Nevertheless, he wondered if he couldn't find some way to heal it without her knowledge. Particularly since his sharp vision caught the beginnings of a bruise peeking out from under the bandage.

Heather laughed and handed Dana a sandwich. "Ethan's the same way. I'm a lot stronger and faster than he is, but he still freaks out over every little scratch I get."

Ethan grunted. "Because some of those scratches aren't so little."

They sat atop Davis Library on UNC Chapel Hill's campus. Minutes earlier, Aidan and Ethan had taken out eight vampires below. And the four of them now were pretty much just hanging around until the network's cleanup crew finished working their magic below—making sure no security cameras had captured the battle, removing blood from the pavement, that sort of thing.

Heather handed Aidan a sandwich.

"Thank you."

Apparently Reordon's kitchen crew at the network had packed them a very nice snack to take along on their hunt.

The two humans below tossed the immortals sitting near the roof's edge a wave.

Aidan and the others waved back and watched the men head

back to their van and drive away.

"This is good," Dana commented after taking a big bite of her sandwich.

Aidan grinned. Yes, it was. And *this* was good. This moment of normalcy, or what passed for such in his world. Just sitting and chatting and sharing a meal, Dana's shoulder brushing his arm.

"It still feels weird," Heather said, "staying up here and doing nothing while you guys do all the fighting down there."

Aidan shook his head. "You have the most important job here, Heather — protecting Dana."

Dana grimaced. "I wish I were already immortal. Then I could protect myself."

A scent rose on the breeze.

Aidan looked to the west. "Do you smell that?" he murmured.

Heather set her sandwich down and followed his gaze. "Yes."

"How many?"

She drew in a deep breath. "Fifteen."

"Excellent. You didn't let the scents from our earlier kills distract you." He handed his sandwich to Dana and rose.

Ethan stuffed the last bite of his sandwich in his mouth and stood, drawing two sais.

The vampires that approached spoke little. Very odd. Insanity rarely bred silence.

Perhaps they simply hadn't fed yet tonight and had no recent kills about which they could brag.

Aidan looked to Ethan. "Ready?"

"Sure."

Dana and Heather stood, abandoning their meal.

Aidan leaned down and pressed a quick kiss to Dana's lips. "This should only take a moment."

"Okay. Be careful."

He hated the worry he saw in her gaze and wished that becoming part of his world would not require her to accustom herself to nightly violence.

Stepping off the edge of the roof, he enjoyed the quick uptake in the wind and the thrill of being able to fall eight stories and land easily on his feet. Perhaps little perks like that would make up for the darker side of becoming immortal for Dana.

He drew his swords as Ethan landed beside him. "They'll be here momentarily."

The sound of a phone number being dialed carried down from the roof.

"Reordon."

"Hi, Chris. It's Heather."

"Everything okay? My boys just called and said they were headed in."

"Everything's fine, but you'd better go ahead and tell them to turn around. Looks like our night isn't over. We're about to create another mess for them to clean up."

Chris laughed. "Will do."

Aidan shared an amused look with Ethan.

The vampires came around the corner a minute later. All looked to be newly turned, their clothing neat, their hair well groomed. Good hygiene tended to be the first thing to go when insanity blossomed.

All the vampires stopped short upon seeing the two men waiting for them.

Aidan read as many minds as he could in the time allowed.

The vampires took in the two men in long black coats sporting swords and concluded they faced Immortal Guardians. They also recognized Aidan, whom they believed had ordered them to attack him in earnest the next time they encountered him so his woman would transform for him.

Damn Gershom for that.

Two vampires yelped as darts struck them in the chest, fired from the library's roof. Eyes rolling back, they sank to the ground.

Aidan grinned. Looked like Dana was trying to protect him again.

The other vampires drew blades and raced forward, eyes glowing, fangs bared.

Another dart hit its mark, dropping a third vampire in his tracks before Aidan and Ethan dove forward and began cutting a swath through the throng.

Aidan didn't think a dozen vampires would be much of a problem but nevertheless kept an eye on Ethan to ensure the younger immortal didn't end up surrounded. One lucky strike from behind was all it would take to end it for an immortal.

Opening the carotid arteries of the vamp in front of him, Aidan spun and blocked the swing of the vampire behind him. The vampire howled in fury when Aidan rid him of his weapon. Drawing two more daggers, the vamp leapt forward.

Aidan swung.

The vampire's head left his shoulders and fell to the ground, his body toppling after it.

Two down.

His swords flashed as two vampires attacked him, one from the left and one from the right.

Two more down.

Bodies began to clutter the ground around them as Ethan slew another vampire, then another.

Aidan took out a vampire that tried to attack Ethan from behind, then stood with his back to the younger immortal's, guarding him and slaying vampires at the same time.

As Aidan's last opponent fell, he turned to help Ethan. Ethan spun at the same time.

They met each other's gaze, then looked around.

No vampires remained standing.

"Are you okay?" Aidan asked, unable to tell if any of the blood that stained Ethan's shirt was his own.

Ethan nodded, breathing heavily. "Just a few flesh wounds. You?"

"I'm good." He had only incurred a few nicks, and those had already begun to heal. He glanced at the sedated vampires sprawled on the sidewalk a few yards away. "Let's — "

Pain struck, so intense it felt as though someone had pressed a power drill to his right temple and was doing his damnedest to bore a hole clear through to the other side.

Crying out, Aidan dropped his weapons and clutched his head.

<hr />

Dana released a sigh of relief as the last vampire fell to the ground. The battle was over, and Aidan and Ethan had emerged the victors. They also appeared unscathed. Good.

She backed away from the edge.

Heather smiled at her. "See, I told you they'd be fine."

"I know. I just— "

Aidan cried out.

Dana's head whipped around. Easing back to the edge, she peered below.

Aidan bent forward, gripping his head. Ethan did the same.

Aidan staggered.

Ethan sank to his knees. Blood began to trail from his eyes and ears.

"Oh shit," Heather breathed and reached inside her coat.

A loud crack split the night, like the sound of a large rock hitting a tree.

Heather's head jerked.

Dana jumped as warm wet liquid slapped the side of her face.

Then Heather slumped forward.

Lunging toward her with a cry, Dana grabbed the back of her coat as Heather tumbled off the roof.

Heather's weight yanked Dana down to her knees, then onto her stomach. Dana shoved her free hand against the curb at the roof's edge to keep from going over herself. So close.

Heart pounding, she drew a knee up and braced it against the edge, too. "Heather!" she screamed. Muscles straining, she tried to lift Heather, but just holding on to her was a struggle.

The fabric in Dana's grasp was wet with blood that had sprayed from whatever wound Heather had suffered and began to slip from Dana's grasp. More blood gushed from the back of Heather's head.

"No," Dana gritted, breathing hard as the immortal's weight pulled at her, luring her farther over the edge. One shoulder and part of Dana's chest dangled over open air. "Heather!" Her muscles trembled. The fabric slipped a little more. "Please," she sobbed.

Then Heather slid from her grasp.

Dana's horrified gaze clung to the other woman as Heather fell eight stories to land with a sickening thud on the ground.

Tears blurring her vision, Dana scrambled to her knees and looked at Aidan.

He writhed on the ground now, blood painting the skin below his nose, eyes, and ears.

Beside him, Ethan convulsed.

Her breath coming in panicked gasps, Dana stood and — with shaking hands — dragged her cell phone out of her pocket.

Before she could call Seth, the phone leapt from her grasp and disappeared behind her.

She spun around.

Her heart stopped.

A man as tall as Seth stood behind her, his chest bare. Long black hair moved with the breeze and blended with the huge dark wings spread behind him.

Clutching her cell phone in one hand, he smiled. "Hello, bait."

Aidan jerked awake. Bright light blinded him. Panic rose, kicking his heartbeat into a gallop. "Dana!" He lunged upward.

Hands clutched his shoulders and tried to restrain him.

"Hold him down! Hold him down!" a male with a British accent shouted.

Aidan fought them with all his might until faces swam into view.

Familiar faces.

He slowed, breathing hard, and surveyed his surroundings. Or tried to.

A sea of black encircled him, the clothing of his concerned brethren.

Bastien and Melanie. Roland and Sarah. Marcus. David. And Brodie.

Again he tried to rise. "Where's Dana? And Ethan and Heather?"

"Easy," David said, resting a hand on his shoulder.

Aidan's rapid heartbeat slowed. His choppy breaths lengthened and became less ragged. But his panic did not recede. He couldn't see Dana. Where was she? Where was *he*?

He glanced down. He sat on what appeared to be a gurney. Blood seeped from the bend of his arm where he had inadvertently yanked out an IV tube. But the ceiling above him, the lights and the walls he caught glimpses of when his friends shifted, did not look like the network's medical facilities. Nor did they resemble those in the infirmary at David's home.

"Lie back and let me finish," David coaxed.

Finish what? Aidan shook his head. "Where's Dana?"

"Do as I say and let me finish healing you," David commanded. Though he spoke softly, his tone advised Aidan not to refuse.

Worry pounding him even more than the pain in his head, Aidan lay back.

David cupped Aidan's head and closed his eyes. Warmth blossomed in those large hands, transferring itself to Aidan and diminishing the throbbing in his temples.

Minutes passed, feeling more like hours.

Aidan fidgeted anxiously, his mind racing. What exactly had happened? Everything seemed fuzzy. He had been… fighting vampires with Ethan. And they had defeated them all, hadn't they?

It took a frustratingly long time to recall that yes, they had defeated the vampires. Then… he remembered nothing but pain.

Had they not defeated the vampires after all? Had one snuck up behind him and gotten in a lucky strike?

What about Dana? Was she all right? Was she safe?

David opened his eyes. His hands cooled. He sighed as he stepped back. "All right. The damage was extensive, but I believe I've healed it all. How do you feel?"

Aidan sat up. "Where's Dana?"

The immortals encircling him shared a grim look.

Brodie cleared his throat. "We believe Gershom took her."

Icy fear clawed at him. "And Heather? Ethan? Are they okay?"

Bodies shifted, parting like double doors swinging open. And Aidan discovered with a great deal of surprise that he was in Chris Reordon's boardroom at network headquarters.

Several Seconds sat at the long table, the laptop computers in front of them casting a bluish tint to their features. On the other side of the table, two more gurneys similar to Aidan's bore Ethan and Heather.

Seth leaned over Ethan, his eyes closed, his hands bearing a golden glow as they cupped Ethan's head. Lisette stood beside them, nose red, nibbling her thumbnail as tears streamed down her cheeks. An IV hanging beside her fed blood into Ethan's veins.

Zach leaned over Heather much like Seth, his eyes closed, brow furrowed in concentration. His hands also bore an unearthly golden glow where they clasped Heather's head.

Both unconscious immortals looked pale as death.

Aidan checked every face in the room. With the exception of Alena Moreno and Scott Henderson, everyone who had been present at the last meeting in David's home was there. Everyone but Dana.

Even little Adira slept in Ami's arms over on the sofa Cliff and Emma had occupied earlier.

Aidan swung his legs over the side of the gurney and rose. Dizziness struck, an indication that he needed more blood.

He staggered.

Brodie grabbed him by the arm to steady him.

Aidan nodded to Ethan and Heather. "What happened?"

David spoke. "When Chris's cleanup crew arrived on the scene, they found you and Ethan unconscious on the ground, bleeding from your eyes, nose, and ears. Three sedated vampires lay several yards away. What was left of the dozen or so you had slain littered the ground around you." He motioned to Heather. "They found Heather at the base of Davis Library. Something had struck her from behind with such force that it laid open her head and caused a great deal of damage to her skull and brain."

Aidan's concern increased. Brain injuries were extremely difficult to heal. Even Seth could not heal all brain injuries, which was why he had been unable to prevent Cliff from slowly losing his sanity.

"Zach is still struggling to repair the damage," David informed him.

Aidan swallowed hard as he stared at the young woman. Heather had been on that roof at his behest. *He* had asked her to stay and protect Dana. What would that cost her if Zach could only partially heal her?

"You and Ethan suffered severe brain damage as well," David continued. "With you, it was as though someone took a sledgehammer to your mental barriers, then—once those barriers toppled—just kept swinging the hammer willy-nilly, wrecking anything in its path. Fortunately, you're an elder and a powerful healer with stronger regenerative abilities that aided me in repairing the damage. Ethan, however, is not faring so well."

"What do you mean?" Aidan asked.

"Ethan's brain is wired differently. Even something as simple as navigating it to read his thoughts is tricky. So Seth is having difficulty healing him and repairing the damage."

Aidan caught David's eye. *Can Seth save him?* he asked telepathically, not wanting Lisette or Ed to hear.

We aren't certain, David responded in kind. *Seth has kept him alive thus far, but Ethan may be… changed… if Seth is unable to make all necessary repairs.*

Changed. "And Dana?" Aidan asked aloud.

David hesitated. "The cleanup crew didn't find her, so we believe Gershom took her."

Gershom had Dana. And nine of the *gifted ones* Gershom had taken had been found dead.

"Was there anything on the roof to indicate she had been injured?" Aidan forced himself to ask.

Bastien moved closer. "No. When we heard what happened, Melanie and I asked Richart to teleport us to the scene. We found no trace of her blood on the roof. Nor did we smell it anywhere on campus. I examined the marks on the roof myself. And it looked as though Dana damned near threw herself off it trying to save Heather, then was teleported away by someone she struggled with briefly."

The images that filled Aidan's mind then sent fury flinging its way through him.

While he had been unconscious on the ground, Dana had been fighting for her life. She had needed him and he hadn't been there for her. Now Gershom had her. What the hell were they going to do?

"How long have I been out?" he gritted.

"Hours," Bastien told him.

Across the room, Heather's eyes flew open. "Oh shit," she whispered, then lunged upright. "Seth!" She started to fumble in her pockets, then stopped as she seemed to forget what she'd intended to do.

Ed hurried to her side as others flowed toward her.

Heather looked around with wild eyes. "What happened?

Where's Ethan? Is he okay? I was going to call Seth, but I can't remember why, just that Ethan needed him…" She trailed off as Ed took her hands. Her eyes met his, took in his grave expression and filled with tears. "No. No, no, no. Don't say it. Please, don't say it, Ed."

"He's alive," her Second told her.

Her throat worked in swallow. Her eyes acquired a bright amber glow. "But?"

"He's in bad shape," Ed said, his hoarse voice telling her without further words that the wounds Ethan had suffered could not be healed with a simple blood infusion.

"Where is he?" she asked.

Ed helped her off the gurney and guided her to Ethan's side.

Tears spilled down her cheeks.

When she reached out to take Ethan's hand, Ed stopped her. "You can't. Not while Seth is trying to heal him."

The word *trying* seemed to hit Heather like a kick in the gut. She gripped Ed's hand. "We were at UNC. I remember his eyes and nose bleeding. Did Gershom fuck with his brain?"

"Yes," Ed confirmed. "Seth is doing what he can to heal him."

More tears dampened her cheeks as she glanced around. "Aidan and Dana were there, weren't they? Are they okay?"

Aidan leaned to one side so she could see him. "I'm okay, Heather."

The crease in her brow relaxed just a bit when she saw he was all right. She searched the crowd around them, then met his gaze. "Where's Dana?"

He drew in a deep breath. "Gershom took her."

"Oh no." Hurrying across the room, she threw her arms around his neck. "I'm sorry. I'm so sorry," she cried, her tears dampening his shirt. "I can't remember all of it, but I think it was my fault. I wasn't fast enough and didn't— "

Aidan patted her back. "It wasn't your fault, Heather. If with anyone, the fault lies with me. I expected Gershom to attack us as he did before, by posing as Seth and striking with words and swords. But he didn't. He again played the magician Sheldon named him. He distracted us with a standard vampire attack, then blindsided us while our guard was down."

"But he has Dana," she sobbed. "And Ethan is…"

Aidan hugged her tight, murmuring soothing sounds he thought woefully inadequate. "Ethan is a fighter. And Seth is the most powerful healer on the planet. Let's wait and see what the two of them can do before we jump ahead to grieving. Okay?"

She nodded. But he could hear all the terrifying *what-ifs* swirling around in her mind.

The boardroom door opened.

Chris Reordon strode in, a laptop tucked under one arm. Closing the door behind him, he wound his way over to the head of the table. "Everyone take a seat."

Aidan guided Heather over to the closest chairs. "Why are we here?" he asked Chris. "Why aren't we at David's?"

Chris set his laptop down and seated himself. "Because the walls, ceiling, and floor of this room are packed with so much soundproofing that even Seth can't hear what's spoken in here if he's outside that door. This is the only place I feel confident that Gershom can't eavesdrop if he tries."

The chairs around the table rapidly filled. Marcus seated himself on the sofa beside Ami and Adira.

"Seth," Chris said, "are you okay with my proceeding, or would you like me to wait?"

"Go ahead," he answered, his eyes closed.

Chris looked to Aidan. "How are you feeling?"

"Scared out of my mind," Aidan admitted. "That fucker Gershom has Dana."

A dark figure abruptly appeared at the far end of the room beside the sofa.

Aidan glanced over at him and found a mirror image of Seth.

An alarm began to blare, *wonk wonk wonking* as Aidan and the other immortals all leapt to their feet.

Adira jerked awake and began to wail.

Aidan reached for his weapons, only to realize he no longer had any. His brethren did, however, and swiftly drew them.

The man threw up his hands as his form shifted into that of Jared. "Easy," he said. "I'm friend, not foe. Seth can confirm it."

"He's a friend," Seth said, opening his eyes.

Ami nodded as she patted Adira's back. "He's not Gershom."

Adira's cries quieted to whimpers.

Chris murmured something into a walkie-talkie.

The alarm ceased. But Aidan's ears continued to ring.

"Were you able to track him?" Seth asked Jared.

"No," he answered, the picture of regret. "Too much time had passed before you summoned me. The trail was too faint. I tried to follow it anyway but couldn't locate him."

Roland scowled at him. "Why did you look like Seth just now?"

Jared lifted one shoulder in a slight shrug. "The Others don't know I've joined your fight. They think I'm still treading their path. I assumed Seth's appearance while I tried to follow Gershom so they wouldn't learn the truth."

The immortals present all looked to Seth, then slowly retook their seats.

Skillet's "Monster" disrupted the quiet.

Seth didn't open his eyes. "Zach."

A cell phone leapt from Seth's pocket and flew into Zach's hand. "Seth's phone," he answered. "Zach speaking."

"It's General Lane," a man announced in an urgent whisper. "I'm in a bind and could use your help."

Heather gasped.

Zach vanished.

Heather swung on Chris. "What did you do?" she demanded. "Why is my father in danger?"

"It wasn't Chris," Seth murmured. "It was me."

Uncertainty filled her features.

Chris nodded. "Seth thought Dana was right about being a likely target of Gershom. So he took measures to ensure we would be able to find her if Gershom got his hands on her."

Aidan retook his seat, hope rising. "What kind of measures?"

Chris nodded at Melanie. "He mind-controlled Melanie and had her plant a tracker under Dana's skin when she took blood and tissue samples for her research."

Melanie's eyebrows shot up. "He did? *I* did?"

David spoke. "We both believed you would agree to help us if we asked, but had we done so, we would've had to erase the memory of our conversation afterward."

She nodded. "Of course I would've agreed to it."

Bastien frowned. "Did the mind control harm Melanie?"

David shook his head. "Because Roland transformed her, Melanie's regenerative capabilities are as strong as an elder's. So the damage done was minor enough for the virus to heal. We wouldn't have proceeded otherwise."

Aidan looked at Chris. "Were you able to track Dana after she was taken?"

"Yes." Chris opened his laptop, then motioned to a large-screen television or monitor that hung on one wall.

The screen lit up with a satellite image that depicted a fairly large building surrounded by forest.

"Dana is being held in a building located in West Texas," Chris told them.

"Texas?" a few repeated.

Aidan shared their surprise. Almost all of their troubles in recent years had originated in North Carolina. "What is it? It doesn't look like a mercenary compound." Aidan saw nothing in the satellite image to indicate that this building was part of a private military company. No training fields. No barracks. No helicopter landing pad. No runways for transport planes. No hangars housing tanks or other combat vehicles.

The building looked civilian in nature.

"As far as we can tell, there is just the one building." Chris tapped some keys on the laptop. The image on the monitor shifted from color to shades of gray and became a little less distinct. "My contacts were able to get me keyhole satellite images. The one you're seeing now is infrared. White indicates heat."

And there were a lot of glowing white bodies in that building.

The video abruptly zoomed in on one wing of the building. "We think Dana is here." He highlighted a room with four figures. "And that these other rooms"—he zoomed out and pointed to many more groups of four—"contain the other missing *gifted ones*."

Roland frowned. "That doesn't look like a hundred *gifted ones* to me."

"No," Chris acknowledged. "We're hoping the building has an underground floor the satellite image doesn't show that houses the rest, like the network."

Heather motioned to the image. "You think it's military?"

Aidan glanced at her. "Why would you say that?" It looked like a regular building to him.

"Because my dad just called Zach. And he wouldn't do that if he didn't think his life was in danger." She glared at Chris.

Chris showed no remorse. "It's hard to see because there are so many damned trees, but some of the images my contacts sent indicate that the building's perimeter is being guarded by men wearing military uniforms."

"Couldn't they be mercenaries?" Aidan asked.

Chris shook his head. "In the hours since I traced Dana to this location, my team has been unable to unearth any information on it. As far as the rest of the world is concerned, it doesn't exist. No construction permits were ever issued. No record of land ownership exists. The power and sewer companies have no record of it. It doesn't even show up on Google fucking Maps. Private military companies aren't shy. They don't hide their shit. They brag about it. Because they know the more badass they appear, the more clients will hire them and pay top billing." He motioned to the map. "But this place? Nothing."

"Shit," Sheldon muttered. "This isn't a fucking Area 51 kind of place, is it?"

Chris shook his head. "I don't know what the hell it is. That's why I called General Lane."

Zach reappeared, General Milton Lane at his side.

"Dad!" Heather leapt up and ran over to embrace her father.

The tight expression on General Lane's face morphed into one of relief. "Heather." He hugged her tight. When she stepped back, he gave her a quick visual scan. "You're okay? Reordon said you'd been— "

"I'm okay," she assured him.

The shoulders of his decorated uniform dipped a bit as he let out a long breath. "And Ethan? He's good, too?"

Biting her lip, she shook her head. New tears welled in her eyes. "Seth is still trying to heal him."

General Lane wrapped his arms around her once more and searched the room for Seth.

Seth's eyes remained closed as he concentrated on his task.

Chris caught the general's attention. "What did you find out?"

Sheldon rose and grabbed one of the extra chairs that had been pushed aside, then rolled it up to the table next to Heather's. Heather thanked him as she and her father seated themselves beside Aidan.

"You were right. It's military," General Lane confirmed. "But it's off-the-books classified. And I mean it's so far off the books that I don't have the clearance needed to check it out. I called in some favors—"

"Dad!" Heather blurted in dismay.

He rested a hand on her arm. "I was damned careful when I did my digging but still ended up acquiring several shadows in under an hour."

Heather covered his hand with hers. "What happened?"

He smiled, the corners of his eyes crinkling with amusement. "Zach happened. It was the damnedest thing I've ever seen. And I've seen a hell of a lot since you stumbled into the Immortal Guardians' world."

All eyes went to Zach as he took a seat at David's elbow.

Zach shrugged. "The military is doing what we've always assumed they would do if they ever found out about *gifted ones*. They're all aflutter over how the men and women Gershom hand delivered to them could be used as weapons against the enemy."

"What enemy?" Aidan asked, perplexed.

"*Any* enemy," Zach replied. "They're holding the *gifted ones* there." He motioned to the screen.

"All of them?" Chris asked.

"I didn't see a specific number, but that's what it looked like in their minds. Right now, they're doing everything they can to determine the full extent of each *gifted one's* talent and researching ways they can utilize it."

Heather shook her head. "Against their will? How can they do that? They can't *make* the captives use their gifts."

Zach sent her a dark smile. "Oh, but they can. They're already coming up with creative ways to force cooperation, including using the deaths of the *gifted ones* who attempted to escape and a few more whose gifts they deemed useless as examples to motivate any who would rather not live out the rest of their lives as lab rats and trained monkeys."

Heather swore. "You were right, Dad. That's exactly what you said they'd do if they ever found out I'm telepathic."

"There's more," her father said.

Zach nodded. "Gershom dropped the word *alien* into a few sentences while conferring with one of the higher-ups."

General Lane huffed a laugh. "Can you believe it? A couple of them actually think the *gifted ones* may be extraterrestrials who are members of some sort of sleeper cell that is quietly infiltrating our society."

A few Immortal Guardians slid surreptitious glances Ami's way.

General Lane, as well as most of the Seconds present, wasn't aware that there was an extraterrestrial in their midst right now. The only one on the planet, in fact. Ami had been ruthlessly tortured by scientists contracted by the military for six months before Seth and David had found and rescued her.

Her face darkened.

Marcus wrapped an arm around her shoulders and drew her closer to his side.

Sheldon looked back and forth between Zach and General Lane. "So this place really *is* like Area 51?" When the general nodded, Sheldon's face seemed to lose a bit of color.

Aidan studied the young Second. "What is Area 51?"

Sheldon shifted uncomfortably. "It's supposedly a military base that investigated UFO crashes and shit. Namely the Roswell crash in 1947."

Aidan didn't like the way Sheldon avoided his gaze. "Investigated them how? What did they do there?"

Tracy cleared her throat. "It's all just speculation really. Rumors circulated on the internet by UFO enthusiasts, conspiracy theorists, and — "

"What did they do there?" Aidan pressed. "What did they do that you don't want me to know about?"

Darnell responded when no one else would. "Among other things, according to rumor they performed alien autopsies."

Aidan clenched his hands into fists. *Autopsies?* "Are you saying that while we're all sitting here with our thumbs up our arses, those bloody bastards could be killing Dana and cutting her up?"

Chris caught Aidan's attention. "I don't believe so. There was no evidence that the *gifted ones* we found dead had been opened up or dissected. The only marks we found on the bodies aside from the bullet wounds were needle marks on their arms where blood had been drawn."

Aidan tried to find reassurance in his words but couldn't.

Zach broke the hush that engulfed them. "I read the minds of the men who followed General Lane and erased all memories of his snooping. Their orders were to kill him and to stage his death so it would appear to have been an accident."

Epithets filled the room.

"Did you kill them?" Heather ground out.

Zach's lips turned up in a faint smile. "No. I didn't want to do anything that might draw both the military's and Gershom's attention. I also erased the memories of the men who objected to your father's inquiries, the men who sent the assassins after him, as well as everyone your father spoke with today so Gershom won't know we're on to him."

Aidan looked from Zach to General Lane to Chris. "So Gershom is working with the military now?"

"Apparently," Chris confirmed.

Lisette shifted. "Do they know what he is?"

Zach draped an arm across her shoulders. "I don't think so. Only two of the men I encountered had actually seen Gershom in person. And Gershom was wearing a uniform in their memories."

General Lane nodded. "Zach showed me. They think Gershom is a four-star general like me."

Aidan looked at the figures in the building on the wall monitor. "He's mind-controlling them all?" That was a hell of a feat. There were a lot of bodies in that building.

Chris grunted. "He only has to mind-control the higher-ups at the facility, those who give the orders."

General Lane nodded. "If the highest-ranking officers say Gershom is a general and treat him as such, the lower ranks will believe it and behave accordingly."

Chris typed something on his laptop. "I had my contacts do a thermal scan of the building as well."

The image on the large wall monitor changed, the shades of gray filling with vibrant color.

The humans and *gifted ones* who had previously been white turned bright red.

"If you'll notice," Chris said, "there are no greenish-yellow figures in the building."

"So no vampires," Aidan murmured. Vampires' body temperatures tended to run a bit cooler than that of mortals.

"No vampires," Chris confirmed. "So I think it's safe to assume they haven't gotten their hands on the virus yet."

Zach's head dipped in a slow nod. "That's good news. At least Dana won't have to contend with vampires."

"No," Aidan retorted. "She'll just have dozens of military men who are armed out the arse."

Zach waved his hand in dismissal. "I'm not worried about them. Dana can handle them."

Aidan regarded him with disbelief. "How? She isn't immortal, Zach. Violence was never a part of her world until I entered it. She's had no combat training. No martial arts. She's never even taken a self-defense course."

"Nevertheless," Zach persisted, "she can handle them."

Lisette eyed Zach suspiciously. "Why are you so sure Dana can hold her own against military men? You've barely spoken with her."

He met her gaze, then shifted in his seat. "Just a lucky guess?"

Her eyes narrowed. "Zach…"

Aidan watched the two, not knowing what to think. He had believed at first that Zach was just trying to put his mind at ease. But now that Lisette was drilling him with her gaze, Zach looked like a schoolboy whose teacher had just caught him dropping a lizard down the back of a girl's dress.

"Fine," Zach grumbled. "There's a *slight* chance that I *might* have mind-controlled Dana. A little bit."

Aidan's breath caught.

Lisette's face darkened with disapproval. "Zach!"

"I said *might*," he reminded her.

Alarm rose once more. Dana was mortal. Mind-controlling her would cause brain damage that her body — lacking the aid of the vampiric virus — could not heal. "How slight a chance?" he demanded.

Zach glanced at Lisette, then reluctantly met Aidan's eyes. "Gargantuan."

Chapter Twenty-One

A IDAN SWORE.

"Damn it, Zach," Seth growled behind Aidan.

"What?" Zach protested, all innocence. "I did it for Aidan."

Dozens of skeptical looks stabbed him.

"Okay, okay. I did it for Lisette. *Ethan* is important to her. *Aidan* is important to Ethan. And we all know how much Dana means to Aidan." He looked down at his wife. "So by the transitive property, I did it for you. This is your fault."

When Lisette opened her mouth to rebut, David held up a hand. "What exactly did you do, Zach?"

He shrugged. "Like Seth, I thought Dana remained a prime target for Gershom and decided to take steps that I believed would protect her to some extent."

Aidan drew in a breath to start shouting as outrage rose within him like lava.

Zach stopped him with a look. "I knew she had lived a typically sheltered mortal life and, without her 9mm, wouldn't know how to defend herself, so…" He frowned. "How can I explain this? I basically planted a how-to-kick-ass manual in her head."

Blank stares.

"What the hell does that mean?" Aidan demanded.

"It means," Zach told him, "that when it comes to hand-to-hand combat, she now knows how to do everything *I* can do. Everything that doesn't require gifts, that is."

Stunned silence.

Sheldon's lips turned up in a big grin. "That is so cool! It's just like with Neo in *The Matrix*."

Aidan shook his head. "I don't know what the hell *The Matrix* is, but this is *not* cool. She's mortal, Zach. Mind control causes brain damage her body can't heal without the virus."

Chris grunted. "You weren't so concerned about that when you mind-controlled my people here at the network."

Aidan slammed his fist down on the table, nearly exploding with fury. "Would you fucking let that drop?" he roared. "The mind control I performed on the guards here took less than a minute. They suffered no more damage than they would have drinking and partying on a Friday night." He turned on Zach. "How long did it take you to plant all that information in Dana's mind?"

Zach glanced over Aidan's shoulder at Seth. "Quite a while, actually."

This just got worse and worse by the minute. "How much damage did it do? Were you even able to heal it?"

"Did you notice any difference in her behavior?" Zach asked in lieu of answering.

Bastien clamped a hand on Aidan's arm when Aidan would have risen.

David looked at Zach. "When did you do this, Zach?"

"Yesterday," Zach said, "while everyone was sleeping at your place. I stayed awake to keep an eye out for Gershom and thought I would take advantage of the opportunity and give Dana the know-how she'd need to survive whatever came." He met Aidan's irate gaze. "Did you notice any difference in her?"

He hadn't. He hadn't noticed any difference at all. "No."

Zach nodded. "There was damage when I finished, but I healed most of it."

"Most?" Aidan repeated. "Not all?"

Zach shook his head. "I couldn't get it all. The damage that remains is similar to that one would have after a concussion. And I feel confident the virus will heal it when she transforms."

Numbness began to seep in. Gershom had Dana and Dana had brain damage.

"I know what you're thinking," Zach said.

"I doubt you do."

"I don't have to read your thoughts to know what they contain. I know you're now worried on two fronts, and I regret adding to your concern. You may think it was ruthless or irresponsible or however you choose to label it, but if you could just look at it without emotion clouding your judgment, you will see that this is a good thing. Dana is now armed with knowledge and skills that will enable her to defeat those guarding her should they try to harm her. She could even make an escape."

Aidan shook his head. "The other *gifted ones* who tried to escape were killed."

"But Dana won't be. She's now like those rough-and-tough marines or SEAL team soldiers in the movies Lisette and Tracy love so much. You know, the ones who go in against all odds, disarm dozens of armed combatants that grossly outnumber them, kick ass, and emerge with only a few scratches. Dana can now, with no forethought, disarm a man twice her size. If there is anything in the room with her that can be used as a weapon, she will find it."

Aidan supposed he could take some comfort in that.

"Well," Chris said, "hopefully it won't come to that. We should be able to formulate a plan, implement it, and get to her in the next twenty-four hours."

Aidan found that hard to believe. "How the hell can we blitz a United States military installation?"

General Lane frowned. "You can't. Can you?"

Chris shook his head. "I don't think that would be the wise play here, in part because we would risk Gershom popping in the instant the first alarm sounded and killing all the *gifted ones* to spite Seth."

More cursing.

Roland folded his arms across his chest. "I say we take a page from Gershom's book and have Seth, Zach, and Aidan do a little mind-controlling on the masses in that building. While *we* free the *gifted ones*, *they* can incarcerate the soldiers, then convince the scientists on site that they're proctologists who have found the answers to all of life's mysteries up the soldiers' arses."

Startled laughter erupted around the table.

Sheldon shook his head. "Dude, you have a serious mean streak."

Roland shrugged. "I've just never favored blindly following orders."

David grunted. "I can vouch for that."

Roland's lips twitched.

Jared, who had been leaning up against the wall beside the sofa, straightened. "Actually, Roland may be on to something."

Aidan stared at him. "You think we should convince the scientists they're proctologists?"

Jared gave his head an impatient shake. "No. I think we should do what *Gershom* always does—play the magician."

Silence.

"Melanie," Seth said, "Ethan could use some more blood."

Aidan glanced over his shoulder as Seth stepped away from Ethan.

Melanie rose and left the room.

Heather's face reflected both hope and fear. "Is he okay?"

Seth hesitated. "I've healed everything I can. I won't know if that is enough—if the virus can heal that which is beyond me—until he awakens."

Melanie dashed back in with two blood bags.

Heather stared at her husband's prone form as Seth started down the length of the table.

Sheldon reached back, grabbed the arm of an empty chair, and sent it rolling down toward David's end. Darnell caught it and scooted over to make room for Seth to sit beside David across from Zach.

Seth gave both Seconds a nod of thanks, then sank into the seat. His shoulders drooping with weariness, he looked up at Jared. "You think we should play the magician?"

Jared stepped forward. "Yes."

Seth nodded. "Tell me more."

<hr />

"So she's crazy?"

The male voice carried to Dana down what seemed like a dark, murky corridor.

"I don't know," another male responded.

Consciousness returned in tiny increments but lent her no

memory of what had landed her... wherever she was.

She fought a frown, keeping her face expressionless as she listened to the murmured conversation and tried without success to pick out a familiar voice.

"What do you mean you don't know?" a third male retorted. "You said her head is full of vampires."

Where was she?

She lay on her back on a lumpy, uncomfortable surface. A bed or a cot?

The light behind her eyelids indicated the room was well lit. Not too clean though, based on the musty scents that tweaked her nose.

How had she come to be there? The last thing she remembered was...

Frustration seared her as she tried to recap events.

Oh shit. The last thing she remembered was watching Heather fall to her death. (Surely even an immortal couldn't survive that much blood and brain splattering the ground.) Then Gershom had grabbed Dana by the throat and —

"Did you really see vampires in her memories?" the first man asked.

"Shut up," the second man snapped. "I'm trying to concentrate."

Were these Gershom's henchmen? Had he handed her over to them while he went back to finish off Aidan, Ethan, and Heather?

Her throat thickened. *Aidan.*

Footsteps approached. "Is she even still alive?" the third man muttered.

Fingers touched her throat.

Dana's eyes flew open.

A man loomed over her.

Grabbing his arm, she reared up and yanked him down at the same time.

Her forehead slammed into his face.

"Ah shit!" he sputtered as blood spurted from his broken nose.

Still holding his arm, she rolled out of bed. Her bare feet hit cold concrete as she looked around wildly.

Small room. Four bare cement walls. Two sets of bunk beds. A sink. A toilet. Fluorescent lights overhead. A heavy door with a small shuttered window like one might find in a prison's solitary-confinement cell.

Two men leapt to their feet across the room.

Dana adjusted her hold on Bloody Nose Guy. Gripping his elbow and wrist, she applied pressure at strategic points.

The man grunted in pain and sank to his knees.

"Whoa, whoa, whoa!" the other men shouted as they lunged forward.

Dana freed one of her hands and yanked a plastic toothbrush off the sink. Clutching the handle tightly, she slammed the head against the porcelain edge and broke off the bristle end, leaving a jagged plastic point. She seized a fistful of Bloody Nose Guy's wavy black hair and yanked his head back against her chest. Shoving the point of the broken toothbrush handle against his neck above his carotid artery, she shouted, "Stay back!"

Both men stopped short, eyes wide, mouths gaping.

Everyone went still, even the man Dana held captive.

"Easy," one of the men facing her said. Though his voice was a little higher with anxiety, she recognized him as the second man she had heard speak. "Take it easy. We aren't going to hurt you."

She increased the pressure on Bloody Nose Guy's neck. "You sure as hell aren't."

"Damn it, Phil," the man on his knees grumbled. "Shut the fuck up."

Everyone quieted.

Dana's heart pounded in her ears. Her breath came in gasps as she glanced around, then down at the man she restrained.

He was tall, muscular and must be twice her weight. Yet she had taken him down in less than sixty seconds.

"How did I do that?" she whispered.

She didn't know how to fight or turn a cheap plastic toothbrush into a weapon. About the only thing she knew to do when threatened was the old knee-to-the-groin trick. But she had just bloodied this guy's nose and now held two others at bay.

"How the hell did I do that?" she whispered again.

"Ah crap," the first man muttered. "She *is* crazy."

"No, she isn't," Bloody Nose Guy said softly. "She's just scared. Back away and give her a minute to acclimate."

Phil and his companion backed away in unison and seated themselves on the lower of the bunk beds across the room.

A minute passed. Then another. Dana really had no idea what to do now.

The man she held cleared his throat. "So… help me out here, fellas. Am I supposed to find the fact that someone her size took me down so fast emasculating or a turn-on? Because I'm sorta goin' both ways."

Though she wouldn't have thought it possible, she laughed. "You sound like…" *Aidan.*

Grief flooded her. Aidan would have fought to his last breath to keep Gershom from taking her. Was he…? Had Gershom killed him?

She swallowed hard, blinking back tears. "There was a man with me."

"Aidan?" Phil asked somberly.

Hope rose. "You saw him? He's here?"

He shook his head. "We haven't seen him."

She frowned. "Then how did you know his name?"

His mouth twisted with a faint grimace. "I read your mind."

She studied him. "You're a *gifted one*?"

The man on his knees cautiously tilted his head back to look up at her. "A what?"

"It's what she and the others call us in her mind," Phil said. "*Gifted ones.* I guess because of our special *gifts*," he finished wryly.

It was only then that Dana realized all the men were dressed alike in gray jumpsuits and white socks.

She glanced down and found herself similarly garbed without the socks.

Releasing Bloody Nose Guy, she stepped back but kept a tight grip on the toothbrush just in case. "You're the *gifted ones* who went missing?"

Bloody Nose Guy eased away from her on his knees, then swiveled around and sat on the floor. "*I'm* sure as hell not where I'm supposed to be."

Recognition struck. "You're the man who disappeared after you went to your father's funeral."

His brows lowered as he drew an arm across his mouth, wiping away some of the blood that stained his lips and chin. His nose bore a lump that hadn't been present in his picture and began to swell as she stared at him. "How did you know that?"

"I saw your file." She looked at the others. "You're sure Aidan wasn't brought in with me? He's about this tall"—she held her hand high above her head—"muscular, and has a Scottish accent."

Phil shook his head. "Sorry. The door was open long enough for them to dump you in here with us, but all I saw was a bunch of military grunts. I'm Phil, by the way." He jerked a thumb at the man beside him. "This is Grant. And the long, tall Texan you took down is Rick."

She nodded, trying hard not to weep as fear for Aidan pummeled her. "I'm Dana." She motioned to Rick. "I'm sorry I hurt you. I saw you looming over me and thought…"

He smiled. "You thought we were the ones who took you."

"Something like that."

Phil took a step forward. "You keep mentioning Gershom. Or thinking his name, I mean. Who is he?"

A sudden impulse drove her to look up at the ceiling, at the corners, and around the small room.

"What is it?" Rick asked, following her gaze.

She lowered her voice. "Are there cameras? Are they watching us or listening to us?"

Grant shook his head. "I've gone over every centimeter of this damned cell, looking for a weak point or anything that would enable us to escape, and found no cameras or mics."

Holding on to the toothbrush like a talisman, Dana returned to the bed upon which she had awoken and perched on the edge. "Gershom is the one who took us."

Rick scowled. "Who *is* he? What does he want with us?"

She shook her head helplessly. "To use us as pawns."

"I told you," Phil declared with triumph. "I *told* you the military just views us as tools!"

Rick nodded somberly. "Yes, you did, Phil. And I totally agree. You are a tool."

Grant laughed.

Dana would have, too, if they were anywhere but there. "What are your gifts?" she asked Grant and Rick.

Rick looped his arms around bent knees and linked his fingers. "I know this is going to sound corny sci-fi, but I'm an empath."

"You felt my emotions when we touched?"

He nodded. "Including your grief. I'm sorry about your friend Aidan. Maybe this Gershom fucker didn't kill him. Maybe Aidan survived."

She nodded, unable to speak for a moment. When she could, she nodded to Grant. "And you? What's your gift?"

His lips turned up in a self-deprecating smile. "I can find missing people."

She stared. "Seriously?"

"Yeah. Ironic, right?" His chuckle held no mirth. "I can locate a missing person if I touch an object they held shortly before their disappearance. I was looking for a woman from Fresno who had gone missing and ended up going missing myself."

"That's messed up," Dana said.

"Yeah. It is."

A strained silence engulfed them.

Rick eyed Dana curiously. "So, what's the deal with the vampires in your head? Are you loco in la cabeza or what?"

She smiled. "I'm not crazy."

Phil nodded. "I tried to tell him as much, but the things I saw in your memories are pretty hard to believe."

She raised her eyebrows. "Are they as hard to believe as a telepath, an empath, a whatever-you-call-Grant and a psychic being kidnapped by the United States military?"

The men shared a look.

"Exactly," she said.

Rick tilted his head to one side. "You're psychic? You can see the future?"

Dana nodded. "When I touch someone and focus my gift, I get glimpses of their future. And sometimes of their past and present."

Rick extended his hand. "Can you tell me if I'm going to get out of here alive?"

Dana hesitated, afraid of what she might see in Rick's—in everyone's—future. But it might help them find a way out of there.

Rising, she slipped the toothbrush up her sleeve, then moved closer and rested her right hand in Rick's. His light brown eyes met and held hers as he curled his long fingers around hers.

Nothing happened. Nothing came to her.

Covering their clasped hands, Dana slowly rotated her left hand over his and slid it up his forearm to the bend of his elbow, which bore a Band-Aid. She drew her hand back to his wrist, then stroked his forearm again… and suddenly saw him kneeling over a soldier, tugging off the man's military uniform.

Her eyes widened.

"What?" Rick asked.

The vision vanished.

Her lips turned up in a slow smile.

Rick's did, too.

A thunk sounded.

They glanced at the door.

"Oh shit," Phil muttered from across the cell. "They're probably coming to take you to the lab."

The door swung open. Two soldiers faced them, weapons raised and pointing at Dana and the others.

One soldier curled his lip at Rick. "What, are you fucking proposing?"

The second soldier motioned to Rick with the tip of his weapon. "Get up, back away, and turn to face the wall. The docs want to see her."

Releasing her hand, Rick slowly rose and eased back toward the wall.

Phil and Grant stood, then did the same.

"Face the wall," the second soldier repeated.

The three men faced the wall, exchanging glances.

The first soldier motioned to Dana with the tip of his weapon. "Now you. Up against the wall."

Dana turned toward the wall. When she took a step, she faked a limp and stumbled to one side.

Soldier One jerked forward. "Hands in the air! Hands in the air!"

Rick spun around. "Whoa, whoa, whoa! Don't shoot!"

Soldier One turned his weapon on Rick.

Phil, can you hear me? Dana thought.

Yeah.

Soldier Two kept his weapon trained on Dana.

She stumbled another step and reached out to grasp the edge of the sink, ostensibly for balance. *Tell them I'm injured.*

"She's injured, damn it!" Rick shouted over Soldier One's threats, catching on before Phil could come to her aid. "Cut her some fucking slack!"

Phil spun around, hands in the air. "Easy! Easy! She's hurt! They fucked up her ankle when they brought her in!"

Rick jerked back when Soldier One advanced on them menacingly, still barking threats. "Okay! Okay!" he shouted back. "I just didn't want you to shoot her, for fuck's sake! I think she's got a couple of broken ribs, too."

Soldier Two took a step inside, eyeing the growing tension between Soldier One and the three male prisoners. "Face the wall!" he called. "All of you! Face the wall! Hands where we can see 'em!"

Dana took another limping step, sliding her hand over to cover the bar of soap as she leaned on the sink for support. Gripping the soap, she dropped her arm to her side and lunged for the wall.

A muffled thud sounded behind her.

Had Soldier One struck one of the guys?

She leaned against the wall, her weight on one leg, her hand tucking the soap in the folds of her too-big jumpsuit as she pretended to cradle sore ribs. When she looked around, Rick was glaring at Soldier One. Blood trailed from one temple.

"Please," she said, infusing her voice with pain and weariness. "Don't hurt them. I'll do whatever you say." *Face the wall*, she told Phil, *but be ready to act.*

He looked at the others.

Rick, Grant, and Phil turned to face the wall, hands raised to appease the guards.

"I realize you boys are just following orders," Rick muttered, "but you don't have to be dicks about it."

Soldier One delivered a scathing, epithet-filled response, then backed up to Soldier Two. "Take care of the woman," he growled, keeping his eyes and his weapon trained on the men.

Soldier Two lowered his weapon, letting it dangle in front of him by its sling. Approaching Dana, he drew out a zip tie. "Face the wall. Hands behind your back."

She nodded, hissing in feigned pain as she faced the wall. "I might need your help walking," she said softly, adding a tremor of fear to her voice. "I think my ankle is sprained."

"Hands behind your back," he repeated, cold as ice.

Dana straightened away from the wall, hopping a bit as though trying to find her balance, then gingerly lowered the toes of her *injured* foot to the floor. Giving her right arm a little shake, she slid the broken toothbrush handle down into her right palm.

"I told you she was hurt," Rick grumbled.

"Shut the fuck up," Soldier One snapped.

"Left hand first," Soldier Two instructed, all business.

So much for engendering a little sympathy. Dana shifted her left arm as though to comply, then gripped the toothbrush handle with her right hand and drove it back. Hard.

Soldier Two howled as the plastic point buried itself in his thigh.

Spinning around, Dana threw the bar of soap, grabbed Soldier Two's weapon and slammed it into his face as he bent forward.

When Soldier One cast a startled look over his shoulder, the bar of soap hit him in the temple like a rock. His head jerked as he staggered to the side.

Soldier Two swore and grabbed for his weapon. But Dana had already pulled the sling over his head. As she yanked it away, he swung at her.

Dana ducked the blow and came up strong, slamming the butt of the weapon into his cheek, then bending to kick out behind her. Her heel slammed into Soldier One's jaw as he hastily regained his balance and turned to her.

Soldier One grunted as his head snapped back.

Dana remained in constant motion, swinging around and knocking Soldier Two's sidearm out of his hand before he could finish drawing it from its holster.

Fury contorting his features, he swung at her.

She blocked the swing with the weapon she held, then slammed her forehead into his mouth. Pain careened through her head as she turned and ducked a swing from Soldier One. Then she was fighting them both, blocking hits and delivering kicks with an expertise she could not explain.

She flung Soldier Two's weapon toward Rick, then deftly relieved Soldier One of his.

When Soldier One reached for his sidearm, Rick pressed the barrel of the automatic rifle to his temple.

"Don't do it," Rick growled.

Soldier Two lunged toward his discarded sidearm.

Dana reached it first and aimed it at his forehead. Her breath came in gasps. Her arms hurt, unaccustomed to the hits they had taken while blocking blows. And her heel throbbed.

"Holy crap," Phil breathed as he stared at her with wide eyes. "Who the hell *are* you? That was like some shit you'd see in a Michael Bay movie."

Quick as lightning, Dana slammed the butt of the gun into Soldier Two's temple.

Knees buckling, the man sank to the floor, unconscious.

Rick followed her lead, knocking Soldier One unconscious. Crouching beside the fallen man, Rick set his weapon aside and started removing the man's uniform.

Grant gaped at Dana. "How did you do that?"

Her heart racing, Dana shook her head. "I have no idea. Phil, how many guards do you usually see?"

He thought for a moment. "Two came to take me to the lab. And there were two more at the end of the hallway, guarding the door to the next section. There are more scattered beyond that, usually in pairs."

She thought quickly. "You're telepathic. Have you caught the names of the two at the end of the hallway?"

"They differ according to their shifts, but the two on duty now should be Edwards and Mitchell." He quieted, looking to one side. "Yeah. It's Edwards and Mitchell."

Grant helped divest Soldier One of his boots and uniform.

Rick stood and tugged off his jumpsuit, revealing a trim, muscular body in white boxer shorts.

"If I can get you past those guards," she said, "can you read enough minds to help me bullshit our way out the back door?"

"I'll sure as hell try," Phil vowed.

Gershom had eluded Seth and the Others thus far by remaining on the move. If he had left shortly after dropping Dana off, she wanted to be far away before he returned with his next victim. She had little hope that in the hours she had been gone, the Immortal

Guardians had miraculously discovered where Gershom was holding the *gifted ones*. So it was up to her to find her way back to them.

Rick hastily pulled on Soldier One's uniform. Grant started on Soldier Two's.

Phil looked toward one wall. "The other guards are wondering what's taking so long."

Dana motioned to Grant. "Help him."

As Grant donned the uniform, Dana and Rick transferred the discarded jumpsuits to the guards.

"The bed," she whispered.

Rick folded Soldier One over his shoulder then dumped him on the bed so he lay with his back to the door.

"What the hell is taking so long?" a male shouted down the hallway.

She looked to Rick, who seemed to be the strongest of the group. "Call them."

He nodded. "Hey, Edwards?" he yelled with a hint of uncertainty.

Dana took the automatic rifle from Phil and backed up to the wall on one side of the doorway.

Rick and Grant curled Soldier Two into a fetal position, then moved to stand over him with their backs to the door.

"What?" a man called back. "What's the holdup?"

"I, uh," Rick yelled in what Dana thought was a pretty good impression of Soldier One. "I think I might've fucked up. The woman fought me when I tried to restrain her, and I may have hit her too hard. I, uh… Shit, I think she's dead."

"Damn it, Cox!" the unseen man grumbled.

Phil backed up to the wall and put his hands behind his head, concealing the 9mm he held.

Footsteps clomped down the hallway, growing closer.

"What kind of asshat can't restrain a ninety-five-pound woman?" a second voice groused. "You're fucking armed!"

The light from the hallway dimmed as two more soldiers entered.

One swore when he saw "soldiers" Phil and Rick leaning over a prone figure on the floor, their heads down. "General Gershom is going to have our asses if — "

Dana knocked them unconscious so quickly they didn't even have time to yelp in surprise. Kneeling beside them, she swiftly divested them of their weapons.

Phil stared at her. "I'm with Grant. Who the hell *are* you?"

Dana shook her head. "Hurry up and put his uniform on so we can get out of here."

Chapter Twenty-Two

THE SUN SANK BELOW THE horizon, painting the clouds above a soft pink and coaxing the sky into ever-darkening shades of purple and gray.

Aidan's nerves jangled as they strode toward the front of the building.

This had to work. It *had* to. But holy hell, he was worried it wouldn't.

He wore a military uniform General Lane had provided. There seemed to be a lot of decorations on it, so Aidan supposed that meant he was posing as an officer. Heather walked on his left, carrying a briefcase. Zach walked on his right. Darnell walked on the other side of him, carrying a briefcase in one hand and a bulging leather bag in the other. All wore military uniforms and were armed.

Behind them, actual army soldiers handpicked by General Lane stuck close, more heavily armed — Tim, Wayne, Jess, and three others. Apparently they all had been with General Lane when Heather, Ethan, and Seth had clued him in to immortals and vampires and were committed to keeping the secret. General Lane did not doubt the soldiers' loyalty. Aidan didn't either after reading their minds. All were fiercely loyal to the general. And all were surprisingly loyal to Seth, because Tim's daughter would've died of cancer if Seth hadn't healed her.

Lisette, Étienne, Krysta, and Sean followed, also garbed in military uniforms.

Chris Reordon and Seconds Brodie, Tracy, and Nicole brought

up the rear.

In front of them all, General Lane strode forward in long, ground-eating strides beside General Gershom — aka Seth.

As soon as Aidan had seen how large their group would be, he had objected, thinking it would give them away.

But Heather had put his mind at ease. "Generals are like America's royalty," she had informed him. "It's very common for them each to have a substantial entourage that accompanies them wherever they go. Their own driver. A security detail. Sometimes a police escort. A secretary. A coterie of various and assorted other assistants who do everything from iron the general's pants to manage his communications equipment. Since we're supposedly accompanying *two* generals, this is pretty much what would be expected."

Aidan glanced at Zach. *Does Gershom bring an entourage like this when he comes here?* he asked telepathically. Zach had read enough minds to have seen it if Gershom had.

I'm not sure, Zach responded, eyes forward. *Either he's found some stooges to serve as his entourage or he mind-controlled everyone here into believing an entourage accompanied him, because they saw nothing unusual in his actions.*

As the generals approached, the soldiers guarding the front entrance snapped salutes, which General Lane and General Gershom returned. The soldiers opened the doors for them so swiftly the two generals never broke stride.

Inside, a man with a lot of decorations on his uniform approached them with a few men of lower rank. All saluted.

"General Gershom." When he turned to General Lane, his eyebrows flew up. "General Lane. I wasn't aware that you— "

General Gershom cut the man off. "I brought General Lane into the loop to help clean up your mess, Nelson."

Nelson stiffened. "What mess?"

"The mess," General Gershom barked, "that landed a fucking self-proclaimed reporter for a conspiracy-theorist website on General Lane's doorstep, asking him to confirm that this is a military installation that conducts experiments on American citizens."

Nelson paled. "What?"

General Gershom snapped his fingers.

Darnell set his bags down, removed a large iPad from his briefcase, then straightened. After folding the cover back, he tapped the glass, then turned it to face Nelson.

The bright screen illuminated an article posted on a conspiracy-theorist website the network had manufactured to look so real that the article appeared to have been shared on social media thousands of times. Whatever that meant.

Nelson's face mottled with fury. "Son of a bitch!"

Darnell regarded him stoically. "It's trending."

Aidan didn't know what that meant but guessed by the officer's apoplectic expression that it was bad news.

General Gershom waved a hand. "No one leaves without my permission until we've identified the source of the security breach." He motioned to Darnell. "My team will need access to your communications hub and your servers to determine whether this was a result of a hack or was leaked from the inside."

"Yes, sir. Immediately, sir." Nelson waved to his men, who promptly picked up Darnell's bags and escorted him, Étienne, Krysta, Heather, Chris, and Nicole away.

"I've made arrangements," General Gershom continued, "to transport the *special cargo* stored here to another facility."

"But sir…"

Aidan shifted anxiously as the conversation proceeded with General Lane and General Gershom taking turns issuing orders the others leapt to obey.

This was taking too long. At least it *felt* like it was taking too long. What if those bastards were already shackling Dana to an operating table so they could autopsy her?

Stop panicking. Zach spoke in his head while the generals continued to turn the place on its ear. *All is going according to plan. A few more minutes and you can see her. She's all right. And you need to keep a lid on your emotions so your eyes don't glow.*

Aidan drew in a deep breath and let it out slowly.

At least the *real* Gershom wasn't present. That would have been a disaster—to walk inside with a faux General Gershom only to discover the real thing waiting for them.

A soldier abruptly turned and motioned for them to follow him.

"This way."

General Gershom followed him, Aidan and Sean on his heels.

Though Zach and Lisette stayed behind to aid General Lane, half of General Lane's men accompanied Aidan's group.

The installation's soldier took them down one corridor, then another and through two security checkpoints.

Heather had been right. These men really did react as though General Gershom were royalty, acceding to anything he asked and offering him the utmost deference and respect. Not one of them questioned or hesitated to obey his orders.

No doubt the real Gershom lapped that shite up since he seemed to have delusions of grandeur.

Or just plain delusions.

When they turned the next corner, Aidan's heart leapt.

Three soldiers carrying automatic weapons approached them, a small female in their midst. Clad in a too-big jumpsuit, she limped a bit on bare feet with her hands secured behind her back.

Dana.

Her eyes lit up when they met his. *Aidan.* The thought came through loud and clear, accompanied by joy and relief.

Then she looked at the tall man beside him, and all color fled her face. *Oh shit. Gershom!*

It's okay, he hastened to assure her.

He captured you, too? she asked.

No, sweetheart. It isn't the real Gershom.

She glanced at his companion. *Are you sure?*

One hundred percent. Since Gershom is so fond of posing as Seth, we thought we'd turn the tables on him. His eyes fell to her legs. *You're limping.* Fury rose. *They hurt you?*

No. I hurt myself when I overpowered the guards.

He stared at her. *I'm sorry, what?*

These men aren't soldiers. They're three of the gifted ones *who were taken. We were just about to make our escape.*

While General Gershom droned on about Aidan-didn't-care-what, Aidan swiftly reviewed Dana's memories.

Holy shite, he muttered mentally. *You overpowered the guards and secured your own release.*

I know. Her brow crinkled. *I've kind of been freaking myself out, because I don't know how the hell I'm doing this.*

General Gershom turned toward the approaching soldiers.

The three males with Dana stiffened. Their hands tightened on their weapons.

That's the asshole who took me, one of the *gifted ones* told Dana telepathically.

This isn't the man who took you, Aidan told them all. *He's only posing as him, much like you're posing as guards, so we can liberate you.*

The men's eyes widened.

A walkie squawked behind Aidan.

Tim mumbled into it, then stepped forward. "General Gershom, sir. The transport trucks have arrived."

General Gershom responded with a curt nod. "Let's load them up as quickly as possible." He motioned to Dana. "Start with this one."

If Aidan was supposed to remain with the others, he deviated from the plan.

Tim motioned for Dana and her faux soldier escort to accompany him back to the front of the building. Aidan fell in behind them, his eyes on Dana. Her hands had been secured behind her back with a zip tie, but her companions had left the tie loose enough for her to free her hands if the need should arise.

Aidan ground his teeth as he again noted her limp.

It seemed to take them forever to reach the front of the building.

Nelson was gone, kowtowing to General Lane, no doubt. The soldiers who remained offered no objections as Aidan and Tim headed outside with Dana and the other three.

Large military trucks were lined up out front, each protected by half a dozen heavily armed soldiers Aidan knew were Chris's men.

Tim guided them to the back of the first truck, then stood aside while Dana's guards helped her inside.

Aidan followed the four into the truck, then let the canvas flap fall back into place. A slice of bright sunlight swept in where the flaps didn't quite meet, alleviating the darkness.

Dana spun around. Jerking her hands from the zip tie, she hurled herself at him.

Aidan wrapped his arms around her and crushed her to him, lifting her off her feet and burying his face in her hair.

"I thought he'd killed you," she whispered, her voice choked with tears.

"I feared he'd done the same to you."

They held each other for a long moment.

"I'm guessing he's Aidan," one of her companions murmured. His thoughts identified him as Rick.

Ignoring him, Aidan lowered Dana's feet to the truck bed and leaned back so he could look down at her. "You're really okay?" he asked, brushing her loose hair back from her face.

She nodded.

"What the hell?" Rick murmured in astonishment. "His eyes are glowing and he has fangs."

Aidan glanced at him.

Rick was tall and slim, the uniform he wore too short in the sleeves and tight across his chest. And he gaped at Aidan.

"I told you she wasn't crazy," another declared triumphantly. Phil, who was apparently telepathic.

The third man just stared, mouth hanging open.

Dana laughed. Keeping her arms around Aidan, she leaned into his side and motioned to the men. "This is Rick, Phil, and Grant."

Aidan nodded to them but was more interested in the foot Dana kept her weight off of whenever she moved. He nudged her toward one of the bench seats that ran the length of the truck. "Sit down and let me see what you've done to yourself."

Dana sank down and propped her foot on the opposite knee. "I hurt it when I kicked one of the soldiers."

Aidan crouched in front of her and examined her cold, dirty foot. The heel was already beginning to bruise. Cupping her foot in his hand, he smiled up at her. "I'll have to see to it you're wearing a good pair of boots next time." His hand heated. The bruise receded, then disappeared.

Dana covered his hands with hers, drawing his gaze. "Did Ethan and Heather survive?"

"Heather did. We're still waiting to see if Seth was able to fully heal Ethan."

Nodding, she blinked back tears. "Where's the real Gershom? Did you defeat him?"

He shook his head. "We don't know where he is. I half expected him to be here when we arrived."

Rick took a step forward. "How did that guy in there look so much like Gershom? Are they twins or something?"

"No. They're more like cousins."

Sunlight brightened the truck's interior as the flap pulled back.

Tim stood outside with four more *gifted ones*.

Dana tugged Aidan's hand. "Your eyes," she whispered.

Aidan closed them while he took a moment to bring his emotions back under control. His fangs retracted. He opened his eyes.

Dana smiled. "You're good."

He brought one of her hands to his lips for a kiss, then rose. "Let's see how fast we can get you all out of here."

Aidan, Seth said in his head. *You're needed at David's.*

Aidan swore and met Dana's gaze. "I'm needed at David's."

Go now, Seth ordered.

Though he was loath to leave Dana, Aidan teleported away.

―――――◦✿◦――――

Gershom stood in the forest, a gentle breeze teasing his hair as he listened to the thoughts of those who thought themselves safe in David's abode. Ever since Seth's adopted daughter had alerted Seth to his presence at the army base last year, Gershom had been carefully testing the extent of Ami's peculiar talent to see just how close he could get before she began to sense his presence.

Close enough to eavesdrop on the conversations and thoughts that cluttered David's home as the sun set.

A slow smile curled his lips.

Once more, he had gotten the best of his nemesis.

It had been too easy really. While that fucker Seth was busy at the military installation, pretending to be *him* and liberating his little *gifted ones*, Gershom would walk right through the front door of David's home—figuratively speaking—and take that which was most precious to him.

Seth wouldn't even realize they were gone until it was too late.

Perhaps Gershom would slay David and a few of the Immortal Guardians while he was there just to dig the knife in deeper.

The notion held great appeal.

Listening to the muted speech, he took a quick head count.

Ami sat on a sofa in David's living room, reading a book to the toddler on her lap. Her husband Marcus sat beside them, so afraid for the two that Gershom could barely find any coherent thoughts in his head.

Roland and Sarah lingered nearby, determined to do anything necessary to protect Marcus, Ami, and their child.

David was there, too, of course, watching over the flock in Seth's absence. It grated a little that Gershom couldn't access that one's thoughts.

Imhotep and Chaak were present as well and were likely the only two aside from David who could offer up a decent fight. The Celt had proven to be a good adversary, but he was at the military installation, fawning over his lover.

The younger immortals Richart and Jenna manned a love seat, their Second Sheldon across from them. Multiple other heartbeats surrounded the house. Network soldiers, no doubt.

He scoffed silently. Did they really believe humans armed with guns could stop him?

The immortal black sheep Bastien was absent, as was his wife. He and Melanie had opted to remain at the network to make a stand with Heather and the vampires should Gershom decide to strike there or should he simply pop in to fuck with Ethan's mind again.

Hmm. Maybe he *should* fuck with Ethan's mind. It would only take him a few minutes to undo all the healing Seth had spent hours performing. Or better yet...

He tilted his head to one side. Perhaps, while the other immortals were struggling to contain Seth's fury after he returned and found Ami and Adira gone, Gershom would stop by the network and nab Cliff. He could deny the valiant young vampire blood until the madness consumed him, then stick him in a room with Ami and Adira. Let nature take its course. Could be interesting.

But first...

He shifted into Seth's form, then teleported to David's living room, appearing beside Ami.

Several gasps sounded.

David rose.

Marcus did, too. "Is it over? Did you get Gershom?"

Ami dropped her book and hugged Adira to her breast as she stared up at him with fear. "That's not Seth! It's Gershom!"

The immortals all leapt to their feet.

In a blur of motion, Marcus scooped his wife and daughter into his arms and raced out the front door.

Gershom shifted back into his natural form and teleported to David's front lawn, appearing directly in Marcus's path.

Immortals poured through the front door of David's home, weapons drawn, David in their lead.

Marcus darted in a different direction.

Gershom again teleported into his path. Then did so again. And again.

Marcus stopped. Lowering Ami's feet to the ground, he moved her and the baby she held behind him and braced himself for a fight.

The human guards that stood just outside the house—fewer than Gershom had guessed—raised their weapons.

"Fire your weapons," Gershom called, "and I'll use telekinesis to send every bullet into Ami."

No weapons fired.

Richart vanished and reappeared behind Ami.

Gershom flung out a hand.

Richart flew backward thirty yards and slammed into one of the huge trees at the edge of David's lawn. Several of Richart's bones broke with audible cracks.

Gershom swung on David, Roland, Sarah, Chaak, Imhotep, and Jenna as they leapt forward. Energy burst from him, radiating outward like a blast wave and sweeping almost everyone—immortals and humans—off their feet.

Only David, Marcus, and Ami remained standing.

As David drew his sword and leapt forward with a roar of fury, Gershom flung a dagger.

Metal glinted in the last of the dying light as the dagger shot around Marcus and stopped half an inch from Ami's neck.

David skidded to a halt, his dismayed gaze going to the blade that hovered so close to Ami's carotid artery.

Triumph filling him, Gershom smiled.

⬥⬦⬥

When Aidan appeared in David's living room, he found it empty.

A ripple of power hit him, nearly knocking him on his arse.

Outside, David roared in fury.

Aidan raced through the front door.

Roland, Sarah, Jenna, Imhotep, Chaak, Sheldon, and all the network soldiers were down on the ground. The immortals grimaced in pain. Some of the network men appeared to be unconscious.

Across the yard, an injured Richart struggled to regain his feet in front of the trees.

In the center of the lawn, Marcus stood with sword in hand in front of Ami, who held Adira tight.

David skidded to a halt as a dagger veered around Marcus and hovered a hairsbreadth from Ami's neck.

Aidan bent to grab a sword Roland or Sarah had dropped and crossed to stand beside David.

David focused his glowing amber gaze on the dagger.

The floating dagger eased away from Ami almost a foot, then darted forward again, nicking the soft skin of her neck.

Gershom smiled and shook his head. "You only *think* you're as strong as me, David."

Marcus drew a second sword.

"Really?" Gershom drawled, then frowned. "Wait. How are you still standing? You're only eight centuries old. You should be flat on your back like the others."

Marcus shook his head. "I'm stronger than I look."

The dagger that threatened Ami abruptly jerked away and flung itself at Gershom.

Aidan's eyes widened.

As did Gershom's as he hastily ducked it. He looked back at Marcus with surprise. "How did you do that?"

Aidan wondered the same thing. Marcus didn't have telekinetic abilities.

Marcus leapt forward and swung his swords.

Caught off guard, Gershom drew his own and fell back a step as

~ 361 ~

he struggled to fend off Marcus's attack, which shouldn't even offer him a challenge since Gershom was so powerful.

What the hell?

"How are you doing this?" Gershom growled, steadily backing away as he blocked blows backed by so much power that sparks lit the darkening night each time their blades met.

Marcus's eyes suddenly flashed golden. "Surprise, cousin." In the next instant, Marcus grew taller and shifted into Seth's form.

Aidan gaped.

Golden fire flashed in Gershom's eyes as his features contorted with fury. "Who are you?" he demanded. "Seth is at the military installation, posing as me. I saw him with my own eyes!"

Seth shook his head with a dark smile. "You studied me so carefully and took such delight in impersonating me when you attacked Aidan. I'm surprised you don't recognize me."

"That's not possible."

"Apparently you aren't the only magician in the family," Seth snarled.

A flash of panic entered Gershom's eyes. "You can't be Seth."

"Oh, but I am. Someone else volunteered to bear your form at the military installation so I could remain here and *bury* your ass."

Aidan had had no idea. He had thought Seth had been the one pretending to be General Gershom.

David shot forward, swinging his blades.

Aidan followed, leaping into the fray.

The three of them surrounded Gershom, whose composure began to fray as one blade bit deep. Then another. And another.

The foliage bordering David's lawn rustled. Dozens of Immortal Guardians strode forward, weapons in hand, ready to take up the fight should Seth, David, or Aidan fall.

Marcus was one of them and crossed to plant himself in front of Ami and their daughter.

Aidan hissed in a pained breath as Gershom's sword cut across his middle.

The metallic scent of blood tinged the air.

Gershom began to rack up wounds.

"Lay down your swords, Gershom," Seth ordered, still hammering away at him. "This ends now."

A red slash appeared on Gershom's cheek as Seth's blade drew blood. Another appeared on his chest when David drew more.

Gershom's face darkened as he roared with fury.

In the next instant, he vanished.

Aidan stumbled as his sword met empty air.

Seth spun around.

Gershom appeared behind Ami and—in the same instant—drew a blade across her throat. Her eyes widened and filled with pain as blood sprayed her husband and daughter.

"No!" Seth bellowed.

The sky above lit with a flash of lightning as thunder filled the clearing like an explosion. Dark clouds swelled in the sky, hiding the first twinkling stars.

Smiling, Gershom vanished.

Marcus spun around and caught his wife and baby as they fell.

"Aidan," Seth snapped as he zipped over and knelt beside Ami.

Aidan teleported away, following Gershom's energy trail to France. To Germany. Australia. Canada. Russia. Japan. And some places Aidan didn't even recognize. But he stayed on Gershom's heels, following the trails of energy he expended each time he teleported to a new destination. He caught up with Gershom in Finland and immediately swung his swords before Gershom could teleport away again.

The Other's wounds must be wearing on him.

Gershom released a bestial sound, like a rabid dog cornered by hunters.

Pain flashed up Aidan's arm as Gershom got in a lucky strike, but Aidan kept moving, kept swinging his swords. He just needed to hold the bastard until Seth could finish healing Ami and catch up.

Gershom vanished.

Swearing, Aidan teleported after him and found Gershom in a cramped alleyway in what he thought might be Lagos.

A man riding a bicycle gaped at them, so startled by their sudden appearance that he nearly lost his balance.

Gershom buried his blade in the man's stomach, then teleported away.

Shite. Aidan caught the man as he fell and swiftly healed him.

He took another few seconds to bury his memory of the incident and plant the suggestion that someone had bumped into him and spilled paint on his shirt. Then he teleported after Gershom to a country road he thought might be in Hawaii.

Gershom swung his swords, cutting down two lads who looked like teenagers.

Seth, Aidan called as Gershom teleported away. He knelt beside the boys and swiftly healed their wounds.

I'm on my way, Seth said in his head.

Hurry, Aidan implored, running so low on energy that his skin began to burn beneath the sunlight.

After burying the memories of the boys, he teleported away again. Following Gershom to China, he found himself on a narrow street, facing a row of homes that had fallen into disrepair.

Gershom's latest victim, an elderly man, sank to the ground as Aidan appeared.

"You fucking coward!" Aidan shouted.

But Gershom teleported away.

Voices floated around the corner.

Grabbing the fallen man, Aidan ducked into the nearest home and found it empty.

Seth appeared.

Aidan knelt and laid the man on the floor. "Gershom is wounding innocents to slow me down."

"Zach," Seth said aloud, then teleported away.

Zach appeared, still clad in a military uniform. "Catch me up," he ordered as Aidan healed the old man and altered his memories.

"Seth, David, and I were kicking Gershom's arse at David's place, so Gershom cut Ami's throat and teleported away."

"Motherfucker!"

"Seth stayed to heal her. I followed Gershom. When I caught up with him, he started injuring innocents to slow me down. Seth is following him now."

Zach nodded. "Get some blood to replenish the strength you've lost, then return to the military installation and guard Lisette and the rest in case Gershom ends up there."

"Zach," Aidan said before the elder could teleport away, "ditch the uniform. Gershom is starting to hit more populated areas, and if you can't bury every memory, we don't want them to connect anything they see with the United States military."

Zach's clothes vanished, giving Aidan a split-second view of bare skin before the black shirt, black pants, and boots favored by Immortal Guardians cloaked his form.

<hr />

Seth doggedly pursued Gershom, struggling to keep his rage under control.

The bastard had slit Ami's throat. He had *slit* her *throat* and terrorized little Adira who, despite her youth, had understood exactly what had happened to her mommy.

Brazil. Norway. Tanzania. Thailand. Greece. Kazakhstan. Chile. Egypt.

Everywhere Gershom took him, the ground began to rumble and quake at Seth's appearance. Clouds gathered.

He ground his teeth, trying harder to leash his temper.

Leave the damage control to me, Zach said in his head. *It's slowing you down.*

He was right. Gershom could cut down a bystander in a second, then teleport away. It took Seth longer than that to heal wounds, bury memories, and plant an explanation for the bloodstains and torn clothing.

I'll heal the injured and bury their memories, Zach continued. *The network can scrub whatever appears on the internet. Just find Gershom's ass and bury him.*

Thank you. If you need help, summon Jared.

He won't be able to keep up. None of the Others can.

Unfortunately, he was right. *Then it's just us.*

As soon as Seth finished healing the couple at his feet, he teleported after Gershom again.

More wounded. Leaving the victims there without healing them went against Seth's every impulse, but Gershom had gotten far enough ahead of him that he worried he would lose him soon.

Gritting his teeth, Seth teleported again and again, his control slipping a little more with each felled man, woman, or child he had to leave behind for Zach.

The gap tightened. Then tightened some more until Seth caught up with Gershom in…

Shit. Times Square. Which bustled with activity.

Gershom grabbed a pregnant woman, drew her back against him, and locked an arm around her throat.

Whimpering, the woman dropped her shopping bag and clutched his arm.

Gershom breathed hard as he tightened his hold and staggered back a step. Blood oozed from multiple wounds as he glared at Seth and raised a dagger.

"Don't," Seth blurted. He tried without success to yank the blade away from Gershom using telekinesis.

His lips twisting in a sneer, Gershom buried the dagger in the woman's chest.

Screams erupted.

Brakes squealed as pedestrians scattered, running into traffic and darting into businesses.

Dropping the woman, Gershom huffed a pained laugh and spat blood.

Seth dashed forward to catch her before she could hit the pavement.

Some valiant men nearby tried to tackle Gershom.

Dark wings burst through the back of Gershom's bloodstained coat and spread wide, knocking the men down.

More onlookers screamed. Some crossed themselves.

Eyes glowing gold, Gershom burst into preternatural speed, racing up the sidewalk, swinging his swords every which way, felling one human after another after another and breeding pandemonium.

"You can't win!" Gershom growled breathlessly. "I'll always find a weakness!"

Once more, he teleported away.

Zach! Seth called.

Almost there, came his response. *I've a few more to heal.*

The screams continued.

Seth couldn't wait for him. *Jared,* he called. *Come to me now, and bring Chris.*

Reaching out to every man, woman and child he could see, Seth seized control of their minds.

All motion ceased.

Running bodies stumbled to a halt.

Drivers braked.

Bicyclers slowed to a careful stop.

Horns sounded in the distance behind Seth as drivers farther back wondered what the holdup was.

He couldn't worry about them right now.

Blank expressions cloaked the faces of every person present as Seth began the arduous task of burying each individual's memory of what had just happened.

Chris Reordon and the faux General Gershom appeared at Seth's elbow.

General Gershom shifted into the form of Jared, who swiftly replaced his uniform with Immortal Guardian standard blacks.

"Oh shit," Chris whispered. "This is fucking worst-case scenario."

"How can I help?" Jared murmured.

"It looks like Seth is taking care of everyone we can see," Chris told him. "You need to catch all those we *can't* see and bury whatever the hell they just saw."

Zach appeared. Foul curses colored the air.

"Heal the injured," Chris ordered, "beginning with the pregnant woman Seth is holding. Then see if you can catch Gershom."

Zach knelt beside Seth and carefully pulled the bleeding woman from his arms.

"If anyone took pictures," Chris told Jared, "or made a phone call or tweeted or otherwise spread the news, give me their names."

"Okay."

Seth worked as swiftly as possible. A hell of a lot of windows looked down on them. The longer it took them to clean this up, the more it would snowball.

Chris dialed a number.

"Yes, sir," a man answered.

"There's been an incident in Times Square. Mobilize four units and get them here ASAP."

"Yes, sir."

"Put the tech team on it and expunge every record of this."

"Yes, sir."

Chris dialed another number.

"Alena Moreno," the head of the West Coast division answered.

"It's Reordon. We have a situation," he announced without preamble.

"Tell me what you need."

Minutes passed as Chris made his calls, Seth and Jared buried memories, and Zach moved from body to body, healing the wounded.

Too many minutes.

And through it all, Seth's anger simmered.

Damn Gershom for this.

Chapter Twenty-Three

THE GROUP THAT GATHERED AROUND David's table two nights later was a somber one.

No meeting had been called. Everyone had just felt the need to stay close. Not just to look after each other, but to be there for Seth.

They had succeeded in rescuing the *gifted one*s Gershom had abducted and removed all knowledge of them from the military, foiling his latest plan. But Gershom would be back. All knew it. And all now knew it would be even harder than anticipated to stop him. Because Seth and the immortals had a weakness he could exploit.

A weakness Gershom lacked.

They cared. About their brethren. About their Seconds and network family. About *all* humans and *gifted ones*.

Gershom would always be able to use that against them. And none knew how to guard against that.

Dana studied the men and women around the table.

Conversation flowed as plates filled with the scrumptious meal Dana wasn't sure who had prepared for them. But the conversation was muted, reserved.

More leaves had been added to the long dining table along with more chairs. All the immortals in North Carolina were present, along with their Seconds. Cliff had come, too, she was pleased to see. And General Lane, who had abandoned his uniform in favor of civvies.

Melanie, Bastien, and Cliff sat on Dana's right.

Aidan, Heather, and Ethan sat on her left.

Ethan had awoken shortly after the trucks carrying Dana and the other *gifted ones* from the military installation had arrived at network headquarters. He had been quiet and had spoken little when Heather, Aidan, Dana, Bastien, and Melanie gathered around him. And the words he *had* spoken had come slowly, sparking fear in those who loved him.

But after more blood infusions and a long healing sleep, he seemed to be his regular self again.

David presided at the head of the table.

Seth occupied the chair at the opposite end.

This was the first time Dana had seen Seth since Gershom had taken her.

Lisette and Zach sat at Seth's right elbow, Jared beside them.

Apparently posing as General Gershom and having Seth pose as Marcus had been Jared's idea. And his helping clean up the mess in Times Square had outed him to the Others. So he was bunking at David's now.

Ami and Marcus sat on Seth's left as usual. Adira sat in her mother's lap, brow furrowed, two fingers in her mouth.

Aidan followed Dana's gaze. *I heard Marcus tell Roland that Adira is afraid to let her mother out of her sight now*, he said softly in her mind.

I don't blame her, Dana thought. *Poor baby. Can't they just bury her memory of what happened?*

He shook his head. *Seth is afraid burying the memory would do too much damage to her still-developing brain.*

The front door opened. Chris Reordon strode in, his battered briefcase in hand.

All called greetings.

Tossing them a wave, he dropped his briefcase and hung his jacket up among the many black coats that adorned the long coatrack.

"Join us for dinner?" David asked.

Chris responded with a weary smile. "Thanks. I'd love to." Shadows darkened the skin beneath his eyes. Had he slept at all since Times Square?

While Darnell grabbed another chair and pulled it up to the table, Sheldon retrieved a plate, heaped it full of food, and deposited it in front of Chris.

Thanking him, Chris tucked into his meal with a gusto that made Dana wonder when the man had last eaten a hot meal.

"So?" David said.

Chris swallowed a mouthful. "Times Square has been taken care of. Alena Moreno and Scott Henderson had their tech teams pitch in and handle everything that popped up on the internet while we handled phone calls and everything on the ground."

Dana stared at him. "So no one knows?"

"No one knows," Chris confirmed, taking another bite.

"That's amazing."

Chris shook his head and motioned to Seth. "What *he* did was amazing. No way would we have been able to contain something this big if he hadn't brought everything to a screeching halt and bought us time."

Seth seemed less than impressed with the feat he had performed. "Gershom still got away."

"But he's running scared," Zach countered. "I followed the bastard for hours before I ultimately lost his trail. For all we know, he may *still* be running." He shook his head. "He might have talked shit to you in Times Square, but you shook him, Seth. You caught him by surprise."

Aidan grunted. "You caught me by surprise, too. I thought that was you by my side, helping me rescue Dana and the others. Having Jared take your place was a stroke of genius."

Voices of agreement circulated the table.

Dana looked to Chris. "How are the *gifted ones* we rescued?"

"Pissed," he answered. "They want payback but know they can't get it without revealing their gifts to the public. And after what they just went through, they know that wouldn't be wise."

Dana nodded. "It would just make them targets again."

"Exactly. We're doing everything we can to help them resume their normal lives, smoothing things over with their employers and the like. We're also providing any who need it with free medical care as well as sessions with therapists on the network's payroll, if they desire it."

"Thank you," she said, thinking of Rick, Phil, and Grant.

Chris smiled. "Don't worry. We're taking good care of them."

Seth cleared his throat. "Now tell them the bad news."

Quiet descended.

Lisette frowned. "What?"

"Tell them the bad news, Chris," Seth repeated.

All eyes went to Chris.

Setting his fork down, Chris sighed and drew a hand down his face. "Just once, I would like to come to this house and *not* be the bearer of bad news." He leaned back in his chair. "After the dust settled at network headquarters and we counted heads, we realized that we didn't recover all of the missing *gifted ones.*"

Aidan took Dana's hand. "Are you saying we left some behind?" he asked, his voice and face expressing the same dismay Dana felt.

Chris shook his head. "No. We got all of them that were housed at the military installation, but fifteen of the missing *gifted ones* weren't there. Scott Henderson's team found three dead this morning in Texas."

"Male or female?" Seth asked softly.

Chris hesitated. "All female."

Aidan swore. "What about the other dozen? Do you think they met the same fate?"

"We don't know," Chris admitted, "but believe that's likely the case. I've got everyone looking for them. Alena and Scott do, too. I'll update you with any progress we make."

Heavy silence.

"You won this battle, Seth," Zach said. "You may think you didn't, but you did."

Lisette nodded. "Dozens of *gifted ones* are alive today, thanks to you."

Zach took her hand and continued. "Gershom's been working behind the scenes all this time, but you brought him out in the open. You scared him. You made him bleed. Until now, Gershom thought himself too clever for us. He thought he was untouchable. Invincible. But I got a good look at him while I was chasing him and he stopped long enough to throw more victims my way. You, David, and Aidan cut that fucker up."

He said it with such satisfaction that even Seth cracked a smile. "At least there's that."

Chuckles lightened the mood.

Roland folded his arms across his chest. "Zach's right," he drawled. "We're making progress. This time we cut him up. Next time we'll bury him."

Hearty agreements from all.

Chris tucked into his meal again.

Conversation resumed, flowing around the table more freely now.

Aidan nudged Dana. "You're not eating," he said aloud. "Are you nervous?"

"A little," she admitted, the butterflies in her belly resuming their flight.

Heather leaned forward to peer around Aidan. "What are you nervous about?"

Sheldon motioned to the immortals sitting around the table with a forkful of chicken. "These guys don't make you nervous, do they?"

Tracy gave her a sympathetic smile. "Too much testosterone in the room?"

Dana laughed. "No. Aidan is going to transform me tonight."

Exclamations of joy filled the air.

Ethan and Bastien clapped Aidan on the back.

Melanie gave Dana a hug. "Welcome to the family!"

"Thank you."

Sarah motioned to Dana's plate. "You're smart not to eat. Anything you down now is going to come right back up."

Dana grimaced. "That sucks."

"It really does," Sarah agreed with a laugh. "But if Aidan is anything like Roland and the rest of the married immortals present, he'll spend the next three or four days pampering the hell out of you."

Looking up at Aidan, Dana raised her brows.

"Your wish is my command," he professed.

"Really?" She eyed him speculatively. Aidan had suggested that he transform her while they made love so the pleasure would dampen the pain of his bite. *Sounds kinky*, she'd said. *But I'll go with it.* And she could think of quite a few commands she'd like to issue as soon as they got naked. "Could my wish be your command *before* you transform me?"

He winked. "Absolutely."

Grinning, she squeezed his hand. "Then I'm not feeling so nervous."

Raising their hands to his lips, he kissed her knuckles.

The tableware abruptly jerked and clinked.

Startled, Dana glanced at the table. Her tea splashed and danced as her glass began to tip. Hastily reaching out, she steadied it.

Aidan and several others did the same.

Dishes began to jump and rattle as the table began to vibrate.

All conversation stopped as hands grabbed silverware that migrated toward the edges.

Confusion and uneasiness filtered through Dana.

What was happening? The ground beneath her feet wasn't shaking. Just the table.

"Seth?" Ami said, her soft voice full of concern.

All eyes went to their leader.

Seth's head was bowed. His eyes glowed a vibrant gold. Arms straight, he gripped the sides of the table so tightly his knuckles shone white. A muscle twitched in his clenched jaw as he drew long jagged breaths in and out through his nose as though battling… what? Pain? Illness?

David leapt to his feet and sped down the table in a blur. Resting a hand on Seth's back, he leaned in close. "What is it?"

Zach rose on Seth's other side.

Seth shook his head, then seemed to reel with dizziness.

The table lurched violently.

Zach hastily gripped Seth's arm and shoulder to steady him.

"Seth?" Ami repeated, resting a hand on his where it clutched the table in front of her.

He closed his eyes. "The *gifted ones*," he gritted, slowly gaining his feet, his arms supporting his weight more than his legs.

Dana saw Aidan and several other immortals surreptitiously grip the edges of the table to hold it steady.

"The ones that are still missing?" David asked softly.

Seth nodded. "They aren't dead."

Zach shared a glance with David. "Are you sure?"

"They aren't dead," Seth repeated. "They're transforming."

Shock rippled through the room.

David swore, his eyes flashing bright amber. "All of them?"

"Yes?"

"Where?"

Seth shook his head, again nearly losing his balance. "I don't know. Gershom is blocking me or otherwise shielding them. I can't lock in on them."

Zach glanced at Lisette.

Nodding, she stood and rested a hand on his arm.

As soon as Seth straightened and staggered back from the table, he, David, Zach, and Lisette vanished.

Dead silence.

"Well, shit," Chris whispered. "And I thought Times Square was the worst-case scenario."

Dana examined the faces around the table and noticed how pale some had become. "I'm not sure I understand what just happened. Is Seth okay?"

Heather nodded. "I was wondering the same thing. Was he angry or sick? I couldn't tell."

"He was both," Roland answered.

Dana looked at Roland, then Aidan, still not sure she understood.

Aidan sighed. "I hope I'm not breaking a confidence here, but some of the youngsters present may not know that Seth feels it whenever a *gifted one* transforms."

Heather frowned. "Feels it how?"

"He once described it as a sick feeling of dread or a burning in the pit of his stomach. It's how he found each of us when we transformed and helped us adjust to our new circumstances. The closer he got, the more he felt it, like a beacon."

Ethan cleared his throat. "I had heard as much, but didn't realize it actually made him physically ill."

"It usually doesn't," Aidan told them, "not to this extent at least. But *gifted ones* don't transform as often as you might think. Humans number in the billions. We immortals only number in the thousands. As far as I know, the only time more than one *gifted one* transformed at the same time was when Richart, Étienne, and Bastien all transformed within days of each other. This... twelve *gifted ones* transforming simultaneously... is unprecedented."

Ethan frowned. "We've been using that word a lot since Gershom arrived on the scene."

Sighing, Aidan shook his head. "And we'll be using it again if Seth can't locate the missing *gifted ones* and Gershom manages to raise his own private immortal army."

"*Merde,*" someone muttered.

———

Days later, Aidan sprawled in a chair in front of Chris Reordon's massive desk at network headquarters.

Chris sat behind it, his eyes on the computer that dominated the center of his desk.

"People," Aidan said suddenly.

"What?" Chris murmured, his eyes still glued to the screen.

"You said people."

"When?" he asked with little interest.

"The last time you bitched about my using mind control here at the network, you said my *people,* not my *guards.*"

Squinting at the screen, Chris leaned closer. "Damn it," he muttered. "I must need sleep or something. I can't seem to bring this shit into focus."

Aidan smiled. "You don't need sleep. You need reading glasses."

"Bullshit," the blond grumbled. "I'm too young for reading glasses."

Rising, Aidan leaned over, braced one hand on the desk, and covered Chris's eyes with the other.

"What are you—?"

"Shut it." His hand heated as Aidan corrected Chris's vision. Then he withdrew his hand and sank back down in his chair.

Chris scowled at him, then looked at the computer. His forehead smoothed out. "I'll be damned. I *did* need reading glasses. Thanks."

"No problem."

"Now, what were you blathering on about?" Chris asked, no malice in his tone.

Aidan laughed. "When I expressed concern upon learning that Zach had mind-controlled Dana, you complained about my not having felt the same concern when I mind-controlled your *people*. Not your guards, but your *people*."

"So?"

"So, I get it now."

"Get what?" Chris returned his attention to the computer.

"Why you won't let the matter drop. My messing with your guards' minds just pissed you off. It was my using mind control on your assistant Kate that infuriated you."

Chris's eyes widened as his brows drew down. Leaping up, he crossed his office and closed the door. "You're just guessing."

"But I guessed correctly." Aidan met his eyes as Chris returned to his seat behind the desk. "And I offer you my most sincere apology. I understand mind control better than you, yet I still panicked when Zach admitted he'd tampered with Dana's brain."

"Because *any* damage is unacceptable," Chris finished for him. "Even that which can be healed."

"Yes."

"Mr. Reordon?" Kate's voice emerged from one of the many devices on Chris's desk.

He pressed a button. "Yes?"

"Roland and Sarah Warbrook are here to see you."

"Thank you. Send them in, please."

Aidan and Chris both stood as the couple entered, holding hands.

Aidan wasn't quite sure how this was going to go but hoped for the best.

"Thanks for coming," Chris said. "Would you have a seat, please?"

Roland and Sarah exchanged a glance, then sank down on Chris's sofa. Aidan turned his chair to face them while Chris leaned back against his desk.

"What's this about?" Roland asked, blunt as usual.

Chris released his breath in a long sigh. "I didn't want to tell you in front of the others, but... Veronica Becker didn't make it."

Roland stiffened.

"Oh no," Sarah whispered.

Leaning forward, Roland braced his elbows on his knees. "How did she die?"

"She was shot in the head, execution style. According to the memories Zach combed through at the installation, she refused to cooperate and repeatedly tried to escape. Because those at the facility thought her gift was one that would aid them the least, they opted to use her as an example to compel the others to cooperate."

Roland swore foully. "Did they torture her?"

"No. She just suffered the one fatal gunshot wound. I'm sorry we couldn't get to her in time," Chris told them with genuine regret. "I really am."

Sarah wrapped an arm around Roland and rubbed his back. "What about her little boy?"

"That's the other reason I wanted to talk with you. Roland, since you're Veronica's only living relative, Aidan suggested I ask if the two of you would like to adopt her son Michael."

Their eyes widened. They turned to each other and stared without speaking for a long moment. Their heartbeats picked up, pounding a rapid beat.

Roland looked to Chris. "Does Seth know about this?"

"Yes. And he's already given his consent if you're interested."

Roland squeezed Sarah's hand and again met her hopeful gaze. "Do you—?"

"Yes," she blurted, then bit her lip. "I mean, only if you—"

"Of course I do." He brought her hand to his lips for a kiss. "You don't know how much I regret that I can't give you children, Sarah."

"But you can," she said softly as she touched his face. "Michael is your descendant. He needs us."

"And," Chris added, "as a *gifted one*, he'll need special guidance. Which is why we don't want to place him with a human family. They wouldn't understand his differences."

Aidan eyed Chris curiously. "Do you know what his gift is?"

"Not yet," Chris said. "Seth might, if you ask him. But whatever it is hasn't drawn the notice of our caregivers yet."

Roland frowned. "Will he be safe with us? We've not yet vanquished Gershom and—"

Aidan spoke before he could finish his thought. "With Gershom still out there, no one else would keep the boy safer. If you adopt Michael, he'll be surrounded by powerful immortals every day.

Hell, you'll probably spend most of your time at David's so he and Adira can play together."

Sarah's face lit with excitement as she squeezed her husband's hand. "That would be so great! You know Marcus and Ami have been worrying about Adira not spending enough time around other children."

Roland's features lightened with hope, then darkened again with uncertainty. "What if he doesn't like me? I haven't been a father in nine hundred years. And you know the other immortals all say I'm antisocial."

Everyone in the room laughed.

"What?" Roland asked, expression puzzled.

Sarah patted his hand. "Sweetie, everyone knows you're Adira's favorite uncle. She adores you. And Michael will, too."

His lips curled up in a smile. "You're sure about this?"

"Yes."

He looked at Chris. "Then let's do it."

Squealing, Sarah threw her arms around his neck and hugged him tight.

Roland grinned. "When can we see him?"

Chris looked up at Aidan. "Tell Melanie and Dana we're ready to see them."

We're ready for you, Aidan told the two women telepathically.

Brimming with excitement, Sarah damned near danced in place while they waited.

Roland looked back and forth between Chris and Aidan. "Seth is really okay with this?"

Aidan smiled. "He thought it a grand idea."

"I'll handle all the paperwork for you," Chris said, business as usual. But Aidan didn't need to read his thoughts to know he was enjoying this. Chris really *didn't* get to give good news very often. And after recent events, he had needed this as much as Roland and Sarah did.

"What about Michael?" Sarah asked. "How is he doing?"

Chris lifted one shoulder in a slight shrug. "About how you'd expect. He's disconsolate. He misses his mommy and doesn't understand why she didn't pick him up from day care or why she hasn't come for him since. The child psychologist we keep on staff recommended that you stay at David's place for a while. Michael will need time to get to know you both and to adjust to his new family life. And she believes his being able to play and interact with Adira will help ease the transition."

"Of course," Roland agreed.

The door opened.

Dana entered and held the door for Melanie.

Melanie entered with little Michael on her hip. The somber toddler rested his head upon her chest and sucked on the index and middle fingers of one hand, just like Adira, as he stared at them listlessly.

Roland and Sarah rose.

Dana closed the door and moved to stand beside Aidan, slipping her hand into his with a smile.

Melanie crossed to Roland and Sarah. "Michael, this is Roland and Sarah."

"Hi," Sarah breathed with a smile as she held her hand out to the boy.

Michael reached out and closed his plump fingers around her index finger. After a moment, he lifted his head, studying her with more interest.

Roland smiled and drew a gentle hand over the boy's dark hair. "Aren't you a handsome lad?"

Sarah winked at Roland. "He has your genes."

He laughed.

Michael leaned toward Sarah, removing his fingers from his mouth long enough to reach for her. Thrilled, Sarah drew him into her arms and cuddled him close.

Aidan quirked a brow at Chris. "Perhaps he's a telepath."

"Or an empath," Chris countered.

"Or maybe psychic?" Dana suggested with a teasing smile.

Aidan grinned and wrapped his arm around her. "My personal favorite."

Leaning up, she kissed his cheek.

Releasing a contented sigh, Dana rested a hand on the arm Aidan had draped around her. The two were curled up on his porch swing, her back to his front, watching twilight gently lower its blanket upon the earth.

He pressed a kiss to the top of her head. "We'll have to go soon."

Nodding, she drew in a deep breath and marveled over the plethora of scents she could detect and isolate now that she was immortal.

In deference to Seth, Aidan had not transformed her the night Gershom's captive *gifted ones* transformed. Neither had wished to add to whatever illness burdened Seth. So they had waited a couple of weeks until Seth was himself again.

Dana had been so ill for three days after Aidan bit her that she barely remembered it. But now...

It was weird to feel so normal yet have so much power, strength and speed at her disposal. In the week since her transformation, Aidan had trained her vigorously. Long hours. Every day.

Dana didn't object. She knew her abduction had terrified him.

Hell, it had terrified her, too.

Fortunately, thanks to the how-to-kick-ass manual Zach had planted in her brain, she already possessed most of the combat skills she needed to defeat multiple vampire attackers. She just had to learn to moderate her strength and speed, which was tougher than she had thought it would be.

Her gaze slid to the large boarded-over hole in the exterior wall of the house.

There had been a few... incidents.

"Hey, guys?" Brodie called through the screen door. "It's almost time."

"Okay," the two answered.

Immortal Guardians and their Seconds would all be dining at David's tonight. David said he and Seth wanted to gather everyone together to formally welcome Dana to the family.

She felt a familiar flutter of happiness.

She had a family again. Aidan had given her that. And so much more.

Ready to embrace her new life, she had sold her little duplex home and shop and had moved in with Aidan.

She grinned.

And Brodie.

It was a little odd, having Brodie there with them. But he was Aidan's Second and a likable guy, and the three of them were adjusting.

Aidan touched a finger to her chin and tilted her head back for a kiss. "Do you regret it?"

"Regret what?" she asked, pressing her lips to his for another kiss.

"Do you regret not sending me on my way when I came to you for that first reading?"

Smiling, she shook her head. "Not for a second."

His eyes darkened with sadness. "I've brought such violence into your life."

"The love and happiness far outweigh that," she replied. "And you've given me the *huge* family I've always wanted *plus* immortality." She shook her head. "My only regret is that I didn't meet you sooner."

He slid a hand over her hair, brushing it back from her face. "We'll have forever together now."

"Forever still won't be enough." Curling a hand around his neck, she drew him down for a longer, more thorough kiss. "I love you, Aidan."

His handsome face lit with a smile. "I've waited nearly three thousand years to hear you say that."

She laughed. "No pressure."

Grinning, he shook his head. "You have by far exceeded all my hopes and expectations. I do love you, Dana. More with every breath I take."

She stole another kiss. "I love you, too."

Thank you for reading *Blade of Darkness*. I hope you enjoyed Aidan and Dana's story.

If you liked this book, please consider rating or reviewing it at an online retailer of your choice. I appreciate your support so much and am always thrilled when I see that one of my books made a reader happy. Ratings and reviews are also an excellent way to recommend an author's books, create word of mouth, and help other readers find new favorites.

Thank you again!

Dianne Duvall
www.DianneDuvall.com

About the Author

Dianne Duvall is the *New York Times* and *USA Today* Bestselling Author of the **Immortal Guardians** and **The Gifted Ones** series. Reviewers have called Dianne's books "fast-paced and humorous" (*Publishers Weekly*), "utterly addictive" (*RT Book Reviews*), "extraordinary" (Long and Short Reviews), and "wonderfully imaginative" (The Romance Reviews). Her books have twice been nominated for RT Reviewers' Choice Awards and are routinely deemed Top Picks by *RT Book Reviews*, The Romance Reviews, and/or Night Owl Reviews.

Dianne loves all things creative. When she isn't writing, Dianne is active in the independent film industry and has even appeared on-screen, crawling out of a moonlit grave and wielding a machete like some of the vampires she loves to create in her books.

For the latest news on upcoming releases, contests, and more, please visit www.DianneDuvall.com. You can also connect with Dianne online:

Website — www.DianneDuvall.com
Blog — www.dianneduvall.blogspot.com
Facebook — www.facebook.com/DianneDuvallAuthor
Twitter — www.twitter.com/DianneDuvall
YouTube —
www.youtube.com/channel/UCVcJ9xnm_i2ZKV7jM8dqAgA?fe
ature=mhee
Pinterest — www.pinterest.com/dianneduvall
Goodreads — www.goodreads.com/Dianne_Duvall
Google Plus — www.plus.google.com/106122556514705041683

Printed in Great Britain
by Amazon